AZURE DYING

BY

C. W. Gordon

Strategic Book Group

Strategic Book Group

P.O. Box 333
Durham CT 06422

www.StrategicBookClub.com

ISBN: 978-1-60976-693-1

This work is dedicated to wonderful wife Joy and my father Ronnie.
I love you both.

Thanks to my brother Gary whose help was invaluable.
You're the best bro.

A very special acknowledgement to the rock band Slayer,
Whose music inspired the dark journey I had to make
In creating this work.
The world needs you guys, keep doing what you do.
Peace.

Walk the streets beneath the shadows

Searching for a cryptic bride

Eat alive the conscience I hate

Without pain I watch you die

I will live through this forever

I have done the things you grieve

As you kneel before its evil

My face is the last you'll see.

—Slayer, "Deviance"

1

Austin, Texas
April

Amy was walking as fast as she could, but she seemed to be moving in slow motion. She wished her legs were long like her sister's so she could walk the distance in half the time. But genetics only allowed one of the girls to have long legs like their dad's, so she was stuck hustling her ass off to get home to the phone before her mother answered her call from Tony. Because of her tardiness the past Saturday night, her mom had taken away her cell phone, stranding her from civilization like a Gilligan castaway.

Humiliating!

To add to the disgrace, she was forced to ride the bus to and from school because her best friend, Megan, was out with a flu. Megan was her only lifeline to the enlightened world since she was without both transportation and cellular communication. The bitch got sick with no consideration of the one person who was counting on her. Amy needed her for support and conveyance. Without her, she was subject to her fascist mother's beck and call. It was bad enough she took away her cell and grounded her for a month, but she had to double-time it home to help with the household chores that belittled her even more. Things like clearing the dinner table and loading—then unloading—the dishwasher, folding the laundry, and vacuuming the entire house. It was times like this she was glad she wasn't a boy; or she'd have her out cutting the grass or, worse yet, hauling the trash to the curb.

Yuck!

Tony would be calling during his break at the HEB at around three forty-five. Her watch read three thirty-four—she had time. If she timed it right, she could be in and answer the phone before her mom. She could squeeze in a couple of minutes before she caught on, making her end the call. She could pass it off as Megan for a little while, but sooner or later, her eavesdropping mother would piece it together and the saga would end abruptly. Any other day, her mom didn't get home from work until four fifteen or four thirty. But today was Thursday, her mom's day off. If she wanted to hear Tony at all, it would be for just a few precious minutes. That was okay with her just as long as she got to hear his voice for another day.

Teenage angst can be soothed by the simplest things at times.

As she drew closer to her street, she thought about how they had met. She and Megan were cruising west Austin around the Arboretum in Meg's Toyota convertible with the top down. The hot Texas sun turning their exposed skin to darker shades of bronze as they sipped cherry lemonade and listened to Beyoncé. Megan eased her car through a strip mall parking lot, looking for friends, when a tall, athletic-looking surfer type caught Amy's eye.

"Stop," she told her buddy.

"Why?"

"Just stop, dummy. Stop and look at what I'm looking at," she told her, pointing to the guy in cutoffs and flip-flops. He wore a cool blue T-shirt and a shell necklace and had sun-bleached hair and a perfect tan. He walked into Best Buy, coolly slipping his sunglasses to the top of his head.

"Oh my god," Meg breathed aloud.

"Told you."

"No shit."

"Park this thing. I'm going in," Amy announced. "I have to see him closer."

Without another word, Megan found a spot, and soon the two girls were walking as fast as they could across the lot, without looking as though they were walking as fast as they could. It would be terrible if a friend saw them in such a state of *uncool*.

2

"My god, Amy, he's gorgeous," Megan said, entering the store. They each removed their sunglasses, letting their eyes adjust to the inside lighting as the cool blast of refrigerated air slapped their skin.

"I totally have to talk to him," Amy told her. "I have to know his name before we leave this stinking place. We have to find him."

It didn't take long. He was browsing the new Linkin Park CD, standing alone, weight on one leg with a hand on his hip. Amy's heart skipped as they approached. She was afraid in equal parts that he'd be either a jerk or a gentleman. A real creep or some miserable choirboy. She just wanted him to be as cool as he looked. She stopped beside him and cleared her throat with her perky blonde friend close enough behind her she could feel her heavy breathing on her neck.

It was like an explosion when he looked at her. He smiled, and she melted like the ice in the lemonade they left in the sun. Big broad smile, white teeth, a hint of stubble on his chin, and deep dark brown eyes that a girl could fall into and never find her way out of.

"Hi, I'm Tony," he offered. "What's up with you guys?"

The next thing she knew, she was neck-deep in love with the nineteen-year-old from Westlake; and for his part, Tony was head over heels for the little brunette with the killer dimples. Amy looked every bit the part of a high school cheerleader that she wasn't, and Tony was the perfect California boy who'd never been west of Lubbock. They struck the image of teenage royalty. However, Amy was just a junior; and the recently graduated Tony was working as a dairy stocker at a local HEB supermarket and going to school at night, majoring in computer drafting.

That's where Mom comes in again. Amy's mother, Sharon, was extremely protective of her two daughters. Since their father's death eight years earlier in a boating accident on Lake Travis, she'd been both a mother and a father to the two girls. Ginger, the oldest, had moved out and was going to school on a grant in San Antonio while Amy finished her last two years of high school. Sharon was proud of her two girls who both turned out beautiful and smart. Conversely, she was not looking forward to living in her house alone whenever Amy's assured departure came about. Living with only one of the girls was bad enough. The thought of living without either of them was mind-numbing. So when

3

she met the handsome and charming Tony Miller from Westlake, she heard the inevitable approach of solitude gaining speed as it rushed toward her like a rising tsunami.

The conversations always started the same way.

"You're only seventeen, baby. All I ask is that you slow down. You've got your entire life in front of you."

"You met Dad when you were eighteen."

"Yes, and I loved your father till the day he died, and today I love him even more," she defended. "But I also got pregnant at nineteen with Ginger and never made it back to school. I missed out on so many things."

"Because of us."

And of course, it always ended the same way.

Guilt.

Robert Crowder was a good man. He loved and provided for his wife and children. Trying to live up to his absence was draining on Sharon. She understood her girls in a way her husband never could. As women. As a woman, she knew what Amy felt; and she was the last person who'd want to stand in the way of her girl's happiness, especially after meeting such a wonderful young man. Tony reminded her so much of her husband, and that's what scared her even more. She saw Amy making the same mistakes for the same reasons. She just hoped that the two kids would take it slow unlike her and Robert. She hated the thought of her baby getting caught up in the undertow of love then being sucked away in the tide, missing out on who *she* was. Missing out on the chance of fulfilling her dreams and settling for being a wife and a mother and nothing else. It was honorable to live that way, but a mature woman should have that choice and not squander it with the childish dreams and desires of youth.

She was only a mother now; it was all she had.

Amy made it to West Haven at 3:40 p.m. She was a mere block away, knowing she would make it in time. The stress she had been under melted away as the warm spring air blew through her long raven curls. She nestled her books to her chest, calming now as she saw her house at the end of the block.

4

She also spotted something else.

A black H2 Hummer was parked on the curb midway on the desolate block. It seemed out of place in the middle-class neighborhood, like one of those newspaper puzzles that ask you to spot the *thing* that doesn't belong in the picture. The H2 definitely did not belong on her street. It was parked in front of the Rondos' house, which was empty until Mr. Rondo got home from work at around six. Mrs. Rondo worked late and would be gone until the wee hours of the next morning, so she had no idea who the slick, expensive SUV belonged to. Amy stopped to examine the vehicle. It was new, no more than a year old, and the owner took great care of it. Black chrome wheels and bumper, windows tinted limousine style so you had no way of seeing inside. She stepped off the curb behind the Hummer and noticed very small writing on the left side of the back hatch between the spare tire and the left taillight. There, painted on the metal in a font she recognized from her computer as Bradley Hand, were three lines written in white:

Think
Of
Your Mother

"What the hell?" she asked herself. It was the oddest thing to put on such a great car. She paused and thought of the day she and Tony would be able to afford such a wonderful vehicle. They would drive through Austin in luxury. Tony a successful businessman and she---

It was her last thought before searing pain ripped through her body, and she blacked out.

Indeed, she was not thinking of her mother.

The phone rang at precisely three forty-five. Sharon Crowder answered, and when the caller began to stammer, the jig was up.

"Hello, Tony," she said, allowing herself an inward smile.

"Hello, Ms. Crowder," he answered sheepishly.

"Tony, you know the drill."

"Yes, ma'am. I'm out of line."

"And so is Amy." She leaned against the wall, expecting her daughter to burst through the door at any minute and react in horror at the site of her mom on the phone. "Look, Tony, you're a fine young man, and nothing would make me happier than seeing you two grow old and gray together and sprout me a grandchild or three."

"But—"

"But"—she smiled again—"rules are rules, and she broke one and she has to do the time. I did the same with Ginger, and I have to be fair. You understand, yes?"

"Yes, ma'am."

"Besides, she'll talk with you tomorrow on a friend's phone like she always does, and she'll talk to you before I get home from work tomorrow. Like she always does. Right?"

Tony answered yes after a nervous laugh.

"Now get back to work before Mr. Alverez fires you."

"Okay, you're right. Sorry, Mrs. Crowder."

"That's okay, son." She started to hang up when she thought to add, "Oh, and uh . . . I'll tell her you *did* call."

"Okay, thanks, Mrs. C," he laughed.

"Don't mention it," she replied, hanging up the phone. "Now, missy, where are you?"

2

Dark. Total, unforgiving blackness.

She came around about a half hour later, feeling as though she'd been hit by a truck.

A truck.

Remember.

The H2.

She was looking at the H2 when whatever it was happened. Now she was in a very dark place, and it was moving. Rolling. She was inside some kind of truck for sure. There was carpet all around her but no doors or windows. The space was small, not like a van. However, what was occupying her mind was the earsplitting music that was bombarding her eardrums. She didn't recognize it, but she knew it was some sort of death metal blaring at such a high volume it felt as though it were coming from inside her head. She rolled over into a kneeling fetal position, covering her ears, while touching her forehead to her knees in an attempt to protect herself from the sonic assault.

"*Help me!*" she screamed, unable to hear her own voice over the mayhem. "*God, please, somebody help me!*"

She left a hand over one ear while pushing a shoulder up to the other as she began to feel around in the dark. From her knees, she could reach the ceiling without fully extending her arms. It was a very small space. Panic was sinking in as she crawled along the sides of the container, looking for a seam or anything she could get her fingers into and pull. It felt as though she were inside a box that was lined with indoor-outdoor carpet. It covered all the walls, the bed, and the ceiling. Running her hands along the ceiling, she felt in the corners what were surely speakers. Small plastic grates that were vibrating. The volume made it impossible to stay at any of the speakers very long. Back in the middle, she felt the ceiling again and realized there was a fixture there, most likely a light. Crying, she moved to the back of the container to where her brain told her she should find a door, but there was none. Instead, she felt two long patches of what felt like a different fabric with bulges behind them. Feeling the seam at the top of the patches, she discovered folded-in zippers on each. Her trembling fingers managed to pull one zipper free, and she unzipped it only to find what felt like worthless thin plastic on the inside. Like a secure trash compartment.

"Please turn that off!" she screamed at the top of her lungs as the pounding music went from song to song with no quiet filler between. It was seemingly one long acoustic attack on her mind. Speed metal with thundering drums, mind-warping guitars, and screaming vocals bombarding her, mugging her. Aggressive, angry music coming at her in an unrelenting torrent of destruction.

The vehicle slowed, and she felt it turn then stop. While it stopped, she began pounding the walls with her hands, screaming for help, clawing at the fabric that cocooned her from the outside world. Frantically, she tore at the wall with her fingernails, only to have two nails painfully break off, forcing an even more terror-filled frenzy. Like a trapped animal, she thrashed at the wall while screaming with everything in her in an attempt for someone—anyone—to hear her.

The vehicle started moving again, gaining speed. Once reaching what was a comfortable cruising speed, it leveled off. Amy fell down in the middle of the hold on her side. Pulling her knees to her chest, she covered her ears and cried. She was a prisoner. Of who or what she had no way of knowing, nor did she have any idea where they were taking her or what would happen when they got there. She cried harder than she'd ever cried in her life.

Now, only now, did she think of her mother.

*

Five p.m. and still no Amy. Sharon had called the school and learned that Amy had indeed gotten on the bus home. The school contacted the driver who said Amy got off at the stop with two other kids who both went in the opposite direction. When he last saw her, she was maybe two blocks from her street of West Haven.

"What time was that?"

"Between three thirty and three forty-five."

The information was relayed to Sharon who was now in the throes of panic. She called Meagan's house, but the poor, flu-ridden girl had no idea where Amy might have been. Her next call went to Tony's cell.

Tony's response was, "Call the police, I'm on my way."

Two uniformed patrolmen came to the house and took all the information Sharon and Tony could offer. When Tony brought up the fact that if her mother had not taken away her cell phone or had at least given her a ride home from school—instead of forcing her to take the bus as an act of discipline—none of this would be happening, Sharon defended herself with force. "Don't tell me how to raise my daughter!" she yelled. The policemen calmed them with the sobering reality that no matter who blamed who, Amy was the one in trouble, and it was Amy who needed all their help.

"Ms. Crowder, the first forty-eight hours are the most crucial. The first forty-eight hours are when the trail is the freshest, and it's when whoever is behind the disappearance usually makes a mistake. We need—*she* needs—the two of you to stay calm and work together." He made eye contact with both, asking, "Can you do that?"

Together, they both felt foolish. This was the first girl Tony had ever truly loved, and it was Sharon's youngest child. Her last child. They both agreed; and when Sharon nearly lost it again, Tony put his arms around her, telling her all would be well, that they'd probably find her "at some new kid's house listening to music."

The mother in Sharon was hopeful but not convinced.

After the police had taken all the information on her description—

from what she was wearing last to the phone numbers and names of all her friends—they requested an APB for her whereabouts. Since Amy was not yet eighteen, they would not have to wait for the mandatory twenty-four hours before filing the report. The alert was for an Amy Lynn Crowder. Five feet two inches tall, one hundred pounds. Long dark hair and blue eyes. Last seen on the three hundred block of West Haven in northwest Austin.

The authorities were now scouring the area for a missing child.

Sharon and Tony waited by the phone, leaning on each other for support. Ginger was on her way from San Antonio to be there as well. It was not like Amy to not be where she was supposed to be. She hated being grounded and on restriction. All she did last week was miss her curfew by an hour and her mom busted her ass good, so the last thing she'd want to do now would be to put her free time with Tony in even more jeopardy. This wasn't good, and they knew it. They saw it in each other's eyes. Sharon, for the first time, saw genuine love for her daughter in the dark brown eyes of the fine young man from Westlake as Tony saw nothing but fear and hope in the eyes of the woman he wanted someday to call his mother-in-law.

They waited the night together with Tony's parents checking in from time to time; they, too, held vigil against all hope.

Forty-eight hours. The first forty-eight were the most important.

They had no way of knowing it was already too late.

3

As the relentless crunching of the earsplitting death metal roared on, Amy felt the truck slow again and seem to go off-road. The jostling and bumping told her she was not on a street somewhere in Austin. She was out of town, out of the city, possibly now in the woods. She cried more, wanting her mother, wanting Tony. Wanting anyone to stop this madness she'd been hurled into. Like a doll caught in a vortex of evil, she was alone and being ripped apart from the inside out.

Why? Why would someone want to do this to her? Who would want to torture her this way? Her mind raced as it had been doing for nearly two hours. There had been several times of slowing and stopping, telling her the truck was maneuvering through heavy traffic. The last half hour or longer had been a steady pace with little or no slowing until now. She knew she was off-road now. The bounces and turns told her as much.

"Let me out of here, you sick motherfucker!"

He found the place he'd scouted a week earlier. Deer woods in the fall that were isolated and far off the beaten path the rest of the year. The sun was setting in the west, causing the sky to illuminate in a glorious glow of varying shades of pinks and purples. He stopped the H2 and killed the music in the hold that was directly behind him.

It was the first time he'd used his new killing jar, its maiden voyage, and it was working perfectly. As soon as the music died, his prey in the hold began screaming her lungs out, trying to find anyone that would help her.

There was no one.

She screamed bloody murder, never realizing her captor was a mere thirty inches away, just beyond the new wall freshly installed in the H2 behind the twin seats in the cab. As she screamed, he checked his watch. He'd allowed himself an hour to do his bidding; then he'd leave this place never to return.

As the girl in the hold cried for a savior, he turned the rearview mirror to look at himself. He studied himself like a detective sifting clues. He considered his blue eyes, the texture of his skin, his cheekbones, and even the hairs in his eyelashes. He studied his face intently because the next time he'd see it, it would belong to a different man. In one hour, he would be changed forever.

As his prisoner in the back continued her ravings, he turned on the light in the hold, causing her to panic even further. Her screams were now maniacal. He broke his stare from the mirror, rolling down his black ski mask to cover his pretty face. As he exited the cab, he had but one thought on his mind.

The jar.

4

Glenn Young was a journalist for the local Austin paper the *Citizen*. He had graduated from St. Mary's in San Antonio in 1992 and had worked for three other papers before landing his job with the *Citizen*. There wasn't anything special about him; he wasn't necessarily gifted with insight or even a knack for good prose. What Glenn Young had was an ability to get under people's skin and get them to open up, sometimes even incriminating themselves. He had done it with sports stars, politicians, business people, and even members of the private sect. Young was a good guy, but he was so persistent when he knew he was on to something that he had gained the reputation as a relentless and remorseless adjutant.

The thirty-eight-year-old Young looked every bit the part of an aggravate. Big round eyes that had a constant look of alarm. A thin graying beard rested beneath a receding red hair that was always unkempt and grown in different lengths. With sloppy, ill-fitting clothes, Glenn Young was the poster boy for disheveled writers everywhere.

He arrived at the paper for work at the usual time of nine o'clock. He'd been made aware, as all the other reporters were, of the Amy Crowder case. It was closing in on forty-eight hours, and every seasoned journalist knew that if the missing person wasn't found in that time, the end result was most likely going to be a bad one. However, he wasn't following the missing person case since he was doing a lead on corruption inside the local political machine.

He loathed politics. Anytime he had a chance to turn a screw on some *hob-knob*, he not only considered it a right, but also his duty. Pulling back the covers of dignitaries, showing them for what he felt most of them to be: power-hungry neophytes grabbing at the brass ring of notoriety.

The receptionist greeted the grizzled reporter as he entered the building with his laptop, briefcase, and a cup of Starbucks.

"Morning, Glenn," said the cute young intern.

"Morning, Jen." She was still in school and was interning at the paper while she sought her degree in journalism. Glenn wanted to know her better, but it would have to wait till she was away from the *Citizen*. Dipping your pen in company ink was a surefire way to get squashed. Not to mention she was far out of his league. "Any messages?" he asked, stopping at the desk. Her smile was electric. Soft short blonde hair, blue eyes that looked like tiny pools of water.

Ah . . . if only.

"As a matter of fact," she answered, sorting through her desk, "a guy named Mangum wants you to call him at your earliest."

"He can suck it."

"Oookaaay," she giggled.

"Bad source. Every time I follow something that prick gives me, I either lose a month chasing a wild goose, or I lose a month's salary because I get suspended by the paper. Brent Mangum can kiss my hairy white butt."

There was dry wit to Young that made his mean words sound as though they were being delivered by a standup comic. You had to laugh, which Jen did.

"There's a letter that's without a return address," she informed him, handing over the small envelope, which he stuffed into his shirt pocket without consideration.

"Hate mail from UT. What else?"

"Jeff Kenny wants lunch, and you never called your mother back from yesterday's conversation," she finished with the same disarming smile.

"I'll call Jeffery if I have time," he said, heading for his cubicle. "And I *know* I won't have time to call Lois. Easter dinner just ain't my style."

14

Arriving at his six-by-six portion of the building, he set down his double espresso and did the normal morning preparations. He stood his laptop on its edge beside his desk and opened his briefcase while turning on his PC. He'd download information he'd written the night before onto the PC later then vice versa before leaving later in the day. That way, no matter what computer he was writing on, he was always up to date.

"Going downtown today?" a familiar voice asked from a few cubicles over.

"Only if my cell's not melting down by two o'clock," he answered without even looking up from his briefcase. The owner of the voice peeked over the white cubicle wall. Steven Sanchez was eyeing Young as he set up shop for the day.

"Think Peterson will talk?" he asked.

"If he does, it'll be to me. I know that much for sure, compadre. And if he hasn't reached out by two, I'm going downtown and pin his ears to the sides of his head."

"That's the bulldog I love!" Steven fired back. Steven was only eight months removed from grad school, and when he got a job at the *Citizen*, he gravitated toward Glenn Young like a moon to a glorious planet. Young wasn't the best writer on the staff and was far from the best reporter. However, he was one the most charismatic at the paper and always saw through to the end . . . even if he was wrong.

He had been working at the *San Antonio Daily News* after a stint with a smaller paper that had the circulation of an eighty-year-old diabetic. He had gotten the break when one of his college classmates dropped his name to the editor when it was mentioned that they were looking for some spitfire to come in and shake things up.

"He's not the best writer, but one thing he can do is stir the shit pot," his buddy had told them. "If you're looking for someone who won't be intimidated or afraid to take a chance, Glenn's your boy."

After subsequent interviews, he landed a job at the paper as a political correspondent. Young had always known he'd been born in the

15

wrong decade. His was a talent better suited for the turbulent '60s. He could rabble-rouse with the best of them, and his view of authority would have matched the visions of Abby Hoffman.

Glenn Young was truly a rebel without a cause.

As a political correspondent for the South Texas newspaper, he was often dispatched to Washington and Austin. It was on one of his trips to DC that his reputation and tenacity were brought kicking and screaming to the forefront.

It seems there was a certain congressman who was embroiled in a sex scandal that apparently left his alleged mistress missing in the Virginia countryside. Young could see through the plot like a clear pane window. It was obvious to him that the esteemed gentleman had this noisy lover removed from the land of the living, knowing he could confess to the affair. But if he was positive that there would never be a body discovered, he'd always be seen as the grief-stricken older politician who fell for a younger woman who was no doubt troubled and had gotten in with the wrong crowd.

If he played it right, not only would he be forgiven for his sexual indiscretions, but he'd also surely become a sympathetic figure.

At his press conference where he was emotionally spent and finding it hard to talk about the missing woman with whom he'd had a torrid affair, Glenn Young saw his opportunity to squeeze the man he just knew was behind her disappearance. In the middle of the conference, Young found the perfect lull to launch his scathing accusations. Question after question he fired, getting the usual political rhetoric that not only answers nothing, but also insults the listener. When the congressman tried to move on to other reporters, Young became more and more belligerent. As the congressman's handler tried to snuff Young's advance, he screamed an out-and-out indictment of murder. The Washington pressroom gasped at the seasoned Texan's bravado and apparent lack of respect for a senior congressman from Capitol Hill. It got so bad that Young had to be removed from the pressroom, screaming as he was being dragged away, "You killed that girl, congressman! We all know you killed that girl!"

The conference was adjourned, and Glenn was escorted to his hotel by the congressman's security detail and told to leave town. Before he'd even checked out of the hotel, the *Daily News* had terminated his employment. By the time his plane touched down in San Antonio, he was an out-of-work journalist.

"Freedom of the press, my ass!"

He was basically blackballed for three years until the body of the young woman was found, with the foul play that led to her demise not implicating the old congressman, but the very handler who had stepped between them at the press conference.

It wasn't a true reprieve, but Glenn was vindicated to a certain extent. The *San Antonio Daily News* would not hire him back, but when he applied to the *Citizen*, he was given a second chance.

Since then, he had riled labor leaders, sports figures, politicians, and big business moguls. Sometimes his aim was a little off or he took a wrong path to get to the right answer; but either way, for as much trouble as he could start, he was equally ardent in finding the truth.

Young didn't have an immense following, but the people who read him on a constant basis felt they knew him and what he stood for. He wasn't a lapdog spouting regurgitated double-talk. He was a writer you could trust to be honest with you.

Sanchez was still looking at Young over the small wall. "Peterson's got two choices, Glenn. Talk to you or talk to the cops. And as tough as you are, I'd rather fight Glenn Young than Austin's finest," Steven acknowledged.

"We'll see, big man. We'll just have to wait and see."

"What's in your pocket?" Sanchez asked, spying the envelope in Young's shirt pocket.

"What?" Glenn asked, confused. Steven tapped his own chest above his pocket. "Huh?" he stammered then realized he'd placed a letter in his pocket at Jen's desk. "Oh, that. Fan mail," he quipped sarcastically. He pulled it out of his pocket and flipped it over the wall to Sanchez. "Open it and tell me if its love or hate at last sight."

The letter sailed past Steven and landed on the floor. He retrieved it, studying the envelope. There was no return address with the address to

17

Glenn typed, not handwritten. "Too small to be a letter bomb," he cracked, to no response.

He opened the letter, taking out the pages.

Page one was a letter produced in bold typeface. It read

Mr. Young,

I trust that you are as earnest and strong willed as I read you to be. This will not be my only correspondence with you. I trust you, above all people, to do the right thing. Please forward the adjoining page to the proper authorities.

D

Before Sanchez could tell Glenn about the first page, he was unfolding the second. The image made his stomach drop. Fear rocked through him as he screamed aloud, *"My god, Glenn! My god!"*

Young heard him, but something in his DNA ignored the sound. It wasn't until Sanchez screamed a second time that he got his attention.

"For god's sake, Glenn, get over here!"

Glenn, along with others in the pressroom, leaped to Steven Sanchez's cubicle to see what the hell was going on. When he arrived, Sanchez was holding an unfolded sheet of printer paper that had the same font-style type on the back, with the front covered in a page-sized digital photograph. Steven was shaking as he handed the photo to Glenn Young while reading the first passage aloud.

"Do the right thing? What the hell is that supposed to mean?" Young asked as he and all who were within earshot gathered around, letting out gasps and cries. Others were shocked into total silence. As he held the photo, Glenn Young's hands—for the first time in years—began to tremble.

It was a digital photo that had been downloaded and transferred to plain printer paper. The photo took up the entire 8.5 x 11 page. It was a snapshot in time. An 8.5 x 11 peek into madness. No one in the newsroom was prepared for the photo, much less Glenn Young. If Jack the Ripper had a digital camera, this might be the sort of thing that would have accompanied his letters to Scotland Yard. Some of the people that had gathered turned away; others were stuck in a macabre trance, not able to break their gaze from the horrible sight. "Jesus," Young whispered. "What the hell is this?"

A woman looking over his shoulder with a hand covering her mouth got a closer look, though not wanting to. "That's the Crowder girl," she said.

"What?" Glenn asked, without turning.

"That poor girl is Amy Crowder."

It was indeed Amy Crowder, though not in a way anyone had ever seen her before. The seventeen-year-old beauty was naked and hanging by her neck from a dead tree limb. The thin rope used caused her slight weight to nearly pinch her small throat in two. There was no blood or visible wounds in the photo. She'd been lynched in the woods, leaving an image eerily reminiscent of war atrocities.

The back of the page held another letter; this one to the police.

Dear Police,

Tell her mother she died sweetly and most assuredly thinking of her. I insisted on it.
I did not rape her; I want that known.
You'll find her in southern Burnet County.
There are no clues to help you, I promise.
Unless this new passion I've discovered subsides, there will be more. I don't intend to stop anytime soon.
The reason is that the experience was even better than I had dreamed.
Most of my dreams are horrible.
This one was bliss.
I've been reborn; I am becoming something greater.
As it stands, I am thrilled with the new me.
As you're dying, think of your mother,

D

Without tearing his eyes from the page, Young asked, "Why hasn't someone called 911?"

5

Everyone in the newsroom who'd touched the letter or envelope was fingerprinted. Glenn Young was being interviewed in a conference room by two Austin detectives, Stanley Bodinger and Eric Cordova. Bodinger was a veteran cop of twenty years. He'd started as a patrolman in rough east Austin and worked his way up to detective sergeant at age forty-four. The youthful Cordova had been put on the fast track as a college grad with a degree in criminology. For the department, having a young Hispanic detective saddling along with one of the city's most tough and streetwise veterans was a plus. Everyone from the governor's mansion to Rosewood Avenue welcomed the diversity.

The two detectives made for a startling contrast. Bodinger was five ten and a rock-hard 185 pounds. He had a graying widow's peak and a full gray goatee. Tanned, with the air of a rattlesnake, Stanley Bodinger looked every bit the part of the cop no one wanted any part of. Cordova was a good six feet tall and over two hundred pounds with a shaved head. Baldness ran in his family, and at twenty-four, he decided to rush the inevitable. Besides, he had a good head for it. To his credit, Cordova knew that no matter how fast he was working up the ladder, the senior officer was the lead investigator. Detective Bodinger was the boss.

"Why do you think this guy sent the letter to you?" he asked Young who was seated at the table with his eyes closed and his head in his hands, trying in vain to comprehend why, indeed, the killer picked him.

"Hell if I know, Detective. He said he trusted me to do the right thing, then he started the second letter addressing the police." He opened his eyes, peeking over his hands. "I guess he knew I'd call you guys."

"But anybody would," Cordova said. "That letter shows up at John Doe Citizen's house, and five minutes later, he's on the phone with a dispatcher. No, he sent this to you for a reason." There was an edge to Cordova. Young guessed it was from playing off the older cop. He was right.

"Look, Mr. Young," Bodinger said, "we all know what happens when one of these whack jobs notifies the press. The police get involved. I really think he just used you as means to inform us that he's out there and his game has begun." He walked across the room and poured a cup of coffee then looked back to his partner. "You know, it wouldn't surprise me if he got Mr. Young's name out of a recent paper and just sent it to him at random."

"You really think that?" Cordova asked, not believing.

Bodinger smiled an easy smile, admitting, "Not for a minute." He walked to the table with his coffee and sat down across from Glenn Young who was still trying to let all this catch up to him. The awful picture, the insanity of the words—and it was all sent directly to him. It was enough to make a saint need a drink.

Bodinger took out a notepad he'd written in earlier; the original letters had already been sent to the crime lab. "Let's read what the letter says: Mr. Young, I trust that you are as earnest and strong as I read you to be." He stopped, giving another calm smile. "He trusts you because he reads your work, that's all." He continued reading. "This will not be my only correspondence with you." He paused, adding, "We'll have to see on that." Bodinger sipped his coffee then finished the letter. "I trust you, above all people, to do the right thing. Please forward the adjoining page to the proper authorities." With that, he slapped the notepad closed, saying wryly, "I think you've done your job, Mr. Young."

Cordova wanted there to be more to it, but he had to admit it was pretty cut and dry. Whoever this D was, he simply used Young as a messenger and nothing more.

"This guy's read your stuff, knows you're a straight shooter, and knew you'd call us and not try to exploit what he's doing," Bodinger assured.

"Yeah, he'll do plenty of that on his own," Cordova added in disgust. Bodinger nodded.

"So let me get this straight," Glenn started. "This sick fuck abducts this teenager, hangs her in the woods somewhere, jerks off to it, and takes a picture. Then he writes two letters, one to me and one to the police, and the only reason I'm involved is because I tell the goddamn truth? Really? You really expect me to believe that?" Young stood up from the table. "How does anyone, including you two, know that this twisted shit wasn't thinking something from left field that hasn't occurred to *anyone*? Maybe I *didn't* do the right thing, and he's gonna be waiting on me tonight when I get home with his pants around his ankles, swinging a meat cleaver!"

Cordova walked closer to the table. He looked at Glenn then cut an eye to Bodinger. "If he's right—and he just may be—we have to put a unit on him." Cordova was almost comically serious on this point.

Bodinger had to stifle a laugh that was brewing somewhere below his naval. The thought of a creep that would do this to poor Amy Crowder then hold a grudge against the one schmuck he chose to deliver his message was not only preposterous, but laughable. He knew that Cordova was in over his head, not that he wasn't a good cop, but nothing in school or the academy prepares you for this kind of craziness. It was Bodinger's gut instinct, based on years of police work and dealing with unbalanced people, that the right answer is usually the first one that waltzes through your mind. This freak—calling himself D—only sent the letter to Young because he knew his first call would be to the police; and if anyone was going to write about him, he handpicked the guy he wanted doing it.

"Look, guys, if it makes you feel better, we'll put a car outside the house for a couple of days. But I really think it's overkill." He stood, downing the rest of his coffee, saying, "The creep's a fan, Mr. Young. Call it what you want, but at least he's talking to someone."

Cordova was still uneasy about Young's safety. He spoke up. "The letter did say it wouldn't be his only correspondence."

Bodinger tossed his cup in the trash. "Yeah?"

"There could be more to Mr. Young's selection than just correspondence."

"Meaning?"

"Meaning, there may be some sort of fixation with this guy. Maybe he sees him as some sort of kindred spirit."

Bodinger grew tired of this line of reasoning. It was a dead end, and he knew it. Inexperienced or not, Cordova should have known better. "Well, I guess we'll just have to see about that, now won't we?" he finished with an edge to his voice that Cordova had never heard directed at him. "Right now, there's bigger fish to fry."

"Bigger than this?" Young asked.

"I have a dead teenager hanging in a tree somewhere in Burnet County if that's even true. If and when we find her, I'll have to go tell her mother that her little girl was executed by a madman," he said, placing his hands on his hips. "Yeah. Excuse me, gentlemen, for shifting my priorities, but I think that's a little bigger than this." He scratched his chin. "Plus, all we have to go on at the moment is a death photo and two letters from the man claiming responsibility."

Cordova felt like a rookie. "I get it," he replied, closing his notebook. "It's about the here and now."

"Correct. I'm really not looking forward to telling Ms. Crowder we know what happened to her child, but damned if we know where she is. We can't find her, but we know she's dead all right—got a picture and a letter to prove it." He walked away toward the door. "That's what's at hand now, this minute. Not speculation."

"Makes sense, boss," Cordova admitted.

"What makes sense?" Young asked him, still worrying for his health.

"We have facts, Mr. Young. Facts are all we can go on to do our job. Speculation clouds the issue, creates more problems than the facts dictate."

"Well, the fact, *Detective*," Young replied, slurring the word intentionally, "is that this fruitcake sent that letter to me." He ran his hand through his reddish flop. "I'm sorry for freaking out, but I'm a little concerned here."

"We understand," Bodinger interrupted, seeing Cordova bristle. "Mr. Young, there will be a patrol car outside your house for as long as everyone involved sees fit. That I promise. I also assure you that you are not in danger. This guy has found his voice . . . you. I suggest that you run any copy you may write by me first before you print it."

The red alarm went off inside Glenn's first-amendment mind, taking priority over his own safety. He fought. "Hell no! I've got first amendment rights."

"*My ass*," Bodinger growled. "We're talking about a psychopath that has promised to kill again. In *my town*. If you print anything about the case, this D guy or that poor dead girl before I approve it, I promise, Mr. Young, it will become your biggest regret. I want this scum off the streets of Austin, and I want it yesterday, and no one in this room is as experienced with how to handle this sort of thing as me." The more he spoke, the calmer his voice grew until it was barely audible. When he finished, he was nose-to-nose with Glenn Young. "I respect you, Mr. Young, truly. But please, don't jack with me on this." He leaned even closer, saying, "My captain will be having the same conversation with your editor in about twenty minutes. This is a matter for the police, not the press."

For the first time all morning, Glenn was more intimidated by the weathered detective than the crazy freak in the letter. Wide-eyed, all he could do was nod his concurrence.

Bodinger turned to Cordova, asking with the familiar smile, "Got anything else?"

Cordova was glaring at Young; he hated the tone he took with him. "No, I got nothing."

"Then we've got all we need for now." They turned to leave. "Mr. Young, if anything about this rings a bell, maybe some clown you've forgotten for good measure or maybe you just have an idea, call us." He opened the door, saying without looking back, "There'll be a car at your house tonight."

In the lobby of the *Citizen*, Cordova seethed. Young had stepped close to insulting him. He might be young, but he was as much a detective as his veteran partner. His pride filled him as he spoke up. "That fucker pushed my buttons."

"It happens," Bodinger answered, still walking. They exited the building and were going down the front steps.

24

"But I felt—"

Bodinger stopped, turning. "Felt what? Disrespected? Get over it." This was a different Stanley Bodinger than the one Cordova had grown used to over the last four months.

Cordova swallowed, saying, "I guess so."

"You've been behind the badge long enough to know we're nothing but the fender that catches all the shit thrown at us from above and below. Let it go."

He knew Stan was right. There was no sense in allowing emotions to interfere; he had to stay on track. "Just something about that guy. He's greasy."

"Most people are," Bodinger said, walking around him. He stepped up a few steps, forcing Cordova to turn, putting his back to the street, looking up at the senior detective. He went on. "You have to remember what's important and what's not. How people feel about you or the way they speak to you means nothing, every rookie knows that. You said it yourself. It's all about the facts. Eric, I've been pounding the streets of the city since before you were born. Now, that's not a slight, I mean that. You know I respect you. But every man starts in his own place. But this, this is the big league. As soon as I saw that picture, read those words . . . ," he trailed off before starting again. "This could be the biggest nightmare this city's ever seen. And they put me, *me* in charge of ending it. Now, I don't really want this assignment. I'm in my forties, I have bad knees, eyes are failing, and I see the light at the end of the tunnel that's showing me a fishing boat and a sexy woman. With bottles of the stuff that makes shit like this fade away." He swallowed before continuing. "But if this is my lot, to find this prick and bring him in, then that's what it is. I'll do it." He leaned closer, like he had done earlier with Young, saying, "But I'm gonna need a focused partner with me. Understand?"

"Loud and clear, boss," Cordova answered. "Loud and clear. I'm riding shotgun."

"For now," Bodinger smiled, putting a hand on Cordova's shoulder. "For now. And for what it's worth, I can't think of anyone better I'd rather have."

6

S haron Crowder fell into Tony's arms, and together they sank to the floor at Bodinger's feet as Ginger sat on the couch hugging her knees, crying hysterically. Cordova squatted beside them, putting a hand on each of their shoulders in a move Bodinger liked. He was proud of the young detective; he still had his empathy. As the family held each other, sobbing, Cordova looked up at his superior who wore a mask of grief. "What now?"

Bodinger gritted, saying, "We have to get a positive."

Cordova nodded as Sharon whispered only loud enough for Tony to hear, "*I'll do it.*" At that, Cordova dropped his head as Bodinger turned away and walked to the door.

It had taken the Burnet County sheriff's department and the Austin PD eight hours to find the body once they received the letter from Glenn Young. A young deputy sheriff recognized the deer woods from his time hunting during the fall. They managed to seal off the crime scene before the television cameras and print media had time to descend on the area. Bodinger and Cordova went over the scene with pathologists and other investigators, looking for anything that could link the heinous act to the perpetrator. On the scene, there wasn't much, but they knew the science had yet to be applied. Once it had, they'd have what they needed.

*

It was midnight as the two detectives sat in silence at their desks. Sharon Crowder had taken it very hard. She saw the rope marks on Amy's neck and her sweet, young face twisted and frozen in death's grip. She had to be pulled from the room, and Tony almost broke his hands from punching the wall in the hallway. Their nightmare only beginning, Cordova had a patrol unit drive them home.

"Was she raped?" Cordova said to the thin air he was staring into.

Bodinger blinked back to life. "Huh? What?"

"Ms. Crowder. She asked me before we came down here if Amy was raped. When I told her no, she seemed relieved." He turned to look at his partner. "But in the morgue, after she saw her . . . All she kept saying was if he didn't rape her, why did he kill her. It's almost like now she wants her to have been raped. Like it would somehow justify it all." He rubbed his face and loosened his black tie. "I'm going home, Stan. I feel like a goddamn zombie."

Bodinger just nodded as his young partner stood from his desk and left.

Zombie? That was an understatement. Stanley Bodinger had put in his share of nights like this. Endless hours of questions, mug shots, interrogations, reports, briefings, not to mention the actual events of chasing down the lowlifes that caused all the hardships in the first place.

All at once, he felt old. He saw some of the expressions Cordova had worn tonight, and he remembered when he felt that way. It seemed so very long ago. It was a time before his promotions, before he fought crime in a suit and tie. Sure there were mistakes, but he was always striding in the right direction. Even when a partner slipped up, forcing him to decide between being a bad partner or a good cop, Bodinger always felt he made the right decision. At least, it was always the right decision for him at the time he made it. Memories started flooding back. The years, the partners, the job, the mistakes.

Some you live down.

Others you live with.

And some even come back to you.

*

Cordova was spent, and Bodinger only wanted to get away from all of it. At the time, they were waiting on crime scene analysis and forensics. The killer had folded Amy's clothes perfectly and left them directly beneath her hanging body. Beside the stack of clothes were her shoes and socks, her purse, and her schoolbooks, everything arranged very neatly. The only other things they had to go on were tire tracks and footprints.

They'd have to wait until the next day to see what the specialists came up with. Tomorrow would be better; tomorrow would bring light. Tomorrow would bring answers.

However, tomorrow would only bring more questions.

7

"What do you mean *nothing*?!" Bodinger yelled across the examiner's room.

"I mean *nothing*," Patrick Adams answered. The seasoned CSI officer was in his mid-thirties and had been investigating homicide scenes for the Austin PD for seven years. The shock of him not finding anything was more than Sergeant Bodinger could take.

Captain Jim Saunders, who was present as well, asked for more. "Pat, for Christ's sake, there has to be something."

"Nope."

"I don't believe this," Cordova said. "Nobody leaves nothing."

"This guy did."

"What about the tire tracks?" Bodinger asked, almost pleading.

Adams pulled a sheet from his stack of papers and read, "Seventeen-inch all-terrain LT315s. Firestone." He peeked over the top of the paper, adding, "They come pretty much standard on any number of stock SUVs."

"No help?" Cordova asked.

"None whatsoever. Other than telling us what size the vehicle is. Like I said, fellas, a stock SUV."

"No make? Not off the tires?" Saunders asked.

"Any number of up to twenty. Your guess is as good as any, Cap."

"Beautiful."

"Footprints?" Bodinger asked.

"A generic brand of work boot you can but at any Wal-Mart for twenty bucks. Size 9. If you can get something out of that, you're better than me," Adams said in disgust. He wasn't liking this any better than the detectives; in fact, it hurt him even more. He was the hotshot CSI specialist who always found the *one thing*. But this time, there was no *one thing*.

D left nothing, like his letter said.

"The letter, picture, envelope—all of them were dusted. Nothing. All we got were staffers at the *Citizen* and postal workers. That's it."

Cordova burst out, "It's at the scene. Whatever it is, it's at the fucking scene!"

"No, it's not!" Adams defended. "Detective, we went over that place with microbrushes and spectra lights. There's nothing there. Went over the body, over her clothes, her belongings—we went over all of it a thousand times, and I'm telling you there is *nothing*."

"Nothing to use at all?" Saunders asked.

"No prints, no blood, no semen, no fibers, no hair, no saliva— nothing. I feel like I'm back in school 'cause this is one for the books."

"You're telling me he committed the perfect crime," Bodinger accused.

"No, Stan. I'm telling you that to catch this creep, you need something more than what I can give you. Unless you have a witness or Leeds comes up with something in the autopsy, we're still standing at square one."

"With our dicks in the wind," Saunders added.

"No shit."

"Goddamn it," Bodinger said, leaving the room with his coat in his hand. Cordova was on his heels, leaving Adams and Captain Saunders alone.

"Any ideas, Captain?" Adams asked, standing while gathering his papers.

"Yeah, but I don't like it."

"What's that?"

Saunders walked into the hall and looked back. "Wait for the next one," he said, turning down the hall. He added to himself, "And hope for a mistake."

*

Dr. Henry Leeds, fifty-six, was a criminal pathologist who'd been working for the Austin PD for the last twenty years. He was not only considered the best criminal pathologist in South Texas, if not the whole state, but he was also known and respected around the country. He was only called in on local cases if the crime was deemed a priority at the highest level. Bodinger was ecstatic that the case was filed up the ladder to the best they had. After the dead end they hit with Adams, he felt like a cold roller in Vegas needing to hit one big seven to turn the tables. Leeds's results would be enormous.

He *had* to find something.

The two detectives were waiting for the doctor in a conference room that adjoined the examining rooms where the autopsies were performed. Stan had waited in that particular room so many times he knew the colored specs in the green floor tile like old friends.

Here we are again.

Cordova was getting antsy. Thus far, in his short career as a homicide detective, he'd dealt mostly with domestic cases and gang hits. This was the first time he'd come face-to-face with a murder without motive. A terrible act of violence without rhyme or reason. He was starting to understand Sharon Crowder's logic. There seemed to be nothing sexual about the case at all, just a random girl plucked off the street and hanged like a great trophy fish snagged in the Gulf. When he first saw the horrible photo, he knew in his gut that the victim had to have been raped; it made the most sense to everyone. After all, she was a sexy young girl who was stripped naked. The numbers added up. Finding out she wasn't raped only posed more questions.

Bodinger's cell phone rang; it was his wife, Susan. "Hi, babe," he answered.

Cordova began looking through his notes at the table while Bodinger explained to his wife that they were still waiting on Leeds; and he would, of course, let her know if "Henry has anything we can use." Cordova laughed to himself. He liked Susan. She was a cop's wife from the get-go. He admired the way she shared in her husband's work no matter how crazy or dangerous it got. She was a real trooper. Not like his own wife who only wanted him sitting at a desk, away from the action.

When he made detective, she was so proud and happy; but when she found out he still had to carry a gun and would still get into some tight spots that meant taking action, she cooled to the idea.

"Baby, when I make captain, then you can relax," he told her.

"And when will *that* be?" she demanded.

"Before I'm sixty, I promise."

As Stan told Susan goodbye, the door of the room opened; and Leeds entered, still in his green scrubs. His salt-and-pepper hair was curly but receding, and his thick mustache matched the colors on his scalp. He was darkly tanned from too many days of sinking putts at the exclusive Falconhead.

"Stan, Detective Cordova, let's talk," he said, entering the room. He sat opposite them at the big table with his glasses on top of his head.

"Hank, I hope you hit something out of the park 'cause right now, we're batting zero," Bodinger confessed, rolling his eyes at Cordova.

"Oh, I got something all right. But it only raises more questions."

They hated the sound of that. Bodinger loosened his tie, leaning on the table with his elbows. "Okay, go ahead," he said with a startling defeatist tone to his voice that neither Cordova nor Leeds had ever heard.

Dr. Leeds opened his folder and took out autopsy photos of Amy Crowder. He flipped through until he found close-ups of the neck. "Okay, fellas, see this deep ligature mark just below the jawline? That's from the nylon rope used to hang her. It's the type any fisherman has for a small anchor, like on a bass boat. Buy it at any hardware store by the foot, untraceable."

"Okay," Bodinger replied, knowing this already.

"But that's not what killed her," Dr. Leeds informed them. His tone was that of excitement, like a schoolboy who knows the answer to the teacher's question. Without moving his head, Bodinger's eyes scanned sideways to Cordova who was looking dead at him.

What? That wasn't what killed her?

"Explain, Hank," Bodinger groaned.

"This mark and the internal injuries caused by the rope were all postmortem. There was zero internal bleeding around the larynx, which is always the smoking gun in a hanging. This girl was dead when he hung her."

"You're sure?" Cordova asked.

Leeds was insulted. "Detective Cordova, I've been doing this for over thirty years. I think I know postmortem trauma when I see it."

"Okay, okay, okay," Bodinger interjected. "So the exam tells you she was dead when her hung her, correct?"

"Absolutely," Leeds said. "There was no eight-ball hemorrhaging of the eyes, and the vessels of the face and neck were never engorged with blood."

"It already settled," Bodinger said.

"Correct."

"How long?" Cordova asked.

"Half hour, maybe forty-five minutes."

"Then what killed her?" Bodinger asked.

"Asphyxiation," Leeds responded, awaiting the next question.

"Oh hell, man!" Cordova said. "He hung her, that's it!"

"No . . . It's not," Leeds replied coolly. "Look closer at the photo."

The two cops leaned in closer. Leeds showed them another mark, flatter and farther below the rope mark. It was faint, not as deep, but there was a hint of bruising.

"What's that?" Bodinger asked, growing tired.

"I really don't know. The bruising is not sufficient enough to suggest strangulation, but the tests shows she died of asphyxiation. However, the trauma to the body is textbook postmortem. He suffocated her before her hung her—I'll stake my career on it."

"How?" Cordova asked.

"Well," Leeds continued, "there were no marks or bruising to her face. So we can rule out smothering. He had to have another way. That brings us to the other mark on her throat. It wasn't severe enough to cause death, but it could have been something put in place to hold the device used."

"Device?" Cordova asked, still skeptical.

"He bagged her," Bodinger said, feeling sick. "He put a bag on her head."

"Her hands and feet were swinging free on the tree, yes?" Leeds asked.

"Right," Cordova replied, "but there were deep impressions from the binds that were used. We felt they were cut off after she died."

"Agreed," Bodinger added.

"Right. And he did. But *before* he hung her," Leeds informed them. Flipping through the photos, he showed them what he meant.

"The widths of the marks are consistent with the lighter mark on her throat and neck. Whatever it was, he used the same thing to hold her in place as it happened."

"He bagged her and used a zip tie to hold it," Bodinger said. "And he used zip ties to bind her arms and legs."

"That's my guess, buy them in any hardware store," Leeds said, sitting back in his chair, satisfied.

It was getting worse by the minute. The room grew quiet. All three men sat with their own thoughts, wondering what kind of madman had descended upon their city.

Leeds had more. He flipped through the photos again and found the one he wanted; it was of her back. "Here," he said, "two small burn marks. Look familiar?"

Bodinger's heart sank. The marks were on the left side of her back, about an inch below her shoulder blade and an inch to the left of her spine. "Taser," he said flatly.

"Bingo. The old kind, directly behind the heart. This girl only weighed a hundred pounds, and her chest depth is a mere four inches. A shot like that, not even at full strength, would not only incapacitate her, but most likely seize her lungs."

"She couldn't scream," Bodinger said.

"Not a peep."

Again, silence filled the room. That explained why no one heard a scream, and on the deserted street, there were no witnesses to see. The neighborhood where the Crowder's lived was full of working families. At that time of day, no one was home except an elderly couple who said they saw and heard nothing.

Cordova spoke up. "Let me get this straight. This creep tased the girl in north Austin. Drives her all the way out past Marble Falls, puts a bag over her head and zip tied it, and watched her suffocate to death. Then after she's dead, he puts a rope around her neck and pulls her up in a tree. Folds her clothes as neat as Mama, puts her things under her, and takes a creepy picture then drives away. Is that right?"

"That's about it, I'd say. At least, that's the idea," Leeds replied.

"God . . . *damn it!*" Cordova responded, slapping the table before walking to the far end of the room.

Bodinger said nothing. This was bad. This was nothing like he'd ever seen. He'd seen all kinds of brutal acts in his years on the force from child molestation to matricide. But this was far beyond anything he'd ever seen. He was beginning to believe that maybe he wasn't the man for the job. When Captain Saunders gave him the case, he actually thought it would be a slam dunk. But now, it seemed as though they were looking in a mirror for a man made of glass. Traces you thought were there vanished. Leeds proved to them that this fiend not only killed the Crowder kid; but he bagged her, watched her die, and then hung her dead, naked body from a withering tree. All before taking a picture and mailing it to that asshole reporter at the *Citizen* with a full confession. He also promised the very lack of evidence that they had indeed discovered. As investigators, all they had to show for it were tire tracks and boot prints matching at least fifty thousand people.

"Hank, this could not have gone worse," Bodinger said.

"Why?" Leeds asked, truly puzzled.

"Because you just showed me that this guy is not only *very* careful, but he's even more insane than we thought."

"Yeah?" Leeds replied.

Cordova spoke, his voice choked up. "He killed her . . . *Then* he hung her. That, my good doctor, isn't just crazy." He walked back to the table, looking at Bodinger. "That's evil."

8

Adam Parker sat alone in his red room, studying the photos he'd taken while listening to the music that flamed the fires in his soul. Deloris never understood his music, and that was always fine with him. He didn't want her to like it; it was his. It was something he could sink his fingers into that never pulled away or rebuked him.

The music—and his jars.

His killing jars.

Now, he had a new killing jar.

As he admired his work, the music told him it was time. He took a shot of vodka then opened the cap of a bottle of amyl nitrate, breathing deeply. The music became colors in his mind. The image of Amy fighting the binds as he pleasured himself became real once again. Her face inside the bag, air snuffed off, hope wilting like the summer sun at dusk. He had to touch himself.

More of the tiny bottle.

More vodka.

More music.

More of losing himself inside his own mind. Not able to stop what he was living within, he pressed on for more. More sex, more violence, more depravity, more insanity . . . more hopelessness.

Amy dying in the bag, human vermin in his killing jar. The music and the chemicals, it was more than he could take. He ejaculated in the trash can next to the desk as the world around him continued to spin like a child's pinwheel. The release was overwhelming. He fell back into his chair as the music roared, and the alcohol mixing with the amyl nitrate nearly caused a hallucination.

He almost saw her.

He knew the truth. He had a viral insanity spawned into him by her. Deloris was the carrier that doomed him to this life of madness. Cursed. As damned to this life as a bee doomed to slave its life away for its queen. She was so much a part of him he could never separate her from himself. No more than he could split away who he was from what he'd done.

It never goes away.

He snapped to his feet, turning over his chair, as Slayer blared behind him. He glared at her portrait above the desk. So pretty, so beautiful . . . So fucking hideous.

"I let myself become *you!*"

Taking the bottle of vodka, he walked out of the red room to the door across the hall. Her room. The door, forever sealed, stopped him. He pulled a long draw from the bottle then placed his back to the door. The sound of her voice echoed through his brain. Calling, haunting, threatening. He took another long pull from the bottle before turning and punching the door. It was on the other side. All the dreams, all the nightmares, and all the deadened hatred. It was a mere few inches away, just on the other side of a sealed door.

"No," he said more to himself than to her. "Not tonight. Tonight, I'm a king. I won't let you ruin this for me."

He walked down the black hall to the dark living room and stood naked in the middle of the floor. He sipped more vodka then realized he needed something else. Racing back to the red room, he snatched the small bottle of amyl nitrate then rushed back to the blackness of the living room. As the music continued, he sniffed it, letting what would happen happen.

He wilted in tears to the floor, curling in a fetal position, screaming to his ghost, "*Why did you do this to me?!*"

There he would pass out and sleep. Then dream. His wonderful dreams and nightmares.

His sweet dreams of unrelenting madness.

9

"You know, Frank, if it was anybody else standing there, I'd cut you off," the bartender said with a smirk.

"And *you* know," Frank replied, "if it was anybody else, they wouldn't still be standing here."

The bartender smiled. "Got me there, partner," he said, pouring another Johnny Walker Black with two ice cubes. "And another for the lady?"

"Of course," he replied smoothly. Toxic Mike set him up, adding the round to Frank's weekly tab. When he turned for his table, Toxic called to him, "Hey, Frank."

"Yeah?"

"Good hunting," he told him, laughing.

Frank Castro shrugged as he maneuvered through the tables like a running back in the open field. He was a regular at Lucky's and knew the floor pattern like an interior designer. He knew how many tables there were, where they lay, and exactly how many steps he could spare between them before he had to plot his avoidance. When he arrived at his table, he was pleased to see that Monica was still there. He half expected her to be gone by now. It had been over three weeks since he'd been laid, and he was beginning to doubt his luck.

"Tequila sunrise for the lady," he said, setting the drink in front of her. She smiled, sipping, as he sat across from her and adjusted his black sports coat.

"Now, where was I?" he asked.

"You were sweeping me off my feet," she replied sarcastically.

"Oh yeah," he remembered, "the law. And all the noble spirits that drive it." In a grand gesture, he raised his glass to the room. "Any sap that wants to change the world need only become a patrolman for the *fine* Austin police department," he said loud enough for several others to hear. There were a few whistles and whoops as he poured down the straight scotch in one long motion, setting the empty glass on the table.

"So I take it you're a drunk?" she rudely asked.

"Me? Nah. I'm what you'd call a social disaster. You see, I understand the game. I know the rules and all that moral responsibility bullshit just like everybody else. The difference is I just don't give a damn."

She giggled. He was a charmer; she had to give him that. Two hours earlier, he walked up to her as she sat at the bar and asked, "I see you're alone. Is it your intention to stay that way?" The line was a little cheesy, but when she turned to face the owner of the baritone voice, she was surprised to see a very attractive, well-dressed man in his forties. Dark hair and eyes with a chiseled face that belonged on a statue. Broad shoulders, standing a good six two and a little over two spins. He was in a black sports coat over a white dress shirt. Pressed Wrangler jeans with expensive boots—Lucchese ostrich, charcoal gray. The alluring scent he gave off was definitely something Calvin Klein.

She went for it, all of it. After all, she was alone on Sixth Street on a Friday night for what was most likely the same reason. The well-dressed thirty-something divorcee with a hint of Asian blood was in the same dry patch Frank was stumbling through. She'd screwed her pillow so many times she'd given it a name—*Sven*. She'd spent two hours with the charming slug and was starting to think she might be able to give Sven the night off.

However, Frank Castro was a seasoned alcoholic. Meaning his solution to any situation was always more alcohol. He'd won her over in the first twenty minutes but then started pounding Johnny Walker like he owed him money. His suave was starting to dim as the booze took over. She was beginning to think this package was all wrapping with no gift. At this point, she wanted to know more.

"Where you from, Frank?" she asked, sipping her drink.

Frank leaned back, saying, "Family's from Cuba. They got out just as my namesake was taking over. I was born in Miami a week before Kennedy got shot in Dallas. We moved West, and I've been an Austenite since I was eight."

"Never wanted to leave?"

"Hell no, I love this town. It's so different. It's like a little spec of California got dropped right in the middle of the state. Besides, I love being a Texan." He leaned back over the table, saying, "But since I wasn't born here, if being from Texas ever goes out of style, I can always tell people I'm from Cuba," he finished with the same bedroom smile that worked so well before.

Frank liked her. She was a looker but not in the usual sense. She was a little curvy like she had to work at keeping her figure from getting away from her. Dark hair and eyes with the slightest almond flavor, suggesting she was at least a third Asian. She seemed very intelligent and secure about herself. She told him she worked in the low level of the state government. He liked that. This could turn out to be a good connection someday.

"Come here a lot?" she asked, still sizing him up.

"I'm like the furniture."

She had another question completely off the topic, but since he was a regular, he should know. "The bartender," she said, nodding to the bar, "why do they call him Toxic Mike?"

Frank laughed; it was a good question. He explained, "Well, ol' Mike there was a truck driver back in the day. Hazmat stuff, chemicals and what not. Well, the short story is there was an accident with a tanker he was hauling, and the corrosive shit he was carrying spilled out and burned his feet right through his boots. Lost his left foot and three toes on his right."

Startled, she turned to the bar.

"Don't look. He'll know I'm talking about him, and he'll get pissed at me," he warned. "The two people you never want mad at you are your barber and your bartender."

She laughed; his charm was returning.

"Anyway," he continued, "he's got prosthetics, so you'd never know. But he had to find a new gig." Lowering his voice, as though he were about to divulge a national secret, he added, "See, it's a little difficult to pass the physical to drive a truck when you got two toes and a stump."

She laughed, spitting tequila and orange juice.

"Stop that!" he laughed. "You'll destroy my spotless reputation!" He glanced to the bar to see Mike shaking his head, knowing Castro was hitting a home run. One man's folly was another man's celebration.

If anyone needed something to feel good about, it was the ex-cop Frank Castro. His work was uncertain at best. Aside from his one employee, the only people he was in contact with were drug dealers, thieves, crooked businessmen, and a bartender with prosthetic feet. That's why he had such a fondness for his best friend, Johnny Walker, who never lied to him or let him down. Frank had been set up and burned so many times he grew to understand his only true friend in the world was his friend in the bottle. The one who was always there. The only one he could trust.

He was an only child. His mother went barren after his birth, so he grew up not having anyone around him. Even as a child, the friends he made—at some point or another—would betray his trust, shaking his early confidence in human nature. He was a popular kid all through school but managed to keep most people at arm's length unless he trusted them unequivocally. When those bonds were broken, the distance he put around himself would grow wider still. Mistrust was in his nature. In his mid-twenties, he decided to put that mistrust to work.

He became a patrolman for the Austin police department. It lasted ten years before his sacred trust was broken a final time.

That was ten years ago.

Now, Frank Castro was simply who he was. Self-employed with a staff of one. Making just enough money to pay his employee, the rent, and cover his love affair with blended scotch. But it wasn't about money with Frank; it was all in the connections. That's how he managed to keep the illusion of success. If you knew a businessman with a taste for Mexican coke and a drug runner who liked sweet cars, a slick middleman could make good cash keeping the two as friends.

Well, *friends* was a relative term. Low places aren't strong in the *real* friends department.

A disastrous marriage in his twenties left him jaded in his views of commitment. The only other true commitment he ever made was to the badge. When that broke his heart, he lost all confidence in the misty vale of human morality. He just wanted to live the rest of his life as he damned well pleased, and if that meant embracing the untrustworthy, he was fine with that. Frank understood the ground rules when dealing with scoundrels.

Don't trust anybody.

J. W. Black had his back.

As the house band started playing an old Paul McCartney song, Monica had another question to ask. It was probably not the right time, but she was interested in Frank. In addition, it meant something to her. "How much money did you make last year?"

Surprised, Frank responded, "Say again?"

"How much money did you make last year?" she asked again, smiling over her glass.

He stared at her for a second then asked, "Is that important to you?"

"Well, Frank, you look the part. I mean you dress nicely, you're handsome, and you smell good. But I just need to know if it's all window dressing."

"Excuse me?"

"I mean, the package is wonderful," she said, getting serious. "I just want to know there's substance under all the pretty paper."

"And to you, the answer lies in my bank account?" he asked, feeling his ire begin to stir.

"No," she defended. "But it's a good indicator."

"Of what?"

She folded her arms, telling him, "If your intentions are honorable."

In his drunken state, it hit him wrong. If he'd been sober, he might have given in and gone along with her. If he wasn't drunk, it wouldn't have insulted him.

But he was.

And it did.

The whole thing seemed to sour in Frank's stomach. The word *honorable* especially held a particular smack to it. He'd left all that stuff behind him years ago. There was no honor in cruising bars for a piece of ass from either side of the coin, man or woman. He took out his cigarettes, glancing at Mike, who gave him a friendly but firm no shake of the head.

Goddamned city ordinance. Can't even smoke in a lousy bar. What's next? No sex in a bed?

He dropped the smokes on the table as the scotch in his brain took him from happy to pissed in a matter of seconds. The gall of it. He'd paid for a whole night's worth of tequila, swooned her, and made her laugh; and now she's going to start being high and mighty.

"You know, Monica—that was your name, right?"

She nodded, looking suddenly aloof.

"Monica, I just want to know one thing."

"Which is?"

"Are we going to do this or not? Because if we are, it don't matter a damn what the balance in my account is. If you think you're too good for me, then I guess, by God, you are. Because all that matters to me right now is getting so far up inside you I make your throat hurt." He leaned forward. "And no amount of money is gonna make that feel different, either way."

Monica's brows wrinkled as she tried to sort out if he was serious or not. When his eyes never wavered, she knew he was. "You insulted me, you son of a bitch."

"You insulted me first," he shot back, standing from the table. "Have fun with your toys tonight. I'm done with this." He walked to the bar where Toxic Mike was waiting.

"Hit me, Toxic."

"I see a distress signal."

"You see a materialistic bitch who's fucking her fingers tonight, that's what you see."

Mike poured three fingers and dropped in two cubes. He didn't need the ice; he just liked the sound the cubes made in the glass. After he sucked it down in one draw, he lit a smoke at the bar.

"Damn it, Frank, you know you can't smoke in here."

"Call a cop," Frank said, dropping five bucks in the tip jar before heading to the door.

"Settle on Monday?" Mike asked, seeing only Frank's wave as the door closed. He turned to the handsome woman Frank had just blown off. "Looks like somebody needs comforting."

Outside, the city was buzzing. Sixth Street on Friday night. A true smorgasbord for the senses. Walking in the cool night air, Frank took in the vibrant aromas that seemed to linger with a life of their own. Every grill was churning. Mexican, Italian, Japanese, and barbeque flooded downtown with an eclectic mix of exotic aromas. Along the street, hot dog wagons and pretzel carts mixed with the many popcorn vendors causing a bouquet that reminded Frank this was his town, his way of life. Music poured out into the street as he headed east toward the parking lot beneath the interstate. Country and jazz mingled with rock and hip-hop. Bands of all kinds playing not just for the night, but for their futures. The street was swarmed with college kids, vacationers, freaks, geeks, and a few local oddities.

Even local icon Leslie was there, passing Frank, wearing leopard panties and matching bra enhanced with a top hat and cowboys boots. The outfit was topped off with a guitar slung over the shoulder and bright orange sunglasses. All fashioned to accent his gray beard and back hair.

"Leslie."

"Frank," they each acknowledged.

The place was like an adult amusement park. Eight city blocks long, all within walking distance of the capitol building, which looked down Congress Avenue like a watchful parent allowing her children to frolic in total enjoyment of their playtime.

"Keep Austin Weird"—it's more than a slogan.

Getting closer to the lot, a moment of doubt crept into his mind. Maybe he was over reactive? Did she really deserve that? Maybe she was trying to make sure he wasn't a creep? A woman can't be too careful.

"Too late now," he said to the night. "Fuck it. It's one in the morning and too late to start over. She'll end up happy. Toxic will see to that."

He reached the lot, finding his car mixed in with all the others. He slipped the lot man an extra five for watching his ride then climbed in. The inside of the car was dry and warm. Sanctuary. A reprieve from the sins of the night.

He started the car, and the radio erupted with a song from Godsmack. As he adjusted to his new surroundings, "Living in Sin" played. Sitting alone in the dark, he felt the lyrics preaching to him like an old evangelist minister from the south:

Broken inside myself, can't seem to break this trend.
I've seen it all, and I've walked it tall.
Lived in this sin…Where do I begin?

He grumbled to himself, knowing he was beyond saving by any measure. He still wanted to feel the inside of a woman and knew of only one sure bet. As the song scolded him further, he removed a small glass vial from the glove box. It was the coke he'd scored the night before. Peeking around the lot, he took two small hits of the powder then checked his nose in the mirror, wiping it clean. The lot guy saw and gave him a thumbs-up. Frank just winked at him as he gunned the engine.

The BMW Z4 he pulled out of the lot was bought through one of his best coke buddies, Tully Pritchard, who owned a low-rent loan company where you could get any amount you wanted as long as you had something to bargain with. It was funny how much a guy could get just by introducing birds of a feather.

Low-place friends.

He headed south out of the lot toward Riverside Drive and east Austin.

"Why not?" he asked himself. "Got nowhere else to be."

Frank reached Vargas Avenue and started looking for the house where he'd last seen her. It had been months, but surely she was still there. He drove to her block and saw that not only was she not there, but neither was the house. Only a pile of black rubble and brick stood in the place of the house where he last felt the inside of her. It was burned to the ground.

"Shit," he said, turning the car.

He drove a little farther and made a block then turned again, taking him deeper into east Austin. This side of town was ruled by gangs. The people who lived here didn't trust anyone, which put Frank Castro right at home. When he trolled the streets as a cop, this was his stomping ground. He'd lived among them for ten years behind the badge and his service .38.

Except for one night, he'd still be here.

Turning onto a new street, he spied some teenagers shooting craps in front of a blacked-out house. He stopped across the street, studying the group. They were acting wired, most likely meth, the bathtub variety. Two he didn't know for sure, but one looked familiar. Through the dark, he realized the kid he knew was indeed the very thug wannabe he'd remembered.

Mario Cohalla. By now, he was nineteen. A good kid dealt a bad hand. He had the brains to get away from all this, but he was stuck in the same cycle as his father and brothers. No matter what potential he had, there was a cell at Gatesville with his name on it.

It was a damn shame.

"Mario! *Que paso*!" Frank yelled from across the street.

The three youths stopped, turning in unison. Frank would let them sort it out among themselves.

"Who's that *pendejo*?" one asked.

Mario turned, adjusting his eyes, then crumbled inside. "Oh shit."

"What?"

"That's fucking Castro."

"Who's that?"

"He's not a *who* he's a *what*."

"Then *what* is he?"

"A real dick."

"Fuck him, *ese*. We'll cut his nuts off!"

46

"No, *vato*, you don't want to get in this fucker's way," Mario warned. "I shouldn't be out here."

"Why not?"

"Probation, *cabrón*!"

The other kid spoke up, "*Ese*, that ain't your probation officer."

"No, he's worse."

"A *pinche* cop?"

"No," Mario told them. "He's *pinche* loco."

Frank yelled, "Mario, don't make me get out of this goddamned car!"

"I said I'm coming, *fucker*!" Mario shot back. When he turned back to his boys, they were losing faith in him. He saw it in their eyes. "Look, I'm going to chill this fucker, and when I get back, I'm taking all that shit!" he said, pointing at the game. The two kids laughed, knowing as much as he that they let him off the hook. "Don't touch none of that shit, understand?"

"Yeah, whatever, *puto*."

"Fuck you, bro. I'm memorizing that shit."

Honk!

When Frank hit the horn, Mario's eyes widened. They saw it. He had to save face. He turned on a dime and stomped across the street with bad intentions, coming to the car with rage in his eyes. When he got within spitting distance, he looked at the man behind the wheel. They locked eyes, just for a second, but long enough for the street in the young punk to realize he was looking into the eyes of mortality. Not doing it physically, he blinked somewhere deep in his soul.

Frank saw it. It was enough for now.

"Still running the streets, *jefe*?" Frank asked.

"What do you want, *cabrón*?"

"You look wired, Mario."

"Yeah? Well, you look worse, bro." He leaned back, saying, "Nice car, *vato*." Frank had the black ragtop up on the silver two seater. He barely fit in the German machine.

"Stole it," Frank said.

Mario turned back to his boys who were watching closely. "You didn't come to show me this fucking car."

"Just looking for somebody."

Mario faked shock. "*Oh really?*"

"Not like that," Frank told him. "A woman."

Mario was relieved. Frank was looking for trim. With that, he could not only help, but also be a hero to his boys. "Who's that, *vato?*"

"Carmen."

"Carmen?"

"Spinoza, dipshit."

Mario laughed. "Bro, she's on MLK now. At the villa."

"No shit?"

"No shit."

"For how long?"

"Hell if I know. Ain't my job to track that *puta.*"

Frank took a deep breath, settling himself. He wanted to get out of the car and stomp some sense into this kid, but there was a higher calling tonight. "What number?" he asked.

Mario looked up, thinking. "Three . . . twenty-seven?"

"You asking me?"

"No, bro, three twenty-seven."

"You think or you know?"

"I know, *vato*. It's three twenty-seven."

They locked eyes a last time. Frank wanted to instill in him the memory of consequence. He knew it wouldn't matter, but for himself, he had to try. Turning ahead, the window hissed closed as the BMW pulled away into the night. Mario felt used, dirty. "Tell that bitch she owes me a *commission!*" he yelled to Frank's taillights. As he moved back to the craps game, whistles and catcalls ensued.

In an hour, Castro was a distant memory.

10

The knock at the door was loud.

Bang! Bang! Bang!

At first, it didn't resonate in her sleep. But on the third or maybe fourth time, Carmen knew there was someone beating down her front door. The twenty-six-year-old woke from her sleep, glancing at the clock on her nightstand.

Three thirty a.m.

"What the hell?" she asked herself.

Bang! Bang! Bang!

"Go away, *cabrón*!" she yelled through the apartment, rolling over and covering her head with her pillow. However, the knocking persisted.

It had been a long night. Carmen had a steady job, but sold herself on weekends to make mad money that her baby daddy could never hold against her. After doing three drunk gangbangers and consuming enough pot to haze Tommy Chong, she was ready to bed down for the night. Her mind and body needed to unwind from the onslaught. With no man in her life, having sworn off relationships due to the obvious circumstances of her existence, the still-young and vibrant woman fulfilled her needs with the cash cow that was her body.

"Use it or lose it, *cariño*," her grandmother told her. "Ir en beneficio de uno defecto." This was coming from a woman who knew and understood the weakness of men. Carmen was willing most of the time and never turned away good money, but this was just out of the question.

Bang! Bang! Bang!

"*Bastante!*" she yelled, climbing from her bed. Carmen stomped through the apartment naked, forsaking cover to rid herself of the annoyance. She slung the door open, ready to spill out a barrage of Spanish abuse, when she saw who was there and stopped.

A total shock.

"Frank?" she asked, now trying to cover herself.

"Hi, baby."

"What? I mean . . . wait," she said, reaching behind the door to the silky robe she'd left hours before. Putting it on, she asked, "What's this?" "Long time, huh?"

It had been at least eight months since she last saw him at her house on Vargas. He was a wreck then; she figured him dead by now. Frank Castro was the absolute last man she thought she'd see on this night.

"Why are you here?" she asked, tying the pink robe.

"I just need a place to sleep, baby. That's all," he said, slurring.

"What?"

"I just have to lay down, and Round Rock is too far to drive," he told her. She looked great. Black hair flowing around her shoulders, her small body wrapped in pink silk. It was so hot he'd forgotten she opened the door totally nude. "Please, baby, I swear. No funny business. I just need to lay down."

The reality was bewildering. For cash, she'd had enough sex to be in a state of numbness only to be woken up out of a sound sleep for the one *pendejo* she would have given her life to just three years ago. There was a time when she loved this drunk ex-cop. Frank was Cuban, but fair skinned, and she dreamed of a day she'd be able to call herself Mrs. Frank Castro, holding her head high while pissing off the white socialites who look down their noses at mixed marriages.

But that was a lifetime ago. A different life altogether. Now she was a statistic on some bureaucrat's spreadsheet. A lost number. One of many so shuffled in and out of the public's consciousness that even her own self-worth was questioned.

And then there was Frank.

He was so strong and smart, so gifted with insight, she could never believe he let one event change him so dramatically. He'd walked out of her life two, maybe three times, but she always knew he'd come back. The last time, she figured it was for good. He'd looked so bad, so defeated. She moved on.

And now here he was.

"Please," he said, taking a step to the door.

Part of her wanted to hug him, kiss him, and tell him he was going to be safe. She wanted to protect him from the demons that chased his mind and ravaged his soul. However, another part of her wanted to slam the door in his face and never see or hear his name again. Torn, she stepped toward him, stopping his advance. "Why me?" she asked.

Frank recoiled. He stood there looking at the one person who was ever in love with him. The one person who would have taken him despite the flaws and warts. The one person who really wanted him and who he turned away from. He owed her a reason; he owed her big time. To show up now, after all this time, looking for comfort after the ache he'd caused. He knew he had to deliver. With all the truth left in him, he told her, "Baby . . . I hurt."

Carmen melted.

This strong man—who could kill his way out of any situation—was so beaten and lost she wilted. Yet again, she wilted to Frank Castro. With a tear in her eye, she stepped back, opening the door. Castro walked through, closing it behind him.

At least for one more night, he'd know peace.

11

A team of homicide investigators attended the funeral for Amy Crowder. With the entire school let out to attend the service, authorities felt the killer, D, may show up out of a sense of awe at the fuss he'd caused. All the local television and print media were there, covering the story of the pretty seventeen-year-old with the bright future who was so brutally murdered. Camera crews from all the local news stations were there filming the grieving students as they entered and exited the chapel. A few were happy to share their feelings for their dead classmate so violently cut down in the youth of her life. Through tears, they would look in the camera, telling the world what Amy had meant to them and the loss they felt as she was being laid to rest. It seemed ghoulish to some, but it was news, and everyone wanted to share in the tragedy.

Aside from the *Citizen*, the only detail given to the media about the killing was that the girl was found hanged in the woods of Burnet County. It had been an "anonymous tip" that led investigators to locate the body. The editors at the *Citizen* agreed not to divulge any report of the letters or the grisly photo in an attempt to force another communication from D while also keeping the valuable details undisclosed. The less the general public knew, the easier it would be to discourage fame seekers from taking credit for a crime they didn't commit.

No other media outlet had any idea the photo and letter even existed, and the APD meant to keep it that way.

To the rest of the world, Amy had died in a random act of violence. Only a handful of workers at the *Citizen* and the homicide investigators knew otherwise.

And of course . . . the monster in the night.

12

The date of death on Amy Crowder's marker read April 13. It was now closing in on Memorial Day, and the trail was so cold it was basically nonexistent. A bright, sunny day found Stanley Bodinger and Eric Cordova sitting in the backyard at the Cordova house as they watched Eric's children play while their wives prepared a barbeque for both families. Sipping Coronas and enjoying the Texas weather, Cordova had a confession.

"I don't sleep, Stan," he said. "Maybe two or three hours at the most. I wake up seeing that picture. That poor girl, dead. It haunts me, bro," he said, sipping his beer. "I swear, buddy, if I ever get the chance—"

"You'll what?" Bodinger asked, like a father talking to a hot-headed son. "Shoot him? Beat him to death? Play hero so you can live with yourself?"

Bodinger had the same feelings, but his years told him emotion was an enemy in a case like this. Procedure was the call, the only call, right or wrong. Anything outside of that was too risky to chance.

Cordova glanced over to his little girl then looked back to his partner. "I can't help it, Stan. Every time I look at my own baby, I see Amy Crowder's face. Dead, filled with horror. I see those autopsy photos. I see the picture that son of a bitch sent." He leaned close so the women couldn't hear. "I can't help wondering what Sharon Crowder's going through right now."

Bodinger thought before speaking. He remembered what being a

54

young cop was like. The days spent putting your own family in the place of the victims you encountered. It was a hopeless proposition at best. You end up chasing your tail, never stopping the pain, and minimizing your professional responsibility.

"Eric," he started, "you're a detective. You've earned this spot way faster than I ever did. You know the evil in the world. You've seen it up close. You've dealt with dead kids before."

"Not like this." Cordova cut him off. "This is something new, at least to me," he admitted, looking at his wife at the grill, laughing with Susan Bodinger. "Yeah, bro, I've seen gangbangers who cut the throat of a woman because she called him a *puto*. I've seen kids shot though the head just because they zigged when they should have zagged. But this shit, this fucker got his fun from watching that poor girl suffocate."

Bodinger glanced around, making sure none of the family was near.

"Then, if that wasn't enough, he stripped her and hung her like some goddamned deer. He did it like a prize, Stan. He glorified himself with that poor girl's dead body."

"Stop," Bodinger told him. "Stop now, Eric, or you're not going to be able to finish this." Bodinger drank from his bottle then positioned himself directly in front of his partner. "If you're trying to think like this guy, stop. You'll never get there. You're normal. Understand? You, me, the kids," he said, waving his hand around the yard. "This, this Eric, is normal. But this guy, this *psycho*, he's not. He won't ever be. Do your kids a favor and stop trying to think like him. They deserve better. They deserve you. Not that. Not *him*."

The two quieted as Cordova's daughter ran to them, hugging her father's legs then running back to the joy of being a child. Bodinger saw Eric well up then catch himself.

"How old is she?" Bodinger asked.

"She'll be three in July."Stan and Susan's kids were both grown with children of their own. Both his son and daughter had given them a grandchild apiece. He understood where Eric was coming from. Not as a cop but as a father.

"The truth," Eric asked, "you ever see anything like this?"

"Only in the movies," Bodinger confessed.

55

"That's why I can't sleep. What if he's getting ready to do it again?"

"Then we'll deal with that when it happens."

"You sound like Captain Saunders."

"Well, maybe he's right," Bodinger told him bluntly. Cordova stiffened as Stan went further. "Eric, you're asking questions no one can answer. We just have to take what we get and work with what we have. This guy could've been picked up in Dallas for knifing a pimp, who knows? Hell, he could be dead by now. What you're doing is torturing yourself." Bodinger let his fatherly tone creep back. "You've been here before. You *have* to let it go, buddy. If not for yourself, do it for them," he said, pointing to Cordova's family. "Maria needs a husband. Those kids need a dad, not a cop," he held his eyes like a mentor teaching a life lesson. "Turn it off, Eric. Whenever you can, and you know when you can, turn it off. You'll all be better for it. I promise."

Susan walked over to the two men. She had a quiet grace that soothed everyone around her. Forty-six with a trim, fit body. Blonde hair she'd tried to keep as Father Time enforced his gray upon her. Her smile was infectious. Eric melted as she made her way to them. There was a strong dignity about her that made even the most hard-boiled toughs bow their heads.

"You two look cozy," she said, making Eric smile.

"Oh yeah," he said, "this one's a charmer."

"I bet," she said, looking deep into Stan's eyes, smiling. She knew there was trouble brewing. Years of being a cop's wife taught her that. "Maria's ready for you to start the grill, honey," she told Eric. "Shoptalk's over, boys."

"Yes, ma'am," Eric said, leaving the two alone with a look Bodinger enjoyed. The look was of a young man knowing what he wanted later in life. Stan and Susan had it—they'd earned it—and damn anyone who didn't understand.

"So," she started. "What's a girl got to do to get a date around these parts?"

"Lower her standards."

She laughed as only she could laugh, turning her head and resting her face against his chest. To Stan, it felt like home. Her inner strength flooding into him. The easy comfort that made all the bad in the world disappear. She was the strong one. She had the grace and power to rule over the worst demons he could ever muster. At least for a few minutes, there was only the two of them in the Cordova's backyard.

"It's a bad one, isn't it?" she asked, still holding him.

"Afraid so."

"Does *he* know?"

"More than I want him to."

Susan let go, looking into the eyes of her husband. There were miles etched into him. Wars won and lost, each leaving the scars of time. He was forty-seven going on eighty. "Can you catch him?" she asked.

"With a break . . . maybe."

"That sounds defeatist."

Grimacing, Stan told her, "Baby, this guy used rubber gloves to mail a letter. He used self-adhesive stamps and envelopes. No prints, no saliva, no DNA, nothing. The crime scene was so clean you'd think the Queer guys pulled it off."

She laughed again, causing Stan to chuckle to himself at the ridiculousness of it. But as she hugged him again, he felt the weight of the case drop on him like a mortar. There was a madman loose, and he had nothing to go on. The city was looking to him to find this menace, and the evidence he had was generic at best.

"I forgot what it was like," Stan told her.

"What?"

"Being them," he said, nodding toward the house. "Having a young wife and small kids. Dealing with all the crazy shit and coming home to a woman who doesn't understand and kids who only know you as Daddy," he finished, saying about his partner, "It's making him think too much."

Susan looked up, asking, "So you're worried for him?"

Resting his bottle on the ground, he told her, "No, I'm worried for her," pointing to Maria Cordova. "I know he's shown her the picture and the letter. It had to freak her out, it *had* to. She's only human. Right now, all he wants is to catch him, and all she wants is safety for their children."

"Even if you catch this guy tomorrow, Stan, that fear will never go away," Susan said, calm in her eyes. "That's the price we all pay. That's why we get buried by our children."

"If you're lucky," he said. Looking deep into her eyes, he asked, "How do you deal with it? Huh? I mean, you, as a woman, right now, how do you deal with all this?"

There was a swelling in her chest. After all the years and sleepless nights. After all the late-night runs to the emergency room and jumping out of her skin every time the phone rang, he finally asked. Stanley Bodinger finally asked his wife the ultimate question. *How do you deal with it?*

She wanted to cry. Instead, she pressed her cheek to his chest, saying, "You just love your man. For as long as you have him, you love your man. Even if it scares the hell out of you."

Stan pulled her up; looking deep in her eyes, he said, "I don't deserve you."

Susan smiled her soft, warm smile. With undying love in her heart, she said, "No, you don't."

They laughed.

On this one day, the Bodingers and Cordovas were still able to laugh and play. For at least one more day.

13

Frank Castro Investigations was located in a tiny strip mall just off I-35 in Round Rock, twenty miles north of the heart of Austin. As he pulled up and parked on Tuesday morning after Memorial Day, he saw about ten Post-it notes stuck to his glass door. Tiffany had yet to arrive, so he would have to open the office, something he hated doing.

After all, what good is it being the owner if the hired help shows up for work after you do?

He peeled off the notes while trying to unlock the door. The metal frame was warped, causing the door to stick. Pulling as he turned the key, the bloody thing finally came loose. The owner of the strip mall was supposed to have it fixed already. "But with the holiday and all," Frank cursed to himself. He went in and kicked on the lights as he read through the notes. One was from an old police buddy he never liked, one was from a woman he met in a bar last month—some redhead whose name he couldn't remember—one was from the owner of the mall wanting his rent, and the rest were from Felix Bryant. The representative of his latest paying client, Florence Cabbershaw.

The wealthy Mrs. Cabbershaw was just certain the wealthier Mr. Cabbershaw was cheating on her. So like a good wife, she hired Frank Castro to tail him and see what he was up to all those lonely nights. In disgust, he wadded all the notes together, tossing them at the wastebasket—missing terribly—just as he noticed the light flashing on the answering machine. "Twenty messages," it read.

"That's just perfect," he groaned, heading back to his office.

The office had been closed for the three-day weekend, but no one seemed to realize that even an ex-cop, private-investigating alcoholic enjoyed national holidays just as much as the next guy. He stopped at the edge of his desk, studying the mountain of papers that had accumulated.

Surely most of this was useless.

And it was. Past due bills; old sports pages; names, addresses, and phone numbers long since worthless, scribbled onto any piece of scrap rubbish that was in reach at the time. He slid all the trash off the desk into his empty waste can just as the door in the front office opened.

"Sorry I'm late, boss," Tiffany whined. "Long weekend, you know?"

Frank put his foot into the trash can and compacted all the paper then picked it up and went back to the front room where his receptionist and personal assistant was. Tiffany Malvern was twenty-five, blonde, sexy, and as incompetent as the summer days are long in South Texas. In contrast to Frank's professional tan sports jacket and white shirt, Tiffany was in her usual miniskirt; heels; and sleeveless, low-cut blouse that perfectly framed her $10,000 breasts.

"What does nine o'clock mean to you?" Frank asked from the doorway that adjoined the two rooms.

"Huh?" Tiffany replied as she turned, seeing him holding the trash can. "What's that?"

"Last month's overhead."

"What?"

"Never mind," he huffed, walking past her and out the front door to the dumpster he shared with the adjacent martial arts school. He dumped the trash and came back, discovering Tiffany was already on the phone. He was about to get furious, thinking it was a personal call, when he realized it was Mrs. Cabbershaw.

"I know you paid a lot of money, ma'am," Tiffany argued, "but doesn't the term *national holiday* mean anything to you people?"

"Jesus!" Frank said, snapping the phone from her. He cut an angry scowl at Tiffany as he uncovered the phone and spoke to his client. "Hello, Mrs. Cabbershaw. Frank Castro. How can I help you?"

Tiffany saw the grimace and knew she'd screwed up. But it was the way she and Frank operated, no big deal.

"Yes, ma'am," Frank spoke into the phone. "Yes, Mrs. Cabbershaw, I do understand. Yes, ma'am, she was outta line, and I *will* deal with her," he said, frowning harder. Tiffany rolled her eyes as she started making coffee. "Yes, ma'am, I understand. Well, I do have some results that look ironclad, but I must say they're probably not what you're looking for." Mrs. Cabbershaw spoke for what seemed forever before allowing Frank to respond. "Mrs. Cabbershaw, this really isn't something you'd want to discuss over the phone. Will it be possible for me to meet with you this afternoon?"

The relived smile he gave indicated that he'd saved the money at the end of the rainbow. He'd smoothed out the old bitty and was going to get paid, something they desperately needed.

"Yes, ma'am, four sounds fine. The football stadium?" he asked, a puzzled look on his face. Even Tiffany stopped and turned. "Oh, I see. You own a suite. Ninth floor, yes, ma'am . . . I'll see you then. Yes, ma'am. Bye-bye," he said. Adding, after she'd hung up, "And bring your checkbook."

"Daddy getting paid?" Tiffany asked in a silly voice.

"No help from you," he scolded. "What was all that crap?"

"What crap?" she asked casually.

"All that *national holiday* and *people like you* crap?"

"Goddamn it, Frank, she was being rude."

"And she's a rich paying customer," he reminded his young assistant. "Paying customers are few and far, and this old gal is loaded. So from now on, treat the natives with baby gloves. All right?"

Tiffany took a deep breath as she poured the water, exaggerating, "*Okay!*" Frank walked past her desk back toward his own office.

"Did you know that she and the old man have a luxury suite at DKR?"

"Where the Longhorns play?"

"Yep. Been there a hundred times and never been up on the inside."

"Sounds like Frankie gets a treat," she cracked, wiggling her ass.

"Only if she brings money, baby. Only if she brings money."

61

*

Frank's meeting with Mrs. Cabbershaw was at four o'clock. At two, he decided to leave with his folder on her husband and get a quick start. Tiffany was at lunch, and the truth be known, he needed to feed the monkey. Frank hadn't had a drink all day. Tiff had even slipped on the Kahlua in the coffee, and he'd been out of beer for his usual breakfast jump start. He was beginning to feel the itch at the base of his spine, and his trembles were getting bad enough that he didn't want his one paying client to lose faith in him. If she noticed the tremors, it could implode the whole deal. He piled into the BMW, dropped the top, and sped out south on I-35 toward Austin.

Frank charged five hundred a day plus expenses. He'd tailed and photographed Mr. Cabbershaw for a full week, so expenses aside, the old gal owed him a cool thirty-five hundred. Not bad pay for a week's work even if the result was something far from what the client expected.

Florence Cabbershaw had come to Frank Castro in need of answers. She was convinced that her husband—the rich Howard Cabbershaw of Cabbershaw, Leonard, and Shull, one of the most expensive law firms in Austin—had a woman on the side. Mr. Cabbershaw was seventy-two years old but in remarkable health. His wife, on the other hand, had suffered her years more severely. She never gave in to the pride of narcissism and, as a result, never opted for face-lifts or breast augmentations even though they could have been easily afforded. The old gal wanted to grow old gracefully without hanging on to the false idols of her own beauty.

Frank really admired that. It wasn't that Mrs. Cabbershaw was some extreme tight ass that never wanted anyone to be happy. Quite the contrary, he found her to be engaging for the most part, full of wit and charm. She just had a base distrust and dislike of people who tried to hide from their age with surgeries and chemicals.

"We all die, Mr. Castro," she told him on their first meeting. "If I am lucky enough to live as long as I have—or longer—then die, I want the world to see every line, every blotch, every blemish I accumulated over the entirety of that life." She smiled before adding, "After all, I earned them, didn't I? Why not be proud of the achievement?"

Frank envied her gracefulness. She was a small woman, barely five feet. He bet she weighed no more than a hundred pounds if you tied cinder blocks to her ankles. He never saw her when she wasn't wearing an immaculate dress, expensive jewelry with her silver hair up, neat and never a stand out of place. She carried herself as Frank imagined the belles of the Old South had. Dignified and proud, but never forgetting the trappings of ladyhood. He knew Mrs. Cabbershaw held ladyhood as a high priority. She once asked him, "What does a lady have if not her grace?"

Frank sped along 35 with the late May wind whipping around him in the open convertible. He had an on-again-off-again love affair with the car. Everyone was at a loss how he could afford a BMW. That was a secret for only him and Tully Pritchard to know.

Two friends scratching backs. Enough said.

The problem he was having, however, as Austin drew closer was that he really liked old lady Cabbershaw. She reminded him of the grandmother he never had. She was wise, comforting, and dependent on him to shed light on her husband's dalliances, no matter the difficulty. Yet she was expecting to find some augmented floozy her husband had been supporting for the last several years. What Frank found wasn't what she was looking for. This was going to hurt far more.

For the challenge ahead, he needed to be at his best, and that meant feeding the monkey that was gnawing at his neck. He knew there was plenty of time, so he exited off 35 and pulled into the neon palm tree–clustered Baby Acapulco, called Baby A's by the locals. He tucked his file beneath his seat, so he wouldn't have to raise the top and went in. It was a Tuesday after a holiday weekend, after lunch, so the place was just as empty as he hoped it would be.

Frank sat at the bar, watching that day's twentieth replaying of SportsCenter. In minutes, a kid no more than twenty-one asked him what he wanted.

"J. W. Black, three fingers. Knock in two cubes," Frank told him. His lack of alcohol and the task before him had him in a sour mood. He needed the welcome rush of the warm scotch. He wanted to tell Mrs. Cabbershaw that her husband kept a nineteen-year-old tramp in a suite at the Driscol downtown, but it just wasn't that way. He really didn't know how she was going to take his news. It saddened him; the noble old woman deserved better.

The kid returned with the scotch. He started to leave, but Frank told him to wait. In one smooth pour, he drained the glass and set it down, telling the kid to "Kill another one just like him." The young bartender chuckled, telling him, "Okay, dude, I'll pour. You just tell me when."

Frank killed two more soldiers and, for the first time all day, started to feel normal. He settled in to the TV and was nursing his fourth when he saw a newspaper on the bar to his right. He reached over and started thumbing through it. Bullshit after bullshit. He was about to toss it when a column by Glenn Young caught his eye. The local scribe was writing about that poor girl they found hung in the woods near Marble Falls back in April. Frank knew of the case but paid it little attention. But this was Glenn Young, the smart-ass that always seemed to push the wrong buttons on the wrong people. He liked the jerk, reading him whenever he found the opportunity.

This was an opportunity.

As Frank read, he began to realize that no one at the Austin PD had a clue who had committed the crime. He read further, sipping his Johnny Walker, when a quote from the author struck him as odd even if he didn't know why at the time. The sentence read: "It seems as though this killer has dropped into our fair city, committed this heinous act, and vanished without a trace even though this reporter knows better."

It was an odd sentence to Frank. He didn't know why; it just felt strange. He continued reading until he got to where the lead investigator was named.

Lead investigator, Detective Stanley Bodinger.

Frank recoiled ever so slightly. He wadded up the paper, tossing it over his shoulder to the floor. A waitress was passing behind him.

"Beautiful," she popped off, "just trash the place."

"Sorry, sweetheart," Frank said without turning. "I didn't like the company that paper was keeping."

*

Frank pulled into the four-story parking garage across from Daryl K. Royal Memorial Stadium at three fifty. He knew he'd done a good job, worthy of the money owed him, but he was hating having to break the news to sweet Mrs. Cabbershaw. He got out, dropping his sunglasses on the dash while retrieving the folder from beneath the seat. He took a deep breath then headed out.

Frank exited the parking garage and walked across the street to the stadium's main entrance. Actually, it was the entrance to the exclusive Texas Club within the confines of the stadium. He'd been in the lobby once, years ago, looking for the Longhorn gift shop adjacent to it after a big game. He never knew where the elevators went and, at the time he was there, didn't care. He was drunk after a game and surrounded by jubilant Longhorn fans. They'd just beaten conference rival Kansas by fifty-two points and assured themselves a shot in the Big 12 championship game. Vince Young was amazing, and they would surely play USC for the national title. However, his best memory of the day was banging a UT pom girl.

Hook 'em Horns for real!

He entered the lobby turning left, went down the hall that was dedicated to Bevo, the Longhorns mascot, and found the elevators at the end. He went up to the ninth floor, and as the doors opened, he was expecting to see tiny Mrs. Cabbershaw standing directly in front of him. Instead, he was greeted by a slight man in his fifties, wearing a neat gray suit with a purple tie and matching handkerchief. The man stepped forward, saying, "Frank Castro, I take it?" His speech was formal and perfect, almost British.

"That's what they tell me," Frank said, exiting the elevator.

"Hello, my name is Felix Bryant, Mrs. Cabbershaw's personal assistant."

"Hello," Frank said, taking his hand. For a gentleman, he had a firm shake. "It's good to match a face with the voice."

"Likewise," Bryant agreed. "Mrs. Cabbershaw is expecting you."

Frank was a little confused. The old gal had never had a meeting with him in which he was met by another person. He had always felt she wanted to keep their association between the two of them, but since he worked with Tiffany, maybe this was her way of showing him that she, too, had employees. He'd spoken with the man over the phone a couple of times, but he never knew he was so trusted.

Making their way down the long hallway to a private suite, Frank asked the man, "Personal assistant?"

"Yes," the gentleman answered. "I've been Mrs. Cabbershaw's closest confidant for the past thirty years."

"Like a butler?"

"If you feel better with that moniker, Mr. Castro," he replied, opening the door to the suite.

The scotch seeped out in another question. "Is that all?" he asked with a smirk.

"Quite," Bryant replied, looking put off. "The lady's chastity is none of my concern."

At first, he came across as gay. However, Frank could read people whether he was drunk or sober; and even though the guy was uptight and proper, by his handshake and mannerisms, he could tell the gentleman liked the ladies.

Fair enough.

Frank entered the suite to see Mrs. Cabbershaw standing square in the middle of the room, as Felix Bryant closed the door and stood by. Her face was business as usual, but as always, there was a small spark that forever caught Frank's attention. He never knew if he reminded her of a child, an old fling, or of someone she'd like to spend time with if she were thirty years younger.

"Mrs. Cabbershaw," Frank said.

"Mr. Castro," she replied with a sly grin.

Frank could tell the old gal loved the cloak-and-dagger stuff. Just the fact that she'd hired a Cuban-born private investigator was lurid enough to revitalize long dormant feelings and urges. He knew, if she was indeed thirty years younger, tonight he'd get the lay of his life.

Too bad she's not thirty years younger.

She was wearing a long ankle-length gray skirt with a long-sleeved purple sweater over a white blouse. Elegant shoes, silver earrings, and matching broach. Her soft face seemed to wear a little more powder than he'd remembered from their last meeting. She had prettied up for him. It was sweet.

The suite was like an expensive hotel room with one glaring difference. Directly across from the door was a glass pane with three rows of stadium seats in front of them and beyond the glass was the football field. One hundred yards of Longhorn history was in front of him. He'd watched countless games there, but this was a view he never believed he'd have the privilege to see.

Awesome.

"Ma'am, I had no idea you were a suite owner," Frank admitted.

"Howard and I graduated class of '58," she informed him. "These suites became available after he'd cemented himself in the local notary. Money wasn't an issue," she smiled sadly, looking at the floor. "But"— she raised her head with a quick jerk, giving Frank a fiery stare—"I need to know what my husband has been perpetrating on me all these years. I want the truth, Mr. Castro, no matter how vile I may feel it to be." She sat in a nearby chair. A table that sat between her and a small couch held a silver coffee set. "Would you like coffee, Mr. Castro?"

Hell no!

"No, ma'am, nothing for me, thanks," he said, sitting opposite her on the couch.

"Felix," she said with a nod, and the dapper Mr. Bryant went back out into the hallway, closing the door behind him.

"I'm impressed," Frank offered.

"Felix is my oldest and dearest friend, Mr. Castro. He's been with me for around thirty years. He's a very dependable and confident man. He's had his issues over the years, but haven't we all?"

Frank flushed, her eyes as penetrating as always. He could write a thousand-page book on the bad decisions that summed his life.

"I don't consider Felix an employee. He's my friend, my confidant. He's taken care of and wants for nothing. We move along life's merry road, overcoming obstacles along the way. He's a true gentleman and a professional unlike that female you employ. What was her name?" she asked, looking highbrow.

Frank knew this was coming, so he was honest with her. "Her name is Tiffany, Mrs. Cabbershaw."

"She sounds young."

"Yes, ma'am, she is."

"Is she pretty?" she asked with a raised brow.

Frank wanted to hide. Yes, Tiffany was a terrible assistant and receptionist, and the only reason he had her around was because she worked cheap, made great coffee, and was so damned hot. Besides, she had a way of making him laugh when nothing else could. She was the pain-in-the-ass little sister he never had. "Yes, ma'am, she's very attractive," Frank confessed. "But our relationship is strictly professional, I assure you."

"Well, I don't approve of her phone etiquette," Mrs. Cabbershaw reprimanded.

"No, ma'am, neither do I. I promise it won't happen again," he said, knowing this would be their last conversation.

"Did you fire her?"

"No, ma'am, that didn't seem appropriate," Frank said, watching her face.

Surely, in 1958, Florence Cabbershaw was a transcendent beauty. Fifty years later, her bloom having wilted years before, Frank waited to see if the moxy he'd grown accustomed to would blare out. Mrs. Cabbershaw wasn't one to give in to vanity, but she acquiesced. A knowing expression washed across her face before she cleared her throat, continuing, "Then a lesson well learned. So let's get down to it, Mr. Castro. What have you found for me?"

As Frank laid the folder on the table between them, he noticed two envelopes sitting to the side of the silver serving tray. He pushed on. "Mrs. Cabbershaw, I followed your husband for six days and five nights."

"Yes."

"Well, what I found is not what I think you were expecting, and quite frankly, I hate to show you these," Frank informed. He truly hated doing this. With great gusto, Florence Cabbershaw sat on the edge of her seat, waiting to see the picture of the strumpet her husband had squirreled away.

The eight-by-ten photos Frank laid out were of a nightclub.

"It's a bar, yes? What's the significance?"

"Mrs. Cabbershaw, that's Charlie's of Austin."

"Every place has a name, Mr. Castro. Get to the point."

"Ma'am, Charlie's of Austin is a classy establishment that caters to"—he paused—"the gay community."

She didn't blink. Her eyebrows rose as though she were waiting for the rest. As Frank's words began to sink in, he watched Mrs. Cabbershaw go through a myriad of emotions. First she was confused, giving way to impatience. Then he watched her eyes shift, thoughts beginning to pour in, as she chewed on this new twist. Soon, a look of total astonishment appeared on the woman. "So this place is a . . ."

"A gay bar, ma'am," Frank said. There, he said it.

Mrs. Cabbershaw sat quietly, allowing this news to filter down through her like coffee in a brewer. Frank remained silent, waiting for her to catch up. Soon, her expression changed again, the anger he was braced for—the very anger she'd been prepared to unleash—simply melted away like an early spring snow.

Frank pulled out more eight-by-ten photos. Mrs. Cabbershaw recognized her husband walking in front of the club. The clothes were some she'd never seen. Slick, silky suits, open shirt with a gold chain. Howard Cabbershaw was a small man and neat as a pin. He'd always stayed fit. Golf, tennis, jogging, weights, low-calorie diet. He was seventy-two, but he looked fifty. She wasn't so much shocked as she was surprised in herself.

"I watched him go to the club on three separate nights, arriving each time alone and at different times," Frank told her. "Seven, eight twenty, and nine forty-five," he informed her. She sat quietly, studying the photos. The mood in the room had changed drastically. The energy she'd displayed earlier totally evaporated. Now, for the first time, Frank Castro saw her as an old woman. Sure, he knew she was old enough to be his mother, but he'd always loved her spunk and energy. Now, with this development, she seemed to wilt more than a little.

"Each night, he stayed until closing, three a.m. *And. . .* Each night, he left with this man," he finished, showing another photo. Howard was

69

walking arm in arm with a man a quarter of his age. White suit, open red silk shirt. Black hair slick and well-groomed. He was dark, obviously Latin. Rings, gold bracelet, expensive watch, several gold chains around his neck. They were both laughing. Frank presented several more shots of the same trek the men made. In each, they looked so happy, giddy even. Howard would talk, and the younger man would laugh. In the last photo, they kissed while crossing the street.

Frank went on. "They left all three nights in Mr. Cabbershaw's Mercedes together."

"He," she started then had to clear her throat. "He arrived alone, and they left together?" she asked, eyes looking more hollow by the minute.

"Yes, ma'am," Frank responded, "all three times."

"And where did they go, Mr. Castro?" she asked, her voice growing distant.

"The Five Fifty-Five condos," he told her.

"Expensive," she admitted, "like his jewelry."

"That's my guess."

"Tell me, Mr. Castro, does this person look like the kind of man who could afford such things?"

"No, ma'am," Frank answered, "and he couldn't."

"Who is he?" she asked, standing and walking to the great window that overlooked the football field.

Frank remained seated. "His name is Patrick Ferrara. He's a failed art student at Texas State. He's been doing odd jobs, mostly waiting tables in local restaurants."

"How old is he, Mr. Castro?" she asked, without turning.

"Twenty-six," Frank told her. "I talked to a lot of the guys inside. They say Mr. Cabbershaw is known as Howie at the club. All the young guys flirt with him and he buys rounds of drinks, but he and Ferrara are an item. No one trifles."

The silence fell like a guillotine. Frank waited for Mrs. Cabbershaw to say something, but she was as engulfed by the silence as the great room. Frank put the photos back in the folder and rested it on the table next to the two envelopes. After waiting as long as he could, he stood and walked beside her. The two stood side by side looking out on the great, historical football field. As excited as he'd been to get the chance to see it from this view, he now felt empty.

"You're telling me my husband…is a homosexual," she said, more of a statement than a question.

"We all draw our own conclusions," he said, still looking out the window.

"Tell me, Frank." She turned for a second. "I can call you Frank?"

"Of course," he replied, smiling.

"Frank, do you know what it's like not to feel like a man? I want you to tell me the truth. I've earned that. Do you really know what it's like to feel like a genderless human? Not to know what it's like to be able to close your eyes and know exactly what being a man feels like?"

Frank thought before turning. She wanted the truth; she was paying for the truth. "No, ma'am, I don't," he admitted.

"Of course not," she said, turning back to the window. "You're a very handsome man. Young, virile, vibrant."

He felt a rush of embarrassment.

"My husband has not touched me in ten years," she said to the glass. "And I'm not talking about sexual things. His hand has not touched a part of my body in ten years. Years ago, I felt he had someone on the side. He was distracted and aloof. He had his improprieties years ago, but they were quick, meaningless trysts. Howard's always had a feminine air to him. He's very vain that way. But I always felt he was a true man."

Frank had no idea how to respond, so he said nothing and let the wounded woman continue. She looked as though he had told her a dear friend had died. She appeared overwhelmingly grief-stricken, on the verge of mourning.

"You know, we met here, back in '55. Fell in love and graduated in '58. That was the year after Coach Royal came. I can't tell you, Frank, the excitement he brought to this place," she said, almost cracking a small smile. "We were so in love. With each other and this place." She turned, walking back to the center of the suite. "You move on, as does everyone, I suppose. We loved this place so much we came every weekend, rain or shine. When the boxes were put in, Howard was one of the first to have a bid." She spread her arms, showing the grandeur of the room. "We've watched every home game from this suite for over thirty years. Good times, Frank," she said; then her face darkened. "Of course, there were bad times as well." She continued to the seats and the table between them before going further. "Frank, we have three children. Two daughters and a son, Phillip, who works at the firm. He's about your age, the youngest, my pride and joy. They all love their father very much, as do I." She stepped close to Frank and looked up into his bold, dark eyes. She looked so weak, so vulnerable. "I expect that you understand the need for decorum?" she asked. "No matter what you think of my husband, he is still a very powerful man in this town even if his indiscretions have gotten the better of him."

Frank was blown away. This woman could ruin that old shit, and all she thought about were the children and *his* reputation. Frank didn't know they still made people like this. He swallowed hard before nodding yes. "Yes, ma'am, I understand your wishes. I won't say a word, I promise you." He paused, adding, "You've earned that."

He understood. He could go to the papers and drop a hint that one of the biggest law firm's lead executors was balling a twenty-something gigolo and make a small fortune. That wasn't Frank's style. He may be an asshole, but he was an asshole who had to live with himself, and that alone was hard enough.

Mrs. Cabbershaw leaned to the table and slid the top of the two envelopes to the side and picked up the one on the bottom. She handed it to Frank, saying, "Do me the courtesy of not opening this here. I assure you the compensation is sufficient."

Frank obliged and slipped the envelope into his breast pocket. "Mrs. Cabbershaw," he started, but she stopped him short.

"Frank, it's okay," she said, looking sadder than ever. "We all play our roles, and this is mine. Howard will come to understand someday what loyalty means. Today is not the day. But I do, *really* do, appreciate your efforts. You are most professional. Even if your receptionist is a tramp."

Finally, something to lighten the mood. Frank laughed and caught a sly grin from the old girl as she asked, "So you and her?"

He knew the insinuation. "No, ma'am, Tiffany and I are purely professional. Besides, I'm old enough to be her father."

Mrs. Cabbershaw giggled, "And?"

Knowing her meaning, he told her, "No. It's okay by me. I just believe she feels I'm a little too old for *her*."

Mrs. Cabbershaw grinned.

Like I'm too old for you.

"You know, Frank," she started, "you really shouldn't drink so much. You're much more charming without it."

Frank was dumbstruck.

"Oh, don't look so surprised," she scolded. "I've got years of experience in that sort of thing, but I do give you king's credit for hiding it so well."

It was the smallest Frank Castro had felt in years.

"Felix," she said in a voice just over her normal tone. Felix Bryant opened the door and stood in the doorway. "Please show Mr. Castro to the elevator."

Frank left with Bryant without looking back. The two walked in silence to the elevator and waited for the doors to open. Once they did and Frank was inside, Felix blocked the door with his hand, asking, "Is she all right?"

"It'd take more than this," Frank said, "but I'm sure you know that." The two locked eyes, and he could see the genuine concern on his face as Felix could see in Frank's the respect he held for the lady in question.

Felix released the door, saying as he stepped back, "Good day, Mr. Castro."

"Bryant. A pleasure."

Frank gathered himself in the elevator and, before he knew it, was outside, heading back across the street to the Manor Road parking garage. He lit a cigarette, his head swimming. In all his life, he'd never known a person as graceful and elegant as Florence Cabbershaw. For an old, burned-out, cynical, drunken ex-cop, the old gal came off as a breath of fresh air.

When he got to his BMW, he slid in, fired the engine, then pulled the envelope from his breast pocket. He opened it, expecting a check for $3,500. He was astounded to see the amount $35,000 stamped onto the cashier's check. His chin dropped open. There were two envelopes; the other must have been for the exact amount. Mrs. Cabbershaw had grossly overpaid for his services. Thirty-five thousand dollars for a week's worth of tailing and picture snapping? He wanted to go back up and confront her but thought better of it. This was her way of closure, and her payment for his silence. If that's what the good lady wanted, who the hell was Frank Castro to tell her otherwise?

He donned his sunglasses and looked at himself in the mirror. "More charming without the booze?" he asked himself. "She ain't the first skirt to tell me that."

With that, the BMW sped out of the garage and headed back to Round Rock.

14

The music pounds. He feels the gun in his hand. The 9-mm Glock feels sexy, even wet, in his grip. It seduces, it lures. Intoxicating to the touch. Adam knows he's out of his mind. No normal person would feel the way he feels. A real man would stop. A real man would not allow the madness to consume his thoughts, his being.

It's been at least twenty hours since he last slept. An insomniac since childhood, the condition is worse now. He's delirious. Drinking vodka, he sniffs the bottle of amyl nitrate, allowing his brain to alter. Shades of black and death cloud his mind. The music beats a rhythm of ruin that his soul has no intention of stopping.

You can't stop it.

The gun. The power of the gun is so seductive. Annihilation at the pulse of a finger. With it, all the fear and pain will disappear forever. He places the tip of the barrel to his forehead and waits for the queue. There must be some sign, some calling that will tell him to pull.

Nothing.

Adam cries to the floor, "Why can't I *stop* this?!"

Only silence follows. Silence within his mind as the thundering metal crashes around him. He just needed to remember to breathe. To fill his lungs with life-giving oxygen. He stopped, taking a deep breath. Sweet breath, life-affirming breath. He craved it.

He loathed it.

He remembered the jar. The bugs dying from poison in his jar, fighting the glass in a vain attempt to find the air that nourished them.

Like Amy.

He was an animal; he knew that. He was a monster that should be obliterated from the world. He was changed into a faceless fiend to be feared. A shadow of what humanity should be. He was the Antichrist. The beast. Alone, forever alone. Alone in his own mind. A mind so corrupt and evil he wished it death. But as hard as he tried, death would not come. With no sleep, gallons of alcohol, and enough chemical inhalants to deluge an army, he lived.

Still, he lived on.

He walked naked to the door. Feeling the scars on his arms, he thumped his head against her door. She was still there. Always. All he wanted was to heal, to feel normal, whatever that was. But he knew in his heart it would never be. The *blue room* was too strong. It owned him like she did. Still.

How does a child tell his mother no?

"This isn't what I wanted to be."

Deloris was causing this. He understood his actions; he understood *he* was the beast. But why? He never asked to be brought into this evil, her evil. In truth, he was a child who only knew the world that was laid in front of him. Feeling the scar on his back, reality was hammered home. His heart told him he was a victim.

But the mind tells a different story.

Adam's mind told him he needed to give it back. *Give it all back.* The black man on the bridge told him so.

"Fuck a bunch of pain," he told him. "Give it back, brother. Give it all back. And to hell with who gets in the way."

Not wanting to be reminded of his lesser moments, he screamed at the door, pounding on it as he screamed, "I'm the worst of *you!*" Backing away, he gathered himself, screaming again, "*I'm the worst of you!*" All he wanted was to be set free. To be free of the nightmare, the pain, the shame. The all-consuming shame that ate away at his guts. The coward in his soul that said *no* only once. Far too late. A time that came when he was old enough to get help and stop the madness. Her madness. But all he could muster was the strength to say *no*. Just once.

Far too late.

"I'm supposed to be more than this?" he questioned his ghosts. "Condescending talk, what I'm supposed to be. Who I'm supposed be. Who is that? Who is that now?"

He slid down the door as the metal music punched its message through the walls. He sobered suddenly. Standing, walking back to the red room, he studied the new pictures he'd hung. Death faces of Amy. The poor girl fighting for air inside the bag like the vermin in his jars. He picked up the pistol off the floor and laid it on his desk.

Another time.

The feelings he had as Amy died filled him. The power and sexual thrill was so much more than just a sadist's need to fulfill a fantasy. It was who he was. However he got here, it was just who he was. Doesn't the world need monsters? What is good without evil? What is light without dark? He was fulfilling a natural world order. He was as much a need to the world as the good of God.

God.

Adam laughed, thinking of God.

"Pathetic God."

Once again, it was time.

"Time to play."

The phone rang, waking Cindy out of a sound sleep. Since it was the housephone and not her cell, she rolled over, letting the machine do the dirty work. Julie's voice came on just prior to the beep, instructing the caller to leave their information. The voice that followed announced, "Julie, this is Carol. If you're there, we'd like to know if you've terminated your own employment, or if you just forgot to call in and take the night off without notice. Call me back, you have all the numbers."

Cindy sat up as sun flooded through her window. It was eight twenty-five, and that was her roommate's boss sounding pissed. Julie Brooks worked as a night stocker at a Wal-Mart in the Four Points area. She noticed Julie's car on the street when she got home last night, thinking it broke down, and she grabbed a ride to work. Confused, Cindy climbed out of bed and checked the window, seeing Julie's car in the same spot.

"Julie?" she called. There was no answer. She trekked back to her room and saw the door open and the bed made. "What the hell?" she asked the walls. "Where did she go?"

Cindy found her purse and fished out her cell. There were no missed calls from Julie but four from her mom.

"Later, Mother," she moaned, dialing her friend's number. It never rang, simply going to her voicemail. "Hi, this is Julie. I can't get to the phone so do what you do and I'll catch up later. Bye-bye," the message ended.

"Where are you, you crazy bitch?" Cindy asked the phone, not knowing it was the last time she'd ever talk to her roommate.

Julie was going to be late for work as she bounded out of the rental house on Anderson Mill Road at nine fifty. She'd already been late far too many times and couldn't afford another screw up. When she reached her car, she was hoping her eyes were deceiving her. Some son of a bitch had backed his H2 so close in front of her that her Toyota's front bumper was pushed down.

"Asshole," she said to the black sky. "Who owns this fucking thing?" Stomping to the curb, she stopped to inspect the damage. "Goddamn it," she whispered. Whoever owned this monstrosity was going to have to pay for her bumper. She walked around the two vehicles to see from the street side if the harm was worse than she'd already seen. Stopping just behind the H2, she placed her hands on her hips, stomping her foot.

Her next thought was of nothing; she had no time to form it. Her body contracted in a giant spasm as electric agony burst through every cell in her body. Everything went black.

She woke to rolling and bouncing as earsplitting music bombarded her from every angle. She recognized it, her dad's kind of thing. Slayer was ripping through a set, one track after another, with no pause between tracks. Whoever burned this music intentionally ran the songs together to make a wall of noise with no seams. The music was as seamless as the inside of where she was. Pitch dark, bouncing from side to side in a place not much bigger than a pickup bed with a camper shell. But this was no pickup. This was a box armed with four powerful speakers, all aimed at her.

"Let me out of *here*!" she screamed, realizing it was too loud to even hear her own voice. She calmed herself, sitting back against the small wall at what she felt was the front of the *thing* she was in. Pulling her knees to her chest, she covered her ears, thinking this was a bad dream. She only had to sit that way for a few more jarring minutes when the vehicle stopped, and the shattering music fell silent.

Her first instinct was to scream, but she fought it off. Whoever this was had the upper hand and the twenty-year-old 103-pound young woman knew she was at his mercy. She was just determined to live through this. Whatever he wanted, she'd give him. Sex? She was no stranger to the ways of pleasing a man even if there was more than one. Just let him do his business and live to tell about it. Resolute, she prepared herself.

A light came on. She could now see where she was even though it only raised more questions. Red indoor-outdoor carpet covered every square inch of her surroundings. With ears ringing, she barely made out the sound of steps moving beside whatever she was in. He was coming.

The back hatch unlocked, and the wall she was facing turned out to be a door that raised bottom to top. As the door stopped at its peak, there was a man—dressed in all black, gloves, and mask—training an automatic pistol at her. Julie felt her face tremble at the sight of the gun.

"Now," he spoke, his voice surprisingly soft. "Just do what I say, and you'll see tomorrow. Understand?"

He wasn't a large man; she could tell that even from inside the hold. Five eight and maybe around 150 with all those clothes on. She could see his eyes were startlingly blue, his neck was thin, and what skin she could make out was pale.

"Do you understand?" he asked again, his tone firmer. *He's trying to sound tough*, Julie thought to herself. Maybe he was and maybe he wasn't, but the pistol convinced her he was as tough as he needed to be. She nodded frantically, with eyes wide and her heart pounding a steady rhythm in her ears.

He went on, "Now, I know you're not going to like this, but I need you to take your clothes off," he told her, gun waving up and down at her.

"Why?" she asked, her voice cracking as tears began to well.

"Because that's what I asked for," he said, taking a step to her, standing directly beneath the open hatch. "Now, I'm going to get what I asked for either way. It would be healthier for you to comply. Trust me."

Trust him?!

"You don't have to rape me," she offered. "I'll do anything you want, I promise." She was shaking all over; every inch of her was in subtle motion as she stared at the masked man with the loaded weapon.

He seemed to laugh a little then look to the ground before telling her, "I am not going to *rape* you." His soft voice was still calm. "But I can't insist enough that I need your clothes, all of them, right here by the door, nice and neat," tapping the floor of the hold with his gun.

Just survive!

Fighting tears, Julie pulled her T-shirt off, revealing her pink bra. Laying it down, she kicked her shoes off and removed her socks.

"Lay them across the shoes," he told her.

After doing so, she had to lie on her back to take off her jeans because of the low roof. After she slid them off, he told her, "Fold the jeans and the shirt, nice and neat, like Mama taught you." Softly weeping, Julie did as he instructed, folding the jeans then the shirt neatly on top. She set them beside her shoes in the doorway. "Panties first, then the bra," he said, his voice still soft, almost warm. From her knees, Julie slid her matching panties over her slim hips, rocking her knees up to free the fabric, she pulled them off, dropping them on the stack of clothes. She knelt beneath the light above her, shivering even though the summer night was warm.

He knew she had a nice body. He'd been watching her work for

80

weeks, prowling the store at night with a shopping cart, milling through the groceries like a run-of-the-mill John Doe Public. He'd seen her running in the aisles, playing with the strapping young men she worked with. Teasing, flirting, taunting. She'd probably fucked all of them by now if not all at once. She was thin like he was. Her skin was pale like his. Eyes blue like his. Her hair, though, was dirty blonde like Deloris's.

"Carpet match the drapes?" he asked, starting to breathe more heavily.

"What?" she asked, trying to understand through the fear.

Calmly, he said, "Raise up on your knees. I want to see for myself."

Julie closed her eyes, raising up on her knees, her head flush with the ceiling. She was neatly trimmed, but what he saw was light brown. Satisfied, he told her, "Okay, now the bra, right here," tapping her clothes with the pistol.

Julie pulled both arms behind her to unfasten the hooks, asking, "Why are you doing this?"

"I'm not here to answer questions," he said, eyes riveted to her. The lace bra fell free, and she slipped it off, laying it with her other things. She folded her arms over herself, concealing her breasts from him.

That was fine; it didn't really matter. "Stay just like you are," he told her, "but turn around and face the other way."

"Why?" she asked, crying more heavily.

"Because I fucking said so," he replied, voice still calm but firmer now. "Do as I say, and you'll be all right. We'll get through this."

"*Through what?*" she whispered, turning as he'd instructed.

"Just a thing, that's all. Just a thing."

Julie sat quietly, facing away from the hatch, hearing him rustling with something at the back of the hold. He couldn't weigh a whole lot, but she felt the vehicle jostle as he climbed in behind her. She could feel his breath on her neck, cascading down her back like an evil mist. Close enough to whisper, he said softly, "I need you to put your hands behind you."

She stiffened, not wanting to give up what little freedom she still clung to. "I still have the gun, baby. Just do it. It's okay." With her heart about to beat its way out of her chest, she did as he instructed. She pulled her hands behind her, crossing them at the wrist. Before she knew it, a thick plastic zip tie slid over them and locked down with a sickening *zip!* "Lay down," he told her, pushing her to the floor, face-first. Another loud *zip* followed, and her legs were bound at the ankles.

"What are you doing?!" she screamed, flipping over on her back, seeing him roll up his ski mask, revealing a face that was almost feminine. High cheekbones, outrageous blue eyes, full bottom lip, not what she expected at all. If he was a girl, she would have called him pretty. Instead, he was her captor; and whatever this was, she wanted no part of it.

Julie continued to scream and plead with Adam as he fished his digital camera from his black jacket, resting it on the floor next to the pistol. He moved toward her, concealing something in his other hand. She didn't know what it was, but she wasn't about to let him do anything else without a fight. Kicking her bound legs, arms unable to help, she was like a fish on a muddy bank. No way to strike, scratch, claw, punch or . . . *breathe.*

The plastic bag went over her head in a flash, and a last horrible *zip!* tightened around her throat. Her air supply was cut off. Panic shot through her like a thunder bolt; she was going to die!

Through clenched teeth, he snarled, "As you're dying, think of your mother."

There was a *click* followed by a flash.

More clicks and flashes as Adam documented his work. Julie was fighting the zip ties, biting at the bag, rolling all over the floor of the modified H2, vainly fighting for life. *Her* life. Her life being snuffed out by a madman.

A rodent fighting the jar.

Adam felt himself getting hard. He pulled it free while operating the camera with one hand—stopping long enough to roll on the condom he'd brought—then proceeded where he'd stopped. One hand on the camera, one on himself.

Moist exhalant filled the bag around Julie's face. With every pathetic draw, the bag would suck into her mouth like a canvas over a yawning cave. Adam knew it took about seven minutes to die from asphyxiation. The brain passes out at three and a half, and death only takes a few more

82

painless minutes. As she started to convulse, he felt his orgasm closing. Her pretty face turning *blue*. Her fingers clawing at the air behind her, her slim legs locking at the knees as her heart fought for the oxygen that wasn't coming. The light was fading, her ears hearing less and less, her brain pulling oxygen from all over her body in an attempt to thwart off death. Her thrashing slowed as his stimulation increased.

"Die sweetly," he said, ready to fill the condom. He moaned to Julie's dying body as his contractions fired pleasure throughout his loins, "Die sweetly, baby . . . Just like Mama wants."

Seven minutes. No blades, no bullets. It took him just seven minutes to let her die sweetly. Her body perfect. Unmarked. He could leave her this way, but that would mean not getting his second thrill.

After collecting himself and placing the used condom in his coat pocket, he retrieved his nylon rope from the cab, heading to a nearby tree. He'd found it several days earlier, knowing it was the perfect location. With a small loop tied on one end, he ran the far end through it, making a larger loop, then tied a C-clamp on the end. He stood at the back of the hold for a while, looking at Julie. Soft, peaceful.

Death and innocence.

Taking her by the ankles, he pulled her to the door where he cut off the ties holding her feet then did the same with her wrists. Her arms fell like those of a rag doll, lifeless. He cut the zip around her throat and pulled the bag free. Her eyes still open in horror, he closed them and kissed her blue lips. Since she wasn't strangled, there was none of the bruising and mottling of the face. The sweet face she had that morning was still there.

Just the lips were blue.

Carrying her small naked body from the hold, he placed her on the ground by the tree then looped the nylon rope around her neck, throwing the end with the clasp over a low branch. He took a deep breath, telling her, "Now . . . we make you famous." Pulling the rope, it tightened around her neck, and she sat up. Another good pull, and Julie's feet were touching the ground, her body hanging like a dead game creature. One more pull and gravity began its sickening tow on her lifeless form. Her small neck almost pinched in two just below her jaw line. Her legs and arms seemed to mock her now. A grotesque caricature of her living, vibrant self.

Death leaves the world with nothing.

He wrapped the end of the rope around the tree twice then fastened it off with the C-clamp. Stepping away, Adam pulled his new erection free, rolling on his second condom. This one wouldn't be as frantic. He had time. Pulling an amyl nitrate popper from his coat, he had time to enjoy himself.

The garage door rolled down behind him, closing him in, sealing him off from the world. Sitting in silence inside the H2, he gazed at his face in the mirror. Again, he'd changed, a little more this time. It was better than the first. "Experience is the best teacher," he said to the reflection.

"Experience, Adam. It's the best teacher in the world."

"Leave me alone," he told her. She lived in his head now. Forever questioning, haunting. Watching his actions from the inside. She liked them. "Not now," he said, exiting the H2. Still wearing the coat, he'd run the air conditioner full blast back from Bastrop County. He needed to shed his clothes, shed everything. Before shutting up the Hummer, he checked to make sure he had everything. Satisfied, he left the garage and entered the kitchen.

Leave with everything, come home with everything.

Inside, he trekked down the dark hall to the bathroom where one of only two white lights in the entire house awaited him. He fished the two used condoms out of his coat pocket and flushed them away along with their wrappers. He removed the surgical gloves, flushing them next. The vortex in the toilet cleaned away any of his stain that might have lingered. He dropped the used zip ties and bag in the trash; they'd go to the curb in the morning. Content, he left the bathroom, turning off the light and receiving the crimson glow from the red room.

He stood there, looking at the many pictures of Amy he'd pinned on his walls. Hundreds of digital photos, in every size his printer allowed, covered the walls. As he admired them, he disrobed completely. His *play clothes* discarded in a pile on the floor, he clicked on the computer that sat beneath Deloris's portrait. Once it was ready, he attached the camera and watched like a schoolboy at Christmas as the new crop of carnage unveiled itself.

"Oh my," he breathed, opening the half bottle of vodka that sat on his desk. As the warm liquid snaked its way through him, his eyes were inundated with the visuals of Julie fighting her binds, struggling to free herself, to rid herself of the beautiful bag that encased her pretty head.

This was more than murder to Adam. This was art. These photos were the real aesthetic wonders that artists had tried to capture over the centuries, but had never been able to find the mark. Even the most horrific images on canvas or caught on film were byproducts of either imagination or luck. These photos, these *works*, were deliberate. The sexual thrill was real. The horror was real. The death was real. This was no Hollywood boogieman. This wasn't some pot-smoking artist's conception. This was *real*.

After all the images loaded, he began printing them out. All 217 of them. Some of Julie in a terrible struggle, making the images blur. He knew he'd have to wait until the brain began blacking out and the subject ceased thrashing around to avoid this mistake a third time.

Don't be in such a hurry.

Shots of her fighting the bag, others of her struggling with the binds, still others of her motionless. Dead, lips blue. Close-ups, an evil eye looking through the plastic, peering into the sanctuary of the bag. Her eyes no longer emanating life, glass eyes, doll's eyes. He felt more vile for having looked inside it. He giggled at his deviance. Some of his favorites were of her in the tree, hanging naked and dead like a victim of war crimes.

As the printer hissed and spat photo after photo of the death of Julie Brooks, Adam drank and hit the popper, staring up at Deloris. Tomorrow he'd write a new letter to Glenn Young.

The *Capital Hangman* was ready to emerge.

15

Glenn Young caught himself slightly trembling as he read the letter. More deliberate than the first, this one was also accompanied by a gruesome photo of a dead girl hanging naked from a tree.

When it came, he opened it in private. Alone in his cubicle, he read D's words:

I insist on calling myself by the letter *D*. It means so much to me. But I know the press will want to burden me with a title. Capital Hangman suits me just fine.

Use it.

Like the first version, she was not raped, nor will they ever be.

They'll find her in Bastrop County, near McDade. White Road, far off to the east.

I look forward to writing to you again.

Your admiring fan,

D

PS:

Is it the voice of God I hear?

Or the sound of Satan escaping, from my own laughter?

Young nearly ran to his editor who called the number Detective Bodinger had left. Glenn was a hard-ass with politicians and superstars, but this was different.

This time, the other guy called the shots. And *this* time, the other guy was insane.

16

Captain Saunders stomped down the hall to the conference room. The fifty-nine-year-old cop was in no mood for bullshit. He had an ulcer, a wife with a drinking problem, a gay son, and a daughter who married a Democrat. Even the Astros were slumping. He'd left his jacket in his office and was sporting sleeves rolled two flips, tie loosened, while woofing down a submarine sandwich from Thunder Cloud Subs.

Saunders burst through the door, startling Bodinger and Cordova who were sitting on the far side of the long conference table. Saunders plopped in the chair across from them, snapping, "Tell me where we're heading and make damn sure you don't tell me in the wrong direction."

Bodinger glanced at his partner then spoke up. "We have a serial killer, Captain."

"Explain," Saunders said with a mouthful of sandwich.

"Well," Bodinger started, "we have a murdered girl on April 13. CSI, autopsy, forensics lead nowhere. Assailant mails a picture of the dead girl and letter to the *Citizen*'s writer Glenn Young.

"June 19, Mr. Young receives a second letter from what appears to be the same person. This of another dead girl, apparently hanged, as was the first. After we discovered the crime scene"—he paused, looking at his partner who turned away—"four days after the slaying, the MO was the same as the first victim. The girl was stunned by a stun gun, suffocated, then hanged. No sexual assault appears to have taken place in either victim. Along with apparent serial traits, the killer corresponded with the media through Glenn Young, signing both mailings the same way."

"How?"

"The letter *D*, Captain."

Cordova spoke. "But he wants to be called the Capital Hangman."

"Fuck him," Saunders said, chewing. After he swallowed his bite, he washed it down with a sip of Cordova's Diet Pepsi, asking, "Where was the new girl?"

"Both girls were abducted close to their homes in Austin, and the bodies were discovered in adjacent counties. The new one in Bastrop."

"What do the county cops say?"

"Burnet's doing everything local, witnesses are zero. We have nothing out there but generic tire and boot tracks that yielded nothing."

"I know that. I made the meeting. Bastrop?"

"Again, nothing at the scene, but the body, her belongings, and the same boots and tires. Match a million in South Texas. They're handing it off to us since Ms. Brooks was abducted within Austin city limits. No one knows where the actual murder took place."

"Wait," Saunders interjected. "I see a girl hanging from a tree, I pretty much know where the killing took place."

"No, sir," Cordova interrupted. "Both autopsies indicate the two girls were already dead when the killer hung their bodies."

"By what means?"

"Asphyxiation," Bodinger told him, aware of the coming response.

"Isn't that the same thing?" Saunders asked, getting impatient.

"No, sir," Cordova answered, "I made the same mistake. The girls died from a lack of oxygen, not strangulation. Their internal injuries, or lack thereof, make that obvious."

He remembered the Crowder kid from April. The scene was clean and the autopsy didn't help, but he'd missed the details of postmortem lynching with the daily grind of running the staff of a police department.

Bodinger continued, "The killer corresponded with Glenn Young in the same manner, the same MO, and the same signature. This guy promised in his first communiqué that he would not stop. Nine weeks later, it looks like he's followed through."

Saunders sat quietly. This was something totally different from normal police functions. This was a grandstand of a serial killer. He couldn't just blow it off as random violence, nor could he pull in too many outside resources to find this creep without setting off bells and whistles. He finished his sandwich and tossed the wrapper in the trash.

"So we got a killer, two victims, and shit-all to find him," Saunders said, before pulling back into thought. "FBI's baseline definition of serial murder is *three* or more killings with a definite interval of time between them, with a series of common factors indicating repeated behavior." Several more seconds passed before he continued. "Here's the news. One, I don't want that clown at the paper saying a goddamn thing about this. You put a muzzle on him, and he don't say what time it is unless he asks me."

"Done," Bodinger replied, having already seen to it.

"Two, it don't matter to me if you use county cops or the local boys, but you need more eyes. Grab two more to help. I don't give a shit who."

"Prince and Reyes," Cordova said. Bodinger nodded.

"Three, I don't want a call to the Feds until I decide. If we need their resources, that's my call and mine alone. Until then, this is a local matter and we'll handle it as such, clear?"

"Yes, sir," the two detectives said in unison.

"All I need is the goddamned paper screaming . . . What was it?" he asked Cordova.

"Capital Hangman."

"Fucking Capital Hangman goddamn *serial killer*," Saunders said, standing. "Stan, do you think we gotta a shot at this asshole?"

Bodinger stood as well. "Jim, right now, we have nothing. This guy's smart. He wears rubber gloves handling the letters, we can't track his tires or his boots, he leaves no DNA on the victims, no witnesses, nothing. He abducts in Austin and disposes miles away. No way to track it. I'm afraid if he hits again—"

"When," Cordova injected.

Bodinger turned toward him, gruffed, then turned back. "We won't find any more help than we have now."

"Well," Saunders said, turning to leave. "I guess we're just going to have to get smarter, gentlemen. That first girl's funeral was a goddamn circus. I don't want that shit again. How much media was at the scene?"

"I squelched it, Captain," Bodinger told him. "Only the paper. The TV boys only know we found a murdered body, no details."

"Keep it that way," Saunders said. "But if it happens again," cutting his eyes to Cordova, "there's no way to keep it under control. Young's editor will be waving the first amendment like a pom-pom after a touchdown. He'll call every TV crew in six counties. Get some help. Get people on the phone, hell, get laid, I don't care. Just get this shit-heel before the press wakes up. I shouldn't have to remind you boys, this is the capital of the country's greatest state. A serial killer here just don't fit well with the powers above, understand?"

"Yes, sir."

"Good," Saunders said, opening the door. "Get this freak, Stan. Whatever you gotta do, get this freak."

"Try my best, Jim," Bodinger answered.

"Try harder."

Stanley Bodinger and Jim Saunders had come up together. Saunders was where he was because he was able to play the game better and finished the race quicker. As a superior, Bodinger could think of no one he'd rather work under. Jim Saunders was no politician; he was a cop. Get to the truth and deal with it no matter what the consequences are. Bodinger liked that about him and liked that about himself.

Saunders left the conference room to the two detectives.

"I'll set up the hired help," Cordova said.

"Get them working with Burnet," Bodinger told him. "We'll take the new lead and see what's what. Don't think it's going to matter much."

"Oh no?" Cordova asked.

"No," Bodinger admitted. "Until he makes a mistake, we're playing his game."

*

The only thing the paper said about the murder was a half page write-up at the bottom of page one.

"Local Girl Found Slain," the bold print stated. Her name and brief history was given, along with the details of the crime scene allowed by Bodinger. He didn't want the killer's entire glory printed; he needed to deny just enough. The hope was that he'd feel slighted and write to Glenn Young complaining about the lack of notoriety. He obviously wanted fame or why else send the photos to a reporter? If they could get him in a steady conversation, he may tip his hand and start a chain of events that could lead to his demise.

But so far, nothing. D seemed the perfect criminal. He left no witnesses, no DNA, and no forensics to speak of. The detectives needed a break, and none were coming.

What were coming were more bodies.

17

Susan Bodinger was curled up on the couch, reading the latest Linda Howard romance novel. It had been years since she and Stan enjoyed an empty house. Now that it was, the only thing that occupied her mind from the deafening silence was reading. Earlier in the day, she'd talked on the phone with her son Brian, a pharmaceutical salesman in Texarkana. He wanted to know how things were going.

"Good," Susan lied, her son hearing.

"Dad?"

"Who else?"

"Bad case?"

"Like you wouldn't believe."

"Can he catch them?"

"If he gets lucky."

"Then he's as good as caught," Brian said, laughing.

"I see you've learned a lot about your father," she cracked, sharing a laugh with her child. If Stanley Bodinger were an animal, he'd be cat, always landing on his feet.

Now, it was six in the evening when she heard Stan's car pull up. She waited, finishing her chapter. He walked in looking like a stray dog. Ruffled, in need of petting. She closed her book, pulling off her glasses, asking, "Bad day?" smiling her smile.

"The worst."

"Oh, yeah? Remember, I've seen pretty bad."

"A grieving father, Julie Brooks's father, told me I was inept and a waste of the taxpayers' money. That was bad enough, but then we had to bury the sweet kid. Yeah, babe," he said, dropping his keys on the table with a loud *clank*, "I say that rates right up there."

Susan closed the book, rising from the couch. In a loving effort, she hugged him. He melted in her arms. He wished he had her strength, her perseverance. Susan was the kind of person who saw the good in everyone, while Stan only saw the bad. They balanced, like two equal sums on the scale.

"Hungry?" she asked, trying not to wilt.

"Got any glass?" he asked.

"Glass?"

"According to Thomas Brooks, that's all I'm fit to eat."

She fought off the urge to anger. Her husband was a good man doing the best of his ability, and if anyone ever thought otherwise, it drew the ire of his wife like nothing else. However, she held it, saying, "Well, we're all out of glass," trying to make him smile. "But I have a roast in the oven. Still hot."

"Still?" he asked, defeated.

"Just for you."

He pulled away from her, holding her at arm's length. "Wouldn't have any alcohol in this dump, would you?"

"Only if you asked me nice."

A small sliver of a smile cracked his lips. "Please?"

"I know the bartender," she said, with a mischievous grin. "See what I can do."

"You do good, baby," Stan answered, hugging her tightly. "You do real good."

She kissed him and left for the kitchen as he flopped on the couch. Feeling like he'd taken advantage, he asked, "So how was *your* day?"

"Well, you know. Had to tell a lot of people no." Susan was a loan officer at a local bank, and Stan thought *his* job was stressful. She never ceased to amaze him. She always carried herself with calm, no matter how dire the situation. She had a cop's mentality, a *good* cop's mentality. Access, determine, then deploy. That was Susan.

Stan just wanted to lock everyone up. Let the judge figure it out. Their kids always knew who to go to with schoolwork, and who to see if there was a bully. As he thought of it, it was a great balance. Yin and Yang. He needed her quiet calm and inner strength, and she needed his fire and brimstone. So did the kids. They were great. Apart and together.

Susan came back with a Whiskey Sour telling him, "It'll be about twenty minutes. I need to warm the vegetables." He took the drink, sat it down, then took her hand. "Baby," he said, looking deep. "I couldn't make it without you."

"And if you ever forget that," she said, sitting in his lap. "I'll kill you." They laughed together before she added, "And I know enough cops to get me off."

Sensing her need to lighten the mood, Stan answered, "Goddamn it, I just bet you do."

"And they'll do it cheap."

"Nothing cheap about you, sweetie," Stan said, swatting her butt as she left to check the oven. He sipped his drink and tried to let the day melt away. Usually he could, but not this time. D had a strangle hold on him. The city was looking to him to find this new menace and make the streets safe.

That was a cruel joke.

The streets are never safe. Pedophiles, drug pushers, pimps, gangs, and just plain rotten people were everywhere. Austin had a feel to it like everything was peaches and cream, unlike its sisters Dallas, Houston, and San Antonio. Hell, even Waco had the Branch Davidians. Austin was the big city with the small-town feel. Things like a serial killer didn't happen here. However, Stan knew better. For half his life, he'd been fighting crime in the state's capital. Austin was big, mean, and nasty, no matter what the pamphlets at the tourist bureau said.

He couldn't stop thinking about an old partner. One that meant the most to him of all the partners he'd ever split a shift with. Best damn street cop he'd ever worked beside. A bruiser with a heart of gold. But like many good things, it ended badly. The guy with the heart of gold had too many vices, and Stan wanted better. He needed better for himself and his family. He had to cut him loose. Hearts were broken; there was no choice.

He had to do it. That's how he lived with it.

"Wonder how he's making it?" he asked himself.

"What, sweetie?" Susan called from the kitchen.

"Huh? Oh, nothing, just thinking too much. Guess I need to practice my own lessons." He sipped his drink, knowing it was a burned bridge that could never be repaired. Susan loved the jerk, everyone did. Except the thugs who got their teeth kicked in for crossing the line. They knew each other inside and out. Like a married couple who finished each other's sentences, they trusted each other with their lives.

But there came that last straw, and Stan did what he had to do to protect his career and possible lives. He made his decision and never looked back.

"Soup's on," Susan called.

Stan was relieved to know. He didn't need to tread that path again, not now, not with everything like it was. There were bigger problems to face. Problems they don't teach you about in the academy.

"The Capital Hangman," he said.

Walking to the doorway, Susan stopped and listened, letting him vent.

"He calls himself that. First it was D. He said he still likes that, that it means something to him, but if the press is going to name him, he likes the Capital Hangman," his eyes scanned up to her. "What kind of man thinks that way? Makes murdering young women a game? You see the movies and books, the real ones and the ones from Hollywood, but you never think you're going to be burdened with the responsibility of catching a madman. A real one. Not one you can close the book on or turn the channel and he goes away."

Susan leaned against the doorway, titling her head as he continued. "In my wildest dreams, I never thought there would come a time when I just wanted to reach over and tag another cop and tell him you're it. You go find him. But I feel that with this case. Baby," he said to her, scooting to the edge of the sofa, "if this is cat and mouse, then we're the mice."

She'd never heard him this way. Not only doubting himself, but the entire force involved. Surely there was something they had, something they could go on. However, the look in his eyes, the weary ache of uncertainty was weighing on him like a granite stone. She walked to him, kneeling in front of him on the sofa. Taking his hands, she said, "We'll get through this, you know that. Nothing will ever be too big for you . . . or us."

Stan blinked away his emotions, finished the drink, then asked, "What if I fail?"

"Then we fail together."

He pulled her close, squeezing her tight. He had his rock. A Gibraltar that would stand the strongest wind. For her, he could press forward. *With* her, he could triumph.

"Of course," she said, pulling back, "I'll divorce you and marry a gigolo."

Laughing, Stan agreed. "You deserve the best, baby. Get what you can."

18

Lost inside the nothingness of himself, Adam only wanted something to call his own. He didn't need the job, since money was never an issue. He took it, however, to soothe his raging mind that devoured his consciousness. He clocked into his job at Delphi Technologies at nine p.m., having driven to work in his *normal* car. Wearing the insipid uniform of a glorified crossing guard, he took his lunch box and folder to his work station at the monitoring desk and settled in. After the day guards left, with calls of *pretty boy* and wolf whistles, Adam turned his attention to his task. He was to monitor the facility by the screens and make security walks twice a night. Since he didn't know what Delphi did, his resolve was lacking.

His mind always wandered. He felt Deloris in his clothes, in his mouth, in his blood. She never took a night off from questioning, tormenting. Asking him what he was doing and pushing him to find the truth about himself.

What was it?

As long as he could remember, the Tidy Man was always the one that supplied their needs. Deloris told him that *he* was the one who gave them their house and arranged things so she could stay home and not have to work, like the mothers of his friends.

What friends?

An outcast from birth, Adam never sought companionship. Alone, not able to justify the way the world saw him, trapped inside, hollow and empty, he sought something to call his own. The job. The job was never enough. At first, he thought it would be. He prayed it would give him that spark of individuality to break away from the cycle of lust and incest. But in the end, it was only a cover. A deception to hide the true beast he was born to be. The predator that feasted on the unknowing.

The screens were playing the same mundane, mind-numbing stillness that ate away his soul. Since her death, all he had was monotony. Day after day, week after week of life-bleeding repetitiveness. The Tidy Man got him the job to occupy his mind. To give him *something to do.*

The gall of it.

The absolute patronization.

A lab rat.

After time passed, assured he was alone, Adam opened the folder, gazing at the pictures of Amy and Julie. Julie had died so sweetly, but Amy was the first. Each, in her own way, held a special place for him. Rooms in his heart quartered off for diverse reasons. Each with her own sanctuary, her own paradise. A place where only he could touch them. Secluded, isolated from the horrors he'd saved them from. Lives of disenchantment. The tragedy of existence. Now, with his help, they could be truly free. Free of the horrors of the world. Free of lies and deception. There were photos of each struggling inside the bag, fighting for breath, like the bugs in his old jar.

He was ten when his obsession took root. Fourth grade. His teacher had given an assignment to the class to collect bugs for a science project. Mrs. Temple. An old strumpet who enjoyed the power of the blackboard. Widowed since forty, the seventy-year-old teacher had passed the last thirty years of her life alone with only the children to occupy her loneliness. Thick and bruising, she very deftly instructed her children on how to alter a simple Mason jar into a gas chamber.

"Line the bottom of the jar with cotton balls," she told them, demonstrating her own technique. "Then pour in just enough rubbing alcohol to saturate the cotton. Make sure the cotton floor of the jar is good and wet with alcohol."

Adam sat, listening intently. He was never much for bugs, so the idea of making something to kill them intrigued him. Temple told them to catch the bugs without harming them in any way then deposit them in the jar, screwing the lid on quickly.

"Then what?" a small girl asked.

"They die," she told her, without emotion. "They die and their tiny bodies are not injured in any way. They can be displayed intact, almost looking alive."

"Shouldn't we poke holes in the lid?" some addle-brained boy asked.

"Now why would you do that?" the old teacher wanted to know.

"So they can breathe," he answered, still not understanding the idea behind the project.

"Randy," she said, calmly, "Haven't you heard a single word I've said? We want them to die. You cannot display a bug collection with the blasted things crawling and flying about. They have to die, and this way is humane and it saves the beauty of the insect's body."

"How do they die?" another child asked.

"The fumes from the alcohol. It kills them slowly and painlessly."

Sure it does.

Some of the girls in the class were squeamish, wanting nothing to do with the project. Temple, never one to force slaying on children, told those opposed to instead write a thousand-word essay on the insect of their choice. The delicate soon grew to accept the idea of entomology.

Adam couldn't wait to get started. Each student was to bring in a poster board displaying at least ten different species of insects. Although not technically an insect, spiders would be allowed, even encouraged.

Bugs.

When Deloris picked him up from school, the little guy was energized.

"So what's got that smile on your face?" she asked, driving him home. Adam smiled very little. Small and delicate, the other boys bullied him, and he was too nervous around girls, so he pretty much lived within himself. She was fine with that. After all, he was hers.

"Mrs. Temple showed us how to make a killing jar to collect bugs," he beamed.

"Bugs? Yuck."

"I know, Deloris, but you drop them in the jar—this jar with cotton and alcohol—and they die. Then we're supposed to glue them on this poster board and label them. I have to have ten. Ten different ones."

"Well, don't expect me to help you. It's disgusting."

"Yeah, a lot of the other girls thought so too. They can write a paper instead, but it's too long. Nobody wants to do that," the little boy informed her, with dead certainty.

Deloris drove to their house on McCormick Street knowing her son could not wait to find a jar and build his awful contraption. She thought it repulsive, but Adam was so excited to get started she was not about to get in his way. As soon as she stopped to open the automatic garage door, Adam bound from the car to enter as soon as it rolled up far enough. Before it had risen completely, the boy was out of sight, rummaging through the kitchen for a good-sized jar. When Deloris entered, he was on his knees atop the counter looking through the cabinets like a jewel thief plying for booty.

"You're not going to find anything up there," she told him.

"Where, then?"

There was a look on his face she hadn't seen in a long time. He looked happy, like how a child should look. He was blessed, or cursed, with the face of an angel. His bone structure and blue eyes, together with his full bottom lip, impressed a sense of femininity. Thin and weak, it was a wonder the bullies didn't kill him. Even at such a young age, they called him *faggot* and *gay boy.* He was too young for anyone to fully know what his sexual orientation would be. Deloris felt he would like girls.

Not all heterosexual men are brutes.

He didn't seem to care for sports or any of the other things most boys his age gravitated toward. He tried video games, but quickly lost interest. He liked words. He was able to read at a second grade level before his first day of school. He enjoyed all types of reading. Comics, children's stories, poetry, even the newspaper was on the child's reading list. Deloris felt he'd be like his father, a big brain instead of a big body.

100

Now, for whatever reason, he was excited about this bug thing. She was glad to see him so determined. She went to the refrigerator and removed a quart jar of mustard. Almost empty, Deloris dumped the meager remains then washed the inside of the jar until it was squeaky clean, all while Adam watched quietly. She was doing this for him.

It felt good. To both of them.

Screwing the lid on, she handed it to him. "This should do," she told him. "Probably still smells like mustard, but I'm sure your creepy crawlies won't mind."

Adam snatched the jar from her hand. Jubilant, he said, "Thanks Mo . . . Deloris."

"It's okay," she told him, not smiling. "Now, didn't you say you needed cotton and alcohol?"

The next day was Saturday, so instead of looking for his tiny creatures in the waning afternoon light, Adam spent the rest of the evening in his room with the encyclopedia, deciding on exactly what his quarry should be before getting a fresh start the next morning. The weather was supposed to be clear and calm on the mid-March Saturday, so his hunting should be bountiful.

Sitting naked at his small desk, with his alcohol-fuming killing jar in front of him, he poured over all sorts of crawlers and fliers he knew to be plentiful in the kingdom of his backyard. It was dark outside, the only light in the room bleeding from a bed lamp a few feet away. The murky light set the tone for his day to come. He was logging both the common names of the insects he'd seek as well as their scientific monikers. This was going to be great; he was going to turn in the best collection of the class.

He heard her enter the room behind him; not turning, he pressed on with his task. She eased her way to his desk, standing beside him with her silk robe open, revealing her entire form. At thirty, Deloris was never a striking beauty, but she was attractive nonetheless. A very handsome woman.

Adam turned. Seeing her as bare as himself, he went back to his work. It was normal, as normal as he knew it to be. Deloris had bred clothing out of him. In her view, clothes were only worn when necessity demanded it. It was the only life he'd known with her since his earliest memories. She loved nudity and would never allow her child to grow up with the same social oppressions that had been forced on her.

"My pretty boy is working so hard," she told him, stroking his black hair. "I'm proud of you." She said the words. Adam heard them, however, they meant nothing. It was the tone that lacked. The feeling. There was no love, no tenderness to the words. It was as though she'd been mandated to utter them, rather than speaking them from her heart.

"Thank you," he said, eyes never leaving the book. He wanted her to leave, let him continue his new passion.

She turned, walking to the door where she stopped and told him, "Before you go to bed, come to my room first. I need you to do our *secret* thing for me, so I can sleep."

His eyes narrowed, his jaws clenched. The ten-year-old swallowed hard before saying all right without turning.

"Don't make me wait too long," she said, leaving the door. "You have a big day tomorrow."

Adam felt chills run up his legs. He didn't understand what she'd taught him to do. He never really wanted to do it, but he always did it for her because he loved her and she wanted him to. Besides, she did sleep better when he did it. He didn't know why, she acted like it hurt. When he asked once if it hurt, she told him no. "It feels so good. It's almost like you're about to *die* from the good feelings. Then it's over, and you're relaxed. And you're able to sleep. Someday, you'll understand. I promise."

Sometimes, for no reason, she'd tell him to be still and she'd put his thing in her mouth. It felt good, but he didn't understand what she was doing. She was always feeling him down there. It never really bothered him, it was just that she seemed to be looking for something. Something he was supposed to have, something he couldn't understand.

It was late. He had to go to her room. The blue room she'd never let him call blue. He'd come back and work more later. He'd finish it, even if he had to stay up all night.

*

Adam woke. He'd fallen asleep at his desk. The monitors were still showing no movements. Peeking at his watch, he guessed he'd been asleep for two hours; it was one fifteen. It was the longest he'd slept in weeks. It was time to make a walk through the building. He stood, closing the folder of pictures and taking his keys.

Another lonely night. Another dark and lonely night.

Just like he wanted.

19

At the moment, life was good for Frank Castro. He paid rent for the two months he owed on the office, plus the next two up front, bought Tiffany a new computer for her desk, and was standing outside the building watching the repairmen fix his front door while supervising the operation with some of Tiffany's Kahlua-laced breakfast blend. It had been a good start to the summer. Florence Cabbershaw had been a goldmine. The hush money she paid him at the end of May was enough to get out of debt with the building owner, take care of a few loose ends, and still sport twenty-five grand in the bank. He was no idiot; he knew the money wouldn't last forever. It just felt good to breathe easy for a while.

The real boost the old lady gave him was a few new clients. Well-paying clients. Frank was a dependable source of information and willing to do about anything that involved getting paid. The wise Mrs. Cabbershaw knew this firsthand. At a function the old gal was hosting for one of her husband's close business ties, a local insurance firm, she overheard they were looking into a fraud case. She stepped in, recommending Frank Castro.

"Thank you, Florence, but we have our own investigators," they replied, being smug.

"I understand," she told them, "but does it ever hurt to have a fresh set of eyes looking at the same old problems?" she finished, giving her husband Howard a knowing glance, which fell dead on him.

A week later, Frank Castro was added to their list of investigators. He wasn't their primary, something he couldn't handle, but he was on their list, meaning that he'd get a monthly check if he did anything or not. Mrs. Cabbershaw just kept surprising Frank at every turn.

Tiffany walked outside with the coffeepot, interrupting the workers at the door. They didn't seem to mind the sexy assistant's disturbance. Topping off Frank's cup, she asked, "How about the sign?"

"What about it?"

"Get a better one. One that says class." Tiffany was talking about the wooden sign planted in the grass in front of their four parking spaces. It was just a small, white sign with two pegs planted in the ground that read, *Frank Castro Investigations* in plain black letters. Through the years, the afternoon sun had faded the words to a miserable gray.

"You think?" he asked, sipping his eye-opener.

"Nothing too fancy, just something to catch your eye," she said with energy.

She was so funny. That was another reason Frank kept her around. As hot as she was to look at, and good as the booze-infused coffee made him feel, there was an air of bubbly excitement with everything she did. Some mornings she'd even come in bitching about her sexual escapade from the night before. Frank always enjoyed the show.

It was the prior fall and money was tight. Frank had pulled an all-night bender with Johnnie Walker, falling asleep in the office—something he hated doing. He was roused the next morning by Tiffany wrestling with the door. In frustration, she swung it all the way open, so hard it bounced back, nearly clipping her heels as she stomped in. She didn't know for sure if he was there. His car was in the lot, but he'd leave it there on occasion if he left with some bimbo or to do coke with Tully Pritchard. A room away, he flipped on his desk lamp as she started her usual ritual at the coffeepot. Tiffany began the conversation like she'd been talking to him all night.

"So Beverly decides she's going home with that creep of a boyfriend and leaves me in Buffalo Billiard's by myself, so I'm already pissed. I mean, *please*. It's one thing to have a life, but you don't ditch a friend, really. But then this guy starts talking to me. Nice guy, really cute. Tall like you, but sandy blonde hair, gray eyes, a real knockout."

Frank stumbled to the doorway between the two offices, shirttail out, needing a shave and a comb; mouthwash would have been nice as well. Eyes puffy and crusted, he cut an image of a river rat.

"You look like shit."

"Please," he said, crossing his arms, "continue."

"Anyway, we hit it off. We leave and go to a couple of other places, dance, and talk. The guy's really got my motor running. I mean, you know me. I'm not a girl that jumps in the sack with just anybody," she finished the coffee, turning with her hands on her hips. "Do I?"

"Hell no," he managed, leaning against the doorway. "Selective, even."

"Thank you. But I mean, after a few drinks and dancing and sweet talking, he's got me needing it. I mean, I invite *him* to *my* place. I never do that, not on a first meeting. But god, Frank, he smelled so good, had these broad shoulders, a great smile. I mean a killer smile."

"It's all about the teeth, baby."

"So we get to my place and start pulling clothes off and feeling our way all over each other and guess what I find out about *Prince Perfect?*" she snapped, almost in accusation.

"Can't wait."

"His dick's as big as my thumb!" she said, holding up her right thumb.

"Well, damn, Tiff. Give the poor sap time to get it up," he tried, caught off guard. He realized the humor, but was feeling too much like a lush to respond appropriately.

"No, Frank, no! You don't understand. It *was* up."

"Really?" he winced.

"Oh yeah. It was rock hard and no bigger than my *thumb*! I didn't think they made them that small." Again, she did the thumbs-up.

Frank snickered, finally feeling a laugh building in his stomach. For the next ten minutes, Tiffany went on about how it's true that size doesn't matter, but there comes a point when it's just not worth the effort. You have to give even the most skilled veteran something to work with. "*Suck it, lick it, jerk it, sit on it,*" she mocked her disappointing lover, gyrating her body, simulating him. "I was afraid I

106

was gonna break it off, Frank! I mean, *goddamn it*!"

Frank burst into laughter.

Trying not to laugh herself, Tiff again did the thumbs-up, "It was *this* fucking big!"

"New sign, huh?" Frank wondered aloud.

"Absolutely. You need it, Frank."

As the workers were finishing, he thought about having the sign painted on the glass door instead. "What do you think about painting the name on the door?" he asked his assistant.

"Oh, yeah, that's way better!" she bubbled. "Gold letters with black trim."

"Sure, baby."

"Who do you wanna call?"

"Like I gotta clue."

"I'll take care of it. Leave it to me," she announced, and off she went, past the workers and back inside. Normally, the two guys would have been put off by the interruption, but Tiffany's interludes were always a welcomed break. After she was inside, the two smiled at each other then rolled their eyes to Frank.

"You oughtta work with her," he confessed, sipping his high-octane coffee.

Too bad she likes boy toys.

It was about three in the afternoon when Tiffany dropped a load of assorted papers on Frank's desk as he thumbed through his little black book looking for a hook up. It had been awhile since his last tryst, and the private dick was ready for some contact. Having Tiffany around—and oblivious to his needs—didn't help.

"What the hell's this?" he asked.

"A month of mail and stray papers. I'll toss it if you want, but I thought you might wanna look through them first."

"Okay," he told her. "I'll ditch what I don't need."

"Cool beans, boss. I'm outta here," she announced, over her shoulder.

"It's not even four."

"I'll come in early tomorrow," she lied, with a sexy smile.

"Whatever," he said, knowing better. She paused at the door. Feeling her eyes on him, he asked, "What?" without looking.

"You're doing good, Frankie."

He let his eyes scan up. "Good?"

"Yeah, real good. That Cabbershaw thing was a good bit of work."

"Glad you're impressed."

"No, jackass, I mean it really opened the door for you. I guess you needed that, huh? Just the right person at the right time."

"Oh, I don't know," he said, leaning back in his chair, feeling full of himself. "Like to think I have what it takes, no matter what the job is. But you're right, if I'd have done that work for someone else, it might not have paid squat."

"Or," she replied, "if someone not as good as you had done the job for her, they might not have gotten paid so well. Hmm?"

Damn. Good point.

Suddenly, Frank got what she was saying. He had it backward. As far as lucky breaks go, this time he was the break and the client was the lucky one. He was simply reaping his true worth.

Convinced of himself, he asked her, "So, baby, who's the man?"

"You're the man, Frank. You are the *man!*"

"That's right, Tits, and don't you forget it," he jibbed.

Trying not to smile, she rolled her eyes, saying as she left, "I hate when you call me that!"

He laughed a belly laugh. "*Hahahaha!*" At least for now, it was good to be Frank Castro.

Frank was alone in his office. Tiffany had done so well arranging the work on the sign that within four hours, the guy showed, did the job, and was gone. It was just too bad she didn't do everything as efficiently.

He placed the pile of mail and papers in his lap, sliding his wastebasket beside his chair. He started dumping everything, old bills and junk mail mostly. He even tossed a couple of newspapers when one caught his eye. It was an article by that pain-in-the-ass, Glenn Young. Another column about a different young woman murdered in the woods outside of town. He thought about the first article he read on the day he saw Mrs. Cabbershaw. He read the entire article.

It was double-talk. Writer gibberish. It seemed as though he was repeating the same story from a month earlier about the other girl that had been found in the woods. And like the first article, the details were sketchy at best. All Young seemed to be interested in was stirring the shit, something Frank liked about him.

"This reporter knows better," he wrote. Just like reading the first story at the bar, it sounded strange. And just like his reading at the bar, Stanley Bodinger was named chief investigator.

"Why's that asshole on both cases?" Frank asked himself, sipping a scotch. "They're nearly two months apart, two separate counties. Saunders has lost his mind," he whispered. "Unless . . ." He stopped. "Nah, stop it. You think too much," he said, folding the paper and tossing it in the trash.

He needed a release. Sixth Street would do nicely.

Hell, maybe Carmen was even free.

It was midnight, and Frank Castro was in the best place in the world; drunk with a sexy woman's ass backed against him. He stayed inside Carmen for over an hour before finally releasing himself inside her. After a brief cooling period, Carmen headed naked to the bathroom, leaving Frank on his back, staring at the ceiling. He was troubled, and for the life of him, he didn't know why. He had a couple of steady clients, there was money in the bank, his BMW was paid off with help from Tully, Tiffany was still herself, and Carmen could always be counted on for a good lay, even in a pinch.

So she cost a Benjamin. It was worth it.

For some reason, there was a sense of foreboding he couldn't shake. Neither scotch nor sex could ebb the feeling. It was like there was a black cloud looming over him. Things were good, the best in a long while, but it seemed fleeting, like the good times you have as a kid a week before summer ends and school starts. No matter how good life is, you know disappointment is just around the corner.

Maybe he was being too negative. After years of boozing, drugging, and womanizing, maybe he was turning paranoid. He should just learn to relax and enjoy the good times, especially since they were so few and far between.

As he rolled on his side, the sexy Carmen returned, falling beside him on the bed. The two nude business partners shared a smile. She was a good kid, better than this. And for her, Frank was more than a drunk and a customer. At that split second, without either saying a word, they both recognized it and smiled. No matter where they went or what happened to either of them, they would always find time.

Even if Carmen charged him.

Frank never saw it as paying a prostitute. Carmen allowed him to meet his male needs, and he dropped a few bucks to help her with whatever she needed. It was two friends helping each other in their own special way.

"I don't love you," he said, grinning.

She smiled, "I know. Me either." She could see there was something weighing on him, even more than usual. Frank was always heavy—most alcoholics are—but tonight was different. Their sex wasn't the usual fire and lust. This time it was softer, like he needed to feel from a place within himself. "What's up with you tonight?" she asked, rolling over and nestling her back against his broad chest. Her hair smelled of gardenias. Frank took a second to breathe her in before asking, "What do you do when the booze doesn't get you as drunk and the drugs don't get you as high or the sex isn't as exciting?" He felt her tense and explained, "No, this was great, but it wasn't what it usually is, was it?"

"No," she replied, after a slight delay.

"I'm getting old, Carmen."

"Oh, please."

"No, I'm *not* old, but I'm going in that direction. Hell, baby, I'm a drunk who hates drinking. A coke head who hates doing lines. I really hate that I put *you* through this."

Without turning, she said, "Don't insult me. If I didn't want you, I'd say no."

"That's not what I meant."

"What, then?"

"I mean I'm slowing down. I feel it, everyday. My life's been a whirlwind, and now I look back and wonder how much of it I wasted. Wasted on booze, drugs, whoring around, trying to party myself to death. Now I'm an age I never thought I'd reach and . . ."

"And what?"

"And it's a little scary," he confessed. "I mean, I pissed away the department, friends, a lot of good people who didn't deserve it. And for what? Cheap thrills and a long joy ride?"

"You're a good man."

"I'm wasted potential."

Carmen rolled over to face him. "Are you finding your soul?" she asked.

"Nothing's that easy," he answered, rolling flat on his back. "I gave up on me as a man a long time ago. I really thought I'd be dead by now. So here I am, closing in on fifty, and the life I was leading was the wrong one. Good thing it only took me forty-five years to figure it out."

Carmen was quiet. He thought she'd protest or laugh, but she just lay there in silence. This was a side of Frank she'd never seen. A side that was mortal; a real, living, feeling man. She'd always liked the jerk, but he was what he was. This was something new.

She liked it.

"When I was a little girl," she started, softly. "My mother would tell me that there were no more good men in the world. Her father was a bad man and my father was a monster. She always said that a woman has to use men to get what they want then cast themselves away, like a boat from the shore. I never wanted to get too close to you, Frank, and honestly, I still don't. But for the first time in a long time, I think maybe Mama was wrong."

"I don't know, baby. I think she was smarter than you give her credit for." He thought of Mrs. Cabbershaw, her dignity, her grace. With the humiliation of her husband's indiscretions, her first thoughts were to protect her adult children and keep the name of the law firm her husband built intact.

The old gal was a better man than he was.

He had made so many mistakes in his life that he needed a Palm Pilot to track them. He'd ruined a police career that could have taken him to the top. He could be captain by now, if he'd only learned to slow down. But nothing was ever fast enough for Frank. He loved living in the moment more than he thought about living in the future. His old partner had warned him so many times to *take it easy,* but he always flew in the face of danger. Almost wanting the dire to happen. He'd also fallen in with some shady characters along the way and had been living in the bottom of a scotch bottle for the better part of twenty years. Gazing down at Carmen, he realized all the ghosts of life's mistakes were not going to go silently into the night. For some reason, Frank was seeing his life as a whole for the first time.

And it was shitty.

Why? Why now?

Maybe it was the way old lady Cabbershaw handled herself. Maybe it was Carmen's ease with him. Maybe it was seeing that damned Stanley Bodinger's name in the paper. Maybe he was just starting to feel what getting old felt like.

Maybe everyone feels this way.

The tagline of the new millennium was that forty was the new thirty and fifty was the new forty. However, at that moment, forty-five felt like an old seventy. He reached down, letting his hand rest on Carmen's right butt cheek. She was a good girl. Like a lot of people in the world, she was a good person who started out behind the eight ball and was never able to get fully out of its shadow. For her, prostitution was a means to an end.

However, Frank was different. Frank went to college, joined the police force, was supposed to be somebody. And now, at forty-five, he was no further along in his life than this hooker who was young enough to be his daughter.

He was torturing himself. He did it from time to time, like most alcoholics do, but usually he knew what started it. This time it was random. He had money, good leads, good clients, got his front door fixed, complete with a new sign, and just got laid.

What was this about?

For some reason, Bodinger's name floated by. It was ugly. For the first time in years, he let his mind recall his face, his aftershave, his personality. The man who had hung him out to dry to internal affairs. Frank sat up in bed, placing his back against the headboard. Carmen never moved. She was lying on her stomach, her arms crossed beneath her chest, asleep. She was peaceful, calm, and beautiful in the soft moonlight that filtered through her window in a blue hue.

Frank closed his eyes and tried to stave off the image of his old partner. He'd made a lot of mistakes, but the last thing Frank Castro could ever be accused of was being a bad partner. At one time, he loved Stanley Bodinger like a brother. They shared everything. When Stan's mom died, Frank was the one Stan turned to for Susan's support at the funeral. And many times, in a predicament—usually caused by alcohol—he could always call Bodinger to bail him out, or at least be there with him. They were a team, a unit. Frank loved being a beat cop with Stanley Bodinger; they were brothers in arms. But when Frank counted on him one last time, at the most important hour, Bodinger took the easy way out, leaving his partner to twist in the wind.

"What's this about?" he whispered to himself. "So he's looking into a couple of murders. Big deal, Frank. Let it go." He slid back down in the bed, snuggling against the sleeping Carmen. He knew she'd be pissed in the morning if she woke to find him still there at sunup. But he didn't care. He deserved to sleep next to a pretty young woman for the night. He'd offer to pay her electric bill for the month; that should do the trick.

As Frank drifted off to sleep, the image of his old partner faded into a mist of contentment. He'd earned a lot of money helping an old woman. Maybe he was feeling this way because he was finding out that he wasn't such a disaster after all. Maybe, in the end, he *was* a good guy. Just one who'd lingered in darkness for years because of a few mistakes.

Mistakes can be forgiven.

Betrayal, however, cannot.

20

July brought drought. The Austin area had not seen serious rainfall since the end of April. It seemed to happen every other summer. A mild winter followed by an inferno that made the most ardent wilt to the heat. This summer was one for the books.

It also added to the frustrations of Stanley Bodinger. He and Cordova were meeting this day with Kevin Kerndon, a freelance criminal psychologist from SMU. Once a member of the FBI, Kerndon had turned in his shield for a post with the university to further his professorial aspirations as well as his writing. He'd published two books on the minds of madmen and offered his services generously. He was one of the best in the field. He was also free from the governmental ties that would involve the Bureau.

After Julie Brooks's murder, he was given every detail of both crimes committed against her and Amy Crowder, in order to put together a profile of what kind of predator D was. The fifty-year-old criminologist was seated in a conference room awaiting the arrival of the four detectives working the case; Bodinger and Cordova, along with sergeants Jefferson Prince and Luis Reyes. Jim Saunders was coming, as was Police Chief Milt Short.

Bodinger and Cordova were antsy to hear Kerndon's take on the two killings. What had started out as a random homicide had turned into every cop's worst nightmare: a serial killer with a taste for his game. The one thing that had the department at a standstill was the lack of forensics at the scene and on the victims. Neither girl's abduction had been witnessed, there was zero blood spill, and the psycho left no DNA to speak of. No hair, no blood, semen, nothing. All they had were two dead bodies and two digital photographs sent to the newspaper by the killer.

If the Titanic wasn't sinking, the iceberg was getting close.

The four detectives entered the conference room at the same time. As they broke the ice with Kerndon, Saunders and Short joined, and all took seats around the long conference table.

Saunders spoke first. "Gentlemen, we all know why we're here. There seems to be a killer in our city who not only loves killing young women, but finds it necessary to announce it to the newspaper. Right now, we have a thumb on Glenn Young at the *Citizen* not to reveal vital information about the two victims' murders until we give the go-ahead. I'm telling you now, if another one happens, and I'm sure it will, the third picture or letter Young receives will blow up on the front page and there's shit-all we'll be able to do about it," he finished, casting an eye to Chief Short. "A serial killer loose in Austin will be on every lip from here to Washington. The mayor and governor will be up all our asses with ice picks, and I for one see no benefit in that. Professor Kerndon has put together a profile of who we should be looking for. I know this ain't the gospel, but it's at least a starting point." He turned to Kerndon, nodding to proceed.

Kerndon, dressed in a navy suit and looking the part with graying at the temples, began. "Officers," he said, sliding manila folders to each man, "from what I've been able to ascertain from the data, we have a very complex criminal on our hands."

Bodinger cut a glance to his partner as if to say *no shit*.

"The very lack of forensic evidence makes these two killings most unique. What puzzles even more is his want for attention. Without the correspondence to the local paper, both of these girls would most likely still be hanging from the trees he used to display them."

"Display?" Saunders asked.

"Yes, Captain. D is using the tree as a prop. Since both victims were dead before he hung them, he sees the hanging of the nude body as an aesthetic creation. He's being an artist, if you will. Surely the act of their demise is his thrill, so the display is his signature. And I'm quite certain he finds the display almost as appealing as the kill itself. But the point is he sent those two photos to the paper for a reason. Without those mailings, all we would have at this point are two missing persons. We would not even be aware of a sadistic killer calling himself D, nor would we be investigating two homicides. No, gentlemen. D wants us to know what he's doing because he needs to feel superior."

"Why Glenn Young?" Bodinger asked.

"What did he say in the first letter? He called Young 'earnest and strong-willed.' I believe that he believes that. Also, he addressed the note on the back of the photo 'Dear Police,' knowing Young would do the right thing."

"But why not just send it to us?"

"That's too direct. It hedges nothing. With Young, he's involved the media."

"Attention," Cordova said.

"Exactly," Kerndon answered. "Just the police knowing isn't enough. He wants the world to know. I'm sure he realizes the restrictions that would be placed on the newspaper, but he's also aware that if he escalates, the papers will be forced to divulge all information. And since he knows there's zero forensics at the scene, he's sure the paper knows just as much as you do."

"Not quite," Bodinger spoke up. "We never told the press or even the girls' families that they were already dead when he hung them. Only we know that."

"And that's *his* secret," Kerndon explained. "As long as the paper says the girls were hung, he knows what no one else knows. That he'd killed them already. That's his power, his entitlement."

"So," Saunders began. "Who exactly are we looking for?"

Kerndon opened his folder, and the other detectives followed suit. "It's going to sound cliché, but here it is. White male, age twenty to forty. Since his crimes have a startling lack of violence . . ."

"Lack of violence?" Cordova asked. "He hung them. To me, that's violent."

116

"Agreed, but there is no bloodshed. Lack of violence in a murder simply means the victim was not stabbed, cut, shot, or strangled. The pathological report states that both victims were suffocated prior to their hanging," Turning to Bodinger, "bagged, if you will. This man likes to watch the struggle. To watch a woman fight for breath with her hands and feet bound gives him sexual stimulation. I wouldn't be surprised if he masturbated during the process. Again, he wants you to know his cravings. He wants you to understand what he's doing."

"Why?" Bodinger asked.

"It gives him control. Control was something he never had as a child, or maybe even as an adult. He was a pawn. But as I stated earlier, the lack of physical violence in the crimes leads me to think he wasn't physically abused as a child. I believe he was more of a victim of psychological abuse. He hasn't passed on violent attributes. He wants to watch the women die slowly, without blood. The line about telling her mother she died sweetly was a pure stab at femininity. I'm certain of it. Leads me to think it was his mother behind the emotional abuse."

"Is he killing his mother with these girls?" Saunders asked.

"It fits. Maybe she was a child-mother that had him at a very early age, or maybe he just likes killing young women. We don't know yet. That book is wide open."

Cordova asked, "The P.S. at the end of the second letter. God and Satan in his laughter, what the hell is that?"

"A ploy."

"Really?" Saunders asked.

"Well, my guess. It rings of authoritarianism. He's getting you to think that he feels overcome with something outside. Beyond himself."

"Copping insanity before he's even caught," Prince chimed in.

"Possibly."

"Bullshit," Cordova grunted, as Kerndon nodded.

Bodinger rested his elbows on the table, covering his eyes with his fingers, exhausted. "Does he think he's being humane? I mean, killing without blood?" he asked.

"No. He just doesn't have bloodlust. In fact, he's probably more sadistic than a bop–and–drop killer who hits a victim over the head, cuts their heart out, and keeps it as a souvenir. Their victims die painfully, but quickly. D likes to watch them suffer as they fight for breath."

"Like a bug in a killing jar," Bodinger said.

"Precisely."

"Why not just strangle them?" Saunders asked.

"Again, it's aesthetics. It's more stimulating for him to *watch* them die as it is to *feel* them die. This man is very hands-off. The stun gun to subdue them. The lack of blood and impact trauma tells me he's far more visual than careful. The lack of evidence is as much a byproduct of his MO as to his caution. And this fellow is very cautious."

"What else?" Saunders asked.

"Judging from the photos he sent, he's attracted to some dark fantasy world. Now, all of these guys are. Their very conduct screams dark fantasies, but I don't mean the crimes. I mean to say, he's overwhelmed and may even be obsessed with some form of fantasy entertainment. Such as a book, a movie, a piece of music, maybe a certain artist's paintings."

"A *Lord of the Rings* freak?" Cordova quipped.

"Possibly, sure. But I think it's something less commercial. Something he sees as *his*, and no one else gets.

"He's stunted sexually. Possibly growing up with a strict parent who viewed sex as dirty. I don't believe he was physically tormented this way, again, the lack of violence, but his view of sex is greatly skewed. He likes bondage, autoerotic asphyxiation, and masturbation. He's inadequate around women, so he plays out the fantasy of what having a woman in his world would be like, and the results are two dead young women. It's possible he's a virgin. It's also highly likely that he's had only one sex partner his entire life, and that that person is gone."

"He killed them?" Bodinger asked.

"Who knows? We are certain, however, that he lives alone, most likely works at odd jobs, or has steady employment where the demands are low."

"Such as?" Cordova asked.

"Mall security, night watchman, hotel desk clerk, the list is endless. His fantasies are such that his mind will wander, and holding a demanding

118

job is just not worth the trouble because his fantasies are the most important things in his life. They *have* been for a long time, and now they're simply not enough. He's probably a subscriber to magazines and websites dealing with bondage and other sexual subcultures. There are websites that have short films, some as short as thirty seconds, of supposed snuff films, even though it's obvious to the trained eye that the murders are fake. You see the same victim several times. It would be in line with D's mindset to watch these films as well, while playing out his fantasies in his mind." Kerndon looked at Bodinger. "Especially ones dealing with strangulation and/or bagging for asphyxiation."

The six officers all shook their heads.

Freaks.

"For D though, it's simply not enough any longer. He's taken his *kink*, if you will, as far as his solo predilection can take it. He needs real partners now. He's not going to stop, and if he stops sending photos to Glenn Young, some poor girl could completely decompose in the woods before her body is discovered. Even at that, I think we've been lucky to find them. Texas is a big place."

"Both victims' bodies were intact, and the families say there was nothing missing from their personal items." Cordova stated.

"I know where you're going, Detective. Souvenirs. We have to look at the photos he sent. We have just one from each crime scene. I bet there are at least a hundred or more of each murder in whatever this guys calls a home. Digital cameras allow you to photograph any kind of perversion imaginable with the luxury of total secrecy. To relive the event, all he has to do is flip on his computer, open a file, and there they both are, in living color."

"Hmm," Bodinger huffed, "*Living* color." All the men shared a knowing moment.

"Gentlemen, the key thing is to know that he's sharing this. That is the only positive we have to go with. He sent the letters to the paper, but the first was meant for you. He wants you aware of what he's doing. He's flaunting his ability by showing what he's done and telling you that there's nothing you can do about it. You have to find a way to speak back to him."

"He reads Glenn Young," Saunders said.

"I want him in here by noon." Short spoke for the first time.

"Agreed." Saunders looked at Prince. Prince and Reyes were on their way out of the room when Kerndon stopped them.

"Not so fast."

"And what do we have him do?" Bodinger asked Saunders, feeling frustrated. "Write an open letter in the paper? This has been a one-way dialogue, and if Young tries anything cute, D's going to see it as a trap and he'll never send another correspondence."

"You're right, Detective Bodinger, absolutely," Kerndon agreed. "Any type of outreach is going to be a red flag to this guy. He's done everything on his terms. If Young writes about the two murders in an editorial, he cannot insult him or direct a remark or question toward him. He won't stop killing, he'll just stop sending photos, and in doing so, will stop telling us where the bodies are. In the first letter, he stated it would not be his only discourse. Unfortunately, he's proven himself a second time." Kerndon cleared his throat, making sure he had everyone's full attention. "He leaves nothing to work with. Crimes of passion are littered with evidence. The reason you have nothing is because that's exactly what he wants you to have. Nothing. There is no passion involved here. This is a cold, calculating machine that feels no empathy, no remorse, no guilt. Even the glue to seal the envelopes and attach the stamps was self-adhesive. No saliva. This is a meticulous man. A meticulous man who is coming into his own. As an adult and a monster."

"But you said his mind wanders, he couldn't hold a demanding job," Cordova argued.

"Yes it wanders, to his fantasies. *Inside* those fantasies we're dealing with a very clever and methodical person." He motioned for Prince and Reyes to be seated, "Please."

"What then?" Saunders asked, dropping his pen on the table. "Just wait for another dead girl and see if his truck plate shows in the picture?" Bodinger finally saw on Saunders the emotions that he'd been feeling for months now. Anger and frustration.

"Look, Captain, I don't have all the answers. If I did, this guy would be in booking as we speak. I'm just telling you what I see and how I believe he'll react. Remember, he sent that first communiqué, something in my opinion that was foolish on his part. He'd had his fun and left no evidence. Why complicate matters? It was because he wanted to share *his secret*. He doesn't have to see his letter in the paper or have Glenn Young spouting about him. He *knows* his secret is shared. In fact, the very lack of response is most likely telling him how much time is being spent on his photos and words. He's building a monument to himself, gentlemen. A monument of sex and death, with the letter D on top of all of it."

"And his mother," Cordova added.

"Yes," Kerndon replied, "I'm sure he hated his mother. I can't say why without more data. But the fact is, in my opinion, D was abused in some way by his mother. What little that helps."

The six policemen sat silently. Tension was building in the room like steam. Kerndon was brought in to help, and all he'd done was show just how far away they were from doing anything constructive about the two cases.

"Fuck this," Cordova spat, standing to leave, kicking the chair beneath the table. "We sit around a table, killing time, just so an expert can come tell us we got nothing but ourselves?"

"Eric," Bodinger tried.

"No, Stan, there has to be something. I'm going back to those streets, back to those neighborhoods, and beating on every door till somebody tells me they saw something. I ain't letting another girl die like that. We all know it's gonna happen, while we sit here wringing our hands wondering what to do. This is *bullshit!*"

"Detective, that's enough!" Saunders scolded.

Bodinger stood, looking directly into Cordova's eyes. This wasn't just a cop he was looking at; it was a father of a little girl. Anger and fear was evident. "Take five, buddy," Bodinger told him. "Cool off. I'll be along."

This wasn't cop–to-cop. It was man-to-man, just what Cordova needed. He calmed down before leaving, as he took his coat, allowing Bodinger to reseat and address Kerndon. "We have nothing. You know that. If we have to wait, we'll wait," he glanced at Saunders and Short, who both nodded. "It's just that there seems to be something that's been missed. We all feel it, all of us. Is there anything you saw that we missed? Anything?"

"No. Excellent police work, Detective. All of you. This guy has just yet to make a mistake. And until he does, all you can do is investigate each crime and sift the rubble until you find something." He leaned back in his chair, taking a deep breath. "The last thing you can afford is to let him make it personal, that he's challenging you as a person. You're nothing more to him than a bug on his windshield, a nuisance. The police are just part of the game. So until there is a witness, we just have to hope he *does* start to get cocky and maybe he'll make a mistake. Until then . . ." he finished, with a lopsided smile.

Stanley Bodinger felt nothing to smile about.

21

Conventional wisdom implies that the majority of sexual degenerates are men. While true statistically, Deloris Parker was the exception that proves the rule. Most deviants *are* men…not all.

Adam sat in his dark hallway, beneath a green light that bathed the black walls in an eerie-colored murk. With Thrash Metal churning away in the front room, he used a piece of chalk to add to his collection of graffiti that covered nearly every wall in the house. Words from his mind rambled like a song from the depths of hell. Depravity seeped from him onto the walls in horrors of chalk. Since her death, he'd let his mind escape with words that spewed out like a severed artery.

Resting, he leaned his head against the wall, nestling a bottle of Bacardi 151 between his bare legs. Sipping, his mind wandered as it had a tendency to do. He remembered her stories. All she had for him were stories. No brother or sister, no aunts and uncles. Even his grandparents were ghosts early in his life. Stories of how she and her two younger brothers played their *secret game.* The rules were meaningless childhood fancy that only served the purpose of distinction.

A winner and a loser.

The loser had to put their mouth on the winner's private parts.

She would get misty-eyed telling of Michael and Brian. Her little brothers, her young lovers. The only thing she'd ever tell him about her parents was that they banished her away from them and away from the boys. "You're dead to us," her father told her. Adam could never even find out anything about his own father. Only that he was gone.

It was early in his life that he met the Tidy Man. He would drop by the house and talk to Deloris for an hour or so then disappear like a phantom. Even at a young age, Adam knew the man was important. He always dressed so well. Deloris was a woman, yet she didn't dress as neatly and properly as he did.

"Who is that man?" he'd ask.

"He's the man that pays our bills. He has money for you that you'll get when you get old enough. But all he is to you is just a man."

"Is he my father?"

"Ridiculous," she'd say. "You're father is gone. Concern yourself with me. I'm all you have, and I'm all you'll ever need."

Need?

He needed a mother, something she forbade him to call her. Since he was old enough to form words, all she ever allowed him to call her was by her name. He thought of Michael and Brian, the brothers she'd *played* with as a child. She was their big sister, the oldest, and she conjured up the *secret game* for them to play on her and she on them. Adam understood the boys he'd never met. Uncles he'd never get the chance to meet. Deloris treated him like another of her little brothers. A sex toy to achieve satisfaction. A lurid secret disguised as fun.

Adam rested the bottle beside him, scrawling in giant letters: *incest*. Beneath it he wrote: *secret game, the epitaph of my oblivion.* He felt the scars on his inner forearms. They felt like bubble wrap.

The first time he cut himself was one year to the day after he'd put his penis inside her the first time. When he was a little boy, Deloris would play with his *little man* from time to time. She'd have him lie still as her hands and mouth explored him. It was all he knew; he didn't know the meaning of any of it. Her hands were always on him, stimulating, massaging the tiny tip, making him laugh.

"You like that, don't you?" she'd giggle.

Of course, he did. He was a child, and it tingled.

When he grew older, she showed him her *tingly* parts and let him touch and kiss her as well. Always nude, he was never fazed by her body. She not only allowed him to explore her, but she also encouraged it. "Go ahead," she coaxed him, "it won't bite."

His first orgasm was not like most boys who discover the pleasure of masturbation on their own. Adam's first ejaculation was administered by Deloris. As the eleven-year-old experienced his first-ever climax, with her hand showing him the way, she whispered to him, "No one can please you like your mother. And no one pleases me like you."

Mother. A word he couldn't even use.

On his twelfth birthday, she stimulated him orally then lay on her back, legs apart, telling him it was time. "You've been waiting to put it there, Adam. It's time, baby. Let Mama make you a man."

The words hung in the air like a curtain. The kids at school always talked about sex with girls and jerking off, but this was his mother. Sure, every adolescent boy wants to know the warm feeling of being inside female flesh, but this was Deloris. Not some girl.

"You're so pretty, baby," she told him, his heart beating a hole in his chest. "It's almost a shame you weren't a girl. You'd have been so pretty. But then, we wouldn't have our secret games, would we?" He wanted to make her happy; it was what she'd seemed to want from him his entire life.

"Why didn't you just *say it*?!" he screamed at the wall, punching the black Sheetrock.

"Why didn't you just say *fuck me, you little shit!*" He slid down the wall as the stereo cranked out another doom-laden punch to his brain. He had sex with her that night. A twelve-year-old boy had sex with his own mother, coming inside her warm and wanting body as she stroked his fine hair, telling him, "Yes, baby, that's it, that's it. Come in Mama. Come inside Mama. Let Mama take all of it away."

He was a sex toy. A pawn in a sick game that never allowed his own frame of mind to be accounted for. For the next year, she was always on him, kissing him, licking him. Sex became as routine as taking out the trash. School was a break, and the jars were always there.

The jars. Filled with creatures tiny and large, all dying when the lid went down, and the master peered through the glass at their pathetic attempts for survival. Adam stood from the floor, walking to the red room. There were three jars there, all filled. He snatched one off the floor, looking at it, filled with death. He remembered the first time. The first time the ten-year-old boy dropped in the grasshopper and screwed down the lid. As the vapors from the alcohol overtook the insect, as it began struggling for its life, something else happened.

Adam felt his *little man* stiffen. It was exciting to watch the creature die, fighting for air, struggling to breathe. At ten, he still wondered what erections were about; Deloris had told him so many things about it. She told him so many wonderful things. But now, now he was aroused by death. A wretched bug dying in a jar.

Again, he felt his arms, the scars. He felt the pain of each tiny mark burned into him. The first time he put the blade to his skin, it hurt. But it was his hurt, not hers. He *caused* it; he *felt* it. The blood felt cleansing as it streamed to his wrist.

"*My* pain, *my* way!"

He felt the scar on the back of his right shoulder. There, always there. Taunting, sneering from behind like a bully on the playground. Picking on a weak little kid, never man enough to stand and look him in the face. He had to use two mirrors to see it, but it was there; he didn't need to see it. It was there; he felt it on his fingers, felt it in his blood.

The black man told him, "Give it back, brother . . . Give it *all* back."

The sonic music roaring from the front, the rum kicking his brain into a state of oblivion, he sought the tiny bottle. Crawling on his hands and knees, he went to the last place he remembered having one. By the speakers in the front room. He crawled down the black painted walls, passed the madness of the graffiti, scuffling in the night, he found it. A tiny popper still fresh. When he popped the cap, it hissed to him like Deloris cooing in his ear as he spilled inside her. One sniff and the colors of his world shifted to black. Rage plumed inside his chest like a flicker catching a sudden draft. Standing, screaming, his pain would never be appeased. His shame would never be diminished. He was the animal of her creation.

"*Is it the voice of God I hear? Or the sound of Satan, escaping from my laughter?!*"

126

*

He'd spotted her a couple of weeks earlier at the liquor store where he bought his rum and vodka. He followed her in his work car, seeing where she lived. That night, he went to work and started formulating his new plan. On his days off, he would wait for her to leave the house and follow her to see where, or if, she worked. Once he was able to time it all out, getting her routine set, all he'd need was an opportunity.

There were always opportunities.

22

Frank wasn't nervous in the least; he had no reason to be. The crowded room had grown quiet, and the head of the group talked for a few minutes, going over the last meeting before getting started on the night's new business. When he finished, he asked the room if there was anyone who wanted to share any thoughts. Frank raised his hand, and the man knowingly acknowledged him, stepping away from the podium, giving Frank the floor.

It was a large room in a recreation center used by several groups for charity functions and fundraisers. Folding chairs had been placed in a large circle with the speaker's podium in the center. Frank was seated directly in front of the podium so the man would be sure to see him. He stood, cleared his throat, and said to the large group, "My name's Frank, and I'm an alcoholic."

"Hi, Frank," the room answered.

"I've been sober for . . ." He checked his watch. It was 7:05 p.m. "Twelve hours."

"*Good job! Way to go! Thatta boy!*" the praises rained.

They meant well, but it sounded hollow.

"I don't really know why I'm here," he confessed. His dark eyes were tired. He showed the kind of tired that goes beyond sleep. Frank was road weary from pounding at life as hard as he could since the day he was born. He was bone tired, the kind of exhaustion that takes years off a man's life. This was a crossroads. He knew that night, in Carmen's bed, that if he didn't change something, he was going to die. That had never bothered him before, but now it did. He'd never been afraid of death, and to some extent, he still wasn't, but now he felt his mortality compounded. Maybe it was Mrs. Cabbershaw; maybe it was having a little success. Maybe he was just getting too damn old to keep doing what he was doing. Whatever the reason, he'd told Tiffany to skip the Kahlua in the coffee and hadn't touched a drop all day. He was uptight, edgy, and pissed . . . But he was sober.

For whatever that was worth.

"Like I said, I don't really know why I'm here. I hadn't planned on it. It's not like I even thought about it. I like to drink. I like it a lot, but this morning, I just didn't want a drink. Even this afternoon, when the itch started getting bad, I still didn't want one."

"And now?" a woman asked from the crowd.

He turned in the direction of the voice. "Now? No, I guess not. I feel like shit, and I know a double Johnny would sure make me feel a lot better, but I just don't want it. I'm tired folks. I'm so goddamn tired I feel it on my soul, like it's etching a groove in me. I was a police officer once upon a time. Made some mistakes, lost a lot of close friends. Friends who deserved better. Drank away the career. A lot of water under the bridge. I've been in some of the worst places you could imagine, doing all the wrong things for the wrong reasons. But until a couple of nights ago, I could always look at myself in the mirror and know I was the best I could be. Now, I know that was a lie." A small introspective smile of shame cracked his lips. "I've left the best years of my life in the bottom of a bottle of scotch. They're not coming back. They're gone. But I still have the rest of my life to try and put back the things I ruined, to make them right, at least to me.

"I'll tell you all right now. I haven't drank today because I haven't wanted to, that's it. Tomorrow if I want it, I'm going to do it. I'm going to be true to myself, that's all I have left."

"One day at a time, brother," the man said from the podium.

"Yeah, I know. One day, one week, one month, one year, one life. I've done so many bad things that I know I can't undo them, not even gonna try. I just want to be able to look at myself and not lie to *me* anymore. If I'm drunk, then it's because I made a decision to do it. I didn't do it just because I was awake." He paused. After a deep breath, he said, "I can't put into words what made me do this. I couldn't say. You might even consider this a waste of time because I won't say I'll never drink again, because I will. But this is the first day in so many years I can't count that I just didn't want it. I hope I feel this way tomorrow. Life's a bitch anyway, guess we'll see." He finished and stepped through the chairs, heading for the door.

The room broke into applause, and the voice from the podium called, "Frank, why don't you stay? You might enjoy yourself."

But he never stopped nor turned to acknowledge any of them. He went through the door and walked to his car. He sat inside and looked at himself in the mirror. He was better than he'd ever given himself credit for, but even now he couldn't see it. All he saw was wasted potential. A bright life drowned in a sea of alcohol and cocaine. When he was a young man in his twenties, his favorite expression was "nothing says freedom like the soft glow of a neon light reflecting in the brown glass of a beer bottle." Twenty odd years later, the words mocked him. A wasted career, not all of which he felt was his fault. Parents dead, no family to speak of, a joke of a profession, and still all he'd ever had that stayed constant—the one thing he'd always counted on for over twenty years—was the booze.

When all else is eliminated, what's left must be the answer.

That was his detective mind working on himself; he hated when he did that. Of course he saw through himself like a cheap wine. He knew he could never go completely dry; he was far too weak for that kind of dedication. But maybe this was the beginning of something. Something that might allow him to get a fingernail grip on today. If today went well, who knows? Hell, he might even look up Bodinger and try to start amends. He didn't have the strength for that today, but it was a start.

Who knows what tomorrow may bring?

23

September

Thirteen-year-old Jimmy Reynolds was still in shock as he was being questioned by Stanley Bodinger. The kid had received the fright of his life, witnessing the murder of four people, three of whom were his closest friends in the whole world. His parents sat with him in their living room as Detective Bodinger sat opposite them over a coffee table.

Jimmy had been given a sedative at the hospital, where he was checked for injuries. A few minor scrapes and bruises on his legs and arms from running through the woods in a blind panic. When he reached the school, he went to the office screaming bloody murder about a man in the woods who just killed his three friends and hung a naked woman from the trees. The police were notified, with the area being found and sealed off. Once detectives recognized the MO as D, they contacted Bodinger. He and Cordova raced south to Wimberley. The father of Jimmy Reynolds didn't want the police disturbing his son any further. The poor kid had been through enough as it was. His mother, on the other hand, knew of the two dead girls from Austin. She also knew that the chances this man was the same criminal were likely, seeing as how her own son watched the man hang another girl like the others. If her son could help catch the killer, he owed it to society.

Jimmy had already told the Hays County sheriff what he had seen, but Bodinger had a much deeper investigation on his hands. If what Jimmy was saying was true, D's body count had just risen to six. Not only had he killed the young woman in the same fashion, but he had killed three teenage boys who had the misfortune of stumbling upon the scene. Like the previous two crimes, the scene was virtually devoid of evidence. Only this time, there was a witness and three shell casings.

Mr. Reynolds sat beside his son, watching every move Bodinger made. The thin, redheaded thirteen-year-old tried to give Bodinger the same information he'd given the Hays County sheriff.

"He was wearing black military pants and boots. He was wearing a plain white T-shirt and had a black mask pulled over his face," the boy recounted, trembling.

"You never got a look at his face, son?" Bodinger asked.

"No, sir. When I got there, he already had my friends on the ground. They were tied up, their hands behind them, their feet together . . . I froze."

"Why were they so far ahead of you?"

"I forgot my cell phone. It was in my backpack. I ran back to the school to get it."

"And when you got back you saw what was happening?"

Jimmy just nodded.

"Were your friends still alive?"

Another nod.

"Was the woman in the tree?"

His face contorted, tears streaming down his cheek.

"That's enough, Sergeant," Mr. Reynolds barked. "Leave my son alone. He's been through enough already!"

"Gary, please," his wife pleaded. "Jimmy is the only person to ever see this man. He has to tell what he knows."

"Not right *now!*"

"Sir, please. Ma'am," Bodinger tried to cool them. "We know this is a hard time. Believe me when I say that. I've done this more times than I can count. I know it's tough." He turned to the father with compassion in his eyes. "In order to get the best jump we can on this, we have to strike fast, while everything is fresh. Jimmy's mind won't be any better for details than it is right now. We have six dead people and your son is the only witness we have in any of these investigations. Sir," leveling a stare, "I need you to think about those six kids and their families."

132

"But he's already talked to the police. Why can't the poor kid rest? Goddamn it!"

"Yes, sir, he did, and Sheriff Lombard is a good man and an excellent law enforcement officer, but this is an Austin investigation. My partner and I have been working to find this guy since the first of April. No one knows more than us, so we have to be able to exhaust all avenues of possibilities."

"I want to, Dad," Jimmy said from the couch. "He killed my friends. I wanna help catch him." There was a slight vapor of anger in his voice. His dad took a deep breath, walking to the window that looked out onto the street. He folded his arms and said nothing. Eric Cordova took his place on the couch beside Jimmy.

"You're a brave man," he said, nudging him with his knee. "Go slow, nobody's in a hurry tonight, okay? Just tell us what you saw and what you did."

Jimmy, along with his three friends, Brandon Taylor, Justin Reeves, and Ronnie Hovey, were cutting class. They rode to Wimberley Middle School together, driven by Reeves's mother, Angela. After dropping the boys off, they ducked behind the gymnasium to go over the plan. Leaving their school gear in the nearby woods, they headed out through the thickets to the deer fields they would be hunting just six weeks later. Wanting to scout their own hunting ground, away from their fathers and older brothers. The boys mostly just wanted to cut class and spend the day in the woods bullshitting and smoking the pot Brandon stole from his cousin.

Halfway to the site, Jimmy realized he'd forgotten the new cell phone his mother had gotten him for his birthday.

"Damn it, guys, I gotta go back. I forgot my cell."

"Fuck it, bro. You ain't gonna get no reception out here anyway," Brandon told him.

"I just want it, okay?"

"We ain't waiting, bitch."

"Didn't ask you to, numb-nuts," Jimmy shot back. "Go on. I'll catch up."

Justin asked if he wanted him to come back with him, but Jimmy didn't want to kill his friend's fun in the sun and told him to go with the others. He'd be back before they knew it.

Four eighth graders. Cutting class and enjoying their youth. It was the way of the world.

So was what awaited them.

The room resettled as Bodinger continued. "Was the young woman in the tree?"

"No."

"What happened?"

"I saw the guys on the ground and the man was holding a gun."

"Go on."

"He was talking to them, but I couldn't hear what he was saying. They were too far away. He laughed I think, it was hard to tell. I was so scared. Then he put his gun inside his belt and went to the back of the Hummer . . ."

"Hummer?" Cordova asked, looking at Bodinger who nodded.

"Yes, sir."

"H2, H3?"

"H2, I think. Black with chrome."

"Did you see the license plate?"

Again the boy started to sob, but got hold of himself. "No . . . I panicked." Mrs. Reynolds cried softly into her tissue, squeezing her son's left arm, letting him know she was there.

"Did you get a picture with the phone?" Cordova asked.

"It doesn't have one," Mrs. Reynolds answered.

"Okay, he went to the Hummer. Then what?" Bodinger pushed.

"He reached in and pulled her out. She was naked. Her hands and feet were tied like my friends. But there was a plastic bag over her head."

Cordova grimaced. They were right. Stan was right all along.

"Did she move at all?"

"No, sir . . . She was dead," again he broke down, this time sending his father out the front door with a loud slam. "The guys started screaming 'cause they knew she was dead too. He drug her to the tree he parked by and put a rope around her neck and pulled her up." The poor

134

kid was crying so bad that Bodinger stopped and told him to take a break. But he refused. "After he got her up, hanging like that, he cut her feet loose. My friends were all screaming and crying. Justin tried to roll away, but he ran back and kicked him, he kicked him so hard, mister . . . He kicked him in the stomach like he was kicking a football. Then he went to the truck and came back with plastic sacks, like you get at the store, and he put them over their heads. They begged him to stop . . . They were screaming and crying. I was so scared, I couldn't move," he turned to his mother, wearing a mask of torment. "I should have done something! *I should have done something!*"

"There was nothing you could've done, son," Bodinger told him. "He would have gotten you too." Those words made Mrs. Reynolds weep harder. Knowing that if her son hadn't forgotten his cell phone, her own gift, he would be in the city morgue like his three friends.

Jimmy fell into his mother's arms and cried it out as Bodinger and Cordova sat quietly. When he was composed, he sat up, starting again. "He . . . put the bags over their heads and tied them off with some kind of plastic strip."

Zip ties.

"They were rolling all over the ground, trying to break free. He just stood there and watched. It was so long I thought it would never end. I had to run and get help, but when I stood to run back to the school, he pulled the gun out of his waist and shot them. He shot them all!" Jimmy cried, "*That bastard killed my best friends!*"

"Then you ran back to the school?" Cordova asked.

Jimmy nodded, unable to speak.

The crime scene verified the kid's story. The young woman died just as the two prior victims. The three boys were actually hogtied with zip ties, their feet bound together and fastened to their wrists as they lay facedown. The bags, still on their heads, were filled with blood, bone, and brain matter. D fired a single 9mm slug through each boy's head, killing them instantly.

"Was the man wearing gloves?"

Jimmy nodded, adding, "Like the doctors wear."

"What happened then, Jimmy?"

"I just ran. I ran all the way to the school."

Bodinger looked at Cordova who said, "From the crime scene to the school is clocked at a little under three miles."

"Through the woods."

"Through the woods," Cordova agreed.

The poor, horrified teenager ran three miles through the woods back to the school thinking the madman was most likely following him. "Did he see you, sweetie?" his mother asked.

"Don't think so. He didn't shoot at me, so I don't think he did."

The two detectives closed their notebooks then stood. They had a witness that told them their guy drives a black Hummer. H2 was the best bet, and three 9mm shell casings. It was more than they had with the other crimes. At least they could match the tires to a certain vehicle. It was better than a picture of a dead girl and crazed letters.

The two men left their cards and numbers, wished the mother and son luck, telling them they'd be in touch. Outside the house, Mr. Reynolds was waiting on the porch. "Fellas, I apologize. I almost lost my son today, and all I'm thinking about now is his protection. The thought that he could have been there . . . ," he trailed off, his voice failing him.

"Your son's a brave young man, Mr. Reynolds," Bodinger told him. He's a good witness, and when we catch this guy, I'm sure he'll help us put him away."

Reynolds eyes began to tear as he walked by the two detectives, heading back inside. The two walked to the car without a word, when Bodinger's cell rang. He flipped his stuff through the driver's side window and pulled his phone off his hip. "Bodinger."

"Stan, it's Jim. Prince just got me the details on the girl. D left her stuff at the scene, same as always, nice and neat. All we had was her name."

"Yeah."

"Well, now we have more," there was a graveness in his voice.

"What is it, Jim?" Bodinger asked, bracing himself.

There was a long pause before Jim Saunders replied, "Stan . . . The girl worked for Frank Castro."

The air sucked out of Stanley Bodinger. The last name he wanted to hear in conjunction with this case was Frank goddamn Castro. "Jesus Christ, tell me it's a mistake," Bodinger said, dropping his head to the roof of the car.

"Afraid not, brother."

He felt his eyes blur, getting dizzy as all the blood rushed to his head.

"You there?" Saunders asked.

"Yeah," Bodinger answered, rubbing his forehead. "Don't wanna be, but I'm here."

"I know, Stan. Bad to worse don't come close."

"He know yet?"

"Not yet," the captain answered, "I wanted you to know first."

"What did she do for him?"

"Receptionist or some such shit. All you gotta do is look at her to see why he hired her. Tiffany Ann Malvern, age twenty-five, a little college, a lot of looks. Probably a treat in the sack. Frank's kind of girl."

Bodinger followed up a long silence with, "I guess I drew the short straw for who's supposed to tell him."

"Not my call, Stan. You want to, it's yours. No, and I'll send Prince."

Bodinger opened the car door and sat inside. Cordova walked to his side and asked what the deal was. "Skeletons keep floating up, brother," Bodinger replied. "Old skeletons better off dead." Cordova knew it must be bad. He walked around to the far side of the car and waited. Stanley thought for a second then realized there was no use in putting off what was now inevitable. D had killed a girl that worked for his ex-partner; sooner or later the facts would have to be dealt with. The devil gets his due no matter who owes him.

He remembered what he told Frank that day on the steps of the courthouse. "Heaven's hung in black, Frank. There are no easy ways. Heaven's hung in black."

No shit.

"I'll do it, Jim. Tomorrow, his place."

"That's probably best. Need company?"

"No," Bodinger lied. "It's best if I do it myself."

"Okay, Stan, just make sure it happens early. If that fucker reads it or hears about it before . . ."

"I got it, Jim," cutting him off. "I'm on it. Don't worry. I can handle Frank."

"Good. 'Cause this shit just got messy, Stan. He broke routine and shot three kids, three juveniles for Christ's sake," he explained. There was a menacing tone in Saunders's voice. Bodinger didn't like it. It was almost threatening. "We have to get back to basics on this one. Interview old witnesses, talk to dead ends, find what's not there. Jesus, just get some kind of result, Stan, please. Tomorrow's going to be a shit storm, buddy. We have to give the people something."

The phone went dead.

"*Goddamn Castro*," Bodinger thought. It was the last person he ever wanted to see for the rest of his life. When Frank left the department, it wasn't a pretty departure, and Stanley Bodinger had been right smack in the middle of it. Accusations of alcohol abuse on the job in conjunction with a dead teenager laid the groundwork for immediate dismissal. The department put pressure on Bodinger, and he did what he thought was his only decision at the time. He dropped a dime on his partner to save his own career and get a dangerous man out of uniform.

That was over ten years ago.

Now, six young people were dead, and one was tied to Frank Castro of all people. All Stanley Bodinger could think of was old man Brooks at his daughter's funeral. How he looked at him and called him a *waste*.

Maybe he was.

Cordova saw him hang up and opened the passenger door. Sitting inside with his partner, he asked, "What's up?"

"The girl," Bodinger said. "She worked for my ex-partner."

Cordova knew enough about Bodinger to know that if he mentioned any ex-partner in a way of importance it could only mean one person.

"She worked for Castro?" he asked, eyes wide.

"Yeah."

"No way," Cordova breathed. "What are the odds?"

Staggering.

Bodinger started the car, flinging his phone into the backseat. "Let's go get a beer. I think I'm gonna need it."

24

Emotion erupted through Adam as the garage door rattled to a close behind him. He cried, laughed, and sang as he made his way into the house, down the hall to red room, clicking on his stereo. Slayer exploded around him with the song "Disciple," which delivers the ominous cry, *"God hates us all! God hates us all!"*

Certainly, at that moment, he felt that God did indeed hate everyone in the world. He fell in his chair, exhausted. The day had taken a part of him he never thought possible. His perfect way of playing out his new game had taken an unexpected turn. He'd acted quickly and decisively, eliminating witnesses while finishing the game. But at what cost?

Instead of one, he killed four.

The girl had been perfect; so damned perfect he jerked off as she suffocated in the back of the H2, this time without a condom. He knew it was stupid, but it was on the inside of the hold; no one would know. She was older than the other two, sexy as hell, and a real prize. But since his plans went astray, he wasn't able to get as many photos as he would've liked.

He stripped off all his clothes, hooking up his camera to the computer. In no time, he'd downloaded all the pictures of his new woman. And this time, it was an honest to goodness woman. No high school kid or drop out from Wal-Mart. This was a working, functioning member of society he'd found to play his game with.

A new secret game.

As the images spat out from his printer, he was already clearing new wall space for his new girl. She should take center stage, a place of honor just beneath Deloris. As he spent the remainder of the day and most of the night tacking up new pictures in his shrine of murder, the wild events of the day replayed in his head like an old home movie. The way it ended had opened a whole new world to him. He was now more than just a freak of nature who was forged from incestuous lust. He was now an executioner.

He felt more alive than he ever had in his entire life. He was growing once again. Evolving into something more than even Deloris could have imagined. He was becoming one with the universe.

Like a god.

He was sitting in his Hummer across the street from Tiffany's rental house at 3:00 a.m. when the sexy blonde got home. After casing her, he knew she went out on Monday nights and usually went home after a night on the town. As soon as she got out of her car, he was moving across the street, dressed head to toe in black, silently approaching her as she unlocked her door and stepped in. As soon as she shut the door, he knocked. Knowing she was drunk and wanting to go the bed, there was no way she'd stop, chain the door, and look through the peephole. Almost as soon as he knocked, the door opened.

Zap!

He hit her between the breasts with his stun gun and she slumped silently to the floor. There was no porch light or internal light from the house, so he pulled her outside and laid her on the small porch. He backed his H2 into her driveway, and opening the back hatch, he slid her inside, keeping her purse. Once he was back in the cab, he drove out of the Round Rock neighborhood and headed south through Austin on I-35. With Slayer blaring, he fished through her purse, finding her cell phone, which he turned off, then dropped the purse in the floorboard. He was heading to Hays County, where he'd scouted a nice secluded spot just outside Wimberley.

This was going to be the best.

Tiffany came to as the H2 sped along a smooth road. It was dark, and she knew she was in a vehicle, but was still disoriented. The alcohol in her blood was making the taser bump even harder to shake off. She went back out and stayed that way for over an hour. When she did manage to wake, she sat up against the back wall. The ride was smooth, but the place she was in was small and dark. She screamed, "*Where am I?*" just before earsplitting heavy metal music exploded around her. She covered her ears, pulling her knees up to her chest. She kept her calm, trying to fight through a night of margaritas and a Taser jolt to the chest, sorting through what memory she had of getting home.

"I got home," she said to herself. "I got home . . . What happened? What happened then? What the hell happened?" She tried to sort it out as the music penetrated her from every angle. It poured into her as her mind cleared. She'd been around Frank long enough to know what this psycho was doing. He was keeping her confused, not letting her get a grip on what was happening. She tried desperately to focus on her surroundings. It was like being caught inside a moving sensory-deprivation chamber. As soon as the vehicle slowed, it would race back to a high speed. The slowing and turning happened more times than she could count, and with each turn, a new bolt of speed followed.

The music she recognized from one of her old boyfriends from high school. It was Slayer, nonstop. Each song ended as fast as the next one started with a zero interval of silence between tracks. The volume never lessened as the earsplitting sonic bombardment carried on unceasingly.

She had to call Frank. Her cell was in her purse and she had no idea where it was. She rolled up on her knees and started feeling around inside the hold. It seemed to be covered in a very fine carpet. Even the walls and low ceiling were covered in the same fabric. Toward the back, there were a couple of long pouches on the side panels and nothing else. All that was in there with her was the mind-numbing Slayer bombardment and two pouches fastened to the walls.

"*Let me outta here!*" she screamed at the top of her lungs.

Nothing.

Slayer played and the vehicle rolled on.

141

Tiffany turned and put her back against what she felt was the backdoor. There was no latch. The inside of the door had been covered with a solid plate, covering the latch, and that was covered in the same carpeted fabric. Her mind was racing. Questions bounced through her mind like popcorn. *Who was this? What were they doing?* She had no answers. If she could only call Frank, he'd kill this fucker and end the nightmare.

The music roared on.

Feeling confident, and well out of town, Adam killed the music just to see what his new beauty would do. Tiffany crawled the short length of the hold to the forward wall and started beating on it, unaware she was mere inches from her captor. Adam laughed as Tiffany screamed, *"Let me outta here, asshole! My boss is gonna kill your sorry ass, you piece of shit! You hear me? He's gonna fucking kill you!"*

"Your boss?" Adam asked himself. "Making time with an old man?" He glanced at himself in the mirror. He hated that face. So pretty, so nonintimidating. He wanted to play with her without the mask, but knew his face would only serve to belie his authority. The mask stayed.

He found the place to go off the paved road, taking a hard right, forcing Tiffany to spill onto her side. Just then, the ride stopped being smooth as Tiffany detected gravel beneath them.

"Oh shit."

She turned and sat back against the wall. She calmed long enough to realize her chest was hurting. The seconds before her blackout played back in her mind, and she recalled hearing a knock on the door just after closing it. She opened it and all went black.

"What was it?" she asked herself. The pain was sharp and jolting. "Stun gun?" She remembered he was close. If it was a stun gun, it was the older model that was pressed against the person, not the new kind to be shot from several yards away. As she tried to reason in her mind what was going on, the vehicle made a sharp right turn, and in seconds she knew they were off the gravel road and in a place off-road all together. It was beginning to be panic time. If she could just find her purse and get to her cell and call Frank, he'd fix everything.

She loved the old worn out drunk with the chiseled face and bad attitude. She'd been with him for two years, and he never once put a move on her. Aside from being a little insulted, she respected his ethic of rank that wouldn't allow him to play around with an employee. She would catch him from time to time sneaking a peak, knowing he wanted inside her, but his professional sense didn't allow him the luxury. Then, of course, maybe, just maybe, he respected her as a woman and didn't give in to primal urges. Whatever the reason, Frank Castro was one of the best men she'd ever known in her life and if he knew what was happening . . .

The vehicle slowed, jostled, then came to a stop. The last few minutes of the ride had been rough, but Tiffany hardly noticed, trying to think of a way to get out of this mess. She had no way of knowing how long she'd been out before regaining consciousness, so she had no idea how far they had driven since the attack. It was obvious her purse wasn't with her, so calling Frank wasn't an option. No matter what was about to happen, she resigned herself not to go without a fight.

Adam sat in the driver's seat enjoying the silence. This was to be his finest hour. The high school girl was a warm-up, and the working bitch was an appetizer. This was a full-fledged woman. Sure, she was only slightly older than the Brooks girl, but she drove a hot car, had a nice house, and obviously had a good job because of the way she kept screaming that her boss was going to kill him.

"Gotta find me first, sweetheart."

Suddenly he felt tired. It was a couple of hours before sunrise, so he decided to take a nap. It was very unusual for Adam to want sleep. Sleep was when the dreams came; awake was much better. He only slept when he ran down so far that his body demanded sleep. For some reason, he wanted to rest up before playing with the hot blonde. Let the fiery bitch stew a little more before she gasped out her dying breath.

He lay across the seat, resting his head against the passenger door armrest. He closed his eyes and thought about his mother. In no time, he drifted off to sleep.

Deloris was young, twenty-five. He was his present age. He knew

143

what she wanted. They were in his house in Austin, a good old home that she told him was paid for by her friend. The Tidy Man, he called him. It was before his renovations of black paint and chalk graffiti. They slept in his old bedroom even though their respective ages didn't match the scene. He was too old and she was too young. As he reclined on his bed, she loosened her robe and let it drop, revealing her tight, sexy body.

"You want me," she purred.

He did. He wanted her more than he ever wanted a woman before. She started molesting him when he was so young, he never had another sexual partner his entire life. In his twenties, his mother was the only sex partner he'd ever had. By the time she died, he had adjusted to the fact that his life was meant to be something different. He knew he was bound to destroy the concept of normalcy just by the sheer fact of his existence. But now, in his dream, he lay on the bed and let his mother crawl between his knees and take his erection in her mouth. It was warm and soft. He tried to imagine someone else doing it. However, to a child, the word mother *means* god. *So if the most important person in his existence wanted to do this, who was he to stop her?*

The scene changed. Now they were in an expensive hotel. They had just been massaged and left alone on two beds to sleep off the effects. He was awakened by Deloris straddling him, guiding his erection into her. As before, he was older, she, younger. He relaxed and let her ride him. She rode him soft then hard and fast. She climaxed then rolled off, telling him to make himself come any way he wanted. He pulled her up on her knees and entered her from behind, driving himself in and out of her as she moaned in pleasure.

Pleasure.

It was all they were about. As he had sex with his mother in his dream, his erection grew painful in his military pants. In the dream, it was hurting to have sex. The pleasure was gone...pain...

Awake.

As always, Deloris was flooding his mind. Dreams. The dreams were always far better than the reality. His raising had been obscene even through the eyes of a child. He knew they were wrong, or at least she was, and she made him this way. Even before the incest, his childhood had been neglectful at best. She took care of him like a sister instead of a mother, leaving him with neighbors or friends for days at a time while she left to do whatever it was she did. He knew the Tidy Man paid for the house, footed their bills, and even set him up with a trust fund so he'd never have to work if he didn't want to. Only seeing the guy once a month for years, the most he'd ever say to the boy was "Is your mother home?"

He hadn't seen the well-dressed man since Deloris's funeral where he followed him to his car in the drizzling rain. Questioning, seeking, trying to find out the truth about who he was and what she had on him. Was it blackmail? Did he love her? What was the reason behind him? Why did he do the things he did? Why did he care for them but only from a distance? But all the Tidy Man talked about was his financial affairs and how he could be contacted by phone.

"You have my number," he said, walking down the small slope to his car, away from her fresh grave.

Adam stopped there, frozen, his world crashing around him. It was all so wrong—everything. Deloris, him, the sex, and the money. As the Tidy Man sat inside, Adam ran to the car. Heart pounding, grief cutting through him like a razor. Needing to know, having to ask, crying, he screamed, *"Are you my father?!"*

He closed the door, the window hissing as it lowered. "Of course not," he said. And he was gone, leaving Adam on his knees, crying as the rain began to pelt him. All he had to say was *of course not.*

Alone. Always alone.

Adam hadn't thought of him in a long time. Even when he cashed the checks from the trust fund, he never thought of the man. He knew his name, but it meant nothing. He was and would always be the *Tidy Man.* Unapproachable, distant, calculating. He saw to everything monetary in his life, even though they hardly ever spoke. For the last four years, the checks came, the grass got cut, and the bills got paid. All Adam had to do was live. If you call that living.

Deloris had thought of everything.

She loved him, he knew that, but not in a healthy mother-child way. She loved him the way you love the family pet. On several occasions, when she'd leave him with friends, there would be some husband or boyfriend that found it funny to smack him around or use him as free labor. He washed cars, cleaned houses, cut grass, and ran errands to the store. He was also a constant source of their entertainment. Once, he even had to let some creep lick his ten-year-old ass while jerking off. Deloris never knew.

And didn't seem to care.

He sat up in the Hummer, realizing he'd been asleep for a few hours. The sun was up; it was eight forty-five. Time to play. Dreaming of his mother made him want to see the bitch in the back even more. He pulled off his thin jacket, wearing only his T-shirt as he tapped the wall behind him, saying, "I've got a gun. I'm coming back there, so don't try anything stupid. Do as I say and we'll both get out of this."

Tiffany heard every word, but had no idea who or what was coming for her. She sat on her knees at the back of the hold, waiting. Her heart was pounding so hard she thought she'd pass out. Her ears were still ringing from the loud music, and she'd sat in dark silence for hours. She was more confused now than she'd been hours before. The back hatch opened violently and bright light flooded the hold, blinding her. As she blinked and let her eyes adjust, she saw a man in a white T-shirt and black pants, wearing surgical gloves, holding a pistol on her. If that wasn't scary enough, he was wearing a black ski mask.

"Stay where you are," he said.

It was easy because she was petrified with fear. She pulled her knees to her chin and tried to bury her face between her thighs.

"I'll shoot if I think you're trying something, understand?"

Tiffany nodded from behind her legs. He went on. "Scoot toward me. Nice and slow."

She thought for a second of some way to get out of the situation, but she was boxed in and the only way out was guarded by a freak with a gun. She did as he said and scooted to the end of the hold. Once she got there, he told her to put her feet together and extend them outside the hatch.

What was this?

Slowly she did as instructed, all the time knowing that if only Frank

146

were there . . .

Zip!

Her feet were bound with a zip tie. He then pushed the pistol in his waistband and climbed up into the hold.

"*What are you doing*?!" Tiffany screamed. Adam then took her beneath the arms, pushing her back inside the truck. She tried to fight, but he flipped her over and pulled her arms back behind her waist, zip-tying them. Tiffany bucked and thrashed as best she could, but he was straddling her back with his full weight on her. She was trapped. Before she knew it, he ripped off her skirt and blouse, leaving her in her thong and bra.

"Sweet!" Adam thought, his heart pounding in grotesque excitement. As the girl thrashed beneath him, he took his knife and cut off her bra and thong, leaving her naked. This total stranger was as naked as Deloris on any given day from his childhood. He wanted to savor the moment, so he rolled off her, climbing out of the hold.

There she was. As naked as the day she was born. Bound for his delight. She was screaming bloody murder but there was no one around to hear it.

"*Frank's gonna kill you, you sick fucking bastard! He's gonna cut your heart out, you sorry piece of shit! You fucking creep! He's gonna kill your punk ass! Frank Castro's gonna cut your fucking heart out!*"

"That name means nothing to me," Adam droned.

"Motherfucker, you do this and *it will!*"

Adam loved it. He loved the power surge. Deloris had never allowed him anything but sex; now he was a real man. A man of power, a man of control. He felt inside a pocket on his thigh and pulled out the clear, plastic bag. Slowly, he climbed into the hold behind the struggling, naked beauty. Without a word, he slipped the bag over her head and twisted the slack in a knot at the base of her neck.

"*Noooo!*" Tiffany screamed. Adam held it there as she thrashed beneath him. He allowed a minute or so to pass then removed it. She gasped for air as he leaned back and pulled another zip tie from the pocket on the wall. Before she could catch her breath, he pulled the bag over her head again then placed the zip tie around her neck.

Zip!

Now the bag was far less forgiving as she struggled to bite through it. He took her arms and flipped her over on her back so he could watch the show.

"Nobody beats the bag, bitch!" he snarled. "As you're dying, think of your mother."

Tiffany was dying and there was nothing she could do about it. This was the sick creep that hung those two girls! The air in the bag was gone and all that was left was her own carbon dioxide that was killing her brain. As she fought the bindings, he straddled her again, pulling his penis free. He stroked it as he squeezed her breasts with his free hand. He pulled an amyl nitrate popper from his back pocket and took a long sniff. His heart rate accelerated, and his mind became a raging inferno of lust and torturous pleasure.

Goddamn it! I can't die like this! Not here! Not now! Not murdered!

Adam paused to fish a condom out of his pocket then stopped. Being inside the hold, he felt safe, tossing it aside. He masturbated without it as the young woman between his legs began to spasm. The light was fading as she tried one last time to buck him off. The pain of suffocation peaked, her ears filled with blood, causing the ringing to echo in her brain. Fading, black drawing closer. The buzz of death kissing her neck, telling her to let go.

"Take me inside you," Adam said, "hold me inside you. Hold me in your eyes, let me take it all! Give it all to me! Give me all there is! Give me all of you, till you have nothing left to take!"

She grew rigid, every joint locking in unison. Her body fighting for life as the brain lurched in the black of her soul for life-giving air. As Tiffany's brain died from lack of oxygen, her last fading glimpse of the world was of her killer through a plastic bag, pleasuring himself to her demise, while screaming insanities. She died with her face frozen in a mask of horror, the bag sucked into her gaping maw, eyes wide in terrific terror, questioning why.

It drove Adam over the edge. He came on his trousers, head spinning, heart pounding. This had been the best yet. As he came back from his blissful release, he studied her death mask he'd created. She was so beautiful; now it was time to capture the moment, to make it live forever, not just inside his mind, but on film as well. He cleaned himself off with the tail of his T-shirt. Then, he pulled his camera from one of his thigh pockets, taking a picture of her face through the bag. Number three. The best yet. He had thought the other two were beautiful, frozen in death. Faces contorted inside the bag, dying as they fought for air. But this one was the big catch. Her eyes so open, so horror-filled. Her mouth a cave of teeth encased in plastic wonderment.

Voices!

What?!

He gathered himself, pulled his pistol from his waistband, and sprang out of the Hummer. He found three teenaged boys, early teens. They were startled by the masked man with a drawn weapon. "All of you, stop where you are!" he bellowed. The three teenagers froze immediately. They were about ten feet from the H2, which was sitting in a soft clearing nestled in woods, thick with deer. "All of you turn around. Turn around and place your hands on top of your heads," Adam instructed.

"Mister, we didn't mean anything," one of the boys said. Another added, "We didn't see anything!"

"Shut up!" Adam screamed. He'd been a pawn his whole life, a puppet for others' amusement. Deloris used his body for her own needs once he was old enough; before that, he was nothing to her. Teachers and kids, employers and contemporaries had always made him feel weak, like a loser. He had no control in his own life. That's why he cut himself, to take control of something, anything. Amy Crowder was in *his* control. Julie Brooks was in *his* control. The dead bitch in the back of his Hummer was still in *his* control. And now, these three snot nosed kids were most definitely in *his* control. He could see them trembling. They must have skipped school and wandered onto his little party.

This was a bad day to skip school.

"Go to your knees," he ordered. All three boys sank to their knees, almost in perfect unison. Two of the kids were still pleading, and one was silent. For some reason, the quiet kid was the one that worried Adam the most. If he was quiet, it meant he was thinking. The other two

149

were trying to bargain their way out of the jam they were in. Telling him about their dads and the things he could get if he just let them go, but the other kid, the one to his far left, never said a word, not one peep. The other two kept jabbering away until finally he'd had enough.

"*Shut the fuck up!*" he screamed, and the two boys fell silent. He knew what had to be done and went to the cab of the H2. He reached behind the seat, retrieving a handful of plastic bags. He stuffed them in his pants pocket then went to the back of the Hummer and fished another handful of zip ties from their hiding place. He walked back, telling the quiet kid, "You there, on the left. Turn around." The kid did as instructed. His eyes were narrow and calculating. Adam knew this was the bad seed of the bunch. The others were loud and boisterous, and this kid probably just went along with them to get free beer and pot, maybe even a shot of teeny pussy once in a while. But he wasn't like them at all. His parents were from the same circle as his friends' folks, but he was really nothing like them. He understood this kid, almost liked him.

Too bad he had to kill his ass too.

"Come here," he told the boy. The kid came to him, all the while keeping his hands on top of his head. Adam handed him the large zip ties and instructed him to bind the other two boys' hands behind them then their feet. As the kid did this, his friends cried and begged him to stop.

"I got to bro, he's gotta piece," the quiet kid answered them each time. Once the two were lying flat on their stomachs, bound and unable to get up, Adam zip tied the quiet kid in the same manner. When he was satisfied they were all subjugated, he placed his sidearm back in his waistband and pulled out three more zip ties. One at a time, he hooked the tie through the binding on their feet and pulled their legs up and fastened them to their wrists. When he was done, it was time to play with the girl. He went to the back of the Hummer as the three boys all rolled to see what he was doing. When the dead Tiffany Malvern dropped naked and bound from the back of the truck, all three boys, even the quiet kid, screamed in unison. They cried and begged Adam to stop as he hoisted her into the tree like a shot deer, ready for dressing.

"Party's over, boys!" he yelled, heading back toward them. He retrieved the bags from his pocket. Irritated with their screams, he kicked the kid on the right as hard as he could. *"Shut up!"* he screamed. Starting right to left, he bagged each boy, zip-tying the bags secure around their necks. Once again, the two on the right screamed and rolled all over the ground, kicking up dirt as sheer panic gripped them in icy realization that they were going to die. The quiet kid simply lay prone, head down as though simply waiting for the inevitable.

Adam watched. He wanted the sexual rush again. But he was disappointed. The sight of watching three teenage boys die by the bag held none of the sexual satisfaction of watching a nude young woman asphyxiate for him did. He wasn't surprised; after all, he was no faggot. He was getting nothing from this and simply wanted it to end. He pulled the 9mm from his pants and walked to the boy on the far right, who was thrashing wildly, fighting for breath. He used his boot to kick the kid over on his stomach then placed the muzzle of the gun in the center of the back of his head.

Blam!

The second boy was like the first, fighting for oxygen, as Adam made his way to him. Placing his right foot on his back, holding him still, again he spotted the gun in the same location.

Blam!

The quiet kid was still lying still. Only his back heaved as his oxygen-deprived body fought for air. Adam knelt beside him, closing his eyes this time as he pressed the barrel to the boy's skull. He liked the kid, almost admired him. Then he pulled the trigger and filled his bag with brains and bone, the same as his buddies.

All three were dead. He had killed four people in that little patch of woods in Hays County. He felt powerful. He'd known power before, from Amy and Julie, but this was different. Amy and Julie were sexual exercises. The blonde slut in the tree was the same. But he had executed three young men. Reminiscent of a mob hit. He searched the boys' pockets and found one had a camera phone. He flipped through the pictures, finding his H2. As far as he could tell, the vehicle was all there was in the image. He smashed it into unrecognizable shards of metal and plastic, stuffing the debris into his pants pocket.

Adam Parker laughed.

He spent the next two hours masturbating and taking digital photos of the scene. He felt godlike. He was all-powerful. Adam Parker was a pawn no more. He thought to himself as he drove out of the woods, "I can't wait to send one of these shots to that bastard at the paper."

25

Frank was in a foul mood. He'd spent the night chowing on ice cream because his alcohol-starved body craved something sweet. After tearing his kitchen apart, he discovered half a gallon of frostbitten Briar's chocolate in his empty freezer. He had to scrape ice out of the carton into the trash can in order to make the shit edible. Standing in his living room, staring at himself in the mirror, he shoveled the frozen fix in his mouth, longing for the warm caress of Johnnie Walker. Shaking from every cell in his body, he growled to the mirror, "Goddamn, this sucks!"

To add to the annoyance, Tiffany did not come in the day before and never answered any of his calls. He just knew she'd found some hard dick on Sixth Street and was banging his lights out for all hours and lost track. That was okay in-and-of-itself, but the least she could do was call him and tell him she was having great sex and couldn't be bothered with making his nonalcoholic coffee. She'd done that before.

"Well," Frank would answer, "when you get your next cookie, think of me."

"We'll share it!" she'd squeal. "Ain't that cute! We're sex buddies without doing it!"

"Bye, Tits."

"Bye, Jackass."

"Be careful."

"Just for you, big *bro*."

That was it. They were sex buddies without the act. Each would tell of their conquests, but never had the urge to jump in together. It really was a big brother and little sister relationship. Even when she messed up, he couldn't stay mad at her.

Frank had been on the wagon for three weeks. For him, it was a record. The worst of the DTs had passed, and now they only came when he was agitated. He was beginning to see what life without the haze felt like. He didn't feel any better about himself or his life situation, but he felt better physically. Maybe that was a start. Maybe the body has to heal before the mind can.

It was 9:30 a.m. when he made the last turn to his office and spied a car sitting in his three-car parking lot. A late model Ford Taurus. As he pulled his BMW into the lot, the driver got out, and Frank's stomach sank. The last goddamn person he ever expected to see that morning crawled out of the Ford like a snake creeping out of crack in the pavement.

"What the hell?"

Stanley Bodinger closed the driver's door and leaned against the car as Frank parked alongside. Frank killed the engine, his mind racing. What was this about? Why was this jerk here, today? Now? It was a little late for an apology, but he knew that wasn't the reason. He wanted to race over and beat the prick within an inch of his soul, but knew if he was here, it had to be important; there was no other way Bodinger would darken his doorstep. He *knew* that.

Frank climbed out of the sports car with a work file from the insurance company and a cup of black coffee. Shutting the door, he looked over the roof at his former partner, wondering what this visit was all about.

"Nice car," Bodinger said.

"Thanks."

"Tully still in business?"

"Didn't get it on my looks."

Bodinger put his hands in his pockets and looked up at the morning sky. It was clear and brilliant blue. He was hoping a simple way would fall from the azure heaven above, but there was none coming. He was going to have to tell his ex-partner the sad and brutal truth.

154

"You look good, Frank."

Frank eyed him with distrust from over the car. Something smelled like fish and it wasn't coming from him. The last words the two had spoken ended with both men swearing never to see the other again. Frank had even told him if he ever did see him out and about, he'd kick his ass and do time for it with a smile.

"Drying out," Frank told him.

"Really? That's good. How a . . . How long?" Bodinger stammered.

"Three weeks. Not much, but it's a start." Frank walked around the front of his car and stopped just a few feet from Bodinger. Stanley Bodinger was a strong man, seeing him acting nervous made Frank uneasy. There was no way he was like this because of him; there had to be something else to it. "So, Stan," he leveled a stare at Bodinger. "What's the news? Why the sudden surprise? I know it's not for old time's sake."

Again Bodinger looked up, then down to the pavement. The morning traffic was buzzing behind them and all he wanted was to jet his way back onto the highway and speed away from Frank Castro as fast as he could. He'd told Saunders he wanted to do it alone, now he was feeling maybe it was a mistake.

Ten years earlier, the two were patrolmen for the Austin Police. Bodinger had seniority and was on the verge of being tapped for sergeant, which would mean he'd leave the squad car and start grooming for detective. He had a wife and kids, kept his nose clean, and worked well within the department. He was perfect for promotion.

Castro was different. He had no family, drank heavily, and was constantly at odds with his superiors. He caroused the bars at night, feeling that the badge gave him a right to be as callous and reckless as he saw fit. The only thing that kept him on the force was the fact that he was a great cop. On the streets, there was no one better to have your back if things went wrong. Frank Castro was a cop's cop when it came to doing the job at street level. More than once, Bodinger reaped the rewards of Castro's tenacity because Frank couldn't have cared less about awards and accolades. All he wanted was to break heads on the streets then party until the next shift. And sometimes during the shift.

Eventually, an event would transpire that sent Bodinger up the ladder and Castro out the door. While Castro never begrudged his partner for playing the game the way he did to get ahead of the curve, he had always felt Bodinger would catch his back if he needed him to.

Things just didn't work out that way. Frank Castro felt betrayed because his partner left him hanging in the wind. Stanley Bodinger felt the same betrayal for a different reason. His partner should never have put him that position. Both men were wrong, and both were right.

And time moved on.

"Frank," he started. "I'm afraid I have some bad news."

"What? They finally find out you don't wear underwear?" Neither of them laughed.

"Frank . . . Tiffany Malvern is dead."

Frank felt a sharp stab in his gut; his legs went numb. The words made no sense; he felt them more than heard them, like a jab of ice. Disbelief overcame him, a chill running up his arms.

"What?" he asked in shock.

Bodinger gritted his teeth, stepping closer. "I can't give you too many details, but she was murdered, Frank. ID is positive. I'm sorry."

Frank sized up his old partner. Good suit, still in great shape, clear eyes, and a firm jaw. But his hands were trembling. He stroked his graying goatee with his right hand while his left rested on his hip; both were unsteady.

"Why you shaking, Stan? I'm the one with morning DTs." Frank said, venom in his voice. "I'd expect some uniform out here to tell me this, not you." He leaned as close as he could, his heart beginning to race. The dots started to connect in his shocked mind. Sure, he loved Tiffany like a little sister and the news floored him, but it was his old partner standing in his tiny parking lot delivering the news that amazed him more than anything. He'd get drunk and cry for Tiffany later, there would be plenty of time for that. Right now, he wanted Stan to tell him why he drew the job.

"Why *you*, Stan?" Eyes piercing.

156

"We discovered she worked for you, and we thought it'd sound better coming from . . ."

"From who? *You?* A *friend?*" Castro cut him off. "Please!" Frank turned, placing his hands on his car with his back to Bodinger.

"Frank, let's go inside."

"No," he answered without turning, shaking his head. He didn't want Bodinger poking through Tiffany's desk, looking through her things. Not now, not yet. "How, Stan? You said 'murdered.' How?" he asked, still facing away.

Bodinger swallowed hard. There was only so much he could share, but this wasn't a grieving parent, this was a former cop turned private detective who knew the rules and knew how to follow evidence. Again, he tried to get Frank to move inside his office. "Frank, let's go in. Get out of the light, just you and me inside. Come on."

Castro stiffened, adjusting his shoulders. He wanted to carry out the threat he'd made all those years before. He wanted to stomp a mud hole into Stanley Bodinger, walk it dry, then stomp another one. The last few weeks made the years he'd spent hating him melt like vapors in the wind. He'd even thought of giving him a call and trying to patch things up. But now, with this, it all flooded back. The old rage was returning like the full moon after the new. He turned, looking at him. Bodinger's eyes were older and seemingly full of regret. Frank paused for a second, realizing the important thing here was Tiffany, not their feelings for each other. Maybe Stan was right, they should go inside away from passersby and prying eyes. It was then he realized that he, too, was trembling.

Without a word, he walked to the building and unlocked the new glass door and entered with Bodinger right behind him. As he flipped on the light, he saw Tiffany's desk and all her things the way she left them Friday before the weekend. The picture of her and her sister, her coffee mug, and her daily calendar of *The Far Side* cartoons. Frank stood in front of the small table that held their coffeemaker and saw her standing there rattling on about some jerk she'd met the night before, never realizing just how infectious she was to be around. Sure, she was hotter than South Texas in July, but it was her personality and her silly way of doing things, making him laugh, that he loved the most.

She really was a kid sister.

And now she was gone forever.

He pulled off his sports coat, dropping it over the back of her chair, then rolled his sleeves up to the middle of his forearms. Turning to Bodinger, he asked again. "How, damn it? How'd she die?"

Bodinger took a breath and started, "Frank, it's complicated."

"How?"

"There's way more to this than meets the eye."

Again, the DTs started. Frank began to shake; he really needed a belt of Johnnie Black. Thoughts started whirling in his mind. Tiffany at her desk, Mrs. Cabbershaw, Carmen, the taste of good scotch, Lucky's, Sixth Street on a Saturday night, his old partner in the newspaper.

"Complicated?" he asked, his chest heaving with his heartbeat.

"And then some."

Frank gathered himself as best he could. He had to ask the question. He was terrified of what he knew the answer would be, but he had to ask. He summoned the strength, thinking of Tiffany. He asked Bodinger, "Is it the same guy you've been looking for since April? Did he hang that sweet kid from a goddamned tree?"

"Frank . . ."

"Did he?!"

No response, only a pained look of remorse.

"Answer me, you son of a bitch! Is it the same *fucking guy*?!"

All Bodinger could do was nod.

"Goddamn you!" Frank roared. He turned, kicking the small table with all his might. The coffeemaker exploded to the ceiling. Cups, sugar, coffee, glass, and wood shattered like bomb shrapnel. There it was; this was the Frank Castro Stan knew. The more things changed, the more they stayed the same. Bodinger backed to the door and let the big Cuban vent. "You've been after this asshole for months, and he's still out there! He killed my friend, Stan! He killed one of the most special people on this putrid planet, and you've been after him for months, and he's still *out there!*"

"It wasn't just the girl this time," Bodinger said.

"What?"

"There were more this time." After a long pause he added, "He shot three kids to death at the scene. That's off the record."

"Off what record? I'm not on the record, remember? I'm the drunk that saved your ass then got the boot for my trouble. Now that I finally think I have a grip on what my life's supposed to be, along you come back into it, telling me someone I love's been murdered by the same freak you've been after for half a year. He's killed some kids, but it's off the record? *Off the record*? Tell me, Stan, you to me, what exactly is *on* your fucking record?"

Frank's eyes were boring through Bodinger, and suddenly he didn't like how it felt.

"Look, I've had about enough of this shit! This asshole's killed six people. I've got the whole state beating down on me. Grieving parents, a pissed Captain, a paranoid partner, and now he's gone and killed the secretary of the one son of a bitch I never wanted to see again!" He was giving back as good as he got. "Trust me, *sunshine*, I don't like this shit any more than you do! But this is what we got, so I guess we gotta deal with it!"

The two pulled back, like two angry dogs catching their breath. At one time, they'd have taken a bullet for each other. They knew each other's moves, what they were thinking, how they would react. Now, they just wanted to be on opposite sides of the world.

Frank slapped a loose coffee cup, sending it to shatter against the far wall. *"Goddamn it!"*

The small room fell silent as the two calmed down. After what seemed like forever, Bodinger said quietly, "I'm sorry, Frank. I'm sorry for your loss. I know it's tough. I've had to tell the parents of the other victims. This ain't any easier, I promise."

Frank sat on Tiffany's desk and picked up the picture of her and her sister. He said nothing. Sadness was overtaking him. She was the kid sister he never had. He honestly cared about her, and for the first time with an attractive woman, it wasn't sexual. He cared for her as a person.

He loved that silly bitch.

"She used to make coffee every morning."

"Yeah?" Stan replied.

"Yeah. It was good too. She'd spike it with Kahlua."

Bodinger chuckled.

"I told her to stop about a month ago. I wanted to see if I could do this." He raised his head and looked at Bodinger. "I wanted to know," he paused. "I wanted to know if I had it in me."

"Well, do ya?"

"So far. But to be honest, right now I could use a stiff one."

"Me too, brother," Bodinger said, sitting in Tiffany's chair. "This whole thing's been one long nightmare. I can't tell you anything else, you know that. Just know we're all over this, and we ain't gonna stop. We finally have a small lead. It's tiny, mind you, but it's more than we've had to date."

"Her parents know?"

"They made the ID."

"Fuck me," Frank said, shaking his head.

"Three kids skipped school and happened up on him right in the middle."

"Oh, Jesus Christ."

"Oldest was fifteen, he capped all three."

"Where did he grab her?" Frank asked.

"Her place, best we can tell. Taser, in the chest. That's all I can give ya."

Frank stared at the picture. She was so young, so beautiful. For some selfish predator to cut her down in her prime was unfathomable. He knew Stan wouldn't share any more details. He'd probably said too much already. Frank wasn't in the forgiving mood, but he was suddenly exhausted. He just wanted Bodinger to leave and let him sort this out on his own.

"Stan, I can't say I always do the right thing. Most times I don't. The thing between you and me is just that. It's between you and me. I'll put that aside right now," he turned a weary eye to his old partner. "Thanks for telling me. It means a lot . . . I'll leave it at that."

Bodinger nodded and stood. He thought about extending a hand in truce then thought better of it. He simply said, "Something I had to do," and he left Frank alone on Tiffany's desk.

160

Outside, Stanley Bodinger exhaled and got in his car. He left quickly, but stopped at the first convenience store he came to and killed the engine. For the next ten minutes, he sat staring at the steering wheel in silence.

Frank placed the framed photo back on the desk then sat in the chair behind it. Tears streamed quietly down his cheeks. They burned. But the empty whole in his heart was burning more. He knew later the rage would come, but for now, all he had were tears for little sister.

26

When Detective Cordova stepped around the edge of Glenn Young's cubicle, the reporter was more than a little surprised. He'd never dealt with the police on the D case unless he called them with a new communication. To see Cordova stride into his place of work without being summoned was a shock.

"So to what do I owe this unexpected visit?" he asked the detective.

Cordova eased into the cubicle, sitting in the chair in front of Young's desk. At first, he said nothing. He didn't like Glenn Young, not in the least. He never liked his work before the case, and after meeting him, he liked him even less. There was an oily quality to the man that repulsed Cordova. He despised him instinctively, the way most people are sickened by snakes. He drew the job of informing the reporter that a letter may be on the way from their new serial killer. He hated talking to Young about anything, let alone the biggest case of his career.

"I just came by to tell you, you should be aware that a new communication from D may be on the way."

That peaked Young's interest. So far, the cops never knew anything about D's crimes until he relayed the killer's communiqué after the fact. Why would Cordova inform him of a new letter?

"What makes you so sure, *Detective*?" There was a condescending way he said *detective* that rubbed against Cordova's grain.

He relaxed before replying, "We just have it on good authority."

Young felt jilted. "Better than me?"

"Firsthand."

"Whose?"

"Not at liberty."

"Bullshit."

"I said what I came to say. Just be ready, that's it," Cordova finished, standing to leave without a second thought.

"You guys are really something, man," Young spat, flipping his pen down on his desk with a loud thud.

Cordova turned. "Meaning?"

"Oh nothing, nothing at all. It's just that if I wasn't the one telling you guys about a couple of kids being strung up like deer meat, you'd have no clue about them, and those two girls would still be rotting in the woods while their moms passed out fliers at the mall, begging for information about their missing daughters. Never knowing they'd both been dead for God knows how long."

Cordova began to boil.

"And now you guys are using me, the one constant in all this, like some kind of errand boy. Do I need to remind you guys who the hell I am, and what the power of the pen means?" he finished, with a smirk of confidence.

Cordova stepped back to the desk, leaning on it with both fists. He managed to quell his fury, focusing on what needed to be said, but a wisp of venom seeped through. "Young, I want you to know up front, I don't like you, never have, and never will. I don't trust you, and I wish to God that this sick creep we're after used someone else. But that's that, nothing we can do about it. Just call if you get a new letter and we'll take it from there. I'm being professional, and I'd appreciate the same in return. If you fuck with me, it won't be pleasant."

As he turned to leave, Young spouted, "Hold on, *ese*."

Cordova snapped around. He wanted to pummel the smart-ass. "*Ese?*"

"Easy, *amigo*, we're all on the same side here, bro. I'd just like a little professional courtesy, that's all. If something's up, I'd like to know. There was some nasty business down in Hays a couple days ago, four dead kids. This got anything to do with that? I heard the boys in blue put the kibosh on the press, pronto-like. Keeping details of a homicide from the press is pretty impressive, especially for you guys. Any comment? Off the record, of course."

Both of Eric Cordova's fists were balled at his side. He took a deep breath, replying, "Just tell us if a letter comes, that's all I have." He turned and left before Young could rile him further. Outside, Bodinger waited in the car. Cordova got in, slamming the door.

"I take it went well?" Bodinger popped.

"When this is over, me and that asshole's gonna dance, bro . . . I promise!"

Bodinger smiled. "Well, you never know, brother. Shit happens to everybody," he said, pulling the car from the curb.

Adam wasn't much for the paper, or news in general, unless he was trying to make it. Since he'd yet to send his letter to Glen Young, he ignored the major news sources. However, as the shift was changing at Delphi, and he was clocking in, he overheard one of the other security guards mention four murders in Hays County while clocking out. The man didn't elaborate. So once they were gone and he was secure inside the building for the night, he found a paper in the break room. Sure enough, on the front page, there was a write up on four people killed in the woods in Hays County, not far from the Wimberley Middle School. The details were obviously muted by the authorities, but there was enough for Adam to recognize his work.

How did they find them without his help? He hadn't sent a picture to Young yet.

The more he thought about it, the more worried he became. Was it possible that someone saw him? Was he starting to slip and allow witnesses? As his shift started, all he wanted to do was leave Delphi and race home. Slayer on his iPod wasn't good enough. He needed alcohol and his popper of amyl nitrate. He did have rum in his thermos, but it was just to stave off the creepy-crawl jitters he got from being stone cold sober for so long. This was going to be a long night. He put his head on the receptionist's desk, closing his eyes.

For the first time in two days.

Once, when he was eleven, after he'd given oral sex to Deloris, she lay on the sheets spouting her worldly wisdom. "Girls are going to lie to you someday and tell you they want love. Don't believe them, Adam. All they want is control of you and your money. There's nothing in the world wrong with sex. It's nature's playtime. But you have to guard your heart. They won't love you, not like me. Your body's going to tell when you're ready. And when that happens, I'll be there for you, baby, I promise. I was there for your Uncle Michael and Uncle Brian. I'll be there for you too. My pretty boy is growing up. When you grow up a little more and your body needs a woman, you'll have me . . . And if you want love? You still have me. I'll take care of everything my baby needs."

"Nobody can please a man like his mother."

Nudity was a rule with her. For the first five years of his life, he hardly ever wore clothes. She explained why their bodies were different, assuring him that *one day* she would show him why it was necessary.

She had her *birds and bees* discussion with her son at such a young age, he really had no idea what it meant. Most children get a talk about sex from their mother or father when they've reached adolescence, as hormones and curiosity overwhelm them. They sit at the kitchen table or take a walk as the nervous parent succumbs to the challenge they'd feared for so long.

Deloris explained sex to Adam when he was eight, as they lay naked on her bed. A discussion complete with show and tell. "Show me what you're curious about, and I'll tell you what it's for." Nothing was off limits.

"Go ahead, touch all you want. I might even want you to."

It won't bite.

His mind always swam in a sea of contradictions. She'd constantly remind him he was having sex with his *mother*, but wouldn't allow him to use the word. As the years passed, he lost the desire to use it altogether. He loved her, but he knew it wasn't the love that a child should feel. He loved her they way you love a big sister. As his mind tried to make even

165

that hold up, he knew there was nothing right about their relationship. There was nothing natural about it. He was being raised by an incestuous pedophile.

As disgusted as she was with them, Deloris allowed him to have his jars. Quart jars filled with dead insects. The only rule was he had to keep them private, in his room. She never went into his room. She hated his music, hated his killing jars, and hated the red light he placed in the ceiling fixture.

"It looks like a horror movie," she complained. "Posters of snarling bands, that red light, jars with dead bugs. Why can't you be normal?"

She asked him that once when he was sixteen and they'd just had sex. Pillow talk. "Why can't you be normal?"

He laughed at the absurdity.

When she saw the scars on his arms, she ignored them. Out of sight, out of mind. Never asking, not even once.

At school, he'd listen to the other boys brag about their sexual conquests. Telling lies, each bigger than the other, trying to one-up their buddies in pubescent battles of testosterone. None of them knowing that the skinny, awkward kid with the girl's face lost his virginity while they were playing in little league. They'd call him faggot and pussy, unaware he was more experienced than the fathers.

His mother saw to it.

Once his body fully matured, she loved taking him to nudist resorts, introducing him as her *friend*. They'd have sex for all hours of the night at these places, with Deloris making far more noise than she did at home. She wanted the other women to know she was having sex with a much younger man. For his high school graduation, when most young men received traditional gifts, Deloris bought him a chrome cock ring that fit around his entire genitalia. "It'll look so good against your dark tan," she said, smiling. "You can wear it to the resort this weekend. I did tell you we were going, didn't I?"

At that point in his life, he had yet to begin to hate her.

That would take a few more years.

Sleep. It was almost foreign to him. An insomniac since childhood, he managed to get by on minutes of sleep for days. As he slept with his head on the desk, he saw the movie again.

The cheap horror flick from the '70s that had fascinated him so much. The killer murdered a pretty girl with a dry cleaner's clear plastic bag. She died with her face frozen in a silent scream, staring at the camera . . . at him.

He saw Deloris, naked and asleep on the bed. Her silver bracelet lying on the table next to the bed. The one charm on it with the script D. Again, the movie and plastic bag. The girl suffocating gave him an erection, even at that early age. He stood next to the bed, staring at her. She was so pretty and yet so miserably ugly. He picked up the bracelet and put it in his pocket. On the floor next to him, beside Deloris's bed, the killer was suffocating the pretty girl. She was naked, as was the murderer, wearing only a black ski mask. Adam, too, was naked in his mother's bedroom. The pretty girl was dying as he stood there watching, his erection growing at the sight of her demise. Deloris woke to see his condition. Taking it in her hand, she pulled him away from the murder. She began performing oral sex on her son.

But he wanted to watch the girl die!

Deloris sucking him.

The girl losing consciousness.

Deloris cradling him, licking him.

The girl's feet kicking the floor, unable to get the naked killer off her.

Deloris forcing all of his penis in her mouth.

The girl was dying now, her last throws of death.

"No one can please you like your mother!"

He snapped awake.

He hated that dream; it was the one that always came to him whenever he'd skipped sleep for too long. It was a catch-22. If he slept, he might dream. That one, among many others too horrible to remember. If he stayed awake, he didn't have to worry about them, but the longer he went without sleep, the worse the dreams. This one was mild compared to some of the others.

He checked his watch; it was 2:00 a.m. He made a walk though the building then came back, draining the rum from his thermos, sitting in silence as the news of his crime scene's discovery loomed large on his mind. He wanted to watch the local news, but they'd removed all the televisions from Delphi a year ago. Adam felt control slipping. The entire event was turning out to be a giant cluster-fuck. Not only did the three kids happen along, forcing him to eliminate them, but now the area was discovered before he could send his taunt to Glenn Young. If there was a witness, he'd have to change things, fast.

First, he would not send anything to Young; that was now off limits. Second, if someone did see him, all they could divulge to the police was the H2. He knew the clearing he used was wide enough that if there had indeed been a witness, they had to be doing it from such a distance that his plates would have been impossible to identify. All the authorities would have to go on was a black Hummer. There were thousands of them, just like his. Still, something had to be done.

Maybe a trip to New Orleans was needed?

If they saw everything, then they saw him shoot the boys and hang the dead bitch from the tree. But he never removed the mask. He'd never removed it in any of his playtimes. It felt good on his face to do his work behind the cover of the thick ski mask. He loved how it looked on him. He even masturbated once wearing nothing but the mask while staring into the mirror. He looked so menacing he could only imagine the horror it evoked in his prey, while concealing his pretty face that intimidated no one.

"All they saw was a man in a mask and a black H2," he assured himself. "There's nothing else to say. Especially if it was another fucking kid. They'd be so rattled the story would have changed three times before the cops heard it," he reasoned. "The other three fuckers showed up out of nowhere, so this had to be a straggler." Adam stood from his chair and sat on the desk as he pondered the possibilities. "There was nothing he could have seen that could identify me. Nothing, *nothing* to lead them back to me." He settled back into his chair, deciding it was too much of a long shot to tie the Hummer to him without the plates. He was certain they could not have been read from the tree line. Even at that, he decided it was time to make an adjustment. He'd put in for some time off, a week should do. He was going to take a trip to Louisiana and see that lowlife, Bodain, for a coat of paint. He hated the black son of a bitch, but he worked off the books.

As "Dead Skin Mask," a song about serial killer Ed Gien, played on his iPod, Adam closed his eyes, watching all three young women die by the bag. His instruction to each of them as their brains suffocated was always the same, and he mouthed those words as the eerie song played the soundtrack to his madness.

"*As you're dying, think of your mother.*"

Adam he thought of his mother, all the time

And he died a little, every day.

27

"You want me to what?" Carmen asked Frank, not believing her ears.

"I want you to come to Tiffany's funeral with me."

She was floored. The day after Frank found out about the girl's murder, he came to her drunk and looking for a place to lay his head and cry off the first scotch he'd had in nearly a month. Carmen let him in, and the sex that ensued was almost animal. Frank took her the way a beast takes his mate; primal, nearly violent. After he came, it took no time until he was ready for more, and this time, it was like he was using her body to pound the memory of Tiffany Malvern out of his mind. By the time he finished the second round, he fell into her arms, softly sobbing for the loss of his friend.

Carmen had known for a long time that Frank had never had sex with his assistant because she struck him as a kid sister, cute and funny, but very off limits. He loved the girl very much and seemed, for whatever reason, to take pride in their plutonic relationship. Maybe he was impressed with his own will power? She didn't know the truth about why, but she did know the truth about the truth, and the truth was that Frank and Tiffany were never an item, just close friends and associates.

"Why me?" she asked, standing naked at her mirror as Frank sat dressing on the bed.

"Don't know anyone else."

"Bullshit, Castro."

"Okay, I don't know anyone else I'd *want* to go with me, and I don't want to go by myself. It's just a funeral, Carmen, not a trip to Vegas."

She knew what that meant. As a professional girl, she made it a policy never to *go out* with her Johns. This wasn't a date; it was a funeral. She liked Frank, a lot, and he liked her, so it made sense that she'd be the one he'd ask to accompany him. It was just a little weird. Carmen knew of Tiffany, but had never met her, didn't care to. It was Frank's personal life and she could have nothing to do with it, or that of any of her clients.

Her business head was telling her no, but the friend in her was saying it was all right to be supportive. Frank had always been supportive of her. Even when he lost track of her for a while, he sent money through her mother. Their relationship worked just the way it was. When he needed sex, she was where he turned because she was a pro and good at what she did. Plus, as time wore on, the feelings were getting stronger. They both felt it, but neither talked of it; it was taboo. Frank would come by, they'd have sex, he'd leave a couple of Franklins, and she'd not see him for a while. It was the best of both worlds. Great sex and good laughs without the turmoil of a relationship.

But now, what he was asking was from way out in left field. His secretary had been murdered by a serial killer, and he wanted her to accompany him to her funeral.

"How will you introduce me?" she quipped, looking at him in the mirror.

"How would you like?"

"That's not what I asked."

"I know it wasn't. I'll do whatever you want, baby, just tell me. I'll tell them you're my sister, my girlfriend, my wife, my maid, my cousin, my slut, my mother's manicurist—just what the hell ever you're comfortable with."

He looked weary. Deep, road-weary from too many long nights and too many empty bottles. He scared her a little as she looked at his reflection over her shoulder. He was grieving. Frank wasn't one to look for sympathy; she knew that. Even after their wild sex and he wept in her arms, it was from a release of emotion and not a need for

171

understanding. If he wanted her to accompany him to the funeral, it was because he needed someone he trusted to help him get through it. Like he said, she was the only one he'd *want* to go with him.

"Friend," she said.

"Huh?"

"Tell them I'm your friend. That's true isn't it?"

"Of course."

"Then tell them the truth. This is my friend, Carmen." She went back to her makeup.

"No problem. I like that. You got it."

"What should I wear?"

"Something black, baby." Frank finished putting on his socks, stopping. He thought of Tiffany. The funeral was in three days, her mom and dad had taken her back to Dallas to be buried in the family plot. He'd only spoken briefly with her dad, who was understandably still in shock. He told Frank the police were doing everything they could to find the monster who killed his baby girl.

Yeah, everything they *can do.*

"It would mean a lot to us, Frank," Russell Malvern said to him, eyes welling with tears, "if you found him first." The two men shared a knowing look into each other's eyes. Frank knew what he meant, and Mr. Malvern knew what his daughter meant to the ex-cop.

"Mr. Malvern," Frank answered, cold as stone, "tell Tiffany's mother that I have every intention of doing just that."

The fifty-year-old Malvern saw it. Like a wolf in the zoo, pacing at the bars, there was a hunger behind the black eyes of Frank Castro. A hunger for vengeance waiting to be set free. Unable to respond, he simply gritted his teeth, nodding his understanding as they shared a firm handshake. The last impression Mr. Malvern had of the private detective was one of fierce determination. The grieving father knew, in his heart, the death of his pride and joy would not go unpunished. Here was a man he could leave it to, all the way to the end.

Carmen saw him drift off, so she stayed quiet. She knew he was hurting, grieving for his dead friend. But once it all stopped—when the grief turned to bitterness, then bitterness to anger—Carmen knew that whoever had done this was going to have hell on his heels. That prick Bodinger was bad enough to deal with, but that was grade school compared to what this *pendejo* would bring to the hunt. There was a debt to be paid. Paid in blood. She knew it might take him years, but sooner or later, the man that killed Tiffany Malvern was going to have to look Frank Castro in the eyes. When that happened, he'd have to settle his debt. His debt with the devil.

Frank was alone in the funeral home with Tiffany. He waited until the family had gone and it was too late for old friends, knowing he'd have the room to himself. She was in Room A off the main hall. It was the biggest room the funeral home offered, usually reserved for the more expensive burials. Her parents spared no expense. He walked slowly to the open casket and saw his beautiful young friend lying in peace. Her mother wanted her dressed as she would have dressed in life. Frank gave a silent salute to Mother Malvern for that. Tiff was wearing a black strapless dress with a gorgeous black lemma wrap around her bare shoulders. Her hair was perfect and her makeup flawless. She looked like an angel. At first, Frank was strong, but as he realized the pretty girl lying before him would never rise from the embrace of her eternal sleep, he began to crack.

"Goddamn it," he whispered. "*Goddamn it, Tiff,*" he said again, as a tear streaked down his dark cheek. He thought of all their talks, all their mornings together. They'd share a laugh while swapping stories about their escapades from the night before. Then they'd share a pot of booze-laced coffee and do what they did most of the time; spurn bill collectors and take dirty pictures of cheating husbands.

This was big. In the landscape of Frank Castro's life, this was huge. This was like taking a part of him away and making him watch it die. This was bigger than Bodinger's betrayal or losing his police career. He knew she was a joke to his clients—everyone thought they were sleeping together—but nothing was further from the truth. Frank had never made a move on Tiffany, and she loved that about him. He was her big brother and she his little sister.

And now she was dead.

Whoever this guy was that was loose in his town had killed a very special person to him. At that moment, he wanted to strangle Stanley Bodinger. This psycho's game was on his watch. He'd managed to kill six people during that time, and one was a friend that meant the world to Frank.

Hell, Tiffany was his only friend besides Carmen.

He pulled a chair close to the casket, leaning in to the body. Even in death, she was so young, so vibrant, and beautiful. The tears started flowing as his voice cracked. "Baby, I swear to you, right here in front of God and all his angels, I'm gonna find the man that did this . . ." Overrun with grief, he stopped to collect himself. "I'm gonna find the man that did this. I swear on my mother's grave, and I swear to you . . . I'm gonna find him. No matter where it takes me or what I gotta do, I'll find him, I promise. And when I do, when I get to him . . . I'm gonna kill him." He paused before telling her, "Oh, baby, I promise. The man that did this . . . He's gonna *know me.*"

Frank stood, taking in Tiffany one last time. She trusted him when no one else would. It tortured him to think that as this maniac was doing whatever he did to her, she thought he was going to come charging in to save the day, and he didn't.

He failed.

He failed her.

"I'm gonna kill him, Tiff, I promise. To hell with Bodinger and the APD. This is mine now. I'm hiring myself to find this fucker, and when I do . . . ," he trailed off. He took a dollar from his pocket, placing it beside her body, between her and the silk lining.

"That's the overtime I owe you." He turned to leave. As he walked from the room, he stopped in the hall, looking back one last time. "See ya in hell, sweetheart. Save me a table by the band."

Adam Parker wanted to watch them bury the last pretty girl he'd played with. He wanted to see how many of her boyfriends showed up and cried. He wanted to see her father weep. He wanted to watch her mother collapse from the anguish. He wanted to spot the cops in the crowd and take note of who they were. Maybe he could find out something about them. Find out who they were and where they lived; he could learn about their families and if they had young daughters or pretty wives he might want to play *bag the bitch* with.

Oh god, to kill some bitch that was connected to a cop working his case!

The thought was almost too thrilling to envision.

Of course, what he never imagined was that he'd already taken the life of someone who was special to someone very dangerous. Adam didn't know who Frank Castro was or what connection he had with the pretty girl, and he couldn't have cared less. She'd said the name, but it meant nothing to him.

"Frank Castro's gonna cut your fucking heart out!"

Adam just laughed. He laughed to himself as he watched them bury Tiffany Malvern.

28

Susan Bodinger gathered the mail from the box and dropped it on the kitchen table as she put her things away, going about her business of settling in for the evening. Stan had gone to Dallas to observe the Malvern girl's funeral, so she was home alone for the night. During the years since their two kids graduated from both high school and college, Susan had grown accustomed to having the house to herself since Stanley's hours were so erratic.

You can never find a cop when you need one.

She went about her way, taking a shower and finding something on the tube to put sound in the house as she read her e-mail and caught up on the day's happenings. After a meal and an hour of *That '70s Show*, she decided to open the mail she'd dropped off hours earlier.

Junk, junk, and junk before a letter from her youngest, Cheryl. She read the easy prose of how her life in San Antonio was going and how she and her husband, Rob, were thinking of having another baby. Her kids were in love. She could not be happier. As she put the letter back in the envelope to save, she saw the last letter. It was addressed to the *Bodinger Household.* The address was typed with no return address. Once she opened it, not only did she realize why there was no return address, but she also wanted her husband beside her immediately. As she unfolded the two-page letter, her heart stopped. The first page was a digital photograph of a crime scene. A young woman was hanging by her neck from a tree. Naked, dead. In front of the tree lay three hog-tied

176

young men, all with bloody bags over their heads. However, the most startling image was a man in a white T-shirt, black pants, and wearing a ski mask, standing between the hanging girl and the three dead boys. Susan's blood chilled. Discovering the second page, she recoiled as she read. It was a typed letter addressed to her husband. The words terrified her.

She called Stanley, hoping he knew that she was already packing for a hotel.

Stanley Bodinger meant absolutely nothing to Adam Parker. Adam knew he'd covered his tracks so well that there was nothing this flatfoot could use to find him. He was simply amused that he could threaten the man put in charge of finding him. How hilarious! The man whose task it was to find him is a matter of public record, and the man snuffing six people can look him up and threaten his family all because of the way the system functions.

Only in America!

Adam threw in a couple of arbitrary threats to Bodinger's wife, insulting her along the way, then closed with a menacing taunt he knew would make the woman of the house shiver in her panties.

It was his chance to jab at the insipid fools trying to catch him. No one in the APD had a clue, and he knew it. The letter to Bodinger was entertainment, nothing more. He'd never even seen Bodinger's wife. He hoped, though, that if she read it first, she'd piss herself.

Bodinger got the call from Susan just as he and Cordova pulled into the cemetery. The service at the chapel had been warm and loving. Tiffany's friends and family coming in droves to pay respects to the murdered young woman, but when he saw Frank Castro with some strumpet dressed as if she was going to a swinger's party, he nearly tossed his cookies. This dead girl worked for the man, and he brought

177

some hooker from east Austin to her funeral? He didn't recognize the pro, but years on the streets told him what she was.

"Old habits," he whispered under his breath.

"What?" Cordova asked.

"Fucking Castro. He brought a hooker with him. What a piece of work."

Cordova looked and saw, shaking his head. All he knew of Castro was what his partner told him, and that meant he'd never like the guy.

Frank stayed at the casket a long while as Carmen backed away and waited. Tiffany's parents liked Frank and knew their daughter's death was unrelated to his work. For some odd reason, they seemed to trust him almost like family. Maybe it was his past, which Tiffany had relayed to them as much as she knew. He was a real man with real flaws, but their daughter admired him so much. When they got together, he was all she ever talked about. Funny stories teamed with unscrupulous work. They knew him through her, and for them, it was enough. She loved the jerk; they knew that. He was someone she looked up to for some peculiar reason. A role model of how, even if you make mistakes, there is always a chance to make it right.

They knew Frank would make this right.

At the cemetery, Bodinger's phone vibrated as he was exiting the car. It was Susan.

"Be quick, baby," he answered.

Her voice was trembling; she was shaken. "Stan, he sent us a letter."

"Who?"

"Him! That maniac you're after! He sent the most horrible picture and a letter that makes my skin crawl. He knows where we live, Stan. He knows where we live!"

Panic ripped through Bodinger like a knife. "Get outta the house, Susan. Right now!"

"I'm in the yard with a suitcase. I'm going to a hotel till you get back."

"Good, get one downtown, by the capital," he demanded.

"I will. I love you. Hurry home."

"On my way tonight, babe. Call me when you get settled."

Cordova looked at his partner over the roof of the car, seeing Stan in a state he'd never witnessed before. "What's up?" he asked after Bodinger closed his phone.

"D sent a picture of the last killings and a letter to my house."

"What?!"

"I know. I guess our boy at the paper ain't good enough anymore. You might wanna call home, brother. If he knows where I live . . . ," he trailed off as Eric was already dialing his wife. Cordova walked away from the car in conversation as Bodinger turned, putting his back against the door, watching the graveside service. He saw Frank and the hooker standing far behind the canopy that sheltered the family from the sun. Frank's face was harsh, almost menacing. The girl looked bored, shifting her weight from one leg to the next. As he watched, he began to realize why she was there. Frank didn't want to come alone. Stan was sure there'd be grief sex afterward; then Castro would get on with his life.

But Bodinger couldn't afford to get caught up in all that. D had just made personal contact with his wife, and he knew he had to get back to Austin as soon as he could. He scanned the cemetery, looking for a black Hummer, and saw none. He knew this was a wild goose. After all, this was Dallas, not Austin. No way the lunatic would make the trip just to see the funeral. Besides, he'd killed before, and those funerals were canvassed with zero results.

Cordova came back to the car with a look of worry.

"Well?" Bodinger asked.

"Nothing, not a thing. But I still don't like it, Stan."

"We're heading home. You ready?"

"Don't wanna wait?"

"Do you?"

"Not a chance, bro, I'm ready. This is a dead end anyway," Cordova said, getting behind the wheel.

As Bodinger opened the door, he heard a familiar voice behind him.

"I'm not letting this go," Frank spoke to the back of Stan's head.

Bodinger shut the door, turning to see his old partner standing there, grief stricken, his *date* well behind him. "That's not going to help, Frank. It won't bring her back," Bodinger replied, feeling a fight brewing.

179

"I'm not a ghost hunter, Stan," Frank said, his eyes piercing. "I want a reckoning. I'm gonna do my part to find this freak. Know that."

"You don't have a part, Frank. This is a police investigation."

"The police have been investigating since April, and the bodies keep piling up." He grew louder, stepping closer. Bodinger recognized a familiar smell.

"You're drunk, Frank. Go sleep it off."

"Not too much to know you dropped the ball on me again, but this time, I'm not getting thrown out with the bathwater."

Bodinger turned, face-to-face, their noses almost touching. "This is a police investigation, goddamn it! And if you sidetrack it in any way, I'll slap you with obstruction so fast *she* won't even miss ya!" he said, pointing to Carmen.

"A beautiful girl is dead, murdered on your watch! *My* friend, Stan. *Mine*! She worked and cared for *me*! And while you're chasing this fucker, he hangs her in a tree and shoots three boys. And I'm supposed to say, 'Go get 'em, boss. You're doing a hell of a job'?"

"Go to hell."

"I'm already there."

Bodinger fell in the car after spitting at Frank's feet. Cordova had stood outside and watched. He wanted to get involved, but the pain of failure in finding D neutered his resolve. He was more worried about his own family now, and truth be known, he's starting to feel that maybe someone outside the restriction of law enforcement might find ways to get results.

Frank kicked the car door as Bodinger slammed it. Cordova turned the car around as the two detectives left the graveyard. "Thanks for the backup," Bodinger grunted as they hit the highway.

"Sorry, Stan. It just seems like unfinished business that's not mine."

"This is *our* investigation, Eric. A *police* investigation, not a washout's stab at revenge. A little support would have been nice, that's all." Bodinger cooled before adding, "No big deal. You're right . . . Probably best you stayed out of it. It wasn't the place for it. Frank should have known better too. It's a goddamn funeral, and he wants to play hero to an eastside whore."

Cordova knew he was right. It was like watching a divorced couple squabble. There are so many scars you know the blade cuts both ways, and all Eric had ever heard was Stan's version.

For now, it would have to do.

Bodinger couldn't shake Frank's image from his mind. He knew he'd follow through on his threat to do his own investigation. He couldn't have it. "When we get back, I'm requesting Captain Saunders put a tail on Castro. As much for his own good as ours. If he even thinks about seeing any of the victim's families or goes near a crime scene, I want the cuffs on him on the spot."

Cordova didn't like it. All he'd ever heard about Castro was from Bodinger, so he drew his conclusions from that. However, now he'd seen him, heard him, and saw the look of a calculating hunter. He didn't seem like an out-of-control alcoholic. He was sure the guy had his demons, but he saw something in Castro even his partner didn't see.

He saw resolve. Something most drunks don't have.

"We're the ones this shit's sending letters to, need I remind you? Let's get back to Austin and see where we stand." After a few seconds, Bodinger punched the dash. "*Goddamn it!*"

Some ghosts never die.

Frank sat on the hood of his BMW, smoking a cigarette with his tie loosened, as Carmen stood in front of him. As Tiffany's family and friends filtered away from the gravesite, she was growing self-conscious of their eyes on her. "I should not be here," she said.

Frank looked at the clear blue sky overhead. "Why not?"

"It's disrespectful."

"I was her close friend, you're with me. That's not disrespectful."

"That man, Bodinger, knows what I am," she reasoned.

"Baby, everybody knows what you are. That doesn't mean you can't care for a friend."

"I didn't even know her."

"I meant me."

"Oh."

Frank sat in silence as they all left. The huge throng of people that had crowded into the chapel had driven to the cemetery, turning the graveyard into something that looked like a parking lot at a Longhorn game. Young and old had all come to pay last respects to Tiffany Malvern. Now, with the pomp and circumstance over, all that remained was dropping the pretty blonde's brass coffin six feet below ground, sealing her away for eternity.

It should have been anyone but her.

Frank and Carmen stayed long after everyone had left. He wanted to watch the cold process of the burial. Now that the tears and sobs were gone, the music had stopped, and the ritualistic send-off had finished, Frank just wanted to feel the earth move as the backhoe filled the hole in, covering her forever. He wanted to hear the machine, watch the man operating it, in remorseless monotony of a man doing an idle job for idle pay. It was getting dark and Carmen needed to get home, but she knew better than to protest. Frank was going to leave when he was damn good and ready. If she made a fuss, he'd tell her to start walking and catch a ride on the highway. She dozed inside the two seater as Frank watched and listened.

His soul felt empty as the machine shoveled the small mountain back into the ground. The scotch had worn off hours ago, and he was feeling as empty as he'd ever felt in his life. In the few days leading up to the funeral, all he was consumed with was doing something for her family. He was right there every time they needed or wanted like a member of the family. He hadn't been in his office since Bodinger broke the news to him. Now it was all over. The backhoe finished and maneuvered its way through the cemetery as a worker in a pickup laid the remaining flowers on the grave; then he, too, left the spot. Twilight was descending. The sky was dark purple, and stars were waking up for the night as Frank walked up the slight rise to Tiffany's final resting place. The dirt was soft, and his expensive boots were covered in the red mix. He stood there for a few minutes, feeling the icy grip of death seize him like the hand of a corpse.

This was the last straw. He'd lost his career, friends, and future.

Albeit to his own doing, but it was all gone nonetheless. So he tried again. Scrounged for clients, doing what he'd been trained to do and doing it well. And now, just as he was starting to see a light—the drinking was under control, money was in the bank, and he was gathering a good client list thanks to old lady Cabbershaw—this happens. He and Tiffany were starting to make something out of that little office in Round Rock. Then, on the whim of a psychopath, he's left standing in a cemetery among the headstones, questioning every move he'd ever made his entire life. One word and one word only came to mind that summed it all up.

Waste.

He'd wasted it all on booze, drugs, hookers, and thrills. And just when he was growing up a little, seeing the error of his ways, and looking forward to putting the savable pieces back in their proper order, this beautiful life was stolen right from under his nose. More to the point, under the nose of the APD and his old partner.

Frank walked back down the rise to his car like a man walking the last mile. Once he got in and drove away, he felt his life was about to change again, for the third time. The hotshot cop was dead long ago, killed by hypocrisy and betrayal. The new man he'd been, the casual private detective with the cool car and hot secretary, was dead in the mound of dirt lying atop a grave in north Dallas, lost forever.

Carmen slept as he slowly pulled the BMW through the cemetery gates and onto the highway, leaving Tiffany Malvern to sleep in peace for eternity along with the man that was once her friend and employer. The man driving the small car was different now; he'd been changed forever. He was as different from the man who entered the graveyard as day is to night. What tiny bit of humanity that had lingered inside him was crushed out of existence. The last flicker of hope that remained inside him was only there because of her. Now she and it were extinguished forever. There was nothing left to save inside Frank Castro. It was all dead now. As dead as the beautiful girl they buried today.

Someone was going to have to pay for that.

29

Bodinger's gut clinched as he stared at the printed photograph. Cordova was looking over his shoulder, Bodinger feeling his breath on his neck. He normally would have been bothered, but the feeling was compromised by his own breathing.

They were at their desks with Saunders and two forensic agents. Bodinger had dropped by the hotel Susan had checked in to and retrieved the letter. After she assured him she was okay and that a cop's wife was built for such drama, he and Cordova took the letter downtown. Using rubber gloves so the only contaminating prints would be Susan's and the postal workers', the two opened the letter with Saunders. The first page was the photo, the dead Tiffany Malvern hanging naked from the tree with the three boys hog-tied and shot. D was standing in the foreground. This was new. He'd set a timer, taking his own portrait with his work. They could see that he wasn't a powerfully built man; some might even say he was slight. But the ski mask had the desired effect. It looked menacing. Coupled with the bodies, it was evil.

But it was the second page that jarred them most. A typed letter addressed to Bodinger.

Dear Detective Bodinger,

I hope you enjoy the photograph I've enclosed. I must say the three blind mice were quite a surprise. I was astounded that one of them had a camera phone he used to take a picture of my fun. I crushed it and dropped the fragments in several places all over the city. The

shot he took only showed my vehicle, so in case you're looking for me that way . . . Need I say more? It's gone now. Sucks to be you, I'm afraid. The young woman was quite fun, more than the mice. I made myself come as her eyes dilated black. The mice got the privilege of watching me hang her dead naked body from the tree before I killed them. I wanted them to know who they were fucking with. I was going to let them die the same way as her, but there was no sexual gratification in it. I decided to end them quickly. Call me a humanitarian if you must.

Speaking of fucking . . . I hope your pretty wife isn't afraid of me. See, I've had my gut full of older women, and there's nothing about her that makes my meat twitch. My tastes these days run more toward the younger of the bunch. Not that watching her fight for air inside the bag wouldn't be a hoot. It would be a hoot, don't you think, Detective? Stripping the old gal down to her pubes and watching her die inside my bag? Huh? Yeah, that would be a real hoot.

But not right now.

Now I'm more interested in the young ones. You see, I've had enough old pussy to last me five lifetimes. As a matter of fact, old pussy disgusts me. Let me ask you, Detective, are you a motherfucker? I am. Quite literally. My mother used to love to bend over and order me to fuck her like an obedient mongrel. I bet you never did that, Detective. I bet you've never dropped a load inside your mother's belly, have you? Ever go down on your mother, Detective? I have. It always tasted like death. My own. I died a little every time I touched her, and she liked to be touched. She died after I told her I couldn't do it anymore. She wanted me to fuck her, and I said no. She died that night. I guess I killed her, huh?

The last time I fucked my mother, she was dead. It was the best I ever had.

I guess I've said enough.

Tell the Cordovas and the rest of the boys in blue I'll be watching.

As you're dying think of your mother,

D

185

Before even reading the signature, Cordova was out of the building, racing home with the image of the madman hot in his mind. As soon as Saunders had copied the letter by hand, the forensic team whisked the letter off to look for prints and DNA. Bodinger knew it was an exercise in futility. D had never given them anything before, so why would he start now? Self-adhesive stamps and envelopes and gloves were the norm as was mailing from a different part of town each time. Three letters with three different postmarks.

"Kerndon's on his way now," Saunders told Bodinger. "He needs to read this."

"Is it real?" Bodinger asked without looking up.

"No reason to think otherwise. Besides, it explains a lot, to me at least."

Bodinger turned, sitting on the desk. He rubbed his hands through his hair briskly, like he was trying to put out a scalp fire, then asked his boss, "And what would that be?"

"Now we know why he hates women."

"But he hates older women. Christ, he said *old pussy* disgusts him. Why kill younger women? Girls?"

"Kerndon will have to make that connection," Saunders replied, sitting next to Bodinger on the desk. "Sure, there's more to it than what he's told us. But it's a start, Stan."

"A start? We have six dead bodies, and *this* is the start? Maybe we ain't as Johnny perfect as we think."

"No argument," Saunders answered. "But we can't just throw our hands up. It's hard for us to admit sometimes that we're not as smart as the bad guys we're after. D's a perfect example. He's smart, thorough, and cunning. He's not some wild madman with a knife that gets lucky and catches a break. This fucker's thought this shit out and plans to make it even harder."

"So what do we do, damn it? When do we tell the people that we know what the hell we're doing? That we know where to start looking?"

"As soon as we do."

"Not good enough!" Bodinger snapped, jumping from the desk. "My partner watched me get grilled by Castro like I was a street punk, and did nothing to back me because he's already thinking we need outside help. And that help is Castro? Frank fucking Castro? You *kidding me*? A guy who got kicked because he couldn't keep his mouth dry for a lousy shift, and my guy meets him once, and he's already doubting me? *Me*! This is more than a start. This shit has to end."

"Stan—"

"That letter came to my house, Jim! My wife saw it before any of us. She read that twisted shit for God's sake! Eric's breaking his neck right now to get home and see if his family's safe. This guy's beyond crazy. He's calculating. He's always a step ahead."

"And?"

"And I can't *stand that*!"

"You're not in this alone, you know. We're all in it together."

"But it's my name in the paper. *My* wife got the letter, *not* yours!"

"You want off this case?" Saunders snapped, having had enough.

"No!" Bodinger shot back before falling lifeless into a chair. Seconds passed before he added, "Of course not. This is mine . . . It's mine to the end." He had the look of a POW from one of the wars. That dead stare. That lifeless stare the vets call the *thousand mile* stare. Empty eyes peering into nothingness, the nothingness of their own soul. Stanley Bodinger was a dog chasing his tail, and there seemed to be nothing he could do to stop the madness. D was beginning to dictate how he would lead his life. His wife was afraid to go home, his partner was questioning his ability, and his boss was doing little to reassure his status on the case in general.

"You want me off?" he croaked.

"Hell no," Saunders answered. "But we do need more men. Tomorrow I'll go to the commissioner and get appropriations for more bodies in the field. We'll start a task force like the New York boys did to catch the Son of Sam. I don't give a rat's ass if it takes half the force and the Texas Rangers. We're gonna catch this piece of shit not just because it's the right thing, but because all our asses are on the line now. All of us."

Bodinger read his face. Captain Saunders was where he was not just because he was a good cop, but he was also a politician. Bodinger

187

expected to see that half smirk most politicians wear when they're trying to screw over some pain in the ass special interest group. However, what he saw in Jim Saunders's eyes wasn't political fodder. He saw fear. And fear was always something Bodinger respected. Fear was the only honest emotion.

"A task force sounds big," he replied. "And maybe big is what we need."

Big would be needed indeed because the detectives were unaware of something very vital. They would find out in the morning with the daily edition of the paper. Unknown to the officers, there was a second letter sent at the same time as the one to Susan Bodinger. Against his better judgment, Adam couldn't resist one last fling with his favorite correspondent.

30

Frank spent the day boxing up Tiffany's things to send back to her family in Dallas. Since her murder, he'd fallen off the wagon and was sipping scotch while packing up her personals at the office. He kept the *Far Side* calendar as his own tribute to her silly sense of humor.

He'd yet to think about replacing her. His business meant nothing now. The only thing that mattered was finding the twisted shit that killed her. He knew intellectually that even if he had what the police were using, he'd hit nothing but a dead end. He had no way of knowing what forensics they possessed or if they had witnesses. All he did know was the madman was still loose, so what they had meant zero. He'd have to start from a different angle, one they hadn't thought of. The problem, however, was that he didn't know what that was. He didn't know where to start.

Going through her things only saddened him; he couldn't afford that. Disgusted with himself, he set the things aside, deciding to go downtown. Maybe he'd get the juices flowing if he just got away from the place he'd last seen her.

"I gotta get out of here for a while," he said to the picture on her desk, the one of Tiffany and her sister. "I can do this later. Right now, I need some goddamn air. I need to breathe."

It was one in the afternoon when he made Eighth Street, parking in an indoor parking garage. He spent the rest of the day shooting the shit with Toxic Mike at Lucky's and bouncing around the streets, going from bar to bar, letting his weeks of sobriety flush away like a bad dream. None of that mattered now. There was only one thing on his mind. Maybe the most important thing he'd ever done. He just didn't know where to start.

As the day passed and night woke around him, the streets began giving birth to the deluge of humanity he was accustomed to. Only now, in this state of mind, the city didn't seem as forgiving as in the past. Instead of happy people out for a good time, he saw a muddled mass of artificiality. People putting on their best fronts to fool the guards at the gate. Toddlers stiff legging toward a busy street, seduced by the bright lights and pretty colors, unaware of the carnage that lay before them. Instead of partiers, he saw fools. Lambs being fattened for the slaughter. As ill equipped to handle the real world as a newborn tossed in a dumpster. It was a strange new feeling to him, one he wasn't accustomed to. He truly felt like a man without a country.

It was two thirty in the morning, and he was getting edgy. The way he always felt during the wee hours while riding in the squad car with Bodinger, knowing there was always something just around the next corner. A new night to scream to the moon that you're alive and making a difference. Not knowing what was next, but living in the now, in the minute. The last ten years had dulled that feeling.

Now, something was stirring inside him. The grief was gone, and he began to recognize what it was. His stride down the busy street quickened to a pace. He felt alarmingly alive. He lit a smoke, letting the night air embrace him, as he walked faster through the crowds. Meaningless faces, each one more vacant than the last, passed him by without care, without thought. The commotions of bands filled the air, the smells of the city barraging him from every direction. His heart raced; he had to get it back. He had to find the—

"Hey, man, watch it!" the big kid yelled. Frank had walked into him as he turned the corner of Lavaca and Sixth. Frank felt the bump but ignored it, moving on. The kid yelled again; this time, Castro heard and turned.

There were four of them. The one in the middle, the vocal leader, was the one who felt assaulted. A college kid, maybe twenty, twenty-one. He stood a good six five and easily outweighed Frank by forty pounds. He looked like a defensive end prowling the streets in his tight T-shirt that hugged every nook of his chiseled physique. Curly blond hair, broad shoulders, and an attitude to match.

"Sorry, kid. Gotta a lot on my mind," Frank said, turning to leave.

"Ain't good enough, fucker!"

Frank stopped. The edge was there. He needed this, he wanted this. His blood had been simmering for days, and now it was at full boil. Ten years of questioning himself. Ten years of self-pity. Ten years of being a joke. Ten years of holding up a stool at Lucky's. Ten long miserable years of his wasted life flashed before him. There was only one person in the whole world he cared about. Just one, and some maniac took her away from him. He heard Tiffany's voice from that day in the office: *"You're doing good, boss. Real good."*

Suddenly the only thing that mattered was letting it out. The kid figured the old guy who looked drunk would apologize, making him feel big to his friends. Frank Castro saw it differently. In a dead run, he dropped a shoulder into the kid's gut, spilling him on the sidewalk flat on his back, as several women screamed. The kid's friends cleared room, backing people away, so their man could work. However, before the big man could react to what was happening, Castro sat up, straddling him, and began raining down the thunder of his right hand. One, two, three, four unblocked shots to the side of the kid's face. Then he dropped a left across his nose, shattering the bridge, sending a crimson gush spewing from his face. His three friends collapsed on Frank in a rush. One caught a thumb in the eye, one a hard kick to the groin, the third a punch to the chest before having his head smashed through the passenger window of a parked car. Chaos ensued. People were running to and away from the mêlée while others sought the police who patrolled the area on horseback.

Pandemonium.

The realization of what he'd done only dawned on Frank once he heard someone yell for the cops. If he got busted for this, then everything Bodinger thought about him would be true. He had to get away. As the commotion escalated, he managed to sprint across the street, past a row

191

of shops, then turned right, heading up Seventh with no one seemingly following. Why would they? In a matter of thirty seconds, he single-handedly left four young toughs bleeding and disfigured in his wake. The last sound sticking in his mind, as he rounded the corner, was of the thug who took it to his eye, screaming over the crowd, *"He poked my fucking eye out!"*

He jogged a block then stepped into a small dive he didn't recognize. It was dark, almost empty. The bartender announced, "Last call, buddy. If you want something, you better get it now." Frank waved him off, eyeing the men's room.

He walked quickly, trying not to draw the attention of the few still there. Inside the restroom, he locked the door, leaning against it. He was shaking. Every cell in his body was vibrating. He stepped to the mirror and looked.

There it was. There was the man he'd lost. He was back. The wolf was back, staring, hungry for his meal, thirsting for blood, stinging for a fight. The beast that had roamed the streets, preying on scum and criminals behind a silver badge. His eyes hadn't looked that sharp in ten years. The rush of recognition made him shake his head, blinking, telling himself he was mistaken. He splashed cold water on his face, but the wolf looked back, still hungry. Not blinking, not flinching. It wanted more. Frank wanted him to have it. He welcomed back his old friend; it'd been far too long. If the wolf wanted to hunt, then Frank would let him hunt; he owed it to him. But first, he had to get out of Austin.

He pulled off the gray sports coat. After removing his sunglasses from the pocket, he rolled it into a neat bundle; then pulling an entire roll of toilet paper from a stall, he wrapped the coat solid, making it look like a package. Now, he had to think of himself. The kids never landed a punch, so there were no marks to hide. He wet his hair, slicking it back straight, then pulled out the tails of his white dress shirt. He unbuttoned it to his navel, exposing his chest, and rolled the sleeves up to his elbows. He donned the sunglasses then inspected his work. He looked nothing like the guy who just pummeled four people. Witnesses were meaningless now. He tucked the bundled coat under his arm, starting to leave, but he stopped. Pulling the shades down slowly, gazing in the mirror, he saw the wolf was still there. He almost smiled.

The parking garage with his BMW was a block away, and Frank crossed the street at midblock and snaked through the alley. He walked to the second floor, finding his silver two seater. Once inside, he was able to breathe normally again. He lit a cigarette, allowing the last twenty minutes to wash over him. He looked in the rearview. Again, he felt the urge to smile but didn't. There was nothing really to smile about. This was the same guy that got kicked off the force. He also knew it was the same guy that always came through in the crunch, and finding Tiffany's murderer was most definitely crunch time. As he pulled the BMW Z4 out of the garage, he knew it had come at last. At last, it was time to get serious about something. And with the wolf back, he might even have a little fun doing it.

Frank never noticed him. He never saw the man sitting in the unassuming car across from his office all morning. He never saw the same car follow him downtown. He paid no attention to the slender young man alone at a table in the corner at Lucky's for most of the day. He was unaware of the eyes on him as he walked the streets in the twilight of the evening. He never saw the same man, one of many faces in the crowd, as he brawled with four college kids.

Frank never saw him.

But Adam was there. And now Adam knew who Frank Castro was. He'd taken a business card out of Tiffany's purse. *Frank Castro Investigations* it read, in Round Rock. So Adam decided to forego his nocturnal ventures and come out during the day to observe the man who, she promised, would *cut his fucking heart out.*

Impressive.

In two days, he'd be heading back to Louisiana to get his H2, his *new* H2 from Bodain. When he got back, things were going to get interesting, he felt. "We'll just see about that Frankie boy. We'll just see."

31

"I want to know if anyone has sold, stolen, or bought a black Hummer in the last year," Saunders told the team of detectives gathered in the conference room. "If a black Hummer's been torched or drowned it comes to me. If a black Hummer took a shit in the woods, I want to be the first to know about it. Understand?"

Reyes spoke up. "Captain, this guy's as methodical and careful as anyone we've ever seen. Do you really think he'd be stupid enough to sell or trade that vehicle knowing we'd be looking for it?"

Saunders leaned on the table with both fists and sighed. "No, Reyes, I don't. But wouldn't we feel like great, fat idiots if he did and we *didn't* check it out?"

Feeling dumb, Reyes didn't respond.

Before another word was spoken, the door smacked open as Chief Milt Short walked in, asking Saunders if he'd seen the morning paper.

"Something tells me I should have."

Short dropped the paper on the table in front of him. The headlines made Saunders spit, "Motherfucker!"

The headline read CAPITAL HANGMAN TERRORIZES AUSTIN.

"Great," Cordova said, "he got his name."

"It's gets worse," Short informed them. "Young gives details about the pictures, tells how he was told *this* and *that* by the detective in charge of the investigation." He cut an eye at Bodinger. "I want you and those two"—pointing at Bodinger and Cordova—"in my office now."

Short stomped out of the room as the rest of the policemen went silent. Before the door closed, Saunders was in the hall following his boss with Bodinger on his heels and Cordova a step behind.

"That prick wasn't supposed to print anything without my approval!" Bodinger roared.

"In case you haven't heard, Stan, there's a little thing in this country called freedom of the press," Saunders snapped, without slowing. "That *prick* was doing us a favor and saw that his job was more important than *you*. The bets are off."

The three men entered Short's office as he closed the door behind them, ranting immediately. "In about twenty minutes, the governor of this state—let me say that again so you gentlemen understand me—the governor of the state of Texas is going to call me and ask me what the hell I'm doing to find this madman killing people in his town. I really hope, for your sake, that you have more for me to tell the man other than what *the son of a bitch drives!*"

The three cops looked at each other, slumping.

Short walked to his desk, saying, "This isn't Dallas, gentlemen. This isn't Houston or Bumfuck, Egypt. This is Austin, Texas. This is the capital of the greatest state in the Union, the only state that could survive on its own. This is the seat of who and what the great state of Texas stands for and represents to the nation and the world. When that sicko climbed the tower in '66 and killed all those people, the city took him down. Not the feds, not the goddamn FBI, *we did it!* Shit like this happens in Seattle and Chicago. Shit like this does not happen in *this town!*" He walked around the desk, stopping directly in front of Saunders. "Jim, we go way back. I know you're the best, but I need this sick shit off the streets, and I need it yesterday." Casting an eye at Bodinger, he added, "And you're in deeper shit than he is because Young names you as the head man in charge. And that's all the people in the city and state are gonna see. *Detective Bodinger couldn't find the freak that killed six kids.* Guess what happens then?" he asked Bodinger. "You're on Oprah, telling the millions at home why this nut job is smarter than *you*." Short walked back behind his desk, taking his seat before saying, "I don't give a shit what you gotta do—go outside the lines, I don't give a damn. I just want this bastard caught, and I want it *ASAP!*"

Bodinger knew this was politics. This was Pontius Pilate washing his hands of the sin while laying the blame on the men doing the job. He lost all respect for Milton Short in that moment.

What did he think? That they weren't trying? That they didn't lie awake at night wondering if D was out there doing his thing and more bodies were piling up? Why would he pull this strong-arm bullshit unless he was trying to distance himself? Besides, the last letter was sent to *his* house, not the paper. D had made this personal for Bodinger even if he never wanted it to get that way.

Susan was sleeping in a hotel for Christ's sake.

Bodinger spoke up. "With all due respect, sir, the last letter and photo was sent to my house, addressed to my family."

"Stan—," Saunders tried to interrupt.

"No, Jim . . . Please," he insisted. Saunders stopped.

"This creep sent that thing to my house knowing my wife would open it and panic. I take that personally, sir. And I'll be damned if I'm not, *we're* not, doing everything in our power to stop this madness. Detective Cordova here has a young, pretty wife and a little girl." He motioned to his partner. "I think he has a vested interest in getting D off the streets. To tell you the truth, sir, I haven't had a good night's sleep in six months. Every time I close my eyes, I see those photos of his and wonder how many he has of each victim and just how much more horrible they are than the ones he sent us. We knew—we all knew— Glenn Young was going to drop this like a bomb if more happened, and he did. So why are we so surprised? Hell, I'm amazed the prick waited this long. As Jim reminded me, it's in the Constitution, and there's shit all we can do about it. So why cry over spilled milk now?"

"Spilled milk, Detective?" Short asked, steeped in sarcasm.

"All I'm saying is maybe we shouldn't have sat on as much as we did. Maybe we should have given as much information as we could to the press, and they could have worked with us. We didn't because we didn't want a panic, but I'm sure we got one now. The phones will be ringing off the hook with crackpots and weirdoes, but maybe, just maybe, somebody out there might actually know something and spill it," he finished, looking at his partner who gave him a nod. As did Saunders.

Short fell in his chair and huffed, "We'll need people on the phones starting now, around the clock. Put some people close to the case on it so they can cull the cranks."

"Of course," Saunders answered.

The room went silent. It hung in the office like a fog and was about to get uncomfortable before Short continued, "I know you men are doing your best, I do. And maybe we took the wrong approach. One we *all* agreed on," He eyed Bodinger who confirmed with a nod. "But what I'm telling you is this thing is going to blow up in a matter of a couple of hours, and we have to be on top of it. We have to know what we're telling the press, and we damn well better know what we're doing to find this asshole." He looked to Saunders. "Is the only detail Young's unaware of is that the girls were all dead when he hung them?"

"Well, I didn't get a chance to study the article, but—"

"That's it," Cordova blurted, scanning the paper. "And nothing about the Hummer."

"They need to know," Bodinger said. "We need everyone in this city looking for a black H2 that's not driven by a soccer mom. Sure, we'll get a ton of wild geese, but we only have to be right once."

"The letter said it was gone now," Cordova added.

"Bullshit," Saunders blurted. "It's somewhere. We just have to find it."

"Can't do it in here," Short said. The men, taking the hint, filed out. However, Short stopped Bodinger, telling him he wanted a word in private. Bodinger was ready for a grilling for stepping out, but at least he had things going in the right direction. He could shoulder a browbeating knowing the train was finally on the right track. Compared to the case, it would be a walk in the park.

"Stan," Short started, "I just wanted to tell you something."

"I'm listening."

"There were those of us a few years ago that didn't trust you for the way you handled Castro. Some of us thought you were a snitch or, worse, a sellout."

Bodinger tensed instinctively. Here it was, the big lie all over again. Short ran his hand over his mouth, breaking eye contact. Bodinger was now starting to dislike the chief more with every breath. He knew the rumors; hell, he lived through them. He was the one that found a dead rat in his locker. He was the one that overheard a rumor to beat the shit out of him in his own yard in front of his kids. He was the one that no one would look in the eye or shake his hand for five years. Short was replaying old news that needed to die.

"But in the last couple of years, you've proved us wrong, Stan. You've become a good detective. A good cop. I trust you on this one. Just don't let D make it personal."

Bodinger couldn't believe his ears. *You've become a good cop?* What was that supposed to mean? He was always a good cop right out of the academy. If they didn't like the way he handled Frank Castro, they didn't stop to realize he handled it honestly, the way a good cop should have. Bodinger had never lost sleep over Castro. As far as he was concerned, the man did it to himself; all he did was confirm what Internal Affairs questioned.

"Was it a good shoot? Yes, it was . . . And no, it wasn't.

"Is that it, sir?" he asked, unavoidable disdain in his voice.

Short heard it loud and clear. He was getting close to making this man-to-man and not chief-to-sergeant. "Yes," he said, going back to his desk, not looking at Bodinger as he left. "Good luck, Detective."

Bodinger stomped down the hall to the conference room where they were waiting on Kevin Kerndon's analysis of the new letter. All the way down the hall, Bodinger kept hearing Short saying, "Those of *us* that didn't trust you."

What the hell was that? Suddenly he was sick of the whole damned thing. He wanted to be as far away from the force as he could get. Did people really still hold Castro against him? If that was the case, he should sell the house, empty the 401(k), and take Susan to Mexico where they could live like royalty for the rest of their days. That's why he'd never got to lieutenant once he made sergeant. Politics made his stomach turn.

And there was always his ex-partner.

32

Patrolman Stanley Bodinger was sitting in his squad car, waiting on his partner, Frank Castro, to come back from his latest sojourn into the night. It was a regular occurrence on their beat in east Austin. It usually happened three times a week for Bodinger to turn his head, allowing his partner to exercise his vices while things were cool. It normally took only an hour or less, and his partner was always better in the long run. Bodinger, on the other hand, hated it. It went against everything that being a cop stood for, but Castro was the absolute best guy to have in the car with you if the shit came down.

The problem was keeping him in the car.

Frank had his problems; Bodinger knew that. But by this time, they knew each other inside and out. They could finish each other's sentences like an old married couple. The only time Castro was loose with the rules was when things were quiet. When the shit storm hit, he was always the first and the best in line. There was no one better in the field than Stanley Bodinger's partner. The entire APD knew that.

However.

He always came back smelling of booze or hooker or both. There were even times Bodinger could swear his partner was wired out of his head on coke. He knew Frank lived on the edge, a real rush junkie. Whiskey and women were his main weaknesses, but he knew the guy liked to dabble in the nose candy when it was an easy turn. As a guy, Bodinger admired Castro in his own way. A man's man who did what he wanted but always took care of business. As the line goes, he wasn't a dirty cop, but he was a cop with real weaknesses. Weaknesses that were detrimental to being a law officer as he saw it. He wanted to drop a dime on him at least a hundred times, but there was no one on the force he wanted more in the passenger side of unit 214 than Frank Castro. When the heat got turned up, Frank was like Clint Eastwood in an old spaghetti Western, doing whatever it took to see justice triumph. As big a prick as he was, he knew where the line was drawn, and he was hell on the people who crossed it.

Bodinger was sitting in a supermarket parking lot at 1:00 a.m., waiting for Frank to burst on the car the same way he always did. It had been an hour since he dropped him off in a seedy neighborhood a few blocks away. Bodinger felt it was a pussy run, and his scumbag partner would show up at any minute, having dislodged his daily quota of semen in some street trash. Waiting for him was the worst part because no matter what the hell he was doing, when he got back, he was going to be altered. It was like a sailor watching the sky turn red. Whatever was coming was never pretty even if it made the asshole a better cop.

Castro was always distracted. He knew the job like his mother's face, so he got bored, needing more. Bodinger would plead with him to turn that energy into something constructive like getting out of the squad car and making detective. Like *he* wanted to do.

"Those guys push too many pencils, bro," he'd tell him. "I ain't one for pencils. Give me the streets, give me the feed. Let the wolf howl. That's where the blood is, that's the line I walk."

The *feed* is what Castro called the adrenaline rush of working the streets of east Austin. The place was a haven of gangs and drug wars. The poor Hispanic people of the east side fought for a square deal every day of their lives, and Castro saw himself as a crusader that made sure the field stayed level. On more than one occasion, he told Bodinger, "Most of these kids are scum and are gonna wind up in Gatesville or dead. But if we can keep the field level, maybe at least one of these little pricks will go on to do something special."

"Like?" Stan would ask.

"Who cares, bro, at least he's alive. And he's out of here."

200

That was the human side of Castro that always stopped Bodinger from squealing on him. Every time he felt it had gone on long enough, Frank would do or say something that made him shake his head, rethink his position. Once, while patrolling at midnight, he made Bodinger stop the car so he could help an old woman looking for her cat in her front yard. Bodinger waited for almost an hour as this tiny little Mexican woman who couldn't speak a word of English, in her pink housecoat, searched the yard for her cat with big Frank Castro helping. After forever, Frank found the damn thing in a shrub, fishing it out for the old lady. It was an old tabby cat with a *blinged-out* collar. Bodinger laughed, watching his macho partner hand the feline to the old woman who was trembling with glee. She shed a tear and kissed the big lug on the cheek before he dropped back in the car.

Bodinger was waiting. "Are you serious?" he asked, fighting off a laugh.

"What?"

"You killed almost an hour with that old woman and a freaking cat for crying out loud."

Castro lit a cigarette, explaining, "Hey, man, she's old. That cat's probably the only thing that gets her up in the morning. *Gotta get up to feed the cat*, you know? Old man's been gone for years. Kids are most likely dead, in prison, or on the other side of the world. But that gray tabby's there every morning like an alarm clock. Keeps her moving, keeps her alive. She needs that cat, brother. She *needs* that cat," he said, winking like a scoundrel. "Serve and protect, partner. Serve and protect."

Bodinger wilted. Castro was right. No matter how screwed up the situation, Castro always seemed to have the right answer. If they were breaking heads on the street or kissing babies at the corner store, Frank always knew the pulse of the people. He was a natural at reading personalities. He knew when to trust a scumbag and when not to trust a socialite. That was just one of the many reasons Patrolman Bodinger bit his tongue every time Castro needed his private diversion. He trusted him. He trusted him not to leave him in a bad situation.

Trust is everything.

Of course, the next night, a call came while Frank was out of the car.

When Bodinger called him on his radio, he had his pants around his ankles, giving it to a hooker in an alley off Canterbury Street, while gangbangers on his dime watched for narcs.

Working with Frank Castro was anything but boring.

This night was no different than any of the rest. They broke up a meeting of some young thugs on a corner with Castro walking up on them as Bodinger made a block. Four teenagers with gang tattoos and years of experience no kids their age should have. The oldest was maybe seventeen. They were sharing a bottle in a paper sack by an old Chevy as Castro walked up on them. He played it low, not wanting to alarm them. His reputation would be enough.

"Fuck me," one said. "*Pinche* Castro. *Puta!*"

"So what are you boys doing up at this hour? It's a school night," he said, saddling up beside them.

"Fuck you, Castro."

"You wish," he said dryly. "You couldn't handle it, son." He turned to the young man holding the bag. "What's in the bag?"

"A 7-Up, *holmes.*"

Castro yanked the bottle from the kid's hand then pulled it from the bag. It was a cheap cognac. Frank hated cognac. He smelled it, taking a small sip. He spat, "How in the hell do you guys expect to grow hair on your balls drinking swill like this shit?" They all groaned, cursing in Spanish, as Frank emptied the bottle on the street. Just as one of the youngsters was about to bow up, Bodinger pulled the unit around the corner, flashing his lights.

"Not tonight, fellas," Frank told them. "Go north and puke in a better neighborhood. Party's over."

"You fucking serious with this shit?" one asked.

"As cancer," Frank said. "When you get too drunk to know when to stop, you ain't gonna be fucking up my watch. Not tonight. Beat it or deal, it's your call."

Seconds passed before one of the thugs asked, "So what's the odds on the deal?"

Frank smiled. He knew this was coming. Street kids only know one way, dry up or force the issue. There is no in-between. He scratched his

202

head, looking dead at the kid, before asking, "If the deal is me, do you really want to find out?"

Again, the reputation served him. The boys climbed into their car, squalling tires as they drove away. Yells and cat calls ensued as they shot the finger and assorted gang signs to the big Cuban cop.

When he got back in the car, Bodinger could tell the shakedown had given Castro a rush. It had been a couple of nights since Frank went on one of his excursions, so when he was acting antsy and told Bodinger he needed to find a *spot*, Bodinger complied as always. "Just don't get clap in the unit, douche bag," Bodinger told him as Frank scurried off into the dark after casting Stan his killer smile.

"Asshole."

The hour passed, and Bodinger was ready for his partner to get back. He hated waiting on the jerk because if a call came while he was gone, he'd have to call him on the radio then drive to his spot *before* they rolled to the site. It could become a disaster in no time. But to his relief, he saw Frank emerge from the shadows across the street, making his way toward him. His step was casual, so Bodinger assumed the trip had been a carnal one. He opened the door and fell in. Bodinger smelled alcohol.

"How much?" he asked.

"A couple."

"I can smell it."

"Your nose works. I'm excited."

The words hit him wrong. "Look, Frank, these little adventures of yours have to stop."

"Do I gotta hear this every goddamn time?" Castro asked, lighting a cigarette.

"All of it sucks, but at least if you're banging a hooker, you come back focused."

Frank rolled his eyes at Bodinger. "I'm focused. Okay? Let's just roll. I'm fine."

Bodinger looked into his eyes and knew he was telling the truth. If he said he had a couple of drinks, it meant he had four. Four scotch rocks to Frank Castro were like a couple of beers to the normal man. He knew his partner was affected, but he was in a place he could function as long as it wasn't too hairy a night. As long as it was usual business, they'd be fine.

But not tonight.

An hour later, while they were patrolling, a call came in to respond to a domestic dispute—a call no uniform cop ever wants to hear. Domestics are usually highly emotional and often violent. Not the kind of situation for a cop with a buzz no matter how good he is. Before Bodinger could give an excuse why they shouldn't respond, Castro was on the mic, acknowledging the call that they were en route.

"You sure about that?" Bodinger asked.

"I'm fine, man. Let's go," Frank assured him; and against his better judgment, Bodinger sped toward the address.

When they arrived, five minutes after the call, Bodinger parked the unit at the curb in front of the house. "Let me do the talking," he instructed Castro.

"Fine by me."

As the two officers approached the porch, scanning the area for anything out of the ordinary, a young man in baggy shorts and a white tank top jumped out of a window on the side of the house and started running up the side street.

"I'm on it!" Castro yelled, taking off on foot behind the runner.

Bodinger sprinted to the door, beating on it. He yelled, "Police! Open the door!"

Instantly the door opened as Bodinger drew his service revolver. A teenaged Latino girl stood before him. She was crying, and there was bruising on her face, her right eye beginning to swell. "Ma'am, is there anyone here with you?" he asked, eyes surveying the living room.

"No."

"The man that just jumped out the side window, do you know him?"

"Yes."

"Name."

"Miguel."

"Is he alone?"

"Yes."

The young woman was obviously used to talking to police and knew the routine. She answered slowly and calmly. She backed away facing him, allowing Bodinger to enter at his own caution. He took a step inside. There was a bad feeling inching up his spine. He didn't like the situation; it smelled funny, like something else was brewing. He stopped one step inside the doorway.

"What's your name?"

"Sabrina Gomez."

"Is Miguel the one that hit you, Sabrina?"

"Yes, he hit me. That *pinche joto* is always hitting me. No more though. Fuck him and all his gang shit!"

"What's his last name?"

"Montoya."

"Is this your house?"

"No—yes," she stammered. "It's my mother's."

"Where is she?"

"San Angelo, her sister's place. My Aunt Rosa."

Bodinger had the revolver pointed up. Easing a bit, he lowered it to his holster although still apprehensive. "Do you need a doctor?" he asked.

"No, I just want them gone."

Them?

"You said you were alone."

"I am."

"Then who else are you talking about if only Miguel ran?"

"His bitch friend, Ryan, was here before, but he left already. That *puta* always starts shit with me. Spoiled little shit thinks he's a gangster. He always gets my man in trouble then splits like a little bitch. I hate that fucker!" she hissed, spitting on the floor.

Bodinger didn't like the sound of that, especially with Castro tracking Miguel on foot. He clicked his shoulder mic. "Castro, where are you?"

Frank Castro was gaining on the kid and couldn't spend the energy to use his shoulder mic. They had crossed countless yards, jumped fences, and evaded cars while Castro yelled, "*Stop running. I'm a police officer! You can't outrun the radio, you stupid shit!*" It was a bluff. With half a bottle of J&B on his breath, the last damned thing he wanted was to get another unit involved.

Frank felt the wolf coursing through him. The longer the chase, the sweeter the bounty would be. He wanted to catch the kid for obvious reasons, but he wanted him to make the chase last. He knew he'd get him sooner or later; it was just that later was more fun. Let your blood get up, let the wolf's fur bristle, get the smell of the hunt full in your nostrils. The fox was smart and fast, but the wolf was relentless.

And once cornered, the fox never wins the battle.

Just when the chase was getting good and Frank was hitting his stride, the kid turned to look at him and tripped over a garden hose in a modest backyard. He hit the ground like a 140-pound bag of fertilizer. *Thump!* Rolling on his knees, he knew he was in trouble; all the air had been knocked out of his body. He was on all fours, trying to suck air into his flattened lungs, when the six two, 215-pound Frank Castro arrived. He, too, was sucking for wind but had more for the confrontation than the skinny kid who was feeling like he'd just been blindsided by a Dallas Cowboy.

"Stay down, asshole," Frank huffed, forcing Miguel facedown on the wet grass. Placing a knee in the middle of his back, he said, "I know you know the drill . . . Don't make me say it . . . I'm outta air."

The wolf wins again!

The pain worsened when the big cop placed his knee in the middle of his back. Hastily he put his hands behind him so Frank could cuff them quickly and get off his agonizing body. Castro cuffed him then jerked him to his feet with one hand. He was about five ten and maybe 140 pounds if you weighed him with his clothes and jewelry.

Castro knew the kid had the wind knocked out of him and let him catch his breath as he finally called back to Bodinger.

"I'm here . . . I'm here," he said into the mic between breaths.

"We may have another one lurking around. The victim says the guy you're after is named Miguel Montoya. He has a buddy that left earlier but may still be around. White male, only name she has is Ryan."

"Your name Miguel Montoya?" he asked the kid whose breath was finally coming back.

He nodded then spit on Castro's shoes. Frank put his foot between Miguel's and shoved him forward, causing him to trip again and land on his chest without being able to break his fall because of the cuffs. He hit the ground harder than the before. The pain returned, his air gone a second time.

"You oughtta learn to play nice, kid, really," he said, clicking his mic, telling Bodinger, "I have Montoya. We're heading back. What was that about a white kid?"

"Only name she has on him is Ryan, says he's a friend of Miguel's. A bad seed, left a few minutes before we arrived."

"Copy that," Castro said, taking a knee beside Miguel. "Where'd your little friend get off to, huh?"

Miguel managed to roll on his side, allowing him to gather some much-needed air. He said as best he could, "Don't . . . know."

"Bullshit."

"He left before you got here. I don't know, fucker. I don't know where he went."

"Bullshit."

"He's grown, *pendejo*! I ain't no *pinche* babysitter!"

Again Castro jerked Miguel to his feet as they headed back to the house several blocks away. "This is all bullshit anyway, *holmes*. That bitch just wants us in jail so she can blow my money and I can't kick her ass for it."

"Got a good job, do you?"

"Fuck you, cop! Fucking *puto* pig!"

It was a damn shame. Miguel fell again, knocking his wind out for a third time, as Frank lit a cigarette. Some people just never know when to shut up.

At the house, Bodinger was talking to headquarters on his shoulder mic, relaying what had happened and that everything was under control. Castro had caught the runner and was bringing him back. Once they arrived, he would relay further information. The most Stan could ascertain was that the girl had riled her boyfriend, and he slapped her around. It wasn't the first time, and growing tired of being a punching bag, she called 911. The other male left during the call, and once they arrived, the boyfriend ran.

Cut and dry.

Castro was towing Miguel by his elbow as the young man cursed him while dragging his feet, falling to his knees from time to time.

"Are you doing this shit because you hate the uniform, or are you just a prick by nature?" Frank asked.

"Fuck you, pig. Fucking *puto*," Miguel hissed then he smelled something. It was whiskey, and it was coming from the cop. "Man! You been throwin' a few, bro?"

"Shut up."

He leaned in, sniffing, then pulled back with a startle. "Damn *holmes*, you smell like a bar, *ese*."

Castro didn't like the sound of that. He wanted to get some distance between himself and Miguel. He'd have a chat with Bodinger about his new aroma to get their stories straight. They rustled a drunk, and he puked on Castro's shirt. That would be the story.

"There's the house, dickwad," Frank said as they made the side yard. "I'm gonna drop you in the front yard on your seat. If you try to run again, I swear to God—"

"I ain't runnin', bro! My arms are cuffed, you drunk shit!"

"Remember that."

"What? That the cop who caught me is higher than I am?"

Frank winced. He hated himself at that moment. His weakness had put both himself and Bodinger in jeopardy. He could take the heat; it was always coming anyway, but his partner deserved better. Stan had goals and a family; he couldn't be the reason it never happened. He leaned into Miguel's ear, whispering, "Don't make an enemy you know you can't conquer. I'd say ask Japan about that, but all you know is they make your video games."

"What?"

"Just shut the hell up, asshole."

Inside, Bodinger saw the girl would be okay but needed to be cleaned up with some local first aid. "I'm going to the car to get my first aid kit," he told her. "We'll get you patched up. You'll be okay. When my partner gets back with Miguel, we'll sort all this out." The girl smiled as Bodinger left for the unit at the curb.

On the way, he thought about his wife, Susan. How he'd never lifted a finger in anger toward her. How they were able to make the tough times better by loving each other. He wondered why everyone else couldn't deal with loved ones the same way. He knew young aggression had to find an outlet, but hitting a woman was never the way to settle anything. He was thinking of his wife when he heard steps running behind him, then a familiar voice yell, *"Gun! Freeze!"* Before he could fully turn and see what was happening, Frank saw Ryan coming up behind his partner with a gun pointed at his back. He shoved Miguel to the ground while drawing his service revolver and dropping to a knee. When Ryan heard the command, he turned on instinct and pointed the 9 mm automatic at Castro who fired two shots. *Bam! Bam!*

Two taps to the chest. The kid was dead before he hit the ground.

"You killed him!" Miguel screamed from the grass. *"You fucking pig, you killed Ryan!"*

"He was gonna kill my partner! *Shut the fuck up!*"

Bodinger was frozen. It all happened so fast he never knew what actually transpired. He heard running then Frank's command. Then the report of the sidearm. The only time he saw the kid with the gun, he was on the ground at his feet, dead.

All Bodinger saw was Frank Castro staring dead ahead with his revolver aimed straight at him, having taken the life of his killer.

That was all he saw.

So began the torment of officer Stanley Bodinger.

The man that saved his life, the debt he could never repay, was owed to a man he dreaded. A man whose sole reason to live was to be in the rush. Frank Castro saved his life that night in east Austin, but the source of his honor would be forever in question. Was it a good shoot or not? That's all Internal Affairs wanted to know.

Was it a good shoot?

A good shoot?

"How dare you question my partner's motive? How dare you question his integrity?"

How dare every damned one of you!

But time, even a few hours, can change how you see things.

Frank Castro saved a life that night. A life forever tormented by what was or wasn't a good shoot. What was *good* was being judged by those never blessed with baptism under fire. Frank Castro saved a good man's life that night.

He paid for it in blood ever since the echo of that last shot faded into the Austin night.

Miguel Montoya was twenty-one and had priors that ranged from petty crimes to possession of controlled substances. On the night of the shooting, he was on probation and ran to avoid violation. Ryan Westbrook, the kid with the gun, had a spotless record. Not even a speeding ticket. The nineteen-year-old had grown up in north Austin, a child of a well-off, upper middle-class family. He'd always had everything he wanted and could not be more opposite of his buddy, Montoya. But during his senior year of high school, he fell in with the wrong crowd and barely graduated. He moved out of his parents' house the last week of school to live in rough east Austin with his new buddies. A year later, after being exposed nonstop to the street-level crimes and daily struggles of the poor community, he was on the road to becoming a criminal. A lifestyle he grew to. He wanted to make his mark on the street, to show his new friends that he belonged among them.

Killing a cop would do nicely.

He'd left as Sabrina called 911, urging his buddy to do the same, but Miguel stayed. He watched from the bushes of the house next door, wanting to do something. Ryan desperately wanted to make a statement to the new brothers who'd adopted him. He had the firearm in his waistband, something neither Sabrina nor Miguel knew about. As Castro took out on foot for Miguel, Ryan was torn on whether to follow them or wait on Bodinger outside the house. Since he had no way of knowing where his friend would run, he decided on the cop in the house. He knew once Sabrina calmed down, this whole thing would blow over; and the cop, at some point, would have to go back to his car. He'd wait for him on the far side of the house and kill him at the curb. With no witnesses, he'd simply disappear back into the neighborhood with the rest of the *suspects.*

It almost worked. It would have, and there would have been a hero's funeral for the cop gunned down in east Austin had it not been for Castro getting back to the house quicker than Ryan anticipated.

The media had a field day. Castro was a hero. The only thing that kept a racial situation from exploding in the community was the fact that the dead teenager with the gun was white. His parents told the authorities they'd been expecting a call like this ever since he moved out. They feared their son was on a path to destruction and readied themselves for the worst to happen at any point.

Cut and dry.

Except for Internal Affairs. At the scene, alcohol was smelled on Castro. Miguel Montoya, not the most credible of witnesses, told the investigators he smelled booze on the officer who apprehended him. There was also a debate on what Frank had yelled to Ryan as he threw Miguel to the grass before drawing his weapon. Frank said he identified himself and ordered the kid to freeze. Miguel told them Frank yelled *gun* then *freeze.* Sabrina collaborated, saying the first word she heard yelled from the yard was *gun.* By their account, Frank Castro never identified himself to Ryan as a police officer; therefore, he didn't know he was turning his weapon on another patrolman. It could have been a rival gang member. That alone changed everything. Then there was the smell of alcohol, making matters worse.

Stanley Bodinger held all the cards.

Bodinger owed his life to his partner, but he had grown weary of having Castro at his side like a ticking time bomb. More importantly, he didn't just want Frank away from him; he wanted him off the force so that no other officer would be subjected to his wild nature. The force was loaded with *cowboys*, officers who were too aggressive and took too many chances. If Castro wound up with one of those kinds of

211

partners, the potential for something catastrophic was immense. He owed Frank his life but owed the city and force much more. He owed everyone, including Frank Castro, safety.

It took a month. Internal Affairs investigated every angle of the shoot and realized that the kill was clean. Frank was grilled for excessive force, but that was argued away with the lighting being bad, and Frank having just run down a man over the course of three hundred yards. However, the alcohol and the orders to Ryan were a different story.

Frank could never talk to Bodinger. IA forbade contact. It wouldn't have made a difference either way. He owed him, sure, but he was going to tell the truth: Frank had been drinking, he heard *gun* not *police*, and the only time he saw the kid with the weapon he was on the ground. He never saw the weapon pointed at Castro.

At the hearing, Castro finally got to Bodinger in the hallway.

"What did you tell them?"

"The truth, Frank."

"Meaning?"

"The truth *goddamn it*." Bodinger was insulted.

"What?" Castro couldn't believe his ears. "You told them I'd been drinking? Why?"

"It's called the truth, Frank. You should try it sometime." Bodinger turned, leaving the courthouse.

Frank was dumbstruck. He never wanted to put his partner behind the eight ball, not for all the tea in China. However, he saved the man's life. If he hadn't acted on his training, Stanley Bodinger would have been another cop killed in the line of duty. Sure, he was wrong about a lot of things, but he stopped the murder of his partner. How could Stan do this?

Frank asked, "You're just going to leave me in the wind? Leave me to die alone?"

"What did you say to me?" Bodinger whirled on him.

Castro closed the gap between them, saying, "Don't you leave me to die like this."

Bodinger's blood boiled. "You son of a bitch, every time you left the unit, every time you went off to play bad guy—leaving me to mind the store—you took a piece of me with you and burned it. Every time you came back smelling like a brewery or a whore or both, I died inside a little more—a little bit of me died every damned time! And *that's* time I could have been doing good instead of babysitting your ass!"

Bodinger was right of course. Castro knew it. But there is a code on the force. He saved his life; so a life, or career, should be offered in return. Besides, they were friends. Frank always remembered Susan's birthday, and Stan always invited him over for beers and brats. He was Uncle Frank to his kids. Stan even cried at the funeral of Frank's mother.

He saved his life.

"Not like this, Stan. Not now."

"When then, Frank?" Bodinger pleaded. "When a civilian dies from your neglect? When a cop dies from it?" He stepped closer, his eyes welling. "What if you missed, Frank? Huh? Ever think of that? You were impaired! What if you missed him and hit me? Then what? Who scrapes the shit up then, huh? Are you the one to tell Susan you screwed the pooch because you were drunk?"

"I wasn't drunk!"

"You're always drunk!" Bodinger growled. "You saved my life, but you're out of control! I can never pay back what you did, but you need to be clean before you get behind the badge. You think I want to do this? You think I *like* doing this? I'm the one that's gonna be scorned, not you! Not the *Great Frank Castro*!"

"That's enough."

"No, it's not."

"Stop."

"No more, buddy. This ends now. You're dangerous to be around. I covered it as best I could. I told them this was the only time, but that's as far as I go. You gotta deal with it from here." As Bodinger again went to leave, Frank, for the last time, said the same thing; but this time, he shouted it the length of the hall. "Don't you leave me to die like this!"

"You left me to die a long time ago, Frank," Bodinger said. "Now we're even."

"You can't do this! I saved your fucking life, you son of a bitch!"

"Well, buddy, paradise is blind," Stan said. Turning away for the last time, he told his former partner, "Nothing's ever easy. Heaven's hung in black, Frank. Heaven's hung in black."

Internal Affairs had leaned on Bodinger—hard. They assured him he'd get the fast track to detective and sergeant if he just told the truth. They promised Frank would go quietly. No jail time, no disgrace. He could even apply with county or state; they'd raise no stink. But thinking the same way as Bodinger, they wanted him off the city force. If the Westbrook kid had been Latino or African American, the incident could have turned into a powder keg for the city. He was a middle-class white kid who'd fallen out with his family, so the city turned the page, dodging a bullet in the process.

All Frank Castro felt was betrayal. His partner had sold him out. Sure, he wasn't the best by-the-book cop, but he saved the man's life, and he sold him out. The broken trust cut through his soul like shards of glass. Broken bonds that could never be repaired. As Bodinger walked away from him and out of the courthouse, all Frank could think of was he should have let the kid shoot before he took him down. Then it would have been his word against that of street trash. He would have killed the perp that took one of Austin's finest. However, the thought was fleeting. He could never do that. The gun was ready to take the life of a man he considered a friend, much less a colleague. He did what was right. He knew it then, and he knows it now. As it was, he was a pariah. A good cop gone bad that saved a life and ruined his own. Forever tragic and soon forgotten.

Frank Castro was removed from the force, and Bodinger got his promotion six months later. The next time they spoke, Bodinger was telling Castro that Tiffany Malvern had been murdered.

Ten years had passed.

Frank always thought he'd be dead by then.

33

It was going to take getting used to. The killing jar was no longer black. That prick Bodain suggested the color, looking up at the clear sky. Swaying to the Louisiana music he was hearing in his head, wearing his chains and beads, reeking of marijuana. The black man with the Cajun accent said, "Up there, man. That's what you want."

Adam hated his head games. The guy he found through criminals and the chop shop underground was a freewheeling, pot-smoking loose cannon with the intelligence of a Neanderthal.

"What?" Adam asked, agitated.

"The sky, brother, the clear blue sky. Paint that glorious bitch the color of the clear blue sky," he said, closing his eyes, extending his arms like he was readying for crucifixion.

Driving to the place was hard enough. Down Louisiana back roads, over dangerous bridges, looking for the turn that brought him in the middle of what was now a drying swamp, only to have to deal with a man who was obviously unbalanced. When Adam arrived in the H2, pulling his *normal* car on a trailer behind him, zydeco music was boiling out of the old garage like a seeping fester. He hated that music, and when Trevor Bodain danced out of the building, Adam wanted to kill him. He wanted to draw the Glock from under the seat and take the top of the idiot's head off.

However, he knew he couldn't. Bodain was good at his work even if he repulsed him as a human. His matted hair going in every direction, four gold teeth, rings on every finger, chains around his neck. He looked like a gangster rapper without good taste. When he suggested sky blue, Adam almost lost it. "Azure? You kidding me?"

"Oh, baby, listen . . . Don't mind if I call you baby, do you? You so damn pretty and all," he laughed.

Adam stared, not blinking.

"Chill, baby, chill. That blue is perfect, bro. I know you went out and done some bad shit. I can see it." He leaned close. "My mama and grandmamma worked voodoo," he said, touching his finger to the middle of his forehead. "I got the gift."

The first bit of work he did for Adam was customizing the inside, behind the front seats. A wall separating the cab from the rest of the vehicle, removing the rear seats, putting in a new floor, sealing off the doors and windows from the inside, and installing four speakers in the cramped area. Bodain knew the pretty white boy was up to no good, but so was everybody else in his line of work.

Don't ask, don't tell.

"You called me and said you needed this beauty painted. Now who in their right goddamned mind would take a stunning machine like this and fuck up the classic black?"

Adam wanted his gun.

"So I know"—he danced a step, celebrating his vision—"you may be in a little scrape and need to change that bad bitch." He stepped closer. "Not only do you need this bitch a color nobody's ever seen on a Hummer, but my price just went up. *Whoo!*"

"I don't give two shits about your price," Adam said, tired of the conversation. "Just paint the goddamn thing. Okay?"

"Cash on demand?"

"Always."

Bodain clapped his hands and danced some more. "Well, sweetness . . . Don't mind if I call you sweetness, do you? You are one pretty motherfucker."

Adam cringed.

"Let's me and you drop that trailer, get you on your way, so I can get started on this *proJECT!*"

216

"How long?" Adam asked.

"Five, six days. I'll call ya," he finished, growing serious for the first time. "Just bring ten grand in cash with you when you come back. You dig?"

"I'll have it," Adam said, without skipping a beat. When he turned twenty-one four years ago, the Tidy Man's three-hundred-thousand-dollar trust fund was open to him. He never touched it. He only used what he needed to get by. The Tidy Man oversaw the finances and management of his money. Taxes were paid and investments grew while Adam simply dealt with his life. The only extravagance he splurged on was the H2 itself, a year before.

And the twelve thousand he paid the blithering Cajun to customize it.

Home again. Naked. The music seething around him.

The song bore into him. The roaring music screamed the words that bit into his soul. Pounding on her door, the door he could never open, he beat with the rhythm. As the words erupted from the speakers, he yelled them at the top of his lungs.

"My symptoms keep me down, won't let me rise above the masses. The last chapter has begun, manic lust leaves the dream in ashes. On and on it keeps getting stronger,

can't deal with this any longer. I know life has betrayed me, that's why the world must pay! The whole fucking world-must-pay!"

He drank his vodka, laughing now. A year ago, it would have been impossible to laugh at the mockery of his life. He changed that. He was new. He had power. He heard the words again, laughing louder as the next lines came. He screamed along, then fell silent.

He sat in the floor of the black hallway, holding one of his jars. It was stuffed to the top with dead mice. He loved dropping them in and closing the lid, watching the time it took for the poor creature to succumb to the lack of oxygen. The best thrill came after there were already several dead rodents inside the jar, dropping a fresh mouse inside and watching it react to the stench of death before dying. Becoming a new ghost to the next unfortunate.

Bugs weren't enough. He'd grown beyond them. When he was in high school and a tough kid messed with him at his locker, he noticed the jar filled with dead bugs.

"Goddamn it, man! You're a creepy little shit!" he said, fists full of Adam's collar.

"Everything dies," Adam told him as he was pinned against the lockers. "Even you."

"What's that supposed to mean?"

"Nothing. Just know someday . . . You will die. And maybe you'll be remembered like them." He pointed to the jar. "I respect death. I embrace it. You avoid it. So who's the coward? You . . . or me?"

The freaked-out teenager couldn't handle it. He challenged Adam to get his ass kicked outside. Adam laughed at him. "You can't hurt me. My pain is more than you can understand. I live in misery every second of my life. You think a cut or black eye is going to change the way I feel?" He pushed him off, saying, "Go ahead, hurt me more. Make me feel *your* pain. I guess mine's not enough."

Nothing happened.

In later years, he wanted more. He went to the pet shop, telling the man he wanted a white mouse. He had to feed *his beast.* The man sold him a white mouse used to feed snakes, asking, "Got a boa?"

"No," Adam said, "my beast doesn't have scales. He's made of glass."

One by one, he dropped them inside, closing them in to suffocate. Clawing at the glass, sniffing their dead comrades gone before them. Each time, he'd get erect, having to satisfy himself without Deloris knowing. She didn't want him jerking off; it diluted his prowess. Something she couldn't have.

"Leave it alone," she screamed at him. "That's mine! You just carry it."

All her rules. The insane ones were the best. Like the color of her room. It was blue. The Tidy Man paid for the entire house to be painted, and Deloris wanted her room blue. A nice, soft, sky blue. Adam asked why blue.

"It's not blue," she scolded him. "It's azure."

"But it's blue."

"How many shades of red are there, Mr. Smarty-pants? Crimson, scarlet, cardinal. Well, there are just as many shades of blue. Navy, royal, and this is azure. My room, Adam, is azure. And you'll call it that."

To him, it was always the blue room. The place where childhood died and madness began. He thought of the last time he was in there. Fours ago, just after her death. That was when he began writing with chalk on the walls. He wrote what he felt and closed the door. It wasn't locked, but he couldn't open it. The door was sealed. Forged shut by his anguish.

As the song played, he sat against the door, thinking of his new mouse. It was going to be so fun watching the new mouse crawl, scratching at the glass, trying to find breath. Frank Castro was going to be a lot of fun.

34

Saunders looked around the room. There were Austin policemen and investigators from surrounding counties where bodies were discovered, like Hays County where the three boys were executed in front of an eye witness. They had gathered to hear Kevin Kerndon's updated profile.

"Gentlemen, I'm not going to waste time. Mr. Kerndon has read the new letter from D and has seen the crime scene photos. Kevin."

Kerndon remained in his seat as he spoke. "The new letter reveals more of D's personality. If what he says is true, he's kind of a sad figure. His mother was dominating and sexually abusive. That was a concern from the start. He most likely suffers from low self-esteem because of it, zero self-worth. He may even have self-inflicted wounds. He's most likely a cutter. His first letter to the newspaper was informative. He was simply relaying his information, letting us in to his *game* if you will. Now, in this new communication, he's taunting Sergeant Bodinger, which means he's healing his self-loathing. Albeit in the most horrendous way."

"He's getting confident," Cordova interjected.

"Absolutely," Kerndon replied, "and with confidence come mistakes. We now know he drives a black H2 Hummer, something we didn't know earlier. One of the young men he killed took a picture with his camera phone, by D's own admission. Something that would never have happened a few months ago."

Bodinger asked, "From what I understand about guys like this, they may take years to kill as many as he's killed in six months. Why so frequent?"

"He's been seething for years. Remember he said he killed his mother, but we don't know when that was. Could have been last Christmas, could have been in 2000. We just don't know. But the genie is out of the bottle now, and all the built-up steam that's been brewing is blowing the rest of his life away. He's becoming more and more obsessed. Before, it was a release. Now, he likes it."

A calm silence fell over the room. They knew he liked it or he wouldn't do it, but the way Kerndon said it, it was like a new page had turned. The animal now had a genuine taste for killing; that made him even more dangerous.

Bodinger remembered a program from the Discovery Channel about man-eating tigers. Tigers usually avoid humans, but once they become man-eaters, it changes them forever. All he could see was a renegade tiger passing up easy prey, searching for man. D was now a renegade animal with the taste for human blood.

"Before, he did these things out of a twisted sense of necessity," Kerndon said. "Now he does it because it's fun."

The temperature in the room dropped as all the detectives adjusted in their seats. Kerndon went on with more interpretation of D's psychosis, followed by each of the involved counties' investigators adding what they had. In the conclusion, Chief Short gave his take on the investigation then adjourned the meeting. As the room emptied, Kerndon took Saunders by the elbow, leading him away from the group.

"What is it?" he asked, knowing Kerndon was about to make a private point.

"Captain, this is just my observation and my experience in investigations like these that make me say this."

Saunders crossed his arms, listening. "Okay."

"All these investigators. All the people from surrounding counties."

"Yeah?"

"It's too much."

Saunders was confused. He'd felt, along with Short and Bodinger, that the more people looking at the picture, the easier it would be to find the hidden clues. He was taken aback. "Excuse me?"

Kerndon knew this was coming and was ready. "Captain, it's been my experience that if you start involving agencies from surrounding areas, the jurisdiction lines become battle lines. Every agency wants to be the one that finds the killer. A tug-of-war of sorts. Although it will not be on purpose, they will get in the way. You'll have statements taken from witnesses by three or four different agencies that will each interpret the words to mean something completely different. I've seen it, Jim, I know. Getting all these people involved will hinder more than help . . . Trust me."

Saunders weighed the words, realizing they made sense. "What do you suggest?"

"The first officers assigned to the case run it. Bodinger's a good man, and so is Cordova. They've been on it since day one. They know more than anybody. Use the surrounding county investigators as liaisons to funnel information here, to you, to Bodinger. Trust me on this. The more you use as a blanket search, the longer it's going to take and more crimes will pile up in its wake. And I don't just mean D."

Saunders fought with it then realized Kerndon was right; it made sense. Instead of each county doing their own investigation, they would conduct interviews and forward all information to his office for him and Bodinger to sift through. The final decisions would lie with them. Except for the three boys D shot, all the other victims were residents of Austin and Travis County. The bodies were found outside of that radius, but it was determined they were murdered beforehand. Saunders had every right to pull jurisdiction on all the surrounding counties except Hays— the boys were murdered there in front of a witness.

"Makes sense, Kevin," Saunders admitted. "I'll arrange it through Short. Won't be a problem."

Kerndon was relieved. "Good," he told Saunders. "Now go catch the son of a bitch."

35

Depression. It was the worst of times. It came to Adam like a foreboding black tide. It left him numb. Being numb was worse than being in pain. Unable to laugh, unable to cry. The searing music fell on deaf ears; the rum was only fueling the lack of feeling. He was stuck in the ugly in-between, not living and unable to die. A human horror film playing out before his own eyes. Not living would be better.

He walked naked inside the black house to the red room and fumbled through the closet until he found the gun. As Slayer blared in the background, he sat on the floor in the doorway of his closet, loading the 9 mm. The feeling of the gun in his hand was powerful. The first time he'd ever fired it at a person was taking the lives of the three boys in the woods in Hays County. It was in that flashpoint of destruction that he truly understood the power of the weapon in his hand. Without thought, he pulled the slide, arming the pistol, then placed the barrel in his mouth. Any twitch of the finger and all Austin could breathe easier. The demon would be dead. The dreams would die with him, and Deloris would no longer haunt his restless mind.

His thoughts drifted back four years, to another time he had dwelt on suicide. It was the day he buried her. The Tidy Man kept his distance, and there was no one left in his world. He was alone against the rest of his life. He wanted to die.

He drove downtown and walked out on one of the many bridges that crossed the portion of the Colorado River called Town Lake. It was late, after midnight. The rain had stopped, and the clearing night sky brought a drop in temperature. He shivered as he walked out on the desolate bridge that teemed with people during the day. The cold night brought only him. He climbed up on the rail beside a lamppost. The white light cast him in a long shadow that he studied for a second. He looked ten feet tall. He felt tiny on the bridge, under the canopy of stars, small and meaningless. The cold wind slapped him, making him shake all over. The water below looked comforting. He'd plunge in and sink into the frigid depth, letting its icy grip take away all the pain.

He was lost in the gravity of his mind when someone said, "What are you doing up there?"

Startled, his head snapped around to see a homeless black man. Layers of tattered clothes laid beneath his grubby face. His eyes were sunken, the corners swathed in a spider web of wrinkles. His beard growing white, his voice raspy.

"Huh?" Adam asked.

"I said," he said as he stepped closer, "what in the hell are you doing up there?"

"Mind your own business," Adam said, turning back to the water.

"I can understand that. But see, I live here. So if you jump, it's kinda like you killed yourself in my house," he explained. "Can't have folks killing themselves in my home. Now can I?"

Adam grew weary. He just wanted to fall off the bridge and save himself the trouble of living out the rest of his life. The Tidy Man could have the stinking trust fund; money was all the jerk thought about anyway.

"Why ain't you jumped yet?" the man asked.

"What?"

"Well, seems to me if you're aim is to kill yourself, you'd have done it by now. But here we stand. Me down here on this nice, strong bridge, and you up there freezing your balls off, thinking about why you shouldn't do it." He paused as they looked at each other. "So, friend, why haven't you jumped already?"

He had no answer. He didn't know himself what kept him glued to the lamppost. No friends or family. The one person who was everything and nothing was dead now. Even if he wasn't in the house when it happened, he felt responsible. The black water below could take it all away. So why hadn't he jumped?

"Something's got you tore up, I can see that. Happy folks don't look down at that cold water thinking about if it's gonna hurt or not. Hell, happy folks don't even come out here on a cold night like this. They stay home in a warm bed. Like you should be."

"You don't know anything about me."

"How can I? We just met. Name's Wilson. You?"

Adam hesitated before telling him, "Adam."

"Nice to meet you, Adam. So now we know each other, why don't you tell me what's got a nice young white boy standing up on that rail."

Adam just wanted him to go away. He wanted to deal with this himself. He didn't need life advice from a filthy vagabond. His mind said to tell the man off, run him away; but his mouth said, "I hurt."

"Of course, you do. It's all over your face. Even I can see that. What hurts, Adam?"

"Every second of every day."

"Whoa, that's big stuff, brother," Wilson said, walking closer. He was standing directly beneath him, close enough to pull his feet off the rail. However, his hands stayed buried in the pockets of his shabby coat. "Something got took away from you, didn't it?"

A puzzling question. Deloris was dead. He lost the only person his life ever had, but was she really taken away? What did he have that *could* be taken away. Jars of dead bugs and mice? A house he didn't own, a car he didn't buy, money he never earned? His temper started to seethe. Deloris *was* the only thing he had, and she was a pedophile. An incestuous, sexual freak who began warping him as soon as he dropped out of her. The sum of his life to that point added up to nothing. Angry, he turned, yelling, "Tell me why! Why shouldn't I jump?! Right now, you tell me why I shouldn't do this shit!"

Wilson's head tilted before he said, "The world heals, brother. The world always heals."

"Bullshit!" Adam screamed. "You tell me right now why I shouldn't jump! The world heals nothing! The world hates! The world loves pain and making you feel small, worthless, and rotten! Look at you! You homeless motherfucker, you live on a fucking bridge! So tell me right now, goddamn you. Tell me why I shouldn't jump!"

Millions of stars overhead waited for the black man to speak. He thought, choosing his words. Adam was ready to die in the icy lake, waiting on the words of the homeless wretch.

"Give it back."

"What?"

"If it hurts that bad, then give it back . . . All of it."

"Give what back?"

"If the world owes you—and by the looks of things, I think it does—take all that pain and give it back," he said again. "Fuck a bunch of pain. Give it back. Give it all back and to hell with who gets in the way."

Adam gritted his teeth. The words hit close to the truth, whatever that was. He had no reason to go on, but for some strange reason, the words made sense. He said nothing.

"Son, whatever's eating at your soul, whatever it is that makes you hurt like this has to have a way of getting turned around. Reverse it. You just have to look in the right place. When you find it, then give it back, brother . . . Give it all back."

His head was spinning. He'd been a victim since birth, never having the upper hand or the power to be anything else. Except for the jars. The creepy little kid that liked to watch bugs die behind glass was a man now. Able to make life-changing decisions. Wilson was telling him it didn't have to be this way. He could do something about it. Act on it.

Give it all back.

He climbed down. He knew what the vagrant meant, and he was right. If pain was what he was put on this earth to endure, then pain was something he could master. He could give back the misery and hopelessness of his childhood, shoving it down the world's throat. He was no longer the obedient pet of a sex-crazed parent who used his body and destroyed his mind. He could turn it all around like Wilson said. Reverse it. Take back what was stolen and give back the refuse of his indignation. He didn't know what it all meant or where it would take

226

him, but at least there was a purpose before him. He could feel it. He'd start with the house. He had to make it *his*.

"Ain't this bridge more comfortable than that damn post?" Wilson asked, smiling.

"Sure," Adam replied, feeling sheepish. "I was gonna do it," he told him. "I was gonna jump. My mind was made up. It was all I knew to do."

"And now?"

"Now I think I'll just start over." The image in his mind was that of the old Etch- A-Sketch game. When you wanted to start over, it was easy. Just shake it up, and the slate was clean. A great calm washed over him. He wasn't cold any longer. He felt like a warm robe had been wrapped around him, soothing him, comforting his troubled mind. "Need money?" he asked.

"Don't we all?"

He gave the homeless man all the money he had on him, forty-three dollars and twelve cents. "Nice talking to you, Wilson. Thanks for the words," he told him, heading back to the car he thought he'd never drive again, back to the house he thought he'd never see again. He'd go back, but he would start changing things. He'd make that pretty little house of horrors a *real* house of horrors.

"That fucking room is blue," he grunted to himself.

Inside the house, the walls were still white and cream, yet to be painted black. He needed something to mark them with. In a drawer in the kitchen, he found a small piece of white chalk some of the painters had left years before. He went to the blue room where he'd found Deloris's dead body just a few days before. The bed was made, the room as spotless as she liked. He stepped up onto the mattress; and on the wall above her bed, he wrote one word. Five letters, each a foot tall. He stepped off the bed and looked at it. It wasn't right, not yet. It was her word. He needed his own word to go with it. He thought, allowing himself to clear before the perfect match came to mind. He stepped back up, and beneath Deloris's word, he wrote his own. Again, five letters, each a foot tall. Stepping off the bed, he stood at the foot and read them together. They were perfect. Five letters each, symmetrical. He straightened out the covers and went to the door. Looking back, he read them again. Satisfied, he closed the door behind him, sealing off the room—and their words—forever.

As the memory played in his mind, he closed his mouth around the gun and wished for the strength to pull the trigger. He knew he was a monster. He knew he was out of control, and the only way this would end was with his death. But there was another part of him whispering in his mind. He wanted to do more. There was still a game that needed to play out.

Castro.

He'd watched him, he'd followed him. Castro was the very type of person he'd grown to hate over the course of his life. Frank Castro was no different than a schoolyard bully. A big brute that had no humility.

He lowered the gun.

Filled with a new sense of purpose, he went to the red room, flipping on the yellow desk light. The walls, papered with photos of the death he'd wrought, flooded his vision. He ignored them, opening his desk drawer that held his mementos. On top was the business card of Tiffany Malvern.

What a glorious subject she was. His best yet.

He stumbled in a drunken haze back down the hall to the dark living room. He turned on the black lights, and the walls glowed with all sorts of florescent drawings of dead women and his sordid poetry. He fumbled in the dark, finding the phone. Squinting to adjust his eyes, he found the number on the card and dialed, knowing he'd get the answering machine.

He left a message for Frank Castro then laughed at having taunted the bully.

36

Frank was sleeping in his office when the phone rang. He ignored it. The scotch in his system made him dull and slow. Sobriety had sucked, and now there was no reason to pursue it. Carmen even cut him off; he was getting too dark for her. The only reason he was sleeping in the office was that he hadn't paid the rent on his apartment in two months.

He woke just briefly to hear a voice on the machine then blacked out. He'd been drowning his sorrows, looking at the pictures of Tiffany she kept on her desk. A silly kid with her whole life in front of her. He cried, screamed, and broke things before passing out on the floor in his office.

However, it wasn't just Tiffany that made Frank crazy, it was his life. Before blacking out, he'd remembered the shooting and Bodinger's betrayal. He remembered his mother and his father wishing him well at the academy. He saw the waste that his life had become. Before he passed out, he saw his life before him as a long and barren landscape. Desolate and dark. His life played out like an afterschool special, full of mistakes and what-ifs. He remembered the partner that betrayed him, knowing all along that Bodinger had been right. He thought about the man he saw in the mirror a few days before. The hungry wolf he used to be on the streets before the streets were taken away from him.

He was a bad man. He was as bad as the scum he used to lock up. He was supposed to be an officer of the law, aimed to serve and protect. All

229

he did, however, was kick ass when it was convenient and put a good cop in jeopardy with his recklessness.

He passed out thinking of Bodinger.

The son of a bitch.

He woke to the phone ringing then fell back out before he could understand what was being said on the machine. He slept in a drunken stupor most of the night. Tossing through nightmares of dead demons and a life filled with regret. During one dream, he heard Bodinger tell him, "Nothing's that easy. Heaven's hung in black, Frank. Heaven's hung in black." The words woke him, as they always did. He traced them back to Lincoln, but the reality was that his old partner used them to bury a friendship. A reliance. Riddled with remorse for Bodinger, he woke up.

As Frank woke from his drunken slumber, there was a different feeling than usual. It was like he was trying to remember something from his sleep that was real and not a dream. The only thought that stuck around was *we're all gonna die anyway, so what in the hell's the problem?*

He rolled over, sitting up on his knees, wondering what the feeling was. Shaking the cobwebs from his brain, he stood on shaky legs in his office. He managed to step around the corner into the front office, past Tiffany's desk, making it to the restroom. After relieving himself, he wanted coffee—and the room to quit spinning. He readied the coffeemaker then flopped into Tiffany's chair to await the brewing.

What would today bring? Not much. The only job he had was the usual cheating spouse business, the kind Mrs. Cabbershaw had paid him so handsomely for, but he was afraid the old man that hired him for this round wasn't about to overpay for his services. He was also doing advisory work on alarm systems for small businesses going up and around north Austin. It was another gig he could trace back to the work he'd done for the old woman. At the moment, Frank was reasonably solvent and could afford not working for a while.

A vacation?

Maybe a trip to the Bahamas was what was called for? White sand, rum cocktails, hot local girls that would suck you blue for twenty bucks—and Frank could hit the town with several grand. Blow it all in a month of parties and decadence then come back to Texas with his head on straight and get busy.

Busy at what? He didn't know where to start.

Again, he looked across Tiffany's desk like he'd done for so long the night before. Whatever it was he was going to get busy on, she had to take priority. Somewhere deep in his soul, he felt somehow responsible. There was no money in it, but he could do the other jobs on the side to pay the bills. No, Tiffany was where it had to start. The more he thought on it, and her, the less the islands appealed. He remembered what her father told him. That he and her mother wanted him to find his daughter's killer before the police. He'd told the grieving man that it was his very intension to do so. The biggest drawback to the whole thing was Bodinger. His old partner made it clear that if he caught him sniffing around, he'd have him locked up. He knew it was no idle threat. He wasn't afraid of Bodinger or the lock up, but he damn well couldn't be of any use to the case if he was behind bars on an obstruction charge.

First things first. He'd go home and pay the rent he owed so he could at least clean up and start feeling human again. He'd wallowed in grief long enough. He went back in the small restroom and splashed cold water on his face. There he was again in the mirror. The man he used to be. The wolf was pacing impatiently behind his black eyes. He didn't like that guy looking back on him, like a bully from his childhood. But there he was, staring him straight in the eyes. Cold, pissed, and ready to do whatever it took.

"Tiffany," he whispered. The sweet kid deserved better than she got. He dried his face and poured a cup of coffee. He tried to straighten his disheveled clothes as best he could while sipping his coffee when he remembered the feeling he had when awoke on the floor.

The phone had rung. There was a message.

He checked the machine on Tiffany's desk, and there was indeed one message. He sat down with his cup then tapped the play button.

"Mr. Castro," the male voice said, obviously as drunk as he'd been earlier. "If you search your heart, you'll know who this is, so I'll skip the formalities. I wanted to fuck your secretary's dead body, but the little fuckers who skipped math class ruined my masterpiece. They ruined it for all of us."

The words hit Frank like a sledgehammer. His heart leaped in his throat, the cup of coffee dropped out of his hand to the carpeted floor. He stared at the machine like it was possessed by demons.

"I'm a tortured man, Frank, like yourself. I've researched you, Frank, and I know who you are . . . What you were. I know you're haunted by that bitch. What a sweet little cunt she was. I know she's in your every thought. She cried for you, Frank. Did you know that? She did. She swore you'd kill me. She swore you'd cut my heart out. Will you, Frank? Will you kill me? Cut my heart out? She said you would. She said you'd cut my fucking heart out, Frank. It would be welcomed, I promise. You see, the mind is a terrible thing. It houses ghosts that we can't exorcise. I'm full of them as I'm sure you are. Maybe that's it. Maybe I found your beloved Tiffany because it's God's way of pitting two tortured souls against one another. Does that sound right to you? Hmm? I watched you beat up those kids downtown. Impressive. I bet you were a handful back in your cop days. Funny how your old partner drew the task of finding me. I mean, of all the shit, right? Hahaha! What a small world it really is. It looks like it's just you and me in the end. The police have nothing. Besides, they're nothing more than ambulance chasers. Running late to my little parties. But you, Frank, you're different . . . Much different."

Frank's eyes began to bulge as Adam went on. He was squeezing the edges of the desk, fighting the urge to slap the machine against the wall.

"You, Frank, are dangerous. You don't have to play by their rules, and that makes me a little . . . Hesitant, to say the least. But I have the upper hand. See, I know you, but you don't know me. It's like the cat and mouse without the mouse knowing where the cat is. How does it feel, Frank? Being the mouse? Big bad Frank Castro, the bad cop with the bad habits, the bully of the block having to peek over his shoulder for a diseased little creep like me! Hahaha! And you've been working as a dirty picture taker for ten lousy years while the man you saved is running such a huge investigation? Oh, and let's never forget poor little Tiffany. Such a sad loss. Quite the cock tease, but you knew that, didn't you? Tell me, Frank, did you hit it? Did she moan beneath you as you rammed that big hard cock inside her soft body? Did you pound her like the cunt she was? I hope you did. But maybe she just teased you like all the rest of us. Maybe that's what tortures you the most. You never found out what the inside of her sweet little pussy felt like. That's what makes me shiver with delight, knowing that I know her far more intimately than you. I shared her death. What's more intimate than death? Nothing. And at the exact moment of her demise, mine was the face she stared into. I saw her fear, all her dreams and hopes, her mortality . . . Her life fade away. All you ever saw was her body. I can just imagine how maddening it must be. Let's add that slut to the mix too. Damn . . . It's quite a quandary, Frank, if I say so myself."

Frank stood from the desk, kicking the chair back against the wall, his chest heaving with emotion.

"I just want you to know one thing before I go. I know who you are . . . I know where you are . . . And I know what you are. And the only time you'll see my face will be . . . as you're dying. Bye for now, Frankie boy."

He turned the desk over with a huge crash. He kicked its legs until they broke off and threw Tiffany's chair through the window, spraying glass and furniture into the tiny parking lot.

"Go to hell!" he bellowed. "Fuck you, *you piece of shit*!" He fell on his knees where the desk once stood, screaming to the faceless psychopath, "You're a dead man! You hear me?! You're a *fucking dead man*!"

His chest was heaving as he turned, looking for something to break, something to throw, something to take his hatred out on. It was then he saw it. Lying on the floor, folded and waiting patiently to be discovered, like a long lost treasure. He saw it. It was then that the wheels in his head began to turn.

There on the floor, among the debris of his explosion, was a copy of the *Austin Citizen*.

37

Newly promoted detective Raymond Washington drew the task of tailing Frank Castro. Bodinger had gone to Saunders, requesting a tail be put on the ex-cop for his own good as well as the citizens of Austin. If Frank went anywhere near the families of the victims or the crime scenes, Washington was to arrest him on the spot, no questions asked. The young hotshot jumped at the opportunity.

The veteran detective Prince, also African American, warned the young officer, "Just don't think for a minute that it'll be that easy. The only way Castro will go with you is if he wants to."

"I'm okay, pops," Washington explained. "I can handle anything he's got. Trust me."

Prince laughed, "No, you better trust me."

Washington arrived at Castro's office early and saw the front window boarded up. He would have left, but the silver Z4 was parked where it had been the entire previous day. Whatever happened to the window, Castro was still inside. After a couple of hours of listening to dispatcher calls, he saw Castro exit the front door. He was clean, as always. Nice sports coat and white shirt, pressed jeans and expensive boots, cleanly shaven, looking like he had an appointment.

"Finally," Washington said to himself, moving his car through the strip mall parking lot, making sure not to get too close to Castro's BMW.

Frank sped out on southbound I-35, weaving through traffic like Tony Stewart. Washington's unmarked Ford cruiser zipped along behind

234

him, following a good three cars back, not to be conspicuous. Heading into Austin at eleven a.m. could mean anything, but to the eager young detective, it was a sign that things could get sticky. He was hoping Castro would go by the Crowder residence. He already had his speech rehearsed and his moves mapped out. If he tried anything tough, Washington would clamp down on it fast, showing Sergeant Prince he was more than able to hit anything Castro could throw.

As the city grew larger in front of him, Washington closed the gap, following a car behind, but in a different lane.

Castro wouldn't notice.

Frank took the upper level at the exchange and Washington casually slipped in front of him then allowed him to pass, hiding like a tree in the forest. He fell back another length as Castro took the MLK exit by the stadium. Not knowing where his lead was heading, Washington managed to file into the same turn lane, placing another car between them.

"Where the hell are you going?"

The light turned, and Frank turned right onto MLK, square in the middle of capital business. The car between them followed, so Washington trailed along, two cars back, as Frank went to the far left lane, stopping at the light in front of the Bob Bullock Museum of Texas History . . . with his blinker on. Still not understanding, Washington flipped on his left signal, waiting on the light. Castro turned left in front of the museum then stopped, turning into the parking garage.

"You gotta be kidding me," Washington whispered. "He's going to the museum?" Still two cars back, Washington also pulled into the line to go down the steep drive of the garage, noticing Castro dropping the top of the convertible. One by one, the cars stopped at the kiosk, shelling out the five bucks to park. There was a car between them when Frank stopped, handing the girl his money. Other cars were driving on the opposite side, up and out of the garage, past the same kiosk. Washington was fishing cash out of his wallet when Frank passed the booth then did a quick u-turn into the other lane going out. The tiny BMW was small enough that he was able to make the move in front of an oncoming car with no fuss. He simply spun the wheel and zip—he was heading back out as Washington was stuck between two cars going in. Besides, his vehicle could never make that maneuver. He'd need a full parking lot to do a U-turn. He was screwed.

As he sat demoralized, Castro stopped on the way out, directly across from him, no more than ten feet. "Tell Bodinger I said to wash his mouth out with gun powder," Frank said, smiling like the cat who just ate the family bird. "So long, dickhead."

Washington dropped his head. He could hear Sergeant Prince laughing already.

Glenn Young was working on a follow-up piece to the massive story he'd just broken two days before. Newspapers around the country were dying, and having a jump like this meant big bucks to the editors. Glenn was the only connection the city had with the Capital Hangman, so that put the paper head and shoulders above the electronic media for the first time in years. For the first time in ages, it actually meant something to work at the *Citizen.*

Glenn was alone in his cubicle, tapping on his keyboard, when a man walked in clearing his throat.

"What is it? I'm busy," he said, without looking up.

"I'm Frank Castro."

It took a few seconds, but Young stopped in mid-sentence, saving the information onto his computer before his head jerked up with a smile. The man, tall and broad shouldered, was wearing a sport jacket with jeans and expensive boots. "Frank Castro? Really?" he asked, almost giddy.

"That's the rumor."

He was blown away. It took less time than he'd expected. "Please, sit," he said, waving to the chair in front of his desk. "I've been expecting you."

"Oh really?" Frank asked, sitting.

"Oh yeah, this is an honor."

"Let's see where it goes before we start sucking each other's dicks," Frank said with a grunt, lighting a cigarette.

236

"Oh, uh . . . this is a nonsmoking building," Young informed him.

"Aren't they all?"

"Yeah."

"Does it look like I give a shit?"

Young chuckled, "I guess not. What can I do for you?"

"Information."

"Like I said, I've been expecting you."

"Why?"

"Because you need a place to start. And you're connected to the last victim. That's a party you can't miss."

Frank was still reading the reporter. He wasn't sure he trusted him, but he needed someone with information that was willing to talk. For now, at least, it looked like Young was bursting to unload. He exhaled smoke, saying, "Cops aren't gonna tell me shit, you know that."

"Right."

"I've done my homework. Seems you're the only other common denominator."

"Right again."

Frank found Young's coffee cup and poured the contents into his trash can then used it for an ashtray. Young laughed. "Man, you're a breath of fresh air. I love it! What do you need?"

"What do you have?"

"Letters from D."

"He calls himself D?"

"Yeah. And pictures too."

"Don't tell me," Frank said, "Bodinger squashed it."

"Like a bug under a tractor."

"More?"

"The last letter he sent went straight to Bodinger's house."

"No shit?"

"Yep. Wife opened it, freaked them all out. But it was only a copy," Young's face reminded Frank of what childhood was like. "I've got the other copy. He sent it to me too."

"That's why the big story."

"Why else?"

Frank sat silently for a few seconds then stood, saying, "I wanna take you for a drink."

"I thought you'd never ask," Young replied. "Let me get my stuff."

"Go ahead. I'll be outside."

As Frank turned to leave the cubicle, a small, wiry man with thick glasses stopped him, saying, "Sir, this is a no-smoking environment," his face screwed in a mask of distaste.

Frank took a long drag off the cigarette then blew smoke in the little man's face. "I know. I'm leaving now," he said, dropping the butt on the carpet, crushing it out with his shoe. "And I don't plan on coming back."

*

Lucky's. Frank's favorite bar in all of Austin. He was sipping his usual J. W. Black while Young nursed a whiskey sour. It was only mid afternoon, so they had most of the place to themselves and could speak openly. They sat at a table in the middle of the room so Frank could see Toxic Mike in case he needed a touch up.

Three attractive young women walked in. Young eyed them, telling Frank, "I love this town. Every year the freshman class rolls over, we get a new crop of strippers."

Frank shook his head. "Back to business, *dick*."

"Okay, sorry," diverting his eyes from the ladies.

"So he sent you the first letter after the first murder. Not the cops," Frank said, leaning back in his chair.

"Right," Young replied. "He said he trusted me to do the right thing. I called the cops, scared the shit outta me to tell the truth."

"Why?"

"This picture," Young said, sliding the photo of Amy Crowder hanging dead from a tree.

Frank looked at it; his stomach clenched. Not that the photo did it, it was that he knew sooner or later he'd have to see Tiffany's. The poor girl in the tree was horrible to look at, but the animal that did it was worse. He'd heard his voice, something neither Young nor Bodinger could say, and he wasn't telling anyone.

"That's just wonderful," Frank said. "Did she die on the rope?"

"Obviously," Young said, not understanding why he would ask. "Why?"

"Her face isn't discolored."

"What?" Young asked, spinning the photo around to get a better look.

"You ever find someone who was hung? Their faces are always either blue, purple, blood red, or nearly black. That girl's face is whiter than yours," Frank informed him, lighting a smoke with a nod to Toxic, who just shook his head. It was an obvious observation he knew the cops caught. Even if Bodinger missed it, the autopsy would have revealed it. She was already dead. Ten years of flatfooting was paying off.

He watched Young study the photo for what had to be the millionth time. The excited man he brought into the bar fell silent, realizing he was out of his league as far as investigation.

"Damn," he finally said, "that makes sense. The blood had already drained to her lower extremities."

"Yep."

"Fuck . . . me," Young said, looking into space.

"You know of any other injuries?"

"No," he answered slowly, as if in a trance. He'd looked at that photo so many times he saw it in his sleep, and he never noticed. This damned guy looks at it for four seconds and sees something so obvious he was ashamed at having missed it.

Son of a bitch.

"You see anything else?" expecting Castro to give him D's address and shoe size.

"Not really," Frank said, "but it's a start. He wants to watch them die one way then display them another. That's fucked up."

"You think?" Young jibbed.

"More," Frank told him.

Young sipped his drink then pulled out more letters from D. Another photo of a dead girl in a tree and ominous words. He almost ignored the words, telling Young, "What he does and what he says are two different things. When he's doing this shit, it's in the moment, it's what he's feeling, it's honest. Probably as honest as this asshole ever gets. But the words are different. He's had time to choose, to think about what he wants to say."

It hit Frank then that he had fallen for the same ploy on the answering machine. D had days to plan out his words. He knew serial killers are cowards at heart, and he'd never attack him one-on-one without a gun. That didn't ease his tension, but it shed a new light.

"None of the victims were related in any way, right?"

"Not in the least," Young told him. "The Crowder girl was a high school kid, the Brooks girl was out of school and working at Wal-Mart. Then of course . . . ," he trailed off for Frank to connect Tiffany himself.

"A real woman," Frank said. "No kid, no underling. A real woman with a life, living on her own."

"Yeah."

Frank thought. The victims were getting older. The three boys were collateral damage to D, nothing more, just as *he* would be if D had a chance. "I want to see the last letter."

Young recoiled. "You sure?" he asked, finishing the whiskey sour.

"Not the picture, just the letter," Frank told him, still not wanting to see Tiffany on the end of a madman's rope. Young slipped the paper from his folder and slid it across the table. Frank flipped it over and read:

Dear Detective Bodinger,

I hope you enjoy the photograph I've enclosed. I must say the three blind mice were quite a surprise. I was astounded that one of them had a camera phone he used to take a picture of my fun. I crushed it and dropped the fragments in several places all over the city. The shot he took only showed my vehicle, so in case you're looking for me that way . . . Need I say more? It's gone now. Sucks to be you, I'm afraid. The young woman was quite fun, more than the mice. I made myself come as her eyes dilated black. The mice got the privilege of watching me hang her dead naked body from the tree before I killed them. I wanted them to know who they were fucking with. I was going to let them die the same way as her, but there was

240

no sexual gratification in it. I decided to end them quickly. Call me a humanitarian if you must.

Speaking of fucking . . . I hope your pretty wife isn't afraid of me. See, I've had my gut full of older women, and there's nothing about her that makes my meat twitch. My tastes these days run more toward the younger of the bunch. Not that watching her fight for air inside the bag wouldn't be a hoot. It would be a hoot, don't you think, Detective? Stripping the old gal down to her pubes and watching her die inside my bag? Huh? Yeah, that would be a real hoot.

But not right now.

Now I'm more interested in the young ones. You see, I've had enough old pussy to last me five lifetimes. As a matter of fact, old pussy disgusts me. Let me ask you, Detective, are you a motherfucker? I am. Quite literally. My mother used to love to bend over and order me to fuck her like an obedient mongrel. I bet you never did that, Detective. I bet you've never dropped a load inside your mother's belly, have you? Ever go down on your mother, Detective? I have. It always tasted like death. My own. I died a little every time I touched her, and she liked to be touched. She died after I told her I couldn't do it anymore. She wanted me to fuck her, and I said no. She died that night. I guess I killed her, huh?

The last time I fucked my mother, she was dead. It was the best I ever had.

I guess I've said enough.

Tell the Cordovas and the rest of the boys in blue I'll be watching. As you're dying think of your mother,

D

As Frank read the words, he heard D's voice. The cadence was the same. Rehearsed. It was made to make him sound intelligent. But it wasn't the rhythm of his words that caught Castro's attention, it was the story. He'd been abused by his mother and his victims were getting older. Could Bodinger have made the same connection? Was he late to the party again?

"Who's the profiler on the case?" Frank asked.

"What?"

"Don't tell me you don't know who APD is using to profile this fucker. I'm not stupid, Young. Don't make that mistake, it ain't healthy."

Young saw dangerous intent in Frank's eyes and knew better than to tempt it. "Kevin Kerndon, some hotshot from Dallas."

Frank thought for minute before asking, "Teaches at SMU right?"

Young laughed. "Yeah. You know him?"

"Know of him. I read one of his books."

"Really?"

"I can read, asshole."

Young loved it. A real son of a bitch doing shit work for free. He wanted to follow Castro around like a sidekick, learning from someone who knew the world's evil firsthand and dealt with it. "I don't know anything about his profile. My guy on the inside can't get close enough."

Frank reread the letter then asked to see the first one again. He read it to himself.

Dear Police,
Tell her mother she died sweetly and most assuredly thinking of her.
I insisted on it.
I did not rape her; I want that known.
You'll find her in southern Burnet County.
There are no clues to help you, I promise.
Unless this new passion I've discovered subsides, there will be more.
I don't intend to stop anytime soon.
The reason is that the experience was even better than I had dreamed.
Most of my dreams are horrible.
This one was bliss.
I've been reborn; I am becoming something greater.
As it stands, I am thrilled with the new me.
As you're dying think of your mother,

D

"Your impression?" Frank asked, sipping his scotch.

"The guy's a nut for sure, but he's diabolical too. If evil does exist, this guy has it down cold."

"Nuts or evil, which is it?"

Incredulous, Young answered, "Both."

"Can't be."

"Why?"

"No, no," Frank said. "You're the hotshot reporter that's seen it all. You tell me."

"You're kidding, right?" Young asked, almost shocked.

"No," Frank said dryly. "Tell me why you think he can be both," he added, folding his arms, leaning back on the chair's two back legs.

Young felt like a student being taught something. When Castro first showed at his office, he just figured they would swap details then spend the day cursing Stanley Bodinger, but Castro was turning out to be something more . . . A lot more.

"Well," he started, "he's a murderer, that much is enough to get you burned."

"Go on."

"He flaunts it, he boasts about it. He fucking takes pictures, man, and sends them to the *goddamn* newspaper. Jesus, Castro, ain't that enough? Now you tell me he killed the girls before he hung them? That's some maladjusted brain matter, dude, I don't care how you read it."

Frank rested the chair back to the floor. Sipping his drink, he said, "If a real psycho kills because he feels it's the right thing to do, then that's just what it is, in his head. It won't matter a damn to him if you, me, or the tooth fairy knows about it. He won't care. He won't care because he lives inside his own head, with his own twisted logic."

Young felt a *but* coming on.

"But for someone to carry this shit out, with no hard evidence left behind. No DNA and no witnesses. Evidently he wears common shoes and has common tires on his vehicle. Bodinger told me they had very little to go on . . ."

"You spoke to Bodinger?" Young asked, in disbelief.

"That's mine."

The stare Young received made him pull back. "Okay."

"For a creep to do all that then take pictures and contact not only you, but the investigating detective personally eliminates your *nuts* argument."

"So?"

"You said it, brother. What else are we left with?"

Young felt a chill as he replied, "Evil."

Frank heard the voice again. Intoxicated, but quite coherent. He was measuring his words and his speech pattern. D was no imbecile killing because a dog told him to. Quite the contrary. D was a cold, calculating predator that preyed on the vulnerable.

Frank finished the scotch, waving to Mike for another.

"Evil, like Manson?"

"Why not? That little shit didn't corner the market on it."

"But who in their right frame of mind would do such things? I mean, surely he's imbalanced somewhere? Right?"

Again, Frank traced the lines to Bodinger about being a real *motherfucker.* "You are smarter than this, right?" Frank asked.

Insulted, Young sat back and downed his whiskey sour before saying, "I guess not. You seem to have all the answers."

"It's not about answers. It's about who you're looking for. And we are not looking for a nut. We're looking for a guy who had a bitch of a childhood that warped him. He's not crazy, Glenn. He's angry."

The light clicked inside Glenn Young's head. The word *crazy* gets thrown around too loosely. D wasn't crazy at all, no more than Jeffery Dahmer or Ted Bundy. He was acting out his emotions. Suddenly, the old renegade cop that got the boot by Bodinger and APD seemed a lot smarter than even he realized.

"You take some classes in this shit?" he asked.

"No," Frank said, swallowing half of his fresh drink. "I just know people." He heard the voice again then added, "And I'm starting to know this guy."

"But you can't get a lot from these letters and pictures as far as finding him, can you?"

"That depends."

"On   what?"

"You," Frank said, pointedly.

"Me? How the hell do you get that?" Young was genuinely confused.

Frank laughed to himself, maybe even let a small smile crack before saying, "You know what he drives, don't you?"

Young felt his heart skip. Castro already knew he had a man on the inside, so of course he knew what the vehicle was even if there was no picture.

"Why?"

"Because the cops found the place without D giving a tip. Means they either had a picture sent by someone else, with the vehicle in it, or someone saw it. Which one?"

"And they kicked *you* off the force?"

"Answer. Which is it."

"The kid with the camera never had a chance, they found no sign of the phone."

"D said as much. He smashed it."

"Right. But there was another kid that was lagging behind and watched the whole thing. That's all I know. I can't get shit out of anybody about the car, but I do have the kid's name. He saw it all, bro, and my guy has his name. Hard as hell since he's a minor, but I have it."

"And you haven't tried to talk to him?" Frank was amazed.

"You showed up today," Young replied, looking sheepish.

Frank settled back into his chair. Was that the way he wanted to go? A kid? Some junior high kid that watched that horrible shit, got grilled by Bodinger, and now would have to talk to him? There was no way the parents would ever allow it, he knew better. If they sat in on Bodinger's questions, the last thing they'd allow would be some private dick with a grudge to quiz their minor son.

"You have to get the make of the vehicle. No way the parents will let that kid talk to me. No way."

"Well, word is they're starting to ease on the information. They may be getting close to putting out a statement about that vehicle," Young said, feeling smart.

"How soon?"

"They're your old buddies, you tell me."

Frank knew if they were serious about letting the public in, the sooner would be the better. D indicated the car was gone, so the faster they had eyes looking for it, the more likely success would follow. Unless the model and make were ordinary.

"I need to know now, damn it," he told Young, in a matter-of-fact tone. "I have a guy in the car business that's good, and he can help, but I gotta know what we're looking for."

"Gimme a second," Young said, flipping open his phone. "If they're really going to open up . . . ," he said, dialing.

Frank liked him. He was a weasel; Frank could work with weasels because he always knew where he stood with them. Self-righteous types were the ones he steered away from; you could never trust them.

"Hey, it's me," Young said into the phone, as Frank waved for him another whiskey sour. Young leaned over the table as he talked, like he was looking for something written on the table top in invisible ink. "I need to know what vehicle the investigators are looking for in the D case." He paused for a while. "Because I *can't wait*, that's why." Another long pause as the drink arrived. He sipped then said, "This has nothing to do with a story, it's about something bigger. That's for me to know, I just need to know the make, man, that's it. Gimme that."

Frank lit a cigarette as he listened to Young grill his inside man at the APD. He knew all these reporters had their guys, their *reliable* sources. It was fun actually sitting in on a conversation that now, ten years later, he could appreciate. Ten years ago, he'd be slapping Young all over Lucky's by now. He smiled to himself. Time moves on.

"Damn it," Young said into the phone, "if they're gonna tell us in a couple of days, what does it hurt to tell me now? I won't write it! Didn't I just say that? Look man, I'm into you for a lot of shit, don't make me . . ."

Frank laughed. The greasy reporter was getting edgy. He loved it.

There was silence as Young listened to the man on the other end. Finally, he smiled. "A black Hummer," he said, looking up at Castro.

"H2, H3?" Frank asked.

Young put his hand up and nodded, asking, "What kind, two, three?"

246

He smiled again. "H2, decked in chrome. Got it, buddy. I owe you. Yeah, same as always, I'll call you. Later," he said, closing the phone.

"Black H2, chromed out," Frank said. "Know how many of those there are in this town?"

"More than I wanna count."

"Exactly. That's why the lockdown on the info. If they told the public, every soccer mom driving one of those things would be stopped at every corner. False alarms would never stop."

"Right," Young agreed slowly, understanding.

Frank sucked down the last of the scotch and extended his hand over the table, "Glenn, thanks."

Young shook his hand, asking, "Now what?"

"Now, I have a place to start."

Young drank a big swallow of his drink then asked, "Really, you to me. How did you know I had more, or could get more?"

"I read a piece you wrote after the Crowder girl. You sounded pretty sure of yourself about a few things. I figured you did. If you didn't, all I'd be out was a few bucks for a couple of drinks. Why not go fishing?" Frank said, standing.

"Catch anything?"

"Not yet . . . But they're biting."

Outside, Castro sat in his car thinking of the possibilities. Bodinger and the boys would be going over everything obvious concerning the H2. Fires, theft, vandalism. They'd scour the state looking for a late model, black H2 recently sold, bought, stolen, or been in a body shop. They'd pull VIN numbers and cross reference the DMV database. They'd interview anyone who'd ever seen a black H2 in the last two years. If it was out there, they'd find it. However, their way would take forever, there had to be another way. And Frank knew just the man to see.

38

"Thanks for meeting with us, Kevin," Bodinger told Kerndon, as he sat. He agreed to meet them for dinner at a restaurant downtown. "Kevin, this is my wife, Susan. Susan, this is Kevin Kerndon."

"I've heard a lot about you," she said from across the table.

"Only the good, I hope."

"You mean there would be otherwise?" she asked with a grin.

"There's always *otherwise*," he replied, glancing at Bodinger, who smiled, rolling his eyes. "It's not unusual to have dinner with a colleague, but it's really a pleasure when they allow me dinner with their lovely spouse," Kerndon smoothed.

"I know this is a little strange," Bodinger said. "I just wanted Susan to hear from someone else what I've been telling her." He glanced to Susan, "an expert."

Susan felt foolish. She knew there should be nothing to fear from the letter. D was a calculating fiend, not someone who would warn you he's coming. But she could never shake the sense of foreboding since the letter arrived. It haunted her every minute. The ghastly picture with the monstrous letter that was sent to their house. *Her* house.

"Don't tell me," Kerndon started, "you're scared."

Once again, Susan felt a little sheepish, hearing the words coming from what, to her, was a complete stranger. Ever since the letter and picture, she'd been leery of everything. Stan had assured her that there was nothing to fear, that it was just D's way of jabbing at them, him in particular. But she felt there was more to it than just a game of cat and mouse. She'd seen in the photograph what this monster was capable of and wasn't in the least bit secure in what her husband called a meaningless taunt. He'd told her that it was D's way of showing he was much smarter than the police, and him in particular.

The waiter came and they placed drink orders. Bodinger, a beer; Susan, a margarita; and Kerndon ordered a 7 and 7. When the waiter left, Bodinger continued. "Kevin, I know the letter coming to my house . . . our house," he said, peeking at his wife, "was simply a way for him to tell me he's smarter than I am. I know I'm the last person he wants to meet up with, so it was nothing more than an insult to me personally."

Kerndon nodded.

"Susan's just a little concerned that it was more than that."

Kerndon stretched his arms out on the table, saying, "Susan . . . If I may?"

"Of course," smiling.

"Susan, what you have to understand, what we all have to understand, is that this man is not functioning with a normal psyche. I've been studying these types of predators for over thirty years . . ."
"Thirty years?" Susan asked. "How old are you?"

"I'm fifty-two. But I've been interested in serial killers since my early days in high school. Fascinated, really. What makes them tick? What sets them off? Why do they do what they do, what makes them see the world the way they do? "And how do they see it?" she asked.

"For the most part, they see themselves as an island, an island in the middle of a hostile and uncaring ocean. The rest of the world is the ocean, and they're the only true sense in an otherwise insensible existence."

"That's sad."

"But that's not where it ends. Millions of people feel the same way. Society breeds that kind of rationale. But we don't have millions of serial killers running around murdering willy-nilly anything that moves. People are basically decent by nature. You may think you'd love to kill the guy that cuts you off in traffic, but in reality, you'd never dream of actually doing it."

The waiter returned with their drinks, Bodinger telling him to wait before coming back for their food order. Bodinger's face was solemn, and the waiter took that to mean a serious conversation was taking place. He was correct.

"So what makes them different?" Susan asked.

"That's the question, isn't it? Why do they feel it's not only necessary to kill, but justifiable to do so? D started out groping for identity. That was his motive, his cry for help, as it were. Now, excuse my language, now the son of a bitch just likes it."

Susan readjusted in her seat, uneasy.

"The man isn't crazy," Kerndon continued, "and for him, it has nothing to do with morality. It's about justification. He feels justified in what he's doing even if he knows it's morally wrong."

"Justified?"

"Why, yes, to himself anyway. That's as far as he thinks. That's as far as any of them think. A serial predator is the most selfish being on the planet. The murders give them a satisfaction that they deem more important than the lives of the victims they destroy."

"That's not making me feel better," she explained, stirring her drink.

Kerndon understood and decided to start over. "Okay. Like I said, I've been studying these kinds of criminals for thirty years. I'm here to tell you they're like snowflakes, no two are alike. There may be tons of similarities, but there really are no two alike. Some use knives, guns, others strangle or bludgeon. Our boy suffocates. Some write letters, others say nothing. Each one of these people is unique in his own way. Sure, they're all vicious, calculating opportunists who feel zero empathy for society, but you must understand—and this is very important—the one thing that they all have in common, all of them, is that they're cowards by nature. That's why they strike out of the blue at an unknowing target. They *must* have surprise in their attack to ensure success. Susan, and I mean this from the bottom of my heart, with total honesty, the absolute *last* person D is going to come after is you. You're a cop's wife. I'm sure you have and know how to use a firearm, and you're house is very secure. Those are not things a serial predator is attracted to. Besides that, he warned you. These type of killers aren't prone to advising someone they want to kill them. It defeats the purpose," Kerndon finished, sipping his drink.

"So what do we do?" Bodinger asked.

"What does your gut tell you to do?"

"Change nothing," he answered flatly.

"Exactly."

"Nothing?" Susan asked.

"Absolutely nothing," Kerndon told her. "Think of this guy as a terrorist. What did the government tell us after 9/11? Don't change the way you live your life. If you do, the terrorists win. This is exactly the same situation. D never sent that letter as a warning that he's coming. Again, that defeats the purpose. He's never, ever going to come after you or Stan. This is a game to him, a ploy to get you to live in fear, change your life in some way. Even if he never sees either of you again, if he knows you're scared and living in terror of what he might do . . . Well, that's the very definition of terrorism."

"I can see that," Susan admitted.

Kerndon knew that at some point Susan Bodinger must have been a stunning woman. Even in her midforties she cut a handsome figure of femininity. He thought about how she must have looked twenty years ago. Blond, tanned, and young. She would have been a sure target for D. Even though the letter stated it was his mother that turned the screws in his head, he seemed to like preying on younger women.

Old pussy disgusts me.

"But he knows where we live," she rebutted.

"That's no stretch," Kerndon said. "He most likely found that out the same way he located each of his targets. Best we can tell, he knew where each of his victims lived. He simply finds who he wants and follows them, tails them home. I'm sure he did the same thing to Stan."

That sent a chill down Bodinger's spine. Thinking about any number of days he'd driven home assessing how to catch the creep, while the very son of a bitch was tailing him. He felt small.

"D's been out of control his whole life because of his mother. He said he killed her, but we may never know that to be true. Now, he has control, at least control as he sees it."

"And to him, that's all that counts," Bodinger added.

"Exactly."

"And his control, it's over us?" Susan asked.

"Yes, and control over each victim. Control is power and power is very intoxicating. Right now, D's drunk on power. And he likes it. These men have never been in power, in any way. Now, through their crimes, they feel real power. Nothing says power more than having the decision of life and death over another person."

The conversation fell silent as Bodinger took the opportunity to wave over the waiter. Each ordered, and he was off again while Kerndon continued. "The only reason he shot those three boys was because they were in the wrong place at the wrong time. D selects his victims in a very methodical way. He sees them, follows them, and knows where and when they do everything. *They* are unsuspecting. You and Stan are not. Trust me, Susan. You are the absolute last woman D will ever come after."

"I told you," Bodinger said to his wife.

He'd felt shame for not being able to assure her. She'd been with him for all these years, waiting for him to come home, knowing each time he left he may never make it back. She always stood by him. Even through the fiasco with Castro, she never wavered. This was the first time his being a cop wasn't enough to make his wife feel secure. In fact, it was his job that had her anxious. Without him investigating D, she would never have been looped into the sordid mess.

She smiled at Stan. It was a good smile, the one he'd been waiting on since the letter showed up. He knew that smile. It said everything was all right; she was good. He hated that it took a profiler to ease her mind, but at least she was comfortable now.

The food came, and they spent the rest of the evening laughing politely and enjoying a good meal, trying to forget that there was a monster loose in their city. A monster who liked watching young women suffocate, naked and bound. Bodinger paid the check and bid Kerndon a farewell. "Thanks, Kevin. I think you did the trick."

"You know I'm right?"

"Of course. She just needed to hear it from someone else. Thanks again," Bodinger said, extending his hand. They shook and Kerndon went to his car, leaving the Bodingers by Stan's Taurus. "Ready to go?" he asked.

Susan was tired now. She'd been living in a constant state of anxiety ever since the letter arrived. Now, hearing the profiler lay it out so clearly, she relaxed for the first time and realized just how exhausted she was.

"Let's go home, baby," she told him. "I really need to get some sleep."

Stan liked that. She'd been an insomniac lately, and seeing his wife's eyes looking sleepy for the first time made him smile inside.

"Home it is, sweetheart, home it is."

As they left the parking lot, they drove past a blue Hummer parked at the entrance.

An *azure* blue Hummer.

He couldn't believe what he was seeing. It was the first time he'd laid eyes on her. Bodinger's bitch wasn't what he thought she'd be. He envisioned some dark-haired woman with a middle age spread. Susan was not at all what he expected to climb in the car next to the cop who was looking for him. She was tall, lean, and very attractive. Her long, strawberry blonde hair flowed with the wind. It was like seeing Deloris all over again. He shook inside the Hummer, killing his music. Memories rushing back like a tidal wave. Deloris coming to him in a fury, like a swirling specter from hell.

That last night, she'd pleaded with him to come to her bed.

"No!" he'd screamed at her. It was the first time her eyes ever showed fear of him. She even trembled.

"Why?" she asked, her lips contorting in anguish. "You have your precious money now? Is that it? Is that it, Adam? You have the goddamned trust fund and you don't need me anymore? You off to find some young teenybopper to fuck so you can leave me alone?"

"No!" he'd yelled, leaving for the door. He just wanted to go, to get away, to breathe fresh air.

"Is it because I'm getting *older*?!"

"It's because you're my *mother*!" he screamed again, stepping toward her, causing her to back away. "You sick bitch! You're my *mother!* You've been fucking your own son for so long, you think it's normal!" he yelled, tears burning his cheek. "You're not normal, *we're* not normal! This is sick! *You're* sick! I don't even know what normal is!" He stomped toward the door. The last thing he said before leaving was, "I'm twenty-one. I'm a grown man. But all I still am to you is a living sex toy. I can't do it anymore, *mother* . . . And I won't. I'm done with it. I'm done with you."

He pounded the steering wheel. Why did she have to look like her? Of all the women in the world, why did *she* have to look like her?

39

Tully Pritchard usually got to his office at Home Town Financing, on the east side, around ten o'clock. Frank Castro knew this. Tully had received a call from his old buddy the day before, telling him he needed to talk, that he was *in the market*. Tully and Frank had a good relationship. Frank had great coke connections and Tully had the means for a burned-out cop to live over his head. Tully was excited about the call. It meant Frank wanted to buy something. Therefore, he'd be willing to barter.

Bartering with Frank Castro was one of Tully's favorite hobbies. Once, he got Frank a reprocessed speedboat for a quarter of the market value. In exchange, Frank landed him a supplier of Peruvian snow at prices equal to local pot. It was great for a year, before the coke runner got busted and sent to the Telford Pen for a dime.

Win some, lose some.

Frank told him he'd be there at opening, so Tully made sure he got to the office early. The coffee was brewed with Kahlua on the side, and he made sure the sexy Candy was going to be available in case Frank needed some creature comfort. Candy was a temp that Tully snagged from a local strip club, who worked on commission during his big deals. She was willing to do whatever was needed as long as she got her cut, be it money or drugs. The five-eight, leggy brunette stormed into the office at ten till, ready to help seal the deal.

"Tully, I'm here!" she called, entering the office. "Is our boy here yet?"

"Not yet, baby, but come in and get comfortable. Frank will be here any minute."

She entered Tully's office wearing a skintight, red miniskirt with a black silk blouse that was at least a size too small. Her ample breasts were pushing the bounds of restriction beneath her overflowing lace bra. "Did I dress well enough?" she asked.

The thirty-eight-year-old slightly built Tully stammered, "Uh . . . Maybe not sleazy enough, but it'll have to do. If we score some good shit, you and me are outta here for the weekend, baby."

"*Yea!*" Candy squealed. "Is he as handsome as you say?"

"Yeah baby, just like you like. He's Cuban…tall, dark, and dangerous. But don't be too aggressive. Frank likes to think he's classy. He's a scumbag like me, but he has an illusion to uphold. Got it?"

"Got it."

The two passed the next couple of minutes making out on Tully's desk before they heard the door open. "That's him, sweetie, act pro," Tully told her, pushing her off his lap.

Frank walked through the receptionist's area then around the corner into Tully's office. There was his old friend at his desk. Wearing a bad leather coat with a black silk shirt and gray tie. The weasel was faking paperwork while the tail of the month secretary stood over the coffeepot.

"Frank!" Tully said, looking up. "Good to see you, buddy. Come in, have a seat." Candy turned, licking her lips and posing by the coffeemaker like a cheesy velvet painting. The two were impossible. If Frank had been in a better mood he might have laughed, but he was feeling dark and determined. He wasn't in the mood for Tully's usual bullshit.

"We need to talk, bro," Frank said, void of emotion.

Tully was slightly startled. This wasn't the Frank Castro he was expecting. The guy he knew always came in smiling with a list of phone numbers and an appetite for pleasure. This guy looked like a son of a bitch. He looked like Frank. Pressed jeans, boots, sport jacket, clean-shaved, and smelling good, but the expression was wrong. If the eyes are indeed the windows to the soul, Tully was looking into a very grim person. He immediately told Candy to leave, saying, "Hey, gorgeous, take a pill or something. Give me and Frank a second to catch up on old times."

Candy didn't catch on and went into her ploy. "Would you like cream in your coffee, Mr. Castro?" she said, pouting her lips and exposing enough cleavage to embarrass Hugh Hefner.

"No, no coffee," Frank said, without looking at her.

Tully was catching a serious vibe. Something was working against him and he needed to get Candy out of the way. "Baby, please. Wait outside."

"But you said . . ."

"Candy!" he barked, attempting to sound tough. "Please . . . outside," he said, gritting his teeth, rolling his eyes to Frank. She finally caught on, after really looking into Frank's eyes. He looked menacing. On closer inspection, she could feel the energy coming off him and had no problem leaving them alone. As she left, Frank closed the door behind her.

Confused, Tully walked around his desk and sat on it, in front of Frank. He knew that Frank knew how he operated, so none of this should have been a shock. The only other explanation was that Frank needed something very special. Maybe he was embarrassed?

"I need something, Tully," Frank said, standing in front of him.

"Of course you do, why else would you be here?" Tully chuckled.

"Something particular."

"What? Like a redhead?"

"No, stupid," Frank said, pacing to the door.

Tully ruminated then said, "Oh, I get it. More than one. Let me check my numbers, maybe—"

"No."

"Maybe Candy's got some friends up at this hour."

"No, damn it," Frank interjected.

"Particular, huh?"

"No girls."

"Maybe that ventriloquist chick with the hot dummy?"

"Shut up."

"She's pretty hot. And that dummy ain't bad for a hunk of wood, let me tell ya."

Frank stepped to him, "Haven't you heard what I said? *No girls.*"

Tully pulled back. His mind jittered trying to think. Then, as it floated by him, he tried to ignore it. The thought was too over the top to consider. However, being who he was, he had to say what he felt.

"You're scaring me, Frank. What's wrong? You start pitching for the other team?"

Frank's eyes narrowed.

The stupid shit!

Quickly, he bent down and took Tully's ankles in either hand, pulling him off the desk. He crashed to the floor, landing square on his ass, nearly breaking his tailbone.

"*Aagghh!*"

Frank dropped to a knee beside him, putting his hand beneath his chin, he shoved his head back hard into the desk. *Thunk!*

"*Owww!*"

"This ain't fun and games, dickwad. This is all business, and I need your utmost attention. *Comprende*?"

"You broke my ass, you *shit*! And you cracked my fucking skull!"

Candy opened the door to see what the commotion was. Frank looked at her from the floor, saying, "He'll be with you in a minute, legs. Why don't you wait outside."

Tully croaked, while wincing in pain, "It's okay, baby. Really, it's good. We're getting reacquainted." Candy was hesitant, but did as both men said and left, closing the door. She sat at her make-believe desk, waiting for more.

More was coming.

Frank stood and walked around the office, looking at the pictures and certificates adorning Tully's dark, paneled office. He was looking at a picture of Tully next to Matthew McConaughey. They met at a bar during the South by Southwest music festival some years earlier. The walls were covered with Tully schmoozing with all kinds of celebrities from Quentin Tarantino to the WWE wrestler the Undertaker. Tully was the guy in Austin to know if you needed to know someone in Austin. Frank hated doing what he did, but he needed Tully's full attention. He was prepared to do whatever he had to. This was for Tiffany.

He went back, helping his friend to his feet, settling back at his spot

258

on the desk. "Look at me," he said. When Tully was able to focus on him, he said, "I'm looking for a black Hummer."Tully knew it was the wrong thing to say, but the words shot out before he could drag them back. "Well, let me call Candy back in here, and you can pretend she's black."

"*Son of a bitch!*" Castro exploded, jerking Tully up by his leather coat and throwing him completely over his desk, crashing through the plate glass window behind him. Tully landed with a thud in the back parking lot in a shower of shattered glass. He rolled over, cutting himself with every move, then fell on his back, staring at the sky.

Frank stood at the desk, admiring his work. He didn't know the wolf was still so strong. He walked out of Tully's office to see the sexy Candy standing, shaking at the massive noise. He winked then said, smiling, "Be right back, baby," exited the building then walked around to the back lot.

When Frank arrived, Tully was on his hands and knees. "*What the hell? Have you lost your fucking . . .*" was all he managed before Castro picked him up by his collar and pants, throwing him back through the broken window into the office he'd just flown out of. He skipped across his desk, crashing on the floor in front of it. Another pained howl echoed through the open window. Frank straightened his jacket, composed himself, then walked back around the building, reentering the front.

"Told you I'd be back," he purred to the shaken strumpet. "You might want to hold his calls, gorgeous, I think he's gonna be awhile," he said, entering the office, slamming the door. Candy left, not wanting to be a witness to a crime scene.

"*Have you lost your fucking mind?*" Tully bellowed, as Frank again jerked him off the floor and slammed him on his desk, knocking his computer to the floor where it died in an array of sparks.

"Listen, you sniveling little shit," Frank barked, "I need your attention! Do I have it now?"

"*Do I have a choice?*"

"No!" Frank yelled, shoving him off the desk, smashing into his chair, overturning on it to the floor with a great *thump*. He walked around the desk as Tully crawled away screaming, "*No mas, no mas, motherfucker! I don't want no more! You goddamned maniac!*"

"You gonna get serious?"

"Jesus, Frank! *What the hell?!*"

"You know the Capital Hangman killed Tiffany. Don't act like you don't."

"Yeah, so? What the hell's that got to do with me?"

"I'm gonna find him. I'm gonna find him if it kills you."

"*Me*? What the hell?" Tully asked, scurrying to his feet. He fell against the wall, spilling the coffeepot, burning his hand. "*Aaaagghh!*"

"Shut up, Tully."

"What's the matter with you? You come in here like Hurricane Frank, breaking shit, killing me?! What the hell's your problem? What the fuck do you *want*?!"

Finally.

"He drives a black Hummer," Frank said. "An H2, chromed out."

"Jesus, Castro. So do about six thousand other people," he said, brushing the glass out of his hair. He tried to sit on the desk again, but it was too painful. He quickly sprang back up.

"I ain't looking for six thousand other people," Frank said, turning. "I'm looking for the asshole that killed Tiffany. He's good. He's got the cops chasing their tails. He even sent a letter to Bodinger's house talking about Susan and how she'd look dying in his bag."

"Bag?" Tully asked, still in a daze from the onslaught.

"Forget it," Frank said. "That's not the point."

Tully stiffened. "He sent a nasty letter to Bodinger's *house*?"

"Yeah. And Stan's still clutching at straws. They got nothing, no prints, no DNA, nothing. Just a kid who saw his ride," he said, pulling a framed picture of Tully and Sheryl Crow from the wall.

"Don't tell me," Tully said, waving his hand. "A black Hummer."

"Exactly," Frank answered, walking back with the picture. "Only thing is, Tully, he knows the cops had a witness. He knows they know he's in a black H2."

"So?"

"So my man about town, I'm sure he changed it. The letter to Bodinger said it was gone. I'm betting it's not."

"No?"

"No."

Tully was still hurting all over as he walked to the coffeemaker. Casting an eye at the broken window, he said, "This shit's gonna cost, asshole," as he reached below the table and came back with a bottle of Crown Royal. Pouring a cupful, he offered the bottle to Frank.

"Why not?" Frank said. He took the bottle, taking a long pull from it, then put the cap back on, setting it on the desk.

Tully let the warm liquid heat up his belly before asking, "What makes you think he didn't ditch it?"

"Because it's not a Volkswagen we're talking about, and he's not stupid. He knows that Hummer's red hot and selling it is not an option. Burning it, dropping it in the lake, leaving it on the road, none of those fit this guy. He's too smart for that. It's an H2, not a Honda. He didn't say he got rid of it, he said it's gone." He slipped the frame beneath his jacket, saying, "It's gone, but it ain't gone."

"You think he stored it?"

"Not quite."

The idea came to Frank while he was sitting in his apartment, reading a copy of the letter to Bodinger that Glenn Young gave him, for a price.

Good coke connections come in handy.

He read the letter then listened to the taped message from the office answering machine. He heard the voice, read the letter, then started the entire process all over. He knew the answer was there. He was privy to something Bodinger didn't have. He had the guy's voice. D was drunk during the call, that much was obvious. As a fellow alcoholic, it's very easy to notice certain traits, and D was definitely a working drunk. Being an alcoholic himself, Frank understood that sometimes ideas seem great while under the influence when otherwise they'd never be considered. D knew the cops had a tip because they found Tiffany and the three boys without his communication. Someone had to either witness the murders or find the scene on their own. Obviously, he felt someone had watched because he said the vehicle was *gone*.

Why would he say that?

If he knew the cops had a lead on his car and he wanted to ditch it in some way, why tell them? You'd just do it and lay low. But he made the effort to send the death photos to Bodinger along with the letter that told them the car was *gone*.

Why?

Frank reread the letter a hundred times, listening to D's sickening voice so much he wanted to puke. He said Tiffany told him he'd cut his heart out.

You goddamn right, I am!

But he was trying to figure out what was going on inside that shit-filled head of his. Why tell Bodinger you got rid of the vehicle? Why tell him? Why say anything about it? Why?

If the cops truly had a witness who saw the Hummer, there was no way they'd have been close enough to get the license plate number. So all they really had was a white male driving a black H2, year unknown.

After another belt of J. W. Black, it clicked.

"Tell them it's gone when it's not," he said to himself. "Get rid of it without getting rid of it." D was smart enough to know that if Bodinger knew what he drove, he'd have to ditch it. But being the smart guy that he is, he'd never try to sell it or destroy it. That left paper trails and investigators.

"You hide something in plain sight," he told the letter before him. "You either chop it or change it. Either way, it's not what they're looking for." Frank stood, walking to his front door. He opened it, letting the warm Texas autumn air fill his lungs. He knew what happened. He knew D never destroyed the Hummer or sold it, like what the APD was surely investigating. No, D was smarter than that. He still had it. It was just different now. He was too smart to take it to a local body shop; they keep records. He'd never trust a shade tree mechanic, he'd have to kill them to shut them up and that was too dirty and left loose ends. He needed someone outside the law, someone with something to hide himself. He needed someone with secrets.

He needed a chop shop.

And one as far from Austin as he could find.

*

Tully finally found a comfortable spot and sat on the corner of his desk. He was pissed that his friend found it necessary to break his ass to get him to help him with his work. He'd met Tiffany a couple of times, and he liked her. Hell, he thought she was hot and wanted to try and hit it, but Frank always stopped him, like some sort of mutant big brother. If catching her killer was what Frank was all about, he'd be more than happy to help. Frank didn't need to strong-arm him.

At least not yet.

"So what are you saying, Frank? It's gone, but it's not gone. What the hell is that shit?"

Frank crossed the room, looking out the broken window. He said slyly, "He had to make it disappear." Looking back to Tully, he added, "Disappear without it being gone."

"Dude, I ain't feeling like riddles right now."

"He told Bodinger it was gone. He's way too clever to sell it or ditch it. They'd have him in a week, even if he drove it a thousand miles away. He's getting arrogant, thinks he's smarter than everybody. No, the smartest thing and the safest thing is to keep it, but make it different. Make it . . . not what they're looking for." He walked to Tully and stood in front of him once again, saying, "He either chopped it or changed it. That's why I'm here."

"What? Me? Why?"

"If you insult my intelligence again, I'm gonna staple your tie to your forehead."

"You're being a dick!" Tully said, "What is this shit?"

"I need some names, bro."

"You need more than that, man," Tully protested, walking from the desk. "Frank, you need a prick with a death wish, that's what you need. And a straight jacket."

"But I got you."

"Then you got shit."

Frank dropped the picture from beneath his jacket, the glass shattering around the photo.

"Oh man, do you have to play the role?" Tully bitched.

"Gimme a reason not to," Frank said, walking to the wall. He started flipping pictures off the wall and letting them smash on the floor. One by one, each celebrity photo taken with Tully Pritchard fell on one another in a pile of glass and wood.

"Okay, stop, goddamn it," Tully said.

"Why, bitch? What are you gonna do about it? You want me to stop, fucking stop me."

"Goddamn it, Frank, it ain't that easy!"

"Anything's easy if you want it bad enough," Frank said, breaking a picture of Tully and Brad Pitt.

"Bro! These are criminals! You want me on their shit list?"

"You wanna be on mine?" Frank asked, cutting a stare that chilled Tully to the bone. Frank was another of his contacts that made him who he was. He always knew Castro was a little left of normal, but the two had always done beautiful business together. He'd never had a cause to see Frank in full armament. Now that he did, he didn't like it one bit.

"Look at it this way, Tully," Frank said. "If you give me a couple of names, maybe they come to see you, maybe they don't. But right now, I'm here, and this ain't a medicine you wanna sip."

It was more than a threat; it was a promise, and Tully knew it. He knew how Frank felt about Tiffany. So as he saw it, he could deal with the devil now or later.

Later was sounding better all the time.

"What, what, *what*?!" Tully implored. "What do you want, Frank? I'll tell you, just stop fucking up my shit."

"I need someone that's not close."

"Fuck you, man! This shit is outta hand!"

"Good, call Bodinger," Frank said. "Tell him how I harassed you. Then I can tell him about your coke habit and the skim deals you work with the insurance companies."

"That's low, bro, even for you."

"Let's face it, Tully. You have clients and friends. You have money deals and all sorts of things that might get dropped if the wrong shit hits the street. The way I see it, you got everything to lose. But me, I got nothing. Career sucks, cops hate me, got no money, drink too much, and my best friend got snuffed by a raving lunatic. I got nothing to lose, brother. And you got everything right in front of you twisting in the breeze if I don't get what I want," Frank finished, taking a few steps back. "I've broke about everything in here, all that's left is you, brother. Your call."

Tully thought. Frank was right. If certain people got wind of some of his actions, he'd lose thousands of dollars, not to mention the contacts that he was planning on making millions with. And besides, getting the shit stomped out of him by Frank Castro wasn't one of the things on his *to-do list* when the day started.

"You're a son of a bitch, you know that?"

"It's for Tiffany, bro. I'm going to do what I have to. Talk to me."

Tully went to the window, peeked out at the brilliant morning through the broken glass, saying, "The Ramirez brothers are—"

"That's San Marcos, too close," Frank cut him off. "I know all the locals, Tully. I could do that myself. I need something outside the loop here."

Tully turned. "Look, Frank, I'm really not the guy you need to be talking   to."
"Then who is?"

He swallowed hard, scratched his head then told him, "There's this guy in Katy, outside Houston. Name's Bullet."

"Bullet? Really?"

"Well, it's what he goes by, a prison name I think. What the hell do I know? A real tough fucker, like you," he said, rolling his eyes and rubbing his ass. "He's the hub of a fairly big operation. Has his fingers in a lot of pies, but getting him to talk won't come easy. Besides, all he could give you is the names of a few shops that may or may not be what you're looking for. No guarantees."

"Where do I find him?"

Tully opened the bottom drawer of his desk. He reached as far back as he could and pulled out a gray metal card index. He opened the top and started flipping through it as Frank said, "State of the art shit."

"Computers crash," he answered, jerking his head toward the pile of plastic and glass on his floor.

Frank smiled.

"Here. This is it, at least the last I heard. Can't promise anything, but for what you're looking for, this cat would be the asshole to know, if anybody does."

Frank snapped the index card out of Tully's hand. The address was handwritten. A rural route in Katy, Texas. A place well off the beaten path, a perfect place for a hood making money off stolen cars. Frank eyed it then looked at Tully with accusing eyes.

"Look, dude," Tully said, "this asshole is a serious hard-ass. If he knows I'm the one that gave you the 411, I'm roadkill."

"I got it, don't worry. Bad-asses like this respond to two things. Violence and cash," Frank said, slipping the card in his breast pocket. He said thanks and started to leave.

"Hey, Frank, what about . . . ?" Tully asked, waving his hands around the destruction that was his office.

"Bill me."

"Oh, you can bet on it."

Tully followed Frank to the front door, hoping now to never see his *friend* ever again. As Frank made his way across the parking lot to his car, Tully asked from the door, "If, by some wild chance, you find this fucker that killed Tiff, what are you gonna do?"

As Frank sat inside the BMW and fired the engine, he told Tully, "If I get to him first,

Bodinger can't book a dead man."

As the BMW backed out and sped away Tully whispered to the wind. "Fuck . . . me."

40

Adam was sitting in the black light of his living room naked, drunk, and feeling melancholy. He held a piece of pink neon chalk, staring blankly at a small patch of clean space on the black wall. He'd been preoccupied all day. Susan Bodinger was crawling through his mind like a worm inside a rotting apple. She looked so much like Deloris. He'd tried to ignore it at first, but it was becoming impossible.

He had never gone back to work at Delphi. He never quit, he simply never went back. The only reason he had the job was to keep up the appearance of normalcy, but he'd grown past that now. He was living beyond the bounds of normal people, whatever that meant.

Adding to that, the Tidy Man, who he hadn't seen in four years, left a message on his machine that his trust fund was being rolled over into a new account with a higher rate of interest which would yield him more money annually. He couldn't have cared less.

He still had money left from the previous four years.

He'd introduced himself on the machine like they were strangers. For as long as he'd known him, his entire life, he'd always tried to keep an illusion of formality. Even when he made Deloris's funeral arrangements, there was a distance to him. Clinical, like a doctor. Since her death, the answering machine was how they communicated, each leaving messages, neither wanting a conversation with the other. Most times when he called, it was about some financial undertaking or matters to do with the house. Adam knew his name, but it was meaningless; he just needed to hear the voice to know this was another time to ignore the message and go back to his daydreams.

He wondered if Susan Bodinger's body was as well kept as Deloris's. His mother started shaving her pubic hair when they started going to nudist resorts and demanded he do the same. A tradition he still observed. Surely Susan's wasn't groomed. She didn't seem the type to trifle with that particular vanity. Besides, Detective Bodinger probably liked his women hairy.

Disgusting.

She was pretty all right, but for all the wrong reasons. She wore her near fifty years like a gown of satin. She was graceful, almost elegant. She was the type of person who enjoyed growing older, looking forward to the next horizon, instead of always looking back at what she used to be, like Deloris.

"You should have seen me before I had you," she'd chide him. She was more than capable of landing a man. She was smart, pretty, and sexy. But it was her own flesh and blood that drove her libido. A warped fetish she could no more control than Adam could control his deeds as the Capital Hangman. Only now was he beginning to understand her weakness.

He wanted to stop thinking of Susan, so he decided to write something. Maybe allowing his mind to wander on the walls would satisfy his need to obsess. He squatted then sat on the carpet by the wall. There, writing close to the floor, he wrote what was bubbling up inside him:

Pain is my god,
Misery my bride.
I hate so-called life,
Release the agony inside.
I am life's sweet chaos,
I am insanity divine,
I am life's little joke,
I am majestic design.
I am your death mask,

I am the truth-bearer,
I am your twisted brother
Looking back from the mirror.
I am . . . the god of pain.
Bless you all to hell
And bring down the bloody rain.

When he finished, he sat and read the words with no emotion. It was his mantra, his declaration to the world. If anyone was to read this, it would be after his death. And that was just fine with him.

He lay naked on the floor beside his words and closed his eyes. Instead of exorcising Susan from his mind, he'd only strengthened her vision. He wanted to know what she felt like, what she smelled like.

What she would look like . . . inside the bag.

41

After relaying the message to Adam's machine, Felix Bryant hung up the phone, feeling a since of loss. It had been four years since Deloris Parker died in her bed; it was the last time he'd been in that house. He knew Adam was still living there, his answering machine attested to that. He'd drive by occasionally to make sure the lawn crew he'd paid for kept the appearance up. He knew where Adam worked—he'd gotten him the job—and he'd call and check on him from time to time. Talking to his superiors, making sure Adam was still functioning in the world since the loss of his mother. But he hadn't seen him in four years. The money kept rolling over, but Adam never spent much more than a hermit. The one extravagance he indulged himself with was a new H2 Hummer off the showroom floor a year earlier.

"Wonder how he's doing?" he asked to himself, not realizing he'd said it out loud.

"What's that, Felix?" Mrs. Cabbershaw asked, entering the study.

He startled then replied, "Adam. I haven't seen him in so long. He never answers the phone and doesn't return my calls when he knows I'm available. He leaves messages at all hours of the night. Some of them are so strange I think he's delusional at times. To be perfectly honest, I really don't know if he even cares about anything."

"And that troubles you?" she asked, gazing at the large bookcase that covered an entire wall.

"In a way, I suppose. Puzzles me is more like it."

"Then maybe you should go and see the young man. Drop by unannounced. It might be fun," she advised, finding the volume she was seeking. "Why you and that infernal woman chose to make your identity a secret is still beyond me."

"Let's not open old wounds," he said, still looking into space. "It was the chosen course, right or wrong. It was what we decided upon, agreed to. I suppose I should have been stronger. But too much water has passed beneath the bridge, old friend. Too late to rectify bad decisions made a lifetime ago."

Mrs. Cabbershaw waited for more, but nothing came. "Go see him, Felix. It will do both of you good. Lord knows the poor boy grew up without a father, and having a mentor now might be what's best for the both of you."

"I don't think he trusts me," he said with a guilty chuckle.

"Well, why in heaven's name should he?" she asked, growing stern. "All you've been to the boy is a cash cow. A way for him never to learn how the world really operates. A boy needs a father to teach him, Felix. You've seen that around here. Howard is no saint, but our children had an influence in their lives, a male influence. Mothers can only do so much, and I, for one, never trusted that woman for a second."

"Please?" he huffed.

She stopped short. He'd heard this for the better part of twenty odd years and didn't need to hear it again, even if it was her money.

"Felix," she softened, "whether he realizes it or not, you love the boy. Go see him. If for no other reason, just to make yourself feel better."

"Might not be a bad idea," he said. "I would like to see the inside of the house, see how he's living."

"I would say he's doing well enough, but I know you. You'll have to see for yourself," she smiled, walking out of the room.

"In a couple of days perhaps," he said.

She stopped long enough to say, "I know you never laid claim to him, and I won't badger old wounds. But there is, after all, something to be said for blood."

He nodded.

"Go see how he's doing, Felix. See if he appreciates my money."

Leaving for her sitting room, she said over her shoulder, "I hope at least someone does."

Felix sat at the desk in the study thinking of Deloris and Adam. He remembered telling Mrs. Cabbershaw that he'd gotten a woman pregnant all those years ago. He relived the conversation they had. He wanted the money for an abortion, but the lady would hear nothing of it.

"Abortion is an abomination, and I'll be to sort to it!" she scolded him. "There are other ways, my dear friend. There are always *other ways*."

Little did he know, Deloris Parker never wanted that abortion. She wanted a son, a child to have . . . as her very own.

42

Frank was sitting inside the rag-tag office of chop shop mogul Bullet, realizing that this entire run may be nothing more than a wild goose chase. The odds that his wild hunch would produce the results he so desperately craved were a million to one. That was what he was feeling on his drive to Katy, Texas, long before his arrival, which was met with less than desired optimism.

He found the sprawling compound on a gravel road far from the lights of the town. Too distant to raise suspicion and far away from innocent ears. It was a place he'd create if he were a major player in stolen cars. No one to hear the mechanical crunch of the shop, nor the screams of trespassers. As his BMW pulled in through the gate, he felt the eyes on him, and the guns ready to take his last breath.

"Jesus, Castro," he whispered. "If you're wrong about this . . . ."

He reached into his glove box and retrieved his .45 automatic, sliding it onto his lap. If he had to blast his way out, he wanted it at the ready. He slid the chamber back, arming the powerhouse, as he drove slowly through the canopy of trees, winding through wrecked cars and rusted hulls. Every so often, he'd see a head bobbing up through the wreckage, taking note of where they were and how many he saw. The numbers were far more than he anticipated.

"Tiffany, baby . . . What have you gotten me into?"

As the number of old cars increased, he realized he was getting closer to the main entrance. There was another gate ahead, and he slowed the car, easing to the closed metal frame. As the car came to a halt at the steel, a huge dark-skinned man with a rifle slung over his shoulder stepped out of nowhere, his hand raised for Frank to stop. He stood next to the driver's door, asking, "What's your business?" Looking as though taking his life would amount to squashing a bug.

"I need to see Bullet," Frank said.

"So does everybody," the man replied, adjusting his sunglasses. "Why you, motherfucker?"

Frank thought before speaking. If this guy was the gatekeeper, he could kill him here, take the car, and there was absolutely nothing anyone could do about it. The BMW alone was worth more than the blood in his veins.

He should have rented a Toyota.

Frank thought about the prison code. All of these guys were ex-cons. The one thing thieves and gang bangers hated was the murder of innocence. "I'm trying to catch a psychopath killing young girls," Frank said. "I'm a private detective. All I want is information, brother, nothing more."

The big man bristled, turned his head, then stared right into Frank's eyes. "Why in the hell would Bullet know anything about a shit like that?"

"Because of what he drives," Frank said, remaining calm.

"Again, asshole . . . why?"

It hit him wrong, deep inside. Frank gritted his teeth, collected himself before telling the guard, "Look, friend, I'm not a cop. I don't give a damn what you guys do, or how you make a living. I just need to talk to the man, and I'll be on my way. Do I get in or not?"

The guard thought for a second, scratching his whiskered chin, then replied, "Not."

That was all it took. Castro kicked the door open, catching the guard at the knees, then exploded out of the vehicle. Before he could react, Frank had delivered five crunching blows to his face as he lay on his back, the last breaking his jaw with a sickening *crunch*. He pulled the rifle off him, tossed it in the car, then searched him for keys. Once he found them, he unlocked the gate and drove through.

One obstacle gone.

Knowing he was in a hot spot, he pushed the car faster than normal, seeing a group of buildings which had to be the main hub just around the next bend. As soon as he stopped the car in front of the main building, three men fell on him from nowhere. Castro sprang from the car quickly, catching the first man with the door, forcing him to the ground before spinning to take out the second with a leg sweep. The third had him dead to rights, a semiautomatic pointed at his head, but Frank dropped to the ground, pressing the .45's barrel to the first man's head screaming, *"Back off or he dies!"* as an explosion erupted overhead. *Boom!* He tracked the sound to his left. Turning, he saw two men. One was in a T-shirt, jeans, and ball cap, holding a shotgun pointed at the clouds. The other was in leather pants and vest with no shirt. The man in leather wore a ponytail of red hair above a graying red goatee. At the blast, all fell silent.

Frank was huffing. His heart beat a rhythm of death he knew from his days on the Austin streets. The wolf had what he desired. This was it, the moment the beast always wanted. Kill or be killed. But the older Castro decided to play it out, to hear them, and not let youthful angst dictate the moment as in the past.

"Okay, I get it," the redhead said. "You're a badass. You gotta be to get this far without an invitation." He stepped forward. "And I don't remember inviting the likes of you."

Frank clicked the hammer on the .45, staring at who he was sure was Bullet. "I'll kill him, know that."

"Fuck him," Bullet laughed. "You're already here, partner. The way I see it, I got bigger problems than his sorry ass."

"I just wanna talk," Frank said, sweat burning his eyes.

"Well, hell, son, let's talk. What the fuck. It's boring around here anyway," he said, waving off the others who'd scurried to the commotion.

Frank didn't like it, but he knew the honor of thieves. Being a scoundrel at heart, his gut told him he was safe. He'd won his passage, at least for the moment. He eased the hammer closed on the pistol as the man on the ground prayed to his god for forgiveness.

Before standing, Frank looked at him. "Remember me," he whispered to him. "This is what death looks like. No matter who's holding the gun." The man squeezed his eyes shut, knowing it was the truth. Looking down the wrong end of a hand cannon was no way to die.

Bullet walked up the steps to his office as two men drove up in an old Jeep screaming that security had been breached. The gatekeeper was slumping in the back seat, the side of his head swollen twice the normal size.

"*What?*" Bullet yelled to them.

"That son of a bitch broke in!" the driver yelled. "He fucked up Hazard pretty bad!"

"Yeah, well, Mr. Hazard has other problems at the moment," Bullet told them. "This man's my new guest thanks to his sorry ass," he said, waving Frank up the stairs. "Get back to work, and get that piece of shit off the ground before he pisses himself," he said, pointing to the man who'd felt Castro's gun.

As the men commenced to restoring order, Frank walked up the steps and into Bullet's office. It was a pigsty, littered with car parts and beer bottles. A worn desk, covered in debris, sat by the far wall with an old lawn chair in front of it, for *guests.*

"What's your name, cowboy?" Bullet asked, kicking room for himself behind the desk.

"Frank."

"Well, Mr. Frank, I must say I'm quite impressed. That was some serious ass–whoopin' I just saw. My hat's off to'ya."

"Thanks . . . I guess."

"No, really. That was some of the best shit I've seen in years. Please, have a seat," he said, pointing to the lawn chair.

Frank was still uneasy. He was in the belly of the beast. No one to help and no one to hear him if he needed them to. The only thing in his favor was the boss himself. If he could work Bullet, the others would oblige. If not, it was going to be sad singing and slow driving for Mr. Castro.

"You must be a heavy hitter, Mr. Frank," Bullet said, leaning back, putting his boots up on the desk.

"Why?"

276

"Because you're here."

"Like I said, I want no trouble. I just need some information. No strings," Frank said, lighting a cigarette, the .45 resting in his lap.

Bullet spoke with a deep southern drawl. "I heard. But just know this ain't some local body shop, brother. If this shit don't pan out, you might be in for a trimming."

"Understood," Frank said, eyes steady. "I wouldn't be here if I didn't think it was necessary."

"Well, in my humble experience, necessity can drive a man to do some pretty foolish shit."

"Agreed."

"Like blowing into an armed compound like he's John fucking Wayne or some shit. That ain't just out of necessity, my friend, that's plain loco."

"If the shoe fits," Frank said, still sizing up Bullet. He was in his late thirties, but his hard life made him look old beyond his years. As Frank was about to speak, a young woman strolled in wearing a thin, pink, baby doll nightie and motorcycle boots with no panties. Without a word, she cozied up to Bullet, nestling her breasts to his face.

"Holly, baby, this here's Mr. Frank," Bullet told her. "Say hi."

"Hi, Mr. Frank," she cooed. She was no more than seventeen, probably some runaway from Houston. "He looks awful serious," she sighed.

"Oh, baby girl, you have no idea. Mr. Frank here is a top-shelf hard-ass, just like me."

"Really?" she smiled at Frank, who was still grim and determined. "I like my men tough and strong," she tilted her head at Frank. He took a breath, wanting her to leave. Bullet recognized it, complying. "We got some man shit to talk about here. Go wait in the bed. I'll be along in awhile," he said, cutting his eyes at Frank, smiling. She kissed his cheek then left them together. Frank watched her leave, her firm cheeks flexing beneath the thin fabric as she plodded away in the heavy boots. "Ain't that something?" Bullet asked.

"Suppose it is."

"What the hell, she'll be gone this time next month and I'll have a new one. Pussy's like a revolving door around this joint."

"Good work if you can get it," Frank said, wanting to get down to business.

"She'll blow you if I tell her to."

"That's good to know."

"She'll kill ya too."

"Like I said, that's good to know," Frank replied, still stoic.

Bullet put his hands behind his head, saying, "Not one for frivolity. I can appreciate that."

"I need information, that's all."

"Like what? Huh? Tell me, Mr. Frank, what did I stop my day to help you with? And remember," he said, eyes firm, "I got a naked teenager waiting to fuck me blue two doors away. So, time's wasting. What do you want?"

"I'm looking for someone."

"That tells me shit."

"I'm looking for a crazy man that killed my friend. He's driving a vehicle every cop in Texas is looking for. He'd need somebody to help him."

"And you think he came *here*?" Bullet laughed.

"No, I don't," Frank answered, crossing his legs. "I think he may have gone to someone you might have control over. Someone inside your loop."

"And exactly how the hell would I know that?"

"Because I have it on good authority you have several fingers in a lot of pies. I bet you're the kind of man that likes to know what his . . . *associates* are doing when they're not chopping hot cars."

"And why should I give a flying fuck?"

"Got no answer for that one. You either will or you won't."

Bullet studied him. His years behind bars gave him a sense to read people, trusting few. He could see Frank had the same knack; he could feel Frank gaining knowledge of him as he sat there. The skills he displayed getting in was one thing, but the no-bullshit attitude was what was even more impressive. Even the sexy Holly couldn't tempt him. He was a serious hard-case on serious business. The way he saw it, there were two courses of action. Steal his fine car and let the boys string his nut sack over the front gate, or have the conversation and send the badass on his way. Good business was the former. Kill him, ending it now. However, for some reason, he liked the guy. In a different time, he'd like to belly up to a bar with Mr. Frank and share some stories. After all, he wasn't a cop; that much was obvious. Besides, even if he knew the boys could take him, how many would it cost in the process, including himself? He was cradling a loaded .45.

"So let me get this straight," Bullet said, lighting a thin cigar. "You have a friend killed and you think you can find the man who did it by his car."

"Yeah."

"That's pretty damned thin, bro."

"I know, but it's all I have right now," Frank lied. He had plenty more. His voice on tape, his letters to Glenn Young and Bodinger, not to mention the much ballyhooed H2.

Bullet blew a smoke ring, letting his thoughts gather. "I know the only reason you're here is because somebody that's already on my dime squealed. Who and why I'll figure out later. That's *my* business. But right now, we're talking about you and your wild goose chase." He leveled a stare at Frank. "Who the hell are you really looking for?"

For some reason, the weight on his shoulders lessened. He relaxed a little, saying, "You watch the news much?"

Bullet laughed, "No, Mr. Frank, can't say I do. What's in the news these days?"

"There's been some dirty business in Austin the past six months. A madman killing girls. He—"

"Hangs 'em in the woods, right?"

Bingo!

"That's the guy. The last time, he shot three kids who'd skipped school. They wandered up on him as he was finishing."

"One of them boys yours?" Bullet asked, his tone changing.

"No," Frank said. "The victim, the young woman they caught him with. She worked for me."

"Yeah, heard about that. Damned fucked up mess. After that one, the other two or three he'd done started getting talked about. Don't they call him the *Hangman* or some shit?"

"Yeah," Frank said, growing darker. "Something like that."

"Hmm," Bullet ruminated. "We got ourselves a first-rate *psycho-*path." He said it like it was two words. "And the closest thing to Dirty Harry I ever saw trying to chase him down. All because he went and lynched the wrong prom queen."

Hearing it from someone else made it sound even worse. "That's about it," Frank said.

"Tell me, Mr. Frank, what you gonna do with this ol' boy, if by some stretch you actually find him?"

Without a second's hesitation he said, "I'm going to cut his fucking heart out."

Bullet chuckled, "I bet he wouldn't be the first notch on that belt of yours."

"He wouldn't."

"Okay, gotta admit, you got me interested," Bullet said, crushing out the cigar. "Lord knows why. I ought to have the boys chop you up for dog rations," he said, watching Frank's reaction, which was nothing. "I'd hate to play poker with you, Mr. Frank. That face don't give a man shit but the creeps. Talk to me. What's the low low?"

"His vehicle."

"Which is?"

"Black H2."

"Your psycho has taste."

"There was a witness during the last murders. All the kid could tell the cops was that he drove the H2. He knows this, I got inside information. He's aware the cops know."

"Hell, Mr. Frank, he just sank it in a river some place."

"Not this guy. He thinks he's smarter than everybody. No, he kept it. He just altered it."

The word *alter* clicked something in Bullet's mind. "Let me bum a cigarette," he said. Frank pulled out his pack, flipping a filter up. Bullet took one and sat back lighting it.   "Altered an H2, huh?"

"I'm staking everything on it."

"Well, you're right about one thing. If he's as smart as you say he is, he wouldn't go to a legit body shop, that's for sure."

280

"Agreed."

"And some local boy who makes extra cash at his house would be too sloppy. Again, if he's that smart." Frank liked what he was hearing. Finally someone was thinking his way, making him feel better about his chances. "But that brings me back to me. Why me, Mr. Frank?"

"It narrows the search. I can eliminate a lot of foot work with one conversation."

"Start at the top, huh?"

"Yep."

"What time frame you looking at?"

"Within the last month."

Bullet let his mind go back to the word *altered*. He thought for a minute, smoking Frank's cigarette, then said, "Well, Mr. Frank, there ain't shit about the last month or so that I can help you with. I mean that. But you said he'd need to alter an H2. That jarred my memory."

Frank sat up. "Go on."

"Now, mind you, this ain't much, but there was a strange request made of one my boys down in Seguin about a year ago. How he found him and knew where to go I still ain't figured out. But like I said before, that's my business."

Frank nodded.

"My guy calls me wanting to get the green light on it. Said this young cat brought in a brand new H2, wanting some weird shit done. Damned thing still had scrape marks from the dealer's sticker. Still had paper floor mats for Christ's sake."

It sounded good to Frank. "Okay, I'm with you. Like what?"

"Some wild shit, bro. Wanted all the rear seats removed and a new floor put in, wanted both rear doors welded shut from the inside, wanted the inside latch on the back hatch covered up. Then, this is the really strange part, he wanted walls put up. One right behind the front seats, and two walls blocking off the back doors and windows. Then, of all the shit, he wanted the very back window painted from the inside. Sounded to me like he was making a . . ."

"A cell," Frank interjected.

"Your word, not mine. But like I said, some crazy shit."

"What happened?"

"Told my boy not to touch it. He said the kid was offering major cash, but I didn't like it. For the very reasons, you understand."

"Understood."

"But he kept on about the cash he was throwing around. Now me, I like cash. And I love a sure thing, but I didn't want him that close."

"So?"

"So I told him to send him to a crazy shit on my roll in Louisiana. A real whack job. A coon-ass named Bodain, works out of Metairie. One of these black, Cajun voodoo motherfuckers."

"How do I find him?" Frank asked, feeling the wolf gnawing at the bars.

"Not so fast, Mr. Frank. So far this has just been two guys talking. Now, we're talking business. Shit like this costs," Bullet informed him, smiling.

"How much?"

"What'ya got?"

Frank knew to bring cash; it was his Plan A before he had to shift to Plan B quicker than he anticipated. "I got five on me right now," he told Bullet.

"Son, I wouldn't get out of bed for five hundred dollars."

"I meant five grand."

"Oh, well, see, we do think alike," Bullet laughed. "Deal." Frank pulled out the wad of cash, handing it over. Bullet smiled, fanning the money, stuffing it in the pocket of his leather pants. "Easiest five grand I ever made."

"Now?" Frank asked, his heart beating loud in his ears. If this was where he could track down D, he'd run to the sun if need be.

"If this guy used any of my shops, and I said *if*, it's that one. Bodain's a crazy shit anyway. I figured it's out of state and easy to cut loose if it turns ugly."

"How do I find him?"

"Hell, Mr. Frank, I'll draw you a map. I'd love to see Bodain's face when the likes of you comes stomping in like Clint Eastwood," he laughed. "Yes, sir, that would be worth the price of a ticket."

282

Bullet drew it all out for him. Through the Louisiana back roads, south of the city of Metairie, a suburb of New Orleans. As Frank studied it, he glanced at Bullet the same way he'd gazed at Tully when he'd given the directions to the compound.

"I know what you're thinking," Bullet admitted. "Trust a sorry sumbitch once, will ya? That's gospel, I swear. Get there at dark though. He'll be high by then. Be an easier mark that way."

"Easier?"

"Well, easier than this shit," he grinned. "Speaking of which, I'm sure there's some pissed off rednecks wanting a piece of your ass right about now."

Frank grimaced, having forgotten. "Yeah, I suppose so."

Bullet smiled, walking to the door. He opened it, yelling, "*Jubal.*" The young man with the ball cap and shotgun walked up on the porch. "Son, make sure Mr. Frank gets off the property in one piece." He glanced back to Frank, smiling. "I might wanna split a bottle with him some day. Be hard to do if those assholes get to him first."

"Yes, sir," the young man said. "Mr. Frank?" he asked, backing out of the door so Castro could leave. Before he left, Bullet extended his hand.

"Been a pleasure, Mr. Frank," shaking hands.

"It was something all right."

At the bottom of the steps, he heard Bullet call him again, "Oh, and Mr. Frank?"

"Yeah?"

"Don't worry about Tully. I'm sure he's in Mexico by now."

For the first time all day, Frank Castro smiled.

43

It's roughly three hundred and seventy miles from Katy, Texas, to Metairie, Louisiana, on US Interstate 10. A hard five-hour drive that Frank made in three and a half. The BMW ate the miles away as he sped to the man he was sure would lead him to Tiffany's killer. After his talk with the criminal Bullet, he was certain this Bodain character would be the man he'd been seeking from the start. The one person who could point him in the right direction. His mood grew darker as he drove, having spilled five grand to get his information, he was in no mood for money talk. He knew this creep would only respond to two things, and since he left all his handy cash at the Katy compound, the only alternative left to him was the one he was the most familiar with.

Pain.

He remembered Russell Malvern at the funeral home, looking like a ghost, having no faith in the system to catch and punish his daughter's killer. "*It would mean a lot to us, Frank, if you found him first.*" Only a naïve kid wouldn't be able to connect the dots to the man's meaning. Find this son of a bitch and kill him the right way.

Frank Castro's gonna cut your fucking heart out!

It was still D's evil voice he heard delivering the words. Drunk, slurring, incoherent. The idea that Tiffany's last minutes in this world were spent with a slimy, putrid waste of human excrement made Frank sick to his stomach. Of all the ways that sweet kid should have spent her life, yet never got the chance to. She'd never find Mr. Right. She'd never have children or grandchildren to grow old with. She'd never see another sunrise or feel a new spring warming her skin. She'd never laugh at a friend in a bar or cry at a sappy movie. D took all that away. He stole it from her. The sick, twisted shit stole her life, and there had to be a life repaid.

In blood.

He followed Bullet's directions, winding his way in the setting sun through the thick cypress growth of the south Louisiana backwoods. Bullet had told him Bodain was a freak, a Cajun steeped in voodoo and drugs. None of that mattered. He knew it was going to be a hard turn, but the so-called freak was going to talk if it killed him. He owed it to himself, Tiffany, and her parents. This was going to happen, one way or another. The one sure way he felt would do the trick was the world's oldest. Force.

As he made the last turn in Bullet's directions, he saw a small clearing to his right, up ahead in the setting twilight. There was a building, a garage with a gravel lot.

"That's it," he whispered. "Time to call the thunder." He could feel the wolf pacing, pawing at the ground, wanting to run free. He felt it pulsing inside him like a torrent of anger and hatred. A beast longing to act on its nature. Needing to feel its true motive in the way of the world. A true animal wanting to eat and not be pacified with weak scoundrels like Tully Pritchard and college kids looking for fun. For the first time in ten years, Frank felt the wolf at one with himself. It was time.

Let the wolf loose, and hell will follow.

He felt strangely detached, like he used to feel in the squad car. There was something about the badge that made him feel as though he wasn't really himself. He felt it again, for the first time in a decade. There was a job to do, as in the past. A job that wasn't going to be pretty, but there had to be a means to an end, no matter the cost. The wolf would see to it.

As he approached the garage, he killed his lights and slipped the car into neutral, letting its momentum carry him quietly to a stop. He killed the engine. Even with his windows up, he could hear loud zydeco music emanating from the garage. He once again pulled his .45 automatic from the glove box and checked the clip. Once he was certain it was ready, he looked in the mirror.

"Failure's not an option," he told the reflection. "I leave here knowing who I'm after." He had no way of knowing how many there were inside or if they were armed. However, unlike at Bullet's compound, he was strangely calm. There was no sense of foreboding or trepidation. He knew in his heart he was where he was supposed to be. It was almost as if Tiffany was guiding him, showing him the way to her killer's identity.

Frank exited the car, pushing the door to with a subtle click. The zydeco music—the jazz meets calypso mutation of the Louisiana melting pot—was even louder once he was outside. The surrounding area was littered with old cars and wrecks, each with its own story of broken expectations, left to rust and decay in the stifling humidity.

Slowly, Frank moved to the main door, pressing his ear to the metal. All he heard was the music and nothing else. Assured the music would mask his entrance, he eased the door open, peeking inside with his automatic weapon at the ready. No one was in the front room, so he slipped in, shutting the door. Immediately to his right, he could see into the garage. There was what appeared to be a 1973 Dodge Charger with the hood up and a man on a creeper beneath it. It had to be Trevor Bodain. There was also a hydraulic floor jack protruding from in front of the left front tire. The man on the creeper was beneath the car, his head facing him. Slowly, Frank walked inside the garage, making his way to the front of the car. With the music blaring, he knew there was no way the man beneath the car could heard him. In seconds, he was standing next to the Charger with the man under it oblivious to him. Frank peeked under the hood and saw the motor mounts were off, with the floor jack holding the engine in place.

Surely it wasn't this easy?

He felt the wolf growling inside him, wanting out. Frank relaxed, letting go of himself and allowing the old friend who'd once stood behind the badge to take over. In one smooth motion, he pulled the man on the creeper halfway from beneath the car while simultaneously twisting the handle of the floor jack, lowering the engine on top of his legs. Just when he knew the man was pinned, Frank stopped the jack.

286

The surprise and instant shock of pain was more than Bodain was prepared for. He let out a primal scream as the engine rested on his knees. "*Aaaahhhh!*" It was then that Bodain locked eyes with Frank Castro. Once Frank was certain Bodain was trapped, he stepped away.

"*What the fuck is this?!*" Bodain screamed.

"It's a shakedown. Shut the fuck up," Frank said, walking to the far side of the garage, killing the music. The sudden silence created a buzz all its own, as though it were a breathing presence in the garage with the two men. As Bodain bellowed in pain, Frank found a large drop cloth and came back to the car. He spread it out between the floor jack and the man on the creeper as Bodain tried frantically to pull himself free.

"You crazy *cracker*! Let me outta here! My legs are *breaking*!"

Frank sat on the drop cloth, leaning back against the front wheel with his firearm in his lap. "If you're going to insult me, at least get it right. I'm not a cracker, I'm Cuban," Frank informed him, lighting a cigarette.

"You fucking spic! I don't give a fuck what your monkey ass is! Raise that *fucking jack!*"

Frank blew smoke in Bodain's face. "You know who I am?" he asked.

"Hell no! A fucking dead man, that's who! My legs are breaking, motherfucker!"

"Not yet," Frank said casually. "I'll tell you who I am. I'm the guy you need to talk to. If I get what I want, you'll be walking in a week. If not . . . ," he finished, resting his hand on the handle of the jack. Bodain's eyes widened. "Now, you and me seem to be in a very unstable situation."

"Fuck you!"

Frank drummed his fingers along the jack handle, saying, "You really should talk to your patrons better than that."

"You sorry ass, tanned excuse for a white man! When I get outta here I'm gonna cut your motherfucking head off!"

"Then you'll have to crawl to do it," Frank said with a wink.

Bodain calmed long enough to see Frank indeed had his hand on the jack handle. One twist and his legs would be crushed. He tried to settle himself, breathing through his nose and exhaling through his mouth, like a pregnant woman in labor.

"That's it, just calm down," Frank said. "Want a smoke?"

"No!"

"Suit yourself," Frank said, crossing his legs at the ankles as he leaned back against the wheel. "Is this a '73 or a '74?"

"Fuck you!"

"Seventy three, I think. A real looker, classic. Big block Hemi. They don't make 'em like this anymore."

"What do you want, motherfucker?!" Bodain yelled, his knees slowly bending in the wrong direction.

"Me? Oh, I'm just looking for somebody," Frank said, smoking his cigarette.

"*Who*, bitch?!"

"Don't know his name, that's the real shitter. Just know what he drives. Maybe you've seen him, maybe not," Frank said, running his hand over the jack handle. "I really hope you can help."

"*What? Tell me, nigga! What?*" Bodain was getting frantic. The pain in his knees was becoming more than he could stand. The engine was pressing down on them and the wheels beneath the creeper were starting to buckle. He didn't know who this crazy man was, but he'd tell him anything to get him to raise the jack and lift the engine off his legs. "Who? Tell me, *who?*"

Frank leaned back against the wheel, saying, "A guy in a black Hummer. An H2. Maybe you did some work, maybe not. I'm not sure. But if you did, you'd remember it."

"*The dude from Texas?*"

"Maybe," Frank said. "You work on a black Hummer for a man from Texas?"

"Which time, *fool?*"

"Which time?" Frank asked. "Explain that, Mr. Bodain. I have all night."

Bodain tried to adjust his legs to get some circulation in his knees before he said, "He's been here twice!"

"Tell me."

"Last year he came in, wanted some crazy shit! I did it!"

"Take out the back seats? Seal off the doors and windows?" Frank asked.

"Yeah, yeah, *yeah!*"

"Get his name?"

"*Parker!*" Bodain yelled. "Fucker's name is Parker!"

"First or last?"

"I don't know! The freak's got one name as far as know, like fucking Elvis!"

"Seen him again, have you?"

"Yeah, fool! Last week, wanted a paint job!"

Frank's heart skipped a beat. He'd been right. Of all the luck. He called it and found it. He hit the lottery with one ticket, he couldn't believe his fortune. Tiffany must have been helping him from heaven. "Painted it, huh?"

"Yeah!"

"What color?"

"Can I have that smoke now?" Bodain asked, eyes watering.

Frank paused at first then slipped Bodain a cigarette. After lighting it for him, he asked again. "What color?"

"Blue," Bodain stressed, shaking.

"What shade?"

"Sky blue, nigga! *Sky blue!*"

"Really?"

"He called it azure. Azure blue."

"His idea?"

"Mine," Bodain said, trembling with his smoke. "I knew he'd been up to something no good, so I told him no one would be looking for an H2 that color."

Frank leaned closer, asking, "Why did you know he'd been up to something?"

"'Cause that pretty boy is a weird little shit! That's why, *motherfucker!*"

"Well, you're right. He's been a busy boy. Killed six people, one of them was very close to me."

"And that shit's *my problem?*"

"It is now. Mr. Parker likes to hang young girls in trees, like deer meat."

"I don't know nothing about that shit!"

"Of course not. You'd be dead if you did." Frank thought for second then went back to the H2. "Azure blue. You painted his H2 azure blue?"

"Yeah! *Fuck*!"

Frank wondered how many azure blue Hummers there were in Austin. His guess was one, the only one. The right one. The temptation to call Bodinger was great, but after reflection he thought better of it.

To hell with him, this is personal.

"How long it take you?"

"A week."

"He stay here? How'd he get around?"

"Fucker went back home."

"How?"

"He drove, *motherfucker!*"

"In what?"

Bodain told Frank about the trailer with the ordinary car on it that Parker pulled with the Hummer. He'd left the trailer and went back to Austin, returning a week later and pulling the car back home.

"The other car. What was it?"

"A Focus."

"Focus?"

"Ford Focus, asshole!"

"What color?"

"Gray. Dark gray."

It made sense; that's how he played his game. He'd trail his targets in the unassuming Focus then come back later, collecting them in his death-dealing H2. An H2 that was now azure blue.

"Know this shit," Bodain hissed. "My boys are gonna cut your fucking ass! They gonna cut your ass long, wide, and deep!"

Frank lit another cigarette. "Let me worry about that."

"You better worry, motherfucker!"

He laughed to himself, saying, "Funny, I don't seem to worry about anything. Now, back to Parker."

"What about him?"

"How old is he?"

"Twenty-five, maybe. Twenty-eight."

"Size."

"Fuck *this!*"

"Uh-uh-uh," Frank said, tapping the jack handle. "We have an agreement. Describe him to me."

Bodain swallowed, trying to adjust himself beneath the weight of the engine. It was useless. He blinked the sweat out of his eyes before telling Frank, "Five-eight, five-nine. Maybe a buck fifty. Little shit. Got a pretty face, like a woman."

"What?" Frank asked, wanting to hear it again.

"He's a pretty boy. Blue eyes, dark hair. Got lips like a girl. Dick sucking lips."

"You like his lips?" Frank asked, smiling.

"*I ain't no fag, bitch!* I'm just telling you what the fucker looks like!"

"How'd you contact him?"

"Got his number on my cell."

"His cell?"

"Houseline. The freak don't have a cell."

"No shit?" It could not be this easy. There had to be something missing. The devil gets his due, always, so Frank knew in his gut there was something else around the corner he'd have to deal with. But for now, it looked as though he'd leave the Cajun's garage with his information after very little trouble.

"Where's the cell?" he asked.

"On my hip."

"Give it to me," Frank instructed, pressing the muzzle of the .45 to Bodain's head. "Make sure the phone is all you pull off your hip."

"Nigga, if I had a gun, you'd be dead already!"

"Get it," pressing the barrel further.

Bodain extended his right arm beneath the car and came back with an IPhone, handing it over. Frank took it. Punching it on, he scrolled through Bodain's numbers until he found it. It read *Parker* and the attached number had a 512 area code. Austin.

"That's our boy," he said, more to himself. He took his own phone and transferred the number. He now had D's home phone number. He'd looked through the answering machine at his office, but the number was blocked by the caller. Now, he had it. He turned Bodain's phone off, tossing it across the garage. He'd gotten what he came for. With the help of one of his computer accounts, he'd be able to track the address by the number. It was only a matter of time. The wolf's fur bristled at the thought.

Frank lit his third cigarette, gazing down to Bodain. "Now, that wasn't so hard, was it?"

"Fuck you! Get this shit off me! My knees are *breaking!*"

Just as Frank took a drag off his smoke, he heard a vehicle outside. Bass was thumping and the engine revved before it went silent. "You expecting company?" Frank asked, still casual.

"That's my boys, motherfucker! Zito's gonna cut you up for fish bait!" Bodain threatened, expecting Frank to jump up and head to the door, but it didn't happen that way. The slick man in the sports coat just puffed his cigarette and sat quietly. "You hear me, shithead? I said my boy's gonna—"

"I heard," Frank said, re-crossing his feet at the ankles. "We'll see, won't we?"

He heard the gravel crunching beneath their shoes as they approached the front, laughing to each other. As the door opened, Frank held his .45 tight in his right hand, still resting in his lap.

"*Zito!*" Bodain screamed as the door opened. Two men entered, one white, one black. Alarmed at the sight, each recoiled slightly. Bodain screamed again. "*Zito! Cut this motherfucker in half!*" Both men went for their weapons as Frank, ever so calmly, raised his right hand, pulling the trigger five times. The powerhouse automatic roared, spitting its death in five short bursts. *Bam! Bam! Bam! Bam! Bam!* The only sound left was the sickening thud of their bodies crashing to the floor, dying in spreading pools of crimson.

"*Nooo!*" Bodain screamed. "*Motherfucker! I'm gonna kill your fucking ass!*"

Frank was numb. He wasn't angry, surprised, or alarmed. He felt nothing. The only other life he'd ever taken was the Westbrook kid in that east Austin neighborhood ten years ago. Like him, these two were people he'd never laid eyes on in his life. The only time he saw them was as he was killing them. Just like Ryan Westbrook. He lowered the gun to his lap, taking another drag on his cigarette.

"Now that's a damn shame," he told Bodain. "I had no quarrel with those fellas or them with me. But they're dead now because of you."

"*Fuck! Fuck! Fuck!*" Bodain screamed.

"It's all on you, buddy. All you had to say was 'back off,' or 'chill out, be cool.' But no, you told them to kill me," Frank said, standing. "You wanna know the funny part?"

"*Fuck you!*"

"I was gonna let you limp away from this. But now," he said, looking at the two bodies in the doorway. "Now I don't feel so generous." He bent over, going face-to-face with Bodain. "You fucked up."

Bodain spit in his face then yelled, "*I'm calling the mojo, motherfucker! I'm calling the mojo down on your spic ass!*"

Frank stood, using his sleeve to wipe his face. The wolf needed one last turn before going back in the cage. He leaned to the floor jack, saying, "Enjoy your wheelchair," as he twisted the handle.

The entire weight of the Hemi engine fell, crushing Bodain's legs, pulverizing them into a mangled, splintered mass of bone and blood. The scream was the worst Frank had ever heard. His face a twisted mask of agony. Frank walked to the jam box and kicked the music on, pumping the volume to drown out Bodain's agonizing wails. He stepped to the two bodies in the doorway. One was dead, a slug through the center of his chest. The other was gurgling blood through a wound in the neck. His eyes open, staring at Frank as he stopped. They looked at each other. To Frank, it was just another lost kid, playing at being a thug. To the young man dying on the floor, he was looking at the devil. An expressionless black void reaching from the bowels of hell to take his life. As Frank turned to leave, he fired a shot through the kid's chest—*Bam!*—ending his struggle. Exiting the garage, he wondered which one was Zito. Didn't matter now; they were both dead, and Bodain would probably be that way as well before anyone found him.

He sat in the BMW, still surprisingly calm. He did what he had to do. There *was* another way, there always is. But he did what he did, there was no turning back. He came looking for Tiffany's killer. He left having killed two men himself and crippling another for life, if he lived at all.

He never did like the man he used to be. Now, he remembered why.

44

After stopping at a liquor store on the way, Frank drove on into Metairie and grabbed a room for the night. He settled in while never letting his mind focus on any one thing. He allowed his conscience to divest itself of his actions by jumping hodge-podge from one item to another. Once in for the night, however, his mind calmed, leaving him alone, subject to its jeopardy.

He'd removed his jacket and was pouring a drink, staring at himself in the mirror a few feet from the bed. He dropped in two rocks then melted them with four fingers of his friend Johnnie Walker. He emptied the glass, never taking his eyes off himself. Another four fingers; this time he sipped, allowing the first blitz of alcohol to catch up to him. His eyes were empty; the wolf was asleep, resting from its bloody rampage. He could still hear Bodain's scream and the sickening crunch of his legs as the big Hemi fell with all its weight. Before he knew it, the glass was empty again.

Four more fingers.

The poor young kid was staring straight into him as he took away his pain. A handsome young African-American, nothing like Bodain. He had a look such that he could have been saved from the life he was in with a good break somewhere in his past. Hell, if the Cajun had just told them to back off, they could have sorted it all out. He could have disarmed them and left them to rescue Bodain after he was gone. Anything else could have been done if only he'd told them to.

"You never gave'em a chance, Frank," he said, to the reflection. "You wanted to hurt somebody tonight. You could have shot a warning, pressed the gun to Bodain's head. You had a chance, Frank. You had time," he took another drink. "You just didn't want to." Leaning close enough to his reflection that his breath fogged the glass, "Did you?" He emptied the glass then poured another with two new rocks.

He hated himself. It was going to be a long night. The only thing that saved him from completely dissolving into self-loathing was his cell phone. He had the number to D's house. In the morning he'd go to the computer in the lobby and logon to his account with Intelius to do a reverse phone search. He frequently used the site in his work. Now, it could pay off big for a lot of people. He not only had to avenge Tiffany, but those two unfortunate young men also would not have died in vain. He could add them to the list of people counting on him to see this thing through.

Pulling himself away from the mirror, Frank fished his cell from his jacket and scrolled to the number. He had to hear his voice. He had to know it was the right man. He had to be certain that Parker was indeed D, the Capital Hangman. Sitting on the edge of the bed, he dialed. After four rings, the machine picked up. The voice he heard was anything but what he was expecting. A woman's voice greeted him. "Hello, you've reached the Parker residence. Neither Deloris nor Adam are able to take your call, so if you'll leave a message, one of us will get back to you as soon as possible. Goodbye."

Frank's brow furrowed. "What the hell?" Questions started flooding his mind. Was this creep married? Were kids involved? Exactly who was Deloris? He called once more, listening closely, letting her voice penetrate his mind. Deloris Parker? The Cajun said Parker was in his mid-twenties, this woman was obviously not that young. She was by no means an old woman, but there were years in her voice, mileage that a twenty-something wouldn't have.

Deloris?

Remembering the letter to Bodinger, he knew D had a problem with his mother. D? Deloris? It had to be. Her message on the machine spoke of herself and Adam. Adam Parker. As the scotch in his blood clouded his actions from earlier that night, he began piecing it together. Deloris and Adam Parker were not a couple, they were mother and child. He said she was dead in the letter. He'd suffered through a tormented childhood and now she was gone, leaving him alone for the first time. Misplaced anger at the world.

Deloris . . . D.

He finished the scotch then reclined on the bed. Tomorrow would bring a new day and a hunt for Adam Parker. He'd have the address by sun up and would be in the freak's house by mid-afternoon. It would all come to a head tomorrow. Tomorrow, Tiffany's killer would meet the wolf inside Frank Castro.

However, unbeknownst to Frank, events had transpired in Austin that changed everything. Adam Parker was already gone.

45

Pain was the foundation of Adam's life. It was such a constant that he looked on it as a sibling. His brother Pain. There was never a time the gnawing emptiness didn't rattle inside him like a tin can. Deloris had lied about so many things that he grew up not knowing what to believe. She had a thousand different stories about his father, none of which could match up with any of the rest. When she died, his father became a ghost. A specter to the real world, nothing to see, feel, or hear. The only proof of his existence was Adam himself. And his pain.

He never tried to escape the pain. He wrapped himself in it like a blanket. It made him cynical and contemptuous of the world, shielding him from the real horrors of broken trust and scorned love. He trusted no one. Not even Deloris, the one human he held a connection to in all the world. He was born into a world of solitary confinement, and he liked it that way.

He saw life as a sort of passion play, with each person having the lead role in their own production. No matter what your bit parts were in the plays of others, the main objective was to star in your own. Growing up the way he did left him with a sense of the true meaning of life. We are all alone. Of all the billions of people throughout history, each one was alone within himself, and the sooner you recognized that, the better off you'd be.

What are we but wisps of air in time? Our lives are so short that leaving a legacy to be remembered is comparable to counting grains of sand. Some people leave a lasting mark, but most do not. We come to life in a screaming blur then live it out seeking comfort and love like sewer rats scrounging for food among the spoils of humanity. It filled him with hate. He hated everyone and everything.

Give it back, brother, give it all back.

The one thing he had was his words. He loved writing on the black walls in his colored chalk, transcribing his messages to the world so he could be studied for years after his death. In a drunken haze, he plopped naked on the floor in his living room, reading one of his favorites. The pink chalk glowed orange in the purple hue of the black light. Feeling like the star in his play, he read the words aloud to himself, annunciating as though he were on a stage reading to thousands.

"Listen to the wind. It may tell the truth, my friend. When alone on a road, a stranger on the highway, losing my mind in the sun, leather boots and a gun, a killer on the road. Sweat tastes sweet when kissing her lips, reminds me of rain . . . bitter pain. Whiskey on my breath, the maker of her death. The blood on my hands, the song of my soul, out of control. Voices echo on and on, beating like a drum. Spirits call my name, calling the game; one more life is all they need, one last vessel I must feed. Stop screaming my name! I am going insane! I'm going to kill again, on the road. Down the long highway with rats on the make, another soul to take. The jungle is my home, along the road alone. Listen to the wind, my friend, always my friend. When alone . . . on the road, my dying friend to the end. Alone on the road . . . a road with no end."

After the reading, Adam fell back on the floor, laughing at the insanity spewing from his own mind. He laughed about Susan Bodinger and her limp-dick husband scouring the state for him as he read his poetry in the black light of his living room. He stretched out on the floor, nudging one of his jars that littered the house. He took it up, rolling it on his chest. A song lyric crept through his mind as he gazed on the death jar, brimming with filth and decay. The lyric was written to be screamed, so he screamed it. *"This is what lives inside me!"*

The laughter returned. Adam laughed, all through the night.

*

As Frank Castro was driving from Katy, Texas, to the backwoods shop of Trevor Bodain in Louisiana, Felix Bryant was easing through the streets of a north Austin neighborhood to a house he hadn't seen in four years. Not knowing what to expect, he nervously anticipated seeing Adam again. He'd lied to him at his mother's funeral, something he'd never forgiven himself for. In Adam's entire life, it was the first and only time he asked him if he were indeed his father. He denied him. In Adam's worst moment, he denied him.

The cock crows.

Felix knew everything. He knew about the self-cutting, the humiliations and the incest. Yet he stayed away, never wanting to get involved in the rigors of parenthood. Never wanting the responsibility of rearing a child, nor the emotional investment. He sought an abortion, something Mrs. Cabbershaw would not be associated with. Felix Bryant was more than a friend to the Cabbershaw's; he was family. So when he came to Florence that spring evening, telling her of a one-night stand that ended with a pregnancy, Florence's maternal instinct flourished, even though Bryant wanted nothing to do with raising a child. Not wanting any part of an abortion, Mrs. Cabbershaw had a conversation with her lifelong friend. Being independently wealthy in her own right, she cut a deal.

"I will set up a trust fund of three hundred thousand dollars for the woman and her child," she told him. "The two will not be able to touch the principle until the child turns twenty-one. Until that time, the interest should be sufficient to provide a comfortable living, I would assume. I'll pay for a modest house in a nice part of the city, middle-class should do. Any other needs that may arise, I'll trust you, Felix, to tend to them in a reserved and frugal manner. Do we have an agreement?"

"Yes, we do. And for that, I will be indebted to you and Mr. Cabbershaw the rest of my days."

They shook on it. That was twenty-five years ago.

It was just four years ago that Adam called him in the middle of the night, gripped in panic and remorse, screaming, "She's dead! Deloris is *dead*!" Felix called the authorities and raced over. There was nothing anyone could do; she was gone. A victim of her own insecurities. Adam

Parker was now alone. A twenty-five year old with money and no direction, a boat without a rudder. Felix watched from afar as Adam spiraled down into the depths of madness, never realizing the obvious. Adam stopped answering his calls, always allowing the machine to take his messages. When he would call back, it was at such odd hours and the messages were so rambling that Felix would disregard them. One came at 2:30 a.m., telling him he wanted to put his *jar* on wheels and take his fun to the streets.

Pointless rambling.

By this time, there was no need or point in telling Adam the truth because too much bitter water had already flowed beneath the bridge. It was best for both men to push forward with their lives, leaving the past where it belonged. Buried with Deloris Parker.

He pulled into the driveway of Adam's house, noticing the yard was well-kept and the house looking as he remembered. The landscapers he'd hired were doing a good job. Fall leaves were starting to turn, and soon they, too, would have to be dealt with. He pushed the thought out of his mind. He sat in the car, trying to convince himself that this was a good thing today. Surely, Adam was home from work and a casual drop-by after such a long time would not be considered inappropriate. He would simply tell him he was in the neighborhood and wanted to see the place.

Foolish.

He didn't remember walking from his Mercedes to the door, but he found himself there, rapping on the frame. When there was no answer, he rang the bell and knocked again. No answer. He waited before repeating, still no answer. Even if he were asleep, he'd be up by now. It wasn't like Adam to lie about and ignore the calling of a visitor. Felix knocked once more, hard, and rang the bell repeatedly. Minutes passed and there was no response. Puzzled, he fished his keys from his suit and tried unlocking the door. If Adam was not home, there was no need for alarm. He had a key and just wanted to inspect the house the Cabbershaws had paid for. Nothing wrong in that.

Except his key didn't open the door. Undoubtedly, Adam had changed the lock. Disappointed, Felix was about to leave when he remembered he had a key to the kitchen door at the back of the house. He decided to give it a try. As he made his way around to the back of the house, he thought about what would happen if Adam came home and found him alone inside his house. He heartened himself with the knowledge that his car was in the driveway, so Adam could not be caught off guard. At the rear of the house, he went to the kitchen door and slid in the key. It turned. He opened the door and stepped in, closing it behind him.

Instantly, Felix knew things had changed. The kitchen was littered with empty liquor bottles, the majority of which were Bacardi 151 rum and cheap vodka. The sink was filled with plates encrusted with weeks-old food. Pizza boxes and beer bottles canvassed the room like dolls on a little girl's bed. Felix could tell Adam wasn't living well. He peered past the kitchen, noticing how dark the rest of the house was. Confused, he went back out and circled the house, looking at the widows. He was surprised to see that every window in the house was painted black from the inside, something he'd missed upon arriving.

"What the devil?"

Making his way back to the kitchen, it seemed the only window in the entire house that wasn't painted black was the window on the kitchen door. Inside, he went to the edge of the kitchen where it joined with the long hall across from the living room. It was as black as night. He chose to find a light in the living room then decided the wall switch was his safest bet, since he had no way of knowing where Adam had placed whatever lamps there were. As he slid his feet across the carpet, his shoes were constantly bombarded with empty bottles of all sorts. Some big and heavy, and others so tiny he had no idea what they were. He remembered the light switch was on the far wall next to the front door. After making his way blindly through the mine field of bottles and pizza boxes, he fumbled on the wall until he found the light switch.

"Jesus, finally," he said, flipping the light.

Click.

The first shock that hit him was that instead of a nice white glow, he was surrounded in the purple hue of a very strong black light. The second shock was much more profound.

"Oh dear god," Felix said, aloud. "Sweet Mary in heaven."

The furniture was decimated. The couch had been ripped apart with cushion stuffing scattered about the room like leaves in an autumn yard. Tables were broken and lamps shattered. Liquor and beer bottles so thick they seemed to be growing from the filthy carpet like weeds. With them were tiny brown bottles he didn't recognize. He picked one up, reading the label: **AMSTERDAM**. It was a popper loaded with amyl nitrate. Felix shook his head, gritting his teeth. There were dozens of them mixed in with the larger bottles, as well as what seemed to be sealed quart jars. As disturbing as it all was, it was the walls that gripped Felix in panic.

They were painted black from ceiling to floor. On them was the rattled scrawl of someone losing touch with reality. Every square inch of the walls was covered in florescent chalk with the ramblings of a mind gone terribly awry. Felix calmed himself, studying the words. Line after line—some several feet in height, and some as small as centimeters—wound around the room like a Mixmaster of delusion. Some of the words were in perfect poetic meter while others were shear madness stomped out in the cadence of primal rage. Hateful words like *murder* and *rape* intertwined around such symbolic odes as love and sympathy. Some of the writings held actual ideas, thoughts that flowed from an active mind, while others were nothing more than hate-filled stabs at humanity. Guttural language that fit more with demonic possession than an educated man. The entire room was filled with these passions. It would take days to read them all and find some sort of order to them.

But there was no order. Not here, not now. Felix understood what had happened, even though his own mind refused to accept it. Adam had gone over the edge.

Guilt fell upon him like an avalanche. "My god . . . What have I done?"

The mere thought of his son sitting in that room at night, scribbling on the walls of his house, with his inner feelings twisting his mind into a conduit of such depravity took his breath away. He circled the room again and again, each lap more horrible than the last.

"What have I done?"

Soon after, he realized there was the rest of the house to see. He wanted no part of it. He wanted to walk back out the kitchen door and never return. He wanted to get as far away from that house and Adam Parker as he could, even if it meant never contacting him again. But he had to see the rest. He *had* to.

Walking back to the hall, he suddenly realized that there was a stench in the air. A mix of body odor and piss. A nauseating bouquet combined with rotten food, stale beer, and assorted nitrates. There was also the fetid stench of rotting decay. Felix fought the urge to vomit then continued, discovering that indeed the rest of the house was as dark as the living room. He knew there was a light switch for the hall a few feet away. He found it quickly.

Click.

The hall came alive with green light. Felix had to adjust his eyes and soon realized the madness had taken a new form. The walls of the hallway were not littered with words, but drawings. Sick, macabre drawings of dead bodies, headless women, and dead babies. Both sides of the hall presented grotesque images so horrible his mind reeled. Women, dead women, with what appeared to be transparent bags on their heads. Their eyes crossed out with tongues protruding in death, as stick figures of men ejaculated on their corpses. Graves with hands reaching out from the soil. Body parts. Heads, legs, arms, and limbless torsos covered the walls. It was a pageant of insanity. At the end of the hall was what appeared to be a self-portrait Adam had done of himself in actual size. He was naked. His eyes seemed to be peering from sunken caves within his skull. His shoulder bones and clavicles stretched beneath his yellowy skin, jutting up like rods holding a canvas tent. Felix thought of the Jews caught in Nazi madness, emaciated forms too pathetic to look at. But unlike holocaust victims, Adam's eyes weren't defeated. The blue gems that flashed from their sockets were filled with rage. The likeness was incredible, the poor boy had an artist's touch, but the work itself was too disturbed to be ignored. He walked toward it, trembling, noticing a pentagram drawn on his lower stomach just above his hairless genitals.

Felix was beginning to hyperventilate; his breathing became erratic.

He extended his arms to the wall, bracing himself with his head down, trying to catch his breath. More and more bottles and debris littered the hall. At his foot, he saw one of the many sealed jars. He'd seen them throughout the house, but this was the first to resonate with him. He stooped, picking it up. It was heavy as he examined it in the murky green light. It was filled with something, but the light made it hard to see. He was still standing at the base of Adam's portrait. He remembered Deloris had the room to the left and Adam, the right. The door to his left was closed. He opened it. Suddenly, bright light exploded in his eyes. Her windows were not painted and the walls still the same pretty blue she loved so much. The room looked pristine compared to the rest of Adam's gallery of disgust. He'd left it clean as a monument to his mother. However, the room was not completely unblemished. Adam had marked it as well. On the wall above her bed were two words, written one above the other:

AZURE
DYING

He had no idea what it meant or why Adam wrote them. Puzzled, he remembered the jar in his hand. What he saw when he gazed on it in the bright light made him jump, "*Oh god!*" he yelped. "*God in heaven!*"

The quart jar was stuffed to the lid with dead mice. There must have been at least a hundred white mice packed in the jar. A putrid display of rotting death sealed inside the glass. He dropped it to the carpet, backing out of the room with his hand over his mouth, trying to calm his heaving stomach. He backed across the hall to what used to be Adam's bedroom. Feeling light-headed, he stopped at the doorway. The air was thick and heavy deep inside the house. The reek and his emotions were making his stomach turn. Tears welled in the corners of his eyes.

How could he have been so blind? How could he have not seen what was going to happen? The man had lived his entire life under the thumb of a dominating woman. After she died, he took a job working at night. Now he understood. He worked at night. He blacked out all light from his house. He lived alone, he worked alone, he thought alone, he did everything alone. For four years, he sentenced himself to solitary confinement, cut off from the world and even the light of day. For four years, he'd been living in this house alone, in the dark, drinking and doing what other awful things his mind told him to do. Adam had become a prisoner in his own mind. He was balancing on the edge of total mental annihilation.

Felix pressed his head against the wall to collect himself. He wanted see Adam's room. At least it was his room before Deloris died; God knows what he'd find. Still, he had to know. He raised his head, dried his tears, then entered the room. Inside, he felt the wall for the switch and hesitantly flipped it.

Click.

Instantly, he was washed in a sea of red light. For a split second, he thought it was a photographer's dark room. But as his eyes adjusted, he found it was no longer a bedroom. The only furniture was a desk on the side wall to his right, with a computer and a chair. Above the desk was a large picture of Adam's mother, Deloris. He expected to see more black walls and chalk obscenities. Instead, he found the walls were covered in some sort of paper. From floor to ceiling, from corner to corner, every square inch of the walls was covered in some kind of loose-fitting paper. A wave of relief washed over Felix as he walked to the desk and looked at Deloris. It had been four years since he last saw her. She was lying in her casket, dressed in white, looking as beautiful as the first time he laid eyes on her all those years ago. The picture was a good one. A close up, her face filled the frame. Smiling her winning smile. Part of him still missed her, even though she was a monster to her child.

Felix backed away and decided to look more closely at the walls. On second glance, he discovered the paper was not just paper, but computer printed photographs.

"What the . . ."

Then reality stabbed him like a dagger. The walls, all four of them, from floor to ceiling were covered with the death photos of Amy Crowder, Julie Brooks, Tiffany Malvern, and the three poor boys who picked the wrong day to skip class. The girls, naked, hanging by their necks. Different angles of all three, hundreds of sickening photographs. Shots only the killer could have taken. The three boys, hogtied, with their heads shot off at close range. The blood, the murder, the insanity!

Felix felt himself seize. His body locked as the ultimate reality unveiled itself like a curtain call. The writings in the living room, the drawings in the hall, the bottles of alcohol and chemicals, the isolation, and the lunacy. Countless jars filled with decomposing vermin. Murder, mayhem, and madness. Adam was the monster! His son was the Capital Hangman!

He turned back to the picture of Deloris. Her smile seemed to change, taking on a whole new meaning. Her sweet smile was now an evil grin as she sat atop an altar of death, looking down, proud of her son's plunge into depravity.

"*Oh, my boy . . . what have you done?*" Felix said to the walls. "*Sweet Jesus, no! Not you! My boy, what have you done?*" He had to get out. It was too much. He had to leave, and leave now. "*My boy, no! Not you! What have you done?*"

When he turned to escape, the flash of Adam, naked, inches away from him, came as a jolt just as the blade of the kitchen knife plunged deep inside his abdomen then up inside his chest. Adam was on him, holding him for the first time in his entire life. He'd longed to be this close to his son, now he was dying at his hands.

Adam's face was a twisted mask of rabid brutality. He hissed, "*No one sees this work till I'm gone!*"

Felix's body went into shock. Cold engulfed him as Adam slid him to the floor, holding the big knife in place. He knew he was dying. How could this be? What happened? Why him? Why now? All he wanted to do was tell him the truth. After all these years, he had to tell him the truth.

"*Adam,*" he moaned, blood erupting from his mouth. Mustering all his might, he slurred, "*Adam . . . I . . . I'm your . . . fa-father.*"

At first, the words sounded Greek to Adam. The word *father* was so far removed from him it seemed like a foreign language. Then, as he held the knife deep inside Felix, he began to understand all of it. The Tidy Man, Felix Bryant, the man that took care of everything was indeed his father.

"*What?*" He began to cry.

Felix's eyes rolled back as his heart stopped pumping blood. Adam had been successful in severing vital arteries. He'd been waiting his whole life for his father to save him. He'd longed and prayed for the day his father would reveal himself and make his life have purpose. But now . . .

Now . . .

Rage erupted inside him like a super nova. He pulled the knife free, holding it in both hands as he knelt beside his father, his sides heaving in despair. "*You!*" he screamed. "*You made me?! You did this, you miserable fuck?!*" Adam raised the blade high over his head. "*You watched and did nothing! You fucking let her do this to me! You lied to me!*"

The knife plunged down.

Again.

Again.

And again.

The blade dug into Felix's chest so many times it was impossible count. A lifetime of anger and pain poured out with every violent thrust. Even after his adrenaline subsided, Adam kept stabbing his father's dead body in a furious frenzy of gore and destruction. Over and over, he killed the man that *created* him until he had no strength to continue.

He could kill him no more.

Naked and covered in blood, he sat beside his dead father and wept. He wept for the child that he never got to be. Then he thought of *her*. He stood, turning to his mother's portrait. Dripping with his father's blood, he stood before Deloris, still shaking with rage. Gritting his teeth and blowing like a bull, he then dropped the knife to the floor.

"*I'm not done yet,*" he growled. "*My life's paid for your disgrace. It's time your life paid for mine!*" He stepped to the picture and placed his right hand on the glass, creating a bloody handprint directly over her face. "I'm not paying anymore," he sneered at the portrait. "You're paying me."

*

Adam sat on the closed toilet seat in his bathroom, covered in blood, with his head in his hands. All he had were questions. Why had she not told him Felix was his father? Why did Felix not tell him himself? He'd asked him at the cemetery and still he denied it. Why was he doing it now? He hadn't laid eyes on him in four years, why the sudden need to barge into his house?

Walking to the sink, he flipped on one of only two white lights in the entire house. The bathroom erupted in bright white light. Out of the corner of his eye, he could see Felix's bloody corpse lying in the tub where he had dragged him several minutes before. He looked back to the mirror. The image shocked him. He hadn't really looked at himself in the mirror in weeks. His face was gaunt. His eyes hollow as his cheekbones seemed to press against the skin in an effort of escape. His face was speckled in a crimson mist of blood that had sprayed from the brutal attack. His entire naked form was bathed in the scarlet film. Placing his hands on the counter, he leaned close to the glass and peered into his own sinister eyes.

Death.

There was no mistake. He'd gone over the edge. This had changed everything. He was now a brutal killer. His mind began to wander, his thoughts rambled from one thing to the next with no continuity. He looked again at how thin he was. He looked down at his blood-covered body and noticed for the first time in as long as he could remember how thin he looked. He fumbled through a nearby closet, finding Deloris's old bathroom scale. The last time he weighed himself, over two years ago, he'd weighed a solid 165 on his five-nine frame. He stepped on the scale and was surprised to see the dial stop at 138. He'd lost nearly thirty pounds.

How?

He paused at that point, trying to remember his last meal. For the life of him, he could not recall the last time he'd eaten. Three days? Five? A week? It had been a little over a week since he returned from Louisiana; assured that he'd eaten there, he tried to remember a meal since coming home.

Nothing.

309

He almost laughed, but the bloody body in the tub stopped him. His attention returned to the man in the mirror. He ran his hands over his eyes, causing a vast smear of blood to cover his pale face. He continued until he wore a glistening mask of crimson, gazing at himself as though studying fine art.

He had changed . . . again.

He was a devil, a destroyer of souls.

Before, he did what he did for gratification, but now he was a beast. He'd crossed his own line. He not only spilled blood, he acted in rage. It was manic and out of control. Passion run amok, something he felt could never happen.

As he peered at his bloody form in the mirror, he needed something else. Walking back into his office, he slid a Slayer CD into his player and zipped through the tracks until he found what he wanted. After pushing the play button, he went back to the mirror, snagging a bottle of amyl nitrate off the floor as he went. The song "Deviance" started. He waited through the first verse, then, as the second started, he sniffed the popper. His heart began to race; his eyes bulged as he felt the veins in his neck throb with his heartbeat. After that subsided, his mind began to alter. As the toxins peaked, he went eye-to-bloody eye with himself in the mirror as the song continued to pound away at his crumbling mind:

"Walk the streets beneath the shadows, searching for a cryptic bride. Eat alive the conscience I hate, without pain I watch you die. I will live through this forever. I have done the things you grieve. As you kneel before its evil, my face is the last you'll see!"

He snapped back, looking now inside the monster that he'd become. Shocked, alone, and feeling unearthly, the song continued, but Adam heard no words, no lyrics, no music. What tiny bit of practical logic that still survived inside his mind evaporated like a wisp of steam. In his heart, he knew the song meant nothing. There was never a song written that could make you do anything you weren't going to do anyway. But like any piece of art that strikes a nerve, these songs told his story. The harsh, unrelenting onslaught of power and mayhem told the life story of Adam Parker. It was the soundtrack to the horror film that was his life. And now, after all these years, *he* was finally the boogeyman instead of the victim.

He turned a bloody gaze to his dead father in the bathtub. He knew he answered to someone else; he'd picked up on that years ago. If he was here, there was someone somewhere who knew it. That meant that when they started looking, this would be the first place they'd start. The house was too incriminating to cover up, and he'd be damned if he was going to change one damned thing.

Let them find it!

He was through the looking glass now. No stopping, no turning back. He walked back to the picture of Deloris, staring at it again. He hadn't eaten in a week and only slept when his body collapsed. Swaying to the banshee screams blaring from his stereo, he hit the popper again, feeling the scar on the back of his right shoulder, the coward bully that never faces him. He saw his mother. She laughed at him. He was a child and wanted to be held, a small boy needing his mother's grace and security. She laughed at him. When he was older, she used him like a sex slave. In his heart, he knew she was dead. But in his warped mind, he *still* had to kill her. By his *own* hands he had to make her pay. Only then could it end.

He washed himself in the sink, not wanting to disturb Felix in the tub. After dressing, he deposited the knife on the kitchen counter and went outside, amazed at how cool it had gotten. A gentle rain had even started to fall. He pulled Felix's Mercedes into his garage after backing the azure H2 out into the street. With his killing jar loaded for a final run, he drove away from the house on McCormick Street as the demonic sounds inside the vehicle pulsed to the rhythms of the autumn rains pelting its skin.

46

Frank rose before dawn. After a shower, he dressed in the same clothes and headed to the computer in the lobby. The only people milling around were staffers and businessmen enjoying their free continental breakfast. He sat at the screen and logged onto his web address. From there, he entered his account with Intelius, pulling up the reverse phone directory. He entered the phone number he'd gotten from Bodain and waited.

It hit. The screen opened with a match, reading,

Deloris Parker
2102 McCormick St.
Austin, TX

He had it. Even though he didn't recognize the address, he had the son of a bitch. He logged out of Intelius then logged onto MapQuest, searching the new address. The screen opened, giving him the location of the street. It was in northwest Austin, close to Cedar Park. His heart leaped. This was it. The only thing between him and the sick creep who killed Tiffany was five hundred miles of highway. If he caught a break and didn't get stopped for speeding, he could get there in six hours. He looked at his watch. Five-forty. He could be there by one at the latest.

He checked out and got on the road. The wolf was awake inside him, thirsty for vengeance and needing to be free of his cage. "We'll get there," Frank said to himself. "It's time the devil gets his due."

*

The sun had risen to illuminate a gray sky. A thick cloud cover swelled overhead, giving the day an already gloomy feel. It was the first week in October, and the autumn winds had descended to the southern states, ending the long hot drought of the summer. Frank needed fuel, so he stopped just outside Lake Charles to fill his tank and stretch his legs. He stood next to his BMW as the pump replenished the thirsty car. The gravity of his actions over the last two days weighed on him like a stone. He'd brutalized someone who considered him a friend, gone toe-to-toe with a compound full of criminals and killed at least two people, maybe three if no one got to the Cajun soon enough. It would be worth it if the information he possessed was accurate. However, if it was wrong . . . If *he* was wrong . . . It was more than he wanted to consider.

The pump clicked off, bringing him back to the present. As he placed the nozzle back on the pump, he noticed something a block away, down a side street from the convenience store he'd stopped at. It was a church. A Catholic church, *Our Lady of the Acadia.* He grumbled inside. Something screeched in his mind like fingernails on a blackboard. For the first time in years, he thought of his sweet Catholic mother. What would she say about all he'd done? How he was living and had lived? It called to him, like a distant echo far from the original source. If the information was right, it'd reconcile his actions with justice. But the battle raging within him was a different matter. He closed his eyes, seeing her warm face, her motherly smile. "Oh shit," he whispered, opening them to see the church. With a heavy sigh he groaned, "What the hell, I got time."

The lot at the church held only one car. Frank parked beside it then climbed out, looking at the gray ceiling hovering overhead. Walking to the front of the church, he felt his legs getting heavy, like a man walking his last mile. He opened the door and stood there, staring at the expanse in front of him. The stained glass windows told the story of Jesus's trial and crucifixion. He hesitated to anoint himself with the holy water at the entrance. He felt like a hypocrite. Again, he heard his mother and saw her face. He dabbed the water on his finger and crossed himself. "A lot of damn good," he whispered. He scanned the church, finding the confessional booth at the back on the far left. After a deep breath, he made his way to it, standing at the door like someone about to enter a haunted house.

"Just do it, asshole," he told himself.

He entered, sitting on the bench. He could feel the priest on the other side of the latticed panel, waiting. He had nothing to say. Well, he had a lot to say, but he didn't know where to start. The silence hung between them like a heavy mist. Frank leaned his elbows on his knees, wanting a cigarette. Deciding there was no use in worrying about offenses, he lit one.

"It's more common than you may realize," the priest told him. "You'll find an ashtray in the right corner."

Frank blew a half-hearted chuckle through his nose. "Of course there's an ashtray," he thought. "This is where souls come to purge their guilt."

Again, he said nothing, letting the silence gather around him like a blanket. He'd spent his life in pursuit of the unattainable. Now, the attainable was waiting on him, but all he felt was guilt. Guilt for all he'd done in the past and guilt for what he was prepared to do. Killing Parker wouldn't bring Tiffany back, or any of the other victims. In reality, the only thing it would do is end the reign of a madman and ease his own anguish. Maybe that was enough. Maybe he was on the right course after all. The wolf lay on the floor of the confessional at his feet, waiting patiently as Frank fought with himself.

"Go ahead, my son," the priest said. "You have something to say?"

Frank took a long drag on his cigarette then started. "There was this woman," he said, slowly. "She meant a lot to me. In the end, I guess I took her for granted." He paused, choosing his words. "I never knew before what she meant to me. I just assumed she'd always be here. But things change. We can't see what trouble's brewing around the next corner. We have no idea what the next day's gonna bring." He fell silent.

"Did you love her?"

There it was. The obvious, in plain English. "Yeah," Frank replied, "I guess I did. But not how you're thinking," he told the priest. "She was just a kid, early twenties. Her whole life in front of her. I liked watching her grow, I guess. I liked laughing at her, like a little sister. She was special, father." He paused. "She deserved better," he said, going back to his cigarette. "A lot better."

"Where is she now?"

"Dead," the word hurt his throat to say. It was too final for such a living soul.

"I'm sorry for your loss," the priest said, his voice calm and strong. Frank needed that.

"A madman killed her. He took her away from all of us."

"I assume the police are involved?"

Frank closed his eyes, his head dropping further. "Sure. Of course they are."

"Your grief is only natural."

"Well," Frank started, "that's really not why I'm here."

The priest hesitated before telling Frank, "Go on."

"See, father, I'm not a good man. Haven't been in a long time. I'm an alcoholic. I use drugs, sleep with strange women. I'm the kind of guy parents pray their daughters never meet. I've cheated, stole, killed, and broken about every one of those commandments in your good book. The laws of God that protect good people from men like me. To a lot of people, I'm nothing more than," he paused, "total destruction. A man to dread. I'm okay with that, you understand. You reap what you sow, right?"

"Yes."

"I've sown bad seeds, father. A lot of them. I was a cop once, and I saved a man's life, a friend, my partner. It cost me my career because," he puffed his cigarette, "well, just because. At the time, I thought I was wronged, that they injured me. But now, looking back all these years later, I understand it was the right thing to do. Again, father, I was the bad guy, *me*. And deserved to be." Frank fell silent before going further. "In the last week, I've left a trail of destruction. Things I didn't want to do, but felt I had to. More of those bad seeds. So up to this point, as I see it anyway, my ledger is pretty tipped to one side. And it ain't the good one."

Frank could hear the priest stirring, adjusting himself before he asked, "So, my son, what do you have to confess?"

"Not a damn thing," Frank said. "Like I said, it's too far along to find salvation now. That lot is cast, so to say."

"Then what are you seeking?"

"I know who killed her, father. I know it like I know my name. Like I said, I had to do some bad things to get his name, but I have it now. I know who he is, and I know where he is." Frank wrestled his emotions, adding, "He told me on my answering machine that death is the most intimate act, and that he knows her intimately. Far more than me. Far more than I ever could."

"Obviously he has no conscience," the priest said.

"To hell with him," Frank replied. "This is about her. Only her family loved her more than I did. He watched her die. I watched her live." He paused, taking a drag on the cigarette. Again, he heard Parker's voice, taunting, laughing at him. "Maybe he's right. I mean, what's more intimate than death? Hmm?" Frank remembered the young man from the night before, looking at him as he struggled for life before he ended it with a bullet. With guilt he said, "To look into a person's eyes as they die, knowing you took their life away, it's the closest two people can get. It's the closest any of us should *never* hope for."

The priest didn't like the sound of that; it was bordering on incrimination. After a long pause he asked, "So what are you asking?"

"If I avenge *this* wrong. If I serve him justice from my own hand, will it balance out the bad I've done? Will it . . . even the score?" he asked, exhaling smoke. "Or is that even possible?"

The priest thought to himself, collecting the right words. He wanted whoever this was to give his information to the police, no matter how he obtained it. "My son," he started, "there is always forgiveness. Simply being here shows your remorse, your want for atonement. You've taken the right step, albeit a difficult one. God can and will forgive. You were once an officer of the law, so you *know*, you truly *understand* what the right thing to do is." He pointed his words directly at him, saying, "If you will do the very thing you know and understand to be the *right thing*. If you open your heart, release your anger, confess your terrible

316

sins, and allow those chosen to act to seize this criminal, then God will light the path on your dark journey. And you can be forgiven."

"The *right* thing," Frank said, knowingly.

"Yes. The laws of God, and man, insist on it."

Call Bodinger. That was the right thing to do.

Not a chance in hell.

Frank crushed out his cigarette, standing in the confessional. He pushed the door open, saying as he left, "Well, padre, it's too late to change who I am. So I guess you'll find me in hell."

47

Adam awoke with the cop tapping on his window. Startled awake, he lowered the glass, blinking sleep from his eyes. He'd fallen asleep in the bank parking lot as the slow rain tapped a lullaby. "Sir, are you waiting on someone?" the cop asked.

Adam had to rouse himself. "Uh, yeah . . . officer. Yes, my friend needs a ride home." He glanced at his hands; blood was still caked around his fingernails. The Glock was under the seat if the cop pushed the wrong buttons. He knew this was basically a suicide mission, but the objective had yet to be met. He couldn't get thrown off this early in the game. "Is there a problem?" he asked, trying to look innocent. He'd spent the night cruising the streets of Austin. His mind racing in all directions at once, never able to fully comprehend what had happened. The Tidy Man had barged into his house, finding his shop of horrors before he was ready for it to be unveiled. Then the murder. The man he'd suspected was his father finally admitted it while dying in his arms. He left for his final game, stalking her as best he could. He knew her address, but her cop husband was turning out to be a bigger pain than he anticipated. He just needed her alone for a few seconds. Just a few seconds is all it would . . .

"Not really," the cop said, snapping him back to reality. "It's just when we see someone asleep in a vehicle, we like to check it out. Make sure they're okay."

"Uh, no . . . officer. Everything's fine. Just had a long night, I guess."

"Yeah, you look tired. Go home and get some sleep. In your bed," the cop said, pointedly.

"Yeah, sure. Thanks, officer, thank you."

The cop backed off, looking at the H2. "Never seen a Hummer this color."

"Yeah, it's special," Adam said, the 9mm at his fingertips.

The cop stepped forward, looking inside at the wall built against the front seats. "Never seen a Hummer like this one, ever."

"No, you wouldn't have." Adam tried to calm himself. "It's custom. A gift . . . from my father."

"He must love you very much?"

In his mind, Adam saw the bloody corpse of his father, the Tidy Man, lying lifeless and butchered in his bathtub. "It would appear so."

The cop scanned the vehicle again before saying, "Well, collect your friend and get some rest. Can't have people sleeping in bank parking lots, now can we?"

"No, sir, of course. I'll make a block to wake up and come back. No problem."

"Good idea. Have a nice day," he told Adam then went back to his unit and waited for Adam to leave.

Adam fired up the H2 and left the lot, slowly. After a block, he knew he couldn't wait for her here; he'd have to find another way. The game's final round was just starting; he had time. He'd get what he wanted, one way or another.

48

Jim Saunders was elbow-deep in paperwork by noon. Like everyone in Austin, he loved the cleansing rain that fell all during the night. Even if it was only a low pressure cell that stalled over the city, dropping several inches of cool, autumn rain, he felt like it was cleansing the city. Crime always slowed when it rained, and maybe if things slowed enough, he and his team might actually be able to piece together some kind of formula to catch the city's serial killer.

The task force had pulled all the VIN numbers of every H2 Hummer purchased in the Austin area over the last four years. Cross-referencing the vehicles with their owners and doing interviews with anyone that remotely came within an eyelash of fitting Kevin Kerndon's profile. Thus far, the results were minimal, but at least they were heading in the right direction. There were a couple of promising leads, however, each had ironclad alibis. Still, the names were on the board of suspects which consisted of only two men.

Randal Clemens, a thirty-year-old divorcee living alone in Georgetown. Had a respectable job with a local marketing firm and spent his free time playing golf with his buddies. But he was raised by a single mother, had minor run-ins with the law as a teenager, and, according to his coworkers, was very aloof. He bought his black H2 two years earlier. He and the vehicle fit the profile.

Calvin Weathers was twenty-seven. A bachelor living in south

320

Austin near Slaughter Lane. His H2 was three years old. He worked as an office manager in a local finance company. With a reputation as a hothead who was prone to blow ups, he too was a product of a single-parent background. His mother had died a year earlier in a car crash in Rolling Wood. Again, it was thin, but he fit the profile. Soon they would widen the search to men with young families, and then women who had purchased an H2 that other people may have access to. They knew the vehicle would lead them to D sooner or later.

Later was looking more plausible.

Around twelve thirty, as Saunders was eating lunch at his desk, Chief Short buzzed him on his office phone. "Saunders," he answered.

"Jim, I need a favor," Short told him.

"Sure, boss, what's up?"

"Well, there's this old friend of mine. A *wealthy* old friend. Her name's Florence Cabbershaw. Her husband has the big law firm."

"Howard Cabbershaw?" Saunders asked.

"The same."

Saunders instantly sat up in his chair. Howard Cabbershaw ran the one of the biggest law firms in the state, much less Austin. If his wife wanted a special favor, and was friends with your boss, you paid close attention.

"I'm listening," Saunders said.

"Well, Jim, we may have a situation. Then again, probably not. Seems the lady has a butler who she's fond of, the guy's been with her for eons, and he went to see his estranged son yesterday."

"Okay."

"He went over late in the morning and the old guy never came back. Mrs. Cabbershaw is beside herself that something's happened to the man. I think he and the son are off bonding, but she says it's out of character for him to run off like that without telling her."

Saunders could hear concern in Short's voice. He was trying not to sound worried, but it seeped through. "You want us to check it out?" Saunders asked.

"If you can spare a couple of people, Jim. I know this is just an old lady worrying about some shit that won't ever amount to a hill of beans,

321

but like I said, she's loaded. And married to one of the most powerful men in this city."

Saunders exhaled, knowing he had to follow through with it. Prince and Reyes, affectionately known to the APD as *Black and Tan*, were due to hit the streets with new VIN numbers soon anyway, might as well send them.

"No problem, Captain," Saunders assured him. "I'll get some guys on it."

"No uniforms, you understand."

"Yes, sir."

"And Jim?"

"Yes, Chief?"

"Keep this on the QT. Understood? Nothing to embarrass the old girl."

"Of course. I've got two good men. It'll be nice and quiet. My word."

"Good," Short responded. "I knew I could count on you. Butler's name is Felix Bryant. The son's name is Adam Parker. He lives at 2102 McCormick, a nice neighborhood, north Austin. "

Saunders jotted down the information and told Short they'd take care of it.

"Thanks, Jim."

Saunders could hear the relief in Short's voice. He figured, just as the chief had, that the father and son had reconciled and were off making hay. His department was stretched thin as it was, but it was for an expensive friend, and for that there was never too little time.

Saunders thought about calling them at their desks, but realized he'd been at his own for hours and needed to stretch his legs. He left his office, walking the hall to where the detectives were gathered working on the D case. As he entered the room, no one looked up. There was Bodinger and Cordova, Prince and Reyes, and a whole team of officers, each doing their part to find the Capital Hangman.

He hated that damned name.

"Reyes, Prince," he said in a voice just over a whisper. The two looked up and Prince waved off his partner and went to the door. "What's up?" he asked.

"Gonna give you two a chance to get some air."

Prince blew relief, rolling his eyes. It was about time. "Shoot, boss."

"Chief Short has a special job for us. There's an old friend, a *rich* old friend who needs a favor. Her butler went to see his son yesterday morning. I think they're on the outs, and the old fella never got home. It's been over twenty-four hours and she's worried. Now the chief . . ." He stopped, noticing Reyes joining the conversation. He lowered his voice another register. "The chief thinks it's nothing, but he feels he owes it to the old gal to check it out. He wants us to do it and I thought of you two."

"No prob, Cap," Prince said. "Just give us the names and the address."

"The butler's name is Felix Bryant. The son is Adam Parker. He lives on the north side, 2102 McCormick. Just run by and check it out. Do a knock and nice and make sure everything's on the up. Okay?"

"Anything for rich friends, right, boss?" Prince said, smiling.

"Just keep it cool, okay?"

"Not a problem," he answered, as he and Reyes went back to their desks to get their jackets. Prince slipped his on as Saunders left, but before he could turn, his partner asked, "Hey, what did Jim say the kid's name was?"

"Parker," Prince said, looking at his notes. "Adam Parker. Why?"

Reyes picked up a clipboard studying the top sheet. "I thought I knew that name," he told Prince. "Adam Parker. He's three from the top. Must have bought an H2 in the last year."

"A bird in the hand," Prince said.

"What?"

"A bird in the hand is worth two in the bush," he explained.

"You mean to kill two birds with one stone."

"Whatever."

Bodinger looked up, agitated by the talking. "What are you two on about?" he asked.

"Nothing, *Big Time*," Reyes jabbed, as they walked out. "Just going to solve the case, that's all."

*

Frank had been driving since before sunup, stopping only for his visit to the confessional. During the entire drive, he had to keep convincing himself that he was on the right track. The chances this was the right guy boggled the mind to comprehend. He thought about the meetings with Tully and Bullet, and how all that seemed to just fall in his lap. The odds that this guy was the Hangman were too high to calculate.

But still, he drove on. He had to, it was all he had. He had to find him before the cops did, before Bodinger. He had to find this man and kill him. He had to do what Tiffany told the son of a bitch he'd do if he caught him. He had to cut his heart out, just like Tiff said. He'd stashed an old hunting knife in his car, beneath the seat, just in case this wild goose chase turned up a real lead. He thought about Bodain and his gold teeth, screaming to him that he was in so much pain. He thought of Tully and how his old buddy was now on the lam because of his actions.

He saw the face of the young man on the floor seconds before he took his life away. He heard the priest telling him to do the *right thing*. "Why start now?"

But the real question was what if he was wrong? What if the guy was a mechanic and did all the work himself? What if he read the voice on his machine wrong? Plain and simple, what if he was wrong all together, about all of it?

He hit Austin at around one o'clock, driving straight to the north side and in particular, McCormick Street and 2102. After making several wrong turns, he found his way to McCormick and soon was a block away from the house he was looking for.

He killed the engine of the BMW, sitting in silence, staring at the house from a block away. The adrenaline rush he was feeling was so strong he had to stop himself from bolting from the car and bull-rushing the front door. The thought that filled his mind was the promise burnt so far deep in his soul he'd never back off from it. He was going to cut the beating heart out of this monster, avenging Tiffany's death if it cost him his life. With that in his heart, he pressed on. He climbed from the small car, surveying the neighborhood. Kids were at school and their parents at work; silence surrounded him. A few early leaves fell as he stepped away from the car toward what was going to determine the rest of his life. He walked to the house not knowing what he'd do if Adam Parker opened the door he was about to knock on. To see, in the flesh, the animal that tortured his beloved little sister standing before him was a thought he struggled to harness. He paused beside a withering old oak to settle his emotions. He recalled his police training. He had to be prepared for anything. If King Kong dropped from the sky when he tapped on that door, he had to know it was going to happen. He crossed the neighbor's yard and soon stepped onto the porch, leaning against the front wall. His heart beat a cadence that could keep time with a jack rabbit as he slipped on a pair of leather gloves prior to pulling the .45 automatic from his waist. Taking a deep breath, he leaned on the doorframe as he knocked.

The wolf growled, "Please let it be him."

Nothing.

He knocked again and rang the bell this time. He half expected the woman, Deloris, to open the door, looking confused as to what this strange man with the menacing look wanted with her son . . . or husband.

Self-doubt crept on him as he waited. It was broad daylight, and he was standing on the porch holding a murder weapon, most likely about to terrorize an innocent woman. He rang the bell again. Not a sound from inside.

A brief wave of relief washed over him as he decided to move around to the backyard. It was when he was at the back of the house that he made a strange discovery. The windows were all painted black from the inside. He pushed the idea aside as he stepped onto the small square porch that framed the backdoor of the house.

Why are the windows painted black?

Putting his left shoulder against the frame of the house, he tapped the barrel of his .45 on the door's glass. He lowered his center of gravity, bracing for the worst, and waited. There was no response. Nothing. Again he tapped, and again there was no response. Assured no one was home, he decided on a little makeshift ingenuity. Glancing around, making sure no neighbors were watching, he used his jacket-covered elbow to break the glass on the backdoor. In one swift blow, the glass broke, then he waited for a response from inside. When nothing came, he slipped his hand inside and unlocked the door, then stepping in, closing it immediately. After his eyes adjusted to the dark, he saw something on the kitchen counter. It was a knife. More importantly, the knife, as well as the entire counter and sink, was covered in blood. Fresh blood.

"It's him," he whispered to himself.

Clicking off the safety on the .45, he stepped toward the large section of the house, noticing how dark it all was. With the windows painted black, there was no way for outside light to infiltrate the glass. He pressed his back against a supporting wall, eliminating blindsides, then called, "I'm armed! Is anyone in the house?!"

Nothing.

Reasonably assured he was alone, he lowered his weapon, stepping into the black living room. Not knowing where any of the light sources were, he pulled the small pen light from his key chain and flipped it on. Every inch of the room appeared to be dark and black. Bottles and all sorts of refuse littered the floor as he searched the walls for a light switch. Seeing the switch by the front door, he kicked the debris aside, making his way to the switch. Once he flipped it on, he was surprised not to find a white light illuminating the room. Instead, there was a strong black light that cast a purple hue around him, illuminating fluorescent chalk writings that surrounded him on all four walls. The writing even ran across the painted windows.

"Jesus Christ."

He paused for a second, reading the ramblings. Hate spewed from every corner of the room. Frank pulled his phone from his pocket and scrolled to his camera. Snapping several pictures of all four walls, he decided he'd study the work later on his computer if he found nothing else here. He snapped shot after shot of the madness scrawled in the glowing chalk. He finished and returned the phone to his belt. Reassured he was alone, he made his way down the hall, realizing it too was covered in insane graffiti. Only there were no words, just depraved drawings.

"Adam," Frank whispered, "you are one sick little man."

He continued down the hall, ignoring the self-portrait, then turned left, opening a closed door. He found a near-immaculate bedroom painted in baby blue. The windows in the room were clean, with curtains. Turning to leave, he noticed two words written on the wall above the bed in white chalk.

"Azure dying," he read aloud. The walls, on second thought, were azure, not baby blue. He knew it had to mean something, but considering what he'd seen in the living room and down the hall, there was no way to know what it was. Turning back to leave, he saw something else that shocked him at the depth of its lunacy. On the floor was a quart jar packed to the top with dead mice. Frank jolted. "Son of a bitch! *Who is this fucking guy?*" He couldn't imagine the kinds of horrors that snaked through Adam Parker's mind, and he didn't want to. He knew now he could let himself off the hook for a lot of his past actions; nothing he'd ever done could rival this.

He left the azure bedroom, easing across the hall to the adjacent room. He felt along the wall, finding the light switch. Prepared for the worst, he flipped the switch. What he got was ten thousand times worse than any of his wildest nightmares. The light washed the room in a deep red, but that was nothing. It was the walls, all four, covered in a kaleidoscope of depravity. Digital photos of naked, dead women covered every square inch of the walls. A lone desk and computer sat on a wall with a chair, but for the most part, every inch of plaster in the room was covered with a photo of one of the dead girls D had murdered.

"My god," Frank said aloud. "I found the bastard. I actually found the sick son of a bitch." He turned from side to side, trying in vain to see a small crack in the madness, but there was none. It was only then that his eye caught a glimpse of something so horrifying he nearly wept. Tiffany. Naked, hanging dead from a tree limb in some forsaken woods in the Texas back brush. A beautiful flower of grace destroyed by the insane gnashing of a madman.

"Oh *Jesus*," Frank snarled. "Evil . . . *motherfucker*. You miserable son of a bitch, I'm gonna enjoy killing your worthless ass!" He wanted to trash the room, to rip all the death photos off the walls, then burn the house of madness to the ground, but he couldn't. Still a cop at heart, he knew he had to save the room for Bodinger. His old partner would need the house intact for the investigation. But the desire to destroy the temple of depravity was coursing through him. After gathering himself, he looked above the desk. Centered on the wall, surrounded by the death photos of the three young women, was the portrait of an attractive woman in her early forties. On the glass, covering her face, was a bloody handprint. The framed photo was the only picture in the entire room not of a dead woman, but death was on her. The blood was recent.

"That's gotta be Deloris. Mama," Frank said. "Bitch, what did you do? What did you do to cause this? Jesus Christ."

Again, he pulled his camera phone from his belt and snapped pictures of every inch of the digital madness. After he'd made sure he photographed every inch of the room, he left and went into the adjoining bathroom. He flipped on the light and was immediately washed in brilliant white light. White light that opposed so vividly against the blood-splashed floor that led to the tub and another grisly discovery.

A dead man.

Wearing a well-tailored suit, the dead man was covered in a wash of crimson that streaked over the edge of the tub and around the corner to the red room. It was obvious the man had been killed in the other room and dragged to the tub. That was enough to startle Frank, but there was more. The dead man looked oddly familiar. Frank stood over the bloody tub, studying him. It was certain he'd been stabbed over thirty times; he was butchered beyond belief. *The knife in the kitchen*, told the dead man. Since he was wearing gloves, he decided to investigate. He felt beneath him, finding no bulge of a wallet in his pants. He then pulled open the inside of his jacket and discovered his wallet inside his breast pocket. Fishing it out, he opened it. The man's license was the first thing to appear. The name rang a bell. Someone from the not-too-distant past.

"What the—"

The license read Felix Arnold Bryant. Then it clicked. He took a bloody towel that was on the floor and cleaned the man's face as best he could. "Mrs. Cabbershaw's man?" he thought. Confused, he stared at the picture on his license. It *was* the Felix that worked for Mrs. Cabbershaw.

What was going on? What in the world was the connection?

"You gotta be kidding me."

Frank slid the wallet back in Felix's jacket and returned to his camera phone, snapping pictures of the corpse and the bloody trail back to the red room. He then scrolled through his numbers, making sure he still had Cabbershaw's phone on file.

This changed everything. He was willing to wait for the creep to come home and avenge Tiffany in his own way, ending this dog-and-pony show once and for all. But with Parker having murdered Bryant, he knew the police were about to get involved. He judged the body had been dead for about a day; surely Mrs. Cabbershaw would be calling the APD soon, wanting answers for her missing manservant. Satisfied he had all the information he needed, he killed the light in the bathroom and quickly shot down the hall to the kitchen. It was then he had another thought.

Bryant's car.

There was no car in the driveway, but the inside door to the two-car garage was on the far end of the kitchen counter. Frank opened the door and looked in. There was a gray late-model Ford Focus next to him; but on the far side, instead of a freshly painted Hummer, he saw Bryant's Mercedes. It had to belong to the dead man. He shut the door and exited out the back where he'd entered, making sure not to step on the broken glass. Shooting around the backside of the house, he briskly walked to his car a block away, his head spinning.

Why was Felix Bryant dead in the Capital Hangman's bathtub? Why was he even there? What was the connection? But the more important question was where was Adam Parker?

Frank reached his car and slid in. He sat for a moment, making sure he hadn't been seen. The rain was starting to fall again in a light mist as he tried to comprehend what he'd discovered. This was D's home, no doubt about it. This was the man who killed Tiffany and the five others. He'd found the sick bastard for sure. He was pleased with himself, and relieved that all his work had indeed paid off. However, the butler of a woman that he had worked for back in the spring was stabbed to death in the man's bathtub. Adam Parker was a psychotic sociopath. How could he be connected to the affluent Felix Bryant, or Mrs. Cabbershaw? Just as Frank started the BMW, he noticed a dark sedan pulling into Parker's driveway.

"Hello," Frank said, to himself. As two men climbed from the car, he recognized them instantly. He knew Prince and Reyes from his days on the force and was already ahead of the game. Cabbershaw had called and given the address. They were on an errand of discretion. Why else send two plain-clothes detectives instead of a unit? The old gal had money and stroke, not to mention being the wife of a very powerful attorney, even if he was light in the trousers.

Frank had a decision to make. Stay and watch the show, or get while the getting was good and call his former client for the skinny on the scum that killed his friend. Deciding that discretion was the better part of valor, Frank eased down McCormick Street past the two detectives as they knocked on the door of Adam Parker. He could only imagine the fireworks that were about to ignite.

49

When Prince and Reyes exited their car, Prince was first to the door. The men fully understood why they were there. To ease the mind of some old woman with a lot of money who had pushed the buttons of the chief of police; that was enough for them. They were just happy to be out of the office for a couple of hours. The fresh rain and cooler temperature was making Reyes frisky.

"I hope he gives us a hard time," Reyes said.

"Why?" Prince asked, trying to ignore the younger man's enthusiasm.

"He's on the VIN sheet, don't forget that. It'd make an easy transition to the list, don't you think? If it's him, he might slip up, say something without thinking."

"I think you watch too many movies," Prince told him. "This is just a stop and knock, nothing else. We'll broach the subject once we're clear of the other matter. Understand, hotshot?"

"Okay, your call," Reyes consented. "Still," he said, rising up on his toes in anticipation as the silver BMW crept away behind them, unnoticed. Prince rang the bell. No one answered. He rang again and knocked; again they waited as no one came.

"Dead end, partner," he told Reyes.

"Wait," Reyes protested. "Somebody with a lot of pull got Saunders to send us out here. *Us*, not a uniform. We can't just go back and say no one was here without looking around. What do you say?"

Prince mulled it over then relented. "All right. Let's look around back." The two detectives plodded around the wet yard to the backdoor. It was Prince who spotted the broken glass. "Don't touch anything."

"No shit."

"Got your flashlight?"

Reyes pulled a small flashlight from his coat, handing it to Prince. "Broke from the outside in," Prince said. Stepping onto the small porch, he shined the light's beam in through the broken glass on the door. "Don't see any . . . Wait."

"What?"

"I be damned."

"What, goddamn it?" Reyes asked again.

Prince handed over the light and told his partner, "Shine it to the right, the kitchen counter."

Reyes did as instructed; his heart skipped. "Oh man, that's blood. We've got blood *and* a knife."

"Yes...we do."

"Now what?"

Prince couldn't answer as he was already on his cell to Jim Saunders who was still at his desk when his cell rang. He answered, seeing Prince's number. "Saunders."

"Captain, looks like no one's home. But we have a broken window on the backdoor, and we see a bloody knife on the kitchen counter."

"You can see it from the outside?"

"Yep."

"Sounds like probable cause to me," Saunders informed him. "Call for backup, two units. And you two don't do shit till they get there, understood?"

"Yes, sir."

"Let me know when you know."

"You got it, boss."

"What?" Reyes asked, shifting his weight impatiently.

"Call two units for backup. We don't move till they get here."

"Black and Tan, baby!" Reyes said, slapping his partner on the shoulder, exuberant as he headed back to their car.

"Yeah, buddy," Prince smiled, shaking his head. "Black and Tan."

*

As Frank drove away from the middle-class neighborhood, heading to his office in Round Rock, he pulled up Florence Cabbershaw's home phone and dialed. In three rings, a woman answered, a young woman.

"Cabbershaw's residence."

"My name's Frank Castro. I need to speak to Mrs. Cabbershaw. It's urgent."

"I'm sorry," the young woman replied. "Mrs. Cabbershaw is not taking calls today."

"She'll take mine," Frank insisted.

"I'm sorry, Mr. Castro, but—"

"Look, bitch, put her on the phone *now*! You don't wanna be the reason she missed this call."

There was silence; then Frank heard the click of the phone going on hold. Soon, the woman came back on, saying, "Very well. I'll see if she'll speak with you."

Frank decided to stop so he could concentrate, pulling into the parking lot of a small store. He lit a cigarette as his head swam in confusion. He knew why the old girl wasn't taking calls; she was wondering where her boy Felix got off to.

Of all the luck!

Halfway through his smoke, the phone clicked again followed by a familiar voice, saying, "Hello, Mr. Castro. What seems to be so urgent you feel a need to be rude to my staff?"

Skipping formalities, Frank answered, "Mrs. Cabbershaw, do you know the name Adam Parker?" He couldn't see her with his eyes, but he saw with his heart her face twist in shock. The silence was deafening over the phone's speaker. Wanting to fire question after question, he held his tongue and waited. He owed her that much.

After what seemed like an hour, she finally said, "I believe I do. Why would *you* ask me that?"

"What's Parker's relationship with Felix Bryant?"

"I really can't see how any of this could possibly be of concern to you," she said, stiffening.

Frank flipped his butt out the window, pressing, "It wasn't my concern until about a half hour ago."

"What on earth do you mean?"

"Mrs. Cabbershaw, I respect you, you know that. I'm in debt to you and your generosity. But this is as important a question as I've ever asked anyone. What is the relationship between Felix Bryant and Adam Parker?" he asked again, resting his forehead against the steering wheel, closing his eyes, and focusing all his attention to his ears and the response coming. He wanted to be able to hear if her voice altered in any way. It took a few seconds, but she finally replied.

"Is this confidential, Mr. Castro?"

"With me? Yes, ma'am. Of course, always."

"I don't why or how you know anything, but if you must know, is it important?"

"Very much so, yes."

She sighed heavily then said, "Adam is Felix's illegitimate son."

Frank leaned back several inches, grimacing, then dropped his head against the wheel with a loud *thud*!

Unbelievable!

"Were they close?" he asked finally.

"Hardly. I don't believe the poor boy even knows he *is* his father."

"But he knows him?"

"Yes. But only as an overseer. Felix takes care of Adam and his mother's finances. I put a large sum of money into a trust fund that he acquired when he turned twenty-one. Felix has worked all the details of their daily business for the young man and his mother for the entirety of his life. He's never told him who he is, and as far as Felix knows, neither did his mother."

What?

Frank felt as though he'd walked in on a movie that had been playing for three hours, trying to catch up in the last ten minutes. "Where's the mother?" he asked.

"Dead, I'm afraid. About four years ago, I believe. Right after Adam turned twenty-one."

He knew it! The woman in the portrait surrounded by death. Mommy dearest. He wanted more but had to be careful; he knew Bodinger would be knocking on her door in less than two hours, and the last thing he needed was for her to tell him that she already knows Felix is dead because Frank *goddamned* Castro told her so.

Choosing his words, he asked, "Would Felix have cause to see his son?"

"Why do you ask?" concern in her voice.

Shit!

It was over. He had to cut bait and run; he couldn't risk anything more. "Mrs. Cabbershaw, in about two hours, a detective named Stanley Bodinger is going to come see you. I'm afraid he's not bringing good news. If you value our confidence at all, this conversation never happened."

"Excuse me? Wha—"

Frank closed his phone. Time was everything now. He had to find this Parker prick before Bodinger. The one thing in his favor was that they'd be looking for a black H2. Frank knew the truth. It wasn't black any longer. It was azure.

There were more questions than answers. Why did she put money into a trust fund for Bryant's son? Why did he go see him yesterday? Who was Deloris Parker? How did he know her? How did she die?

In the end, none of that mattered; they were all things that could be sorted out later. The important thing now was to get to the office and download the pictures from his phone. Frank was sure he'd get a clue from the neon ravings on Parker's walls.

In truth, Frank had the answer, but only part of it was in Adam Parker's graffiti.

50

It had been an hour since Prince called in to Saunders about the broken window on Adam Parker's backdoor. He was tidying up some paperwork when his cell went off again, another call from Prince.

"Saunders. What do you guys have?"

When Prince answered, his voice was so pumped with adrenaline it almost cracked like an adolescent teenager. "Captain, you are *not* going to believe this."

At their desks, Bodinger and Cordova were still sifting through VIN numbers and making phone calls, setting up interviews with H2 owners who'd purchased over the last four years. The two hated this. It was like the proverbial needle in the haystack. The more they looked, the more they came up with den mothers, car poolers, and weekend warriors. The very few single men within Kerndon's age profile that had purchased such vehicles were all seemingly too far above the curve socially to fit the profile of a degenerate psychopath like D.

"I tell you, bro," Cordova said. "There has to be something more we can do other than this shit."

"It's in here, Eric. We just have to be patient. We'll find it. He ditched it, burned, or sold it. Hell, he might have left it on the east side with the keys in it just so it would get stolen then never turn it in." Bodinger sat back, stretching his arms over his head. "It's not a Camry, after all. It's

336

a high-profile automobile. It'll turn up." He was about to start scanning the numbers again when Jim Saunders stepped around the corner, his face was white. "What's up, boss?" Bodinger asked, feeling his tension.

Saunders stood there a moment before saying, "I think Prince and Reyes just stumbled onto your boy."

"Which boy?" Bodinger asked, controlling himself.

Saunders nodded to the table, "That one."

51

Frank was at his office in Round Rock. He fixed the cable from his phone to Tiffany's computer and pulled up the photos he'd just taken in Parker's house. The photos were much clearer on the big screen of the computer. The writings were shear madness. Hate-filled diatribe that made Frank wonder how such a sick mind could function in the world. Line after line he read of murder, incest, hate, and brutality. Some of the lines were actually constructed in poem form, although they read more like song lyrics. Songs filled with such inner pain and torment they spewed forth as odes to such atrocities as rape, murder, and genocide.

"Okay, I get it," Frank groaned, "you're a mad dog that needs to be put down. Now, tell me something. Show me something I can use, you miserable fuck." He could see in some places that Parker had used his hand to wipe away words that no longer held his interest to put down new ideas of revulsion. Old writings mixed with newer ones, creating a menagerie of psychosis.

After reading chalk writings for nearly an hour, he went to the photos of the red room. The pictures of his victims, dead and naked, hanging like prize game. The moniker of the Capital Hangman suited the fiend. Some of the photos, even of Tiffany, were close ups. As in the photo Young shared with him, he could tell there was no discoloration on the girls' faces. They were dead when he hung them. With no bullet or stab wounds, he came to the conclusion he'd bagged them before hanging them. He referenced it from Bodinger's letter as well. It wasn't enough to just hang them—Frank was sure Parker got a sexual rush from seeing the girls hang naked—but he needed to be close to them as they died. He needed to feel their life force leave their bodies. The sick creep probably bagged them from the front so he could watch the life fade away from their eyes.

He remembered something from one of the letters: "*As you're dying, think of your mother.*" The letter to Bodinger indicated that he'd been molested by his mother, the same woman in the framed picture hanging in the red room with the bloody handprint covering her face. "He told all of them," Frank whispered. "He wanted them to think of their mothers as they died. The sick shit told them all the same thing as they died, I know it. His mother screwed his head up so bad he wants his victims' last thoughts to be of their mothers." He remembered the first letter he used to announce himself to the world, the letter he sent to Young, starting the whole fiasco. He told them to tell the victim's mother she died thinking of her, that he insisted on it.

"It all comes back to Mama, don't it?" he asked the computer screen. "Seems like all these assholes have dead mamas the rest of us have to pay for."

He stared at the picture of Deloris Parker, trying to see around or through the bloody hand, to get a better bead on her. After all, she was most likely the major catalyst in the creation of this monster. As he studied her face, he began to realize she looked vaguely familiar. In the photo, she was probably in her late thirties to early forties. Mrs. Cabbershaw told him she died four years ago. She even gave him Parker's age, that he was twenty-one when she died. He'd be twenty-five now. Looking at the frame and the style of photo, Frank gathered that the portrait was most likely shot about five to ten years ago. Aging the picture a few years to the time of her death, he deduced she'd been in her mid-forties when she died. If what he confessed in the Bodinger letter was true, he seemed to have a hand in her death. As long as it wasn't psychotic gibberish.

Blonde, midforties, attractive.

As he focused on her, the mad writings and letters along with the message left on his machine kept ping-ponging through his mind. He didn't try to focus on them, or any one thing. Instead, he allowed all of Parker's madness to bounce around inside his head like popcorn popping in a cooker. He wanted it all to swirl inside, looking for anything he could connect.

"I'm a tortured man, Frank, like yourself."

"I was going to let them die the same way, but there was no sexual gratification in it."

"Ever go down on your mother, Detective?"

"She said you'd cut my fucking heart out, Frank."

Blonde, mid-forties, attractive.

"I'm a tortured man, Frank."

"I wanted to fuck your secretary's dead body."

"Are you a motherfucker? I am. Quite literally."

"She cried for you, Frank. Did you know that?"

"Order me to fuck her like an obedient mongrel."

The victims were getting older.

"I hope your pretty wife isn't afraid of me."

"Will you, Frank? Will you kill me?"

"The mind is a terrible thing."

He didn't know Bryant was his father.

"Ever drop a load inside your mother's belly?"

"My mother used to bend over and order me to fuck her like an obedient mongrel."

"Stripping the old gal down to her pubes."

Bloody hand on the portrait. His father's blood.

"Watching her die inside my bag."

Blonde, mid-forties, attractive.

"Are you a motherfucker?"

He didn't know Bryant was his father.

"The last time I fucked my mother she was dead."

Blonde.

"It was the best I ever had."

Mid-forties.

"I hope your pretty wife isn't afraid of me."

Attractive.

340

"I've had my gut full of older women."
Bryant told him!
"She cried for you, Frank."
The bloody hand on the portrait! His father's blood on his mother's face!
"I hope your pretty wife . . ."
They both lied to him his entire life.
"Isn't afraid of me."
Someone has to pay.
"As you're dying, think of your mother."
As you're dying, think of your mother.
Above his mother's bed. Her azure bedroom where she abused him.
Azure Dying.
"It always tasted like death. My own."
As you're dying.
"I died a little every time I touched her, and she liked to be touched."
Azure Dying . . . Think of your mother.
"Your pretty wife."
"Watching her die inside my bag."
Susan?
"Yeah, that would be a real hoot."
Deloris Parker.
"Your pretty wife."
Blonde, mid-forties, attractive.
"Strip the old gal down to her pubes."
Someone has to pay.
They lied to him.
His father's blood, his mother's face.
"Watch her die inside my bag."
Susan Bodinger?
"I hope your pretty wife isn't afraid of me."
It hit Frank like an electric current. He'd never known anything as certain in his life as he knew this. "Stan can case the house all he wants, he's not going back . . . He's never going back." He looked one last time at the screen before, saying, "He's going after Susan!"

The blood-stained portrait of Deloris Parker was still big and bright on the computer screen as Frank tore out the door.

Stanley Bodinger was standing in the living room of the man they'd been chasing for over six months. The man that brutally killed six people that they knew of and taunted them with photos and letters was quite obviously insane. The madhouse he called a home was enough to attest to that, but his very own photographic evidence in the red room was enough to seal the deal. Not to mention the dead man in the bathtub and the murder weapon covered in prints left on the kitchen counter. The dead man's car was even in his garage. They knew from the tip that the stabbing victim's name was Felix Bryant and the father of the man who lived in the house. It felt good to finally have a real name for the fiend they'd been chasing. Adam Duane Parker. It's how they'd refer to him from now on. No more Capital Hangman and, most assuredly, not D.

An entire crime unit had descended on the house at 2102 McCormick. Forensics, detectives, the coroner, and every investigator that ever had anything to do with the case were there. Bodinger's team made it clear, however, that only the minimal personnel necessary to do the job was allowed inside the house. The last thing they needed was some big foot gawker stepping in evidence that Parker had so blatantly left for them.

When Jim Saunders arrived, he wasn't ready for what awaited him. He walked through the now well-lit house and saw the trash-strewn floors, smelled the foul odors, and above all, saw the walls covered in madness. He walked up to Bodinger, saying, "What do you have out?"

"An APB on Adam Duane Parker. We pulled his work file from a chemical lab he worked at as a night watchman. Delphi, in the Cameron business district. The woman," he stopped to check his notes, "Cabbershaw told us he worked there, but that was all she knew about him. The dead man in the tub *is* her butler, and she says he did come by to check on him. Been four years."

"Four bad years, you ask me," Saunders said, looking around the room.

"This ain't the main event though."

"No?"

"You won't believe this," Bodinger said, leading his boss down the macabre hallway to the red room. Saunders gazed at the artwork on the walls of the hall along with the portrait that stared at him from the end.

"Is that our boy?"

"I'm guessing."

"Certifiable," he said in a low voice.

"What's that?"

"Nothing. Where we going?"

"Here," Bodinger said, showing him the room with the death photos of his victims literally wallpapering every square inch of wall space.

"Jesus Christ on a pogo stick," he lamented. He walked the room, looking at the pictures, making extra sure not to touch anything. "All of them?" he asked.

"Yes, sir. All six. Even the three boys."

"What kind of . . . Never mind," Saunders stopped. "No one knows. That's the problem. Crazy makes its own rules. Who's that?" he asked, pointing to the blood-stained portrait of Deloris.

"Don't know. I'm betting it's the mother he said he killed in his *own way*. Cabbershaw told us her name was Deloris Parker. Mrs. Cabbershaw never met her, so she has no idea what she looks like."

"It's her. I know it."

Bodinger nodded.

"What was the connection again with this guy and the old lady?"

Bodinger had met with Mrs. Cabbershaw briefly, telling her the sad news of her friend's murder. She wept openly but pulled herself together with great inner strength. Bodinger was impressed by the woman. She personified dignity.

"She footed the bill for the butler as best as I can tell," Bodinger explained. "Seems he knocked up Ms. Parker back in the late eighties. He came to her, requesting money for an abortion, and the old gal would have nothing to do with it. Instead, she set up a trust for the kid that he got when he turned twenty-one."

"When was that?"

"Four years ago, he's twenty-five."

"How big is the trust?"

"Three hundred grand."

"A man with money living like this? Guess the trust had nothing to do with the mother's death?"

Bodinger looked around the room, smelling the fetid odors that saturated the walls. He nudged one of the death jars at Saunders's feet. "You think this is somebody who gives a damn about money?"

The Captain looked down then jumped back after seeing what the glass cell was filled with. *"What the hell is that?"*

"Dead mice. There's about twenty of those jars in the house, all of them stuffed with dead rodents or bugs. I guess he liked to watch things die. Looks like the mice couldn't cut it anymore."

"Sick bastard. You're right, cash is the *last* thing on this guy's mind."

"Bryant took care of the bills here at the house with the money that Cabbershaw supplied to the woman and her child. Best she knows, Bryant didn't have any type of relationship with either the mother or the kid . . . till now," he finished, flipping his small notebook closed.

As the two stood there, watching photographers chronicle every inch of the room, Cordova came in from his talks to the neighbors. "Tell me, guys. Either of you ever see anything like this before?"

Saunders lowered his head, huffing his response. Bodinger simply said, "Never."

"Well, I got it from the neighbors that the guy's mother did die four years ago. It was ruled accidental."

"What accident?" Saunders asked.

Cordova frowned. "She choked on her own vomit."

"Jesus Christ. This just keeps getting better."

"How old was she?" from Bodinger.

"Forty-seven."

"She got off lucky, you ask me," Saunders added.

"Maybe she died of a broken heart," Cordova said, eyeing the room.

"Cut it out," Bodinger told him. "Anything else from the neighbors?"

"The usual stuff. Lone guy, worked at night, and slept all day, but there was one thing. The neighbors did say that he played his music

C. W. Gordon

loud, very loud. Said it was always metal, the heaviest metal. Always. Some nights they thought of coming over or calling somebody. But they never did."

"Why?" Bodinger asked.

Cordova swallowed saying, "They said that the times the music wasn't playing, there were still sounds. Sounds that freaked them out."

"Like?"

"Screams Stan. I mean, they could tell it was him, but the sounds were beyond screams. Painful, guttural...like a wounded animal."

The three men studied each in silence before Saunders spoke up. "I guess some nights, the kid wore his headphones."

"The clincher is," Cordova added, "a year ago, he bought a new Hummer. H2, a jet black one."

They all looked to one another before Saunders said, "Find this piece of shit. Find him today. I want this prick in lock up by midnight."

Cordova informed, "Every cop, trooper, and deputy sheriff in South Texas has a description and tag number. He can't go far. We'll get him."

As sure as he was, there was still something eating at Bodinger. Parker said in his letter the Hummer was gone. He could be driving anything. He told them as much, but Saunders felt it was just a ploy. "No, he just kept it in the garage. It's gone, but his other car is here along with Bryant's. I'm telling you, Stan, he's in that Hummer."

Maybe he was. Maybe they'd find him within the hour. But something just wasn't sitting right. And Detective Stanley Bodinger couldn't stop the icy fingers from creeping up his spine.

52

Once Deloris died, Adam was left with such a void in his life that he had no options. The pain of *her* was replaced with the pain of emptiness. After he stood on the bridge and the homeless man told him to give it back, give it *all* back, he understood. The world had tortured him. It was time to torture the world back. His mother lived out her sexual deviance at his expense. Why not live out his at the expense of whomever he desired? *How*ever he desired? After four years of isolation, pain, and self destruction, he knew what had to happen. He had to become what Deloris had spawned.

Not forgetting his new father. The cold and calculating man that oversaw his life from a distance—never getting close, never revealing himself—was a specter in his life. A ghost with no soul. Adam was a mix of deviance and cold precision. Deloris and Felix made him who he was. He was a monster preying on defenseless women with such precise calculation that he had baffled the police to the point of hopelessness.

Now, it was over.

Amy Crowder, Julie Brooks, Tiffany Malvern, and three unlucky school kids were the result of his deep-seeded desire to destruct. He wanted to watch the world burn in a holocaust of filth. Adam Parker wanted to masturbate to the total destruction of humanity.

One person at a time.

He became the god of his own universe. Pain would have retribution, no matter what the cost. Discarded and left alone, the only friend he knew was pain. Pain he had to share. Pain so total he had to seek the devil in himself to make it a reality for the rest of the world to see. Reality, as he understood it.

Oblivion.

He was the infection of a twisted society. Left alone to fend off the demons of his mind, with no friends, no family, nothing. Only himself and his mind. His own twisted and warped sense of reality. A reality that spoke of nothing but pain and apathy.

No one cared.

Not even his putrid father. A man so immersed in logic and calculation he never saw the pain of his own child. He turned a blind eye to the truth that his own offspring was doomed to a life of chaos. He would make the world pray for death. Adam would leave his mark. He'd make the whole world his own twisted, warped playground. Death had a new companion, and it looked a lot like Adam Parker.

He sat alone in the back of the Hummer, on the side street next to the Bodinger house. Feeling beneath his shirt, he ran his fingers over the cowardly scar on the back of his right shoulder.

He spoke to himself, "The reason is now, the time is now." Climbing from the H2, he whispered, "My face is the last you'll see."

Frank sped through Austin from Round Rock, trying not to catch the attention of the local law. The last thing he needed was to be pulled over. His luck, Mrs. Cabbershaw dropped a dime on him to Bodinger and the heat was already on him. The risk was worth it, however. He knew the Bodingers lived on the south side below Oltorf Avenue. He had to pass the capital, the university, and all of downtown to get there. A call was no good; Parker could be there without Susan knowing. He had to see for himself and warn her face–to–face.

It was late afternoon and he was going to get bogged down in traffic on the interstate, so he decided to jump off the highway and hit the side streets. The BMW zipped through more than a few parking lots to avoid cramped intersections as Frank maneuvered the two seater with a clarity he hadn't felt in years. The adrenaline was flowing as he continued south. He had to save her, he *had* to. Part of him still blamed his old partner for his exit from the force, but there was something new growing inside him. A part of humanity that felt the reticence to admit he'd been wrong all along. He was a cowboy that put a good cop's life and career in danger every time he climbed into the unit with him.

Maybe Bodinger was right after all. It took ten years, less alcohol, and the death of a close friend at the hands of a serial madman for him to see it.

"Nothing's ever that easy. Heaven's hung in black."

Frank was a few blocks away when he decided to call the house. He scanned through the numbers on his cell, realizing the only number he still had for Bodinger was his office extension at the APD.

"Goddamn it!"

He swerved to miss some kids playing football in the street and dodged a huge black German shepherd that was following a jogger. He glanced at his watch; it was five fifteen.

"Be home, Susan," he said aloud. "Please, baby, be home."

Frank and Susan genuinely liked each other. She liked his warm smile and sense of humor, often referring to him as a big loveable goofball, while Frank felt her empathy every time they spoke. They'd had a few heart-to-hearts all those years ago, and she always shot him straight. He liked that, but there was never anything in her voice or words that made him feel small. It was like she could see the danger he was in, and as a true friend was trying to stem the inevitable crash. She honestly cared for him.

But that was ten years ago. They hadn't seen each other or spoken in all that time, and he knew she was nowhere near ready for what he was about to spring on her. Of course, Stan was keeping her up-to-date with the case, and she herself was the focal point of the letter Parker sent to them, but Frank knew how Stan and Kerndon would interpret that message. They would say there was nothing to it, that it was just a psychotic mind playing out a game of cat and mouse. A terrorist ploy to simply scare them. There was no way he would actually act on it.

348

Parker's voice, again, tripped through his mind.

How does it feel, Frank? To be the mouse?

The jar full of dead mice.

"Shit!"

Things would have stayed the way they were if Bryant hadn't gotten involved. Without his miserable timing, Frank would have found Parker in his house of horrors and killed him then and there. An anonymous tip later and Bodinger would be standing in the house on McCormick Street wondering who it was that killed the Capital Hangman in his own home.

But that wasn't meant to be. Mrs. Cabbershaw said Parker never knew Bryant was his father. When he told him, and saw his madhouse, Parker exploded and killed him in a fit of violent rage. That changed it all. Parker knew his house would be a secret no more, that whoever was behind his financial dependence would send others to look for Bryant, which she did. The cops would get involved, which they did. He would have time to act out one last fantasy floating around in that swamp of a mind.

Susan Bodinger.

It was clear to Frank, staring at the portrait of who he believed to be Parker's mother. With the bloody handprint covering her face, she looked enough like Susan so that, in Parker's twisted way, he saw a surrogate antagonist to his life. His bullying letter was now heartfelt. He most likely wanted to kill his mother all over again, if in fact he actually killed her at all. Now that he knew who his father was, the total betrayal he must have felt would have been overwhelming. He'd have to act on it. The one thing that bought him more time was the Hummer. No longer black, he could linger right under the noses of everyone without fear. What he didn't know was that Frank was coming. Frank knew who he was and where he was going. Frank Castro even knew his one edge.

Azure.

Azure Dying . . . think of your mother.

The pieces snapped in place like a child's toy. He pounded the steering wheel, "Oh goddamn it! Goddamn it!"

When Frank turned onto the Bodinger's street, he was relieved to see no blue Hummer. The house sat on a corner lot, but he didn't feel he had time to circle the block looking for Parker's killing jar. There was a small sedan in the driveway he assumed was Susan's, and he pulled in behind it. Jumping from the BMW, he stepped quickly to the front door of the nice brick house and banged on the door. When an answer didn't arrive fast enough for him, he banged again, a wave of relief washing over him as he heard a woman's voice from inside yell, "Hold your water. I'm coming!" Frank felt his blood pressure drop instantly.

Susan opened the door and Frank saw what he knew he'd see if everything was all right, the look of someone who hadn't laid eyes on him in ten years. Taken aback, Susan said, "Frank?" squinting her eyes.

"Susan, are you all right?" he asked, stepping closer.

"What? Of course, Frank, what are you doing here?" she asked, a dishtowel over her shoulder as she was preparing a meal.

"Please, may I come in?"

"Well, sure, Frank, of course you can," she answered, stepping back, allowing Frank to step into the house. "Frank, what on earth is all this about? It's been . . ." She paused to count.

"Ten years," he informed her.

"Okay, ten years. Frank, you're a nervous wreck. What's going on?"

"I'm sure Stan's been keeping you up to speed on the whole *Hangman* case."

She took a breath, still trying to sort him out. Her kind eyes, the eyes you'd never associate to Stanley Bodinger, soothed him. Frank calmed and listened.

"Yeah, sure. Stan's been working night and day on this one. Of course I know about it."

"Then you know Parker's seen you. You read the letter, yes?"

"Parker? Who's Parker?" she quizzed.

That's right. She doesn't know any of this, it's all happened so fast.

"Look Susan, I won't get into all the details of the whys and hows, but the Hangman's name is Adam Parker. Stan's finding all this out . . . right about now, I'd guess. The deal is, I've seen inside this guy's house and I'm telling you as a friend, until he's caught, you're not safe here."

She looked deep into his eyes, trying to catch up. "How do you know, how do *you* know all this Frank?"

"It's a long story."

"I've got time."

"No, we don't. Have you seen a light blue Hummer lately? Around the neighborhood, while you're going around town, doing your errands, going to and from work?"

"A what?" she asked, still not grasping him.

"You know Parker drove a Hummer, yes?"

"Yes, an H2."

"It's painted blue now. Azure blue. Have you seen one?" Frank was starting to sound more and more desperate.

She crossed her arms, saying, "I can't say I have, no."

Realizing how this must all sound, he stopped. "Susan," he started slowly. "He killed my friend. She worked for me. She was my secretary, assistant, whatever you want to call it. I liked her, she was like a sister to me, and this Parker freak killed her like the others."

"I know," she replied, sympathy in her eyes.

"And you know me too. You know I couldn't let that lie and not try to get to the bottom of it. You know I'd have to try to find him myself. Well, I did. I found his house and the place is a nightmare, right out of horror movie. I'm sure Stan and half the APD are there right now, but Parker's not. And I think he's coming here for you."

"They assured me he wouldn't dare."

"That was before."

"Before what?"

"Before he found out who his father was."

"What? Frank, what on earth would that have to do with me?" Her face was a mask of confusion as a bell went off in the kitchen. "Walk with me, I have to check dinner."

"Stan hasn't called you?"

"No, but then he's been so busy I usually eat alone and leave the rest on a plate for him."

"Convenient," he said, walking into the kitchen behind her.

"Just years of being a cop's wife. The kids are grown and my work keeps me busy most of the time, but my hours are nowhere as radical as Stan's. Of course, you'd know that," she said, looking in the oven.

351

"Unfortunately," he was starting to think he'd made a mistake. The more he thought on it, the more he was convincing himself that Parker would simply run for the hills. He wouldn't stop on the way to nab the investigating detective's wife.

It was absurd.

Susan took the casserole from the oven and tapped the door closed with her knee. "Hungry?" she asked.

"Not me, not today. After what I've seen today, I might not eat for a week," Frank said, walking to the window above the sink. Pulling the curtain open, he saw the side street, no cars. Their privacy fence blocked the rest of the view. He felt stupid. He'd managed to track down the killer from nothing more than hearsay and the words of con men and convicts. That much he got right. But he must have misread Parker's intentions for leaving the house and pulling Bryant's car in the garage. He most likely was heading to Mexico with a bag of Cabbershaw money.

He'd missed this one. But it was okay; at least Susan wasn't in danger. Now he'd have to convince her not to tell Stan about this or he'd be explaining his case to him through bars in the city lockup. Satisfied, he closed the curtain just as Susan said, "That's funny. I don't remember leaving that drawer open." It was the silverware drawer.

The next thing he knew, he was in pain. Serious pain.

Adam beat Susan home by just five minutes. He'd gone over the fence in the backyard, unlocking it from the inside, then broke in through the kitchen door. Once inside, he managed to maneuver through the house without Susan noticing. She'd come home from her job at the bank, going straight to work on dinner. He was ready to abduct her when Frank knocked at the front door. Not knowing who it was or how long they'd stay, he hid in the service room with the washer and dryer just off the kitchen. Through the quiet house, he could hear Frank lamenting his case as to why she should leave with him.

"Fucking Castro?" he puzzled. "How in the *hell*?" He heard him tell her about his house, Felix Bryant, and the H2 being a different color.

"How in the hell does he know this?"

He'd known all along Castro was a wildcard. A renegade who never saw past his own nose. He knew at the time that dealing with him would be a challenge, so he let it drop. He'd regretted leaving the phone message once he sobered up, but it was water under the bridge. Castro had less to go on than Bodinger and the APD. How in the world did he track him?

Bodain!

He squeezed his eyes together and sank to his knees in front of the washing machine, cursing the Cajun outlaw. "You dirty son of a *bitch!*" He hoped Castro killed the mindless big mouth, with his gold teeth and crazy music. Once he gathered himself, he was determined not to leave without his prize. There was no going back, for there would be nothing to go back to. By now, the cops would be all over his house and he would be the most wanted man in all of Texas. Having the H2 a different color bought him the time he needed, or so he thought. Castro had changed that for sure.

All he'd brought with him was his Taser. While Susan was busy elsewhere, he went into the spare bedroom upstairs and pulled the comforter off the bed, bringing it downstairs with him as a cover for her body once he paralyzed her with the Taser. He'd need more to deal with Castro. While they talked, he slipped into the kitchen, taking a large kitchen knife from the drawer, but didn't have time to close it as she and Frank headed to the kitchen. Once Castro had his back turned and Susan was preoccupied with her casserole, he made his move out of the service room and went straight for Castro with the Taser.

Frank's entire body seized as he fell to the kitchen floor. It took a few seconds for him to realize what had happened. It had been years since he had to be tased as part of his police training. All officers who carry a Taser have to be subjected to its effects in order to carry one for the state. His mind was semi-alert, but his body was locked in a giant spasm as he heard the buzzing of what sounded like a tattoo needle and the muffled and shocked groan of Susan succumbing to the same effect. He could tell he hit her a second time to subdue her longer.

His mind was murky, but he knew he had to get to his feet. He'd left his gun in the car, so his only option was to stop him one-on-one. Frank could take anyone in a street fight, but the odds weren't in his favor with his body painfully locked in a huge cramp. He heard Parker drag Susan past him toward the backdoor then lay her on the floor as he draped a thick blanket of some sort over her then roll her up in it.

"*Move, Frank, move!*" he commanded himself. Just as he was about to try and stand, Parker came back. Frank tried to turn his head, but couldn't, and once Parker was behind him, Frank felt another searing pain. Again he went to the floor, but this time it was different. The pain wasn't electric. It was dull, deep, and localized, like a very hard punch. An agonizing pain shot through his left back below his shoulder blade, his neck convulsing back toward it. Parker was gone, and as Frank again lay on the floor, he realized why the silverware drawer had been left open.

As the crime unit scoured the house on McCormick Street, Stanley Bodinger couldn't shake the uneasy feeling that was looming over him. He should be happy. They knew who they were looking for, they had enough evidence to convict him, and there was a statewide man hunt for Adam Parker and his H2. His driver's license picture was being flashed on every news channel and website that could be reached. But there was still something he didn't like about it. He killed the father and left, leaving the victim's car in his garage.

Where did he go? And why?

If what Mrs. Cabbershaw had told him was true, surely Parker knew he couldn't just leave the dead man in his tub and not expect someone to come looking for him. After all, there was a lot of money involved here. The Cabbershaws were no faceless wannabes in the city of Austin. Even if Parker didn't know who was really behind his trust fund, he knew Bryant was linked to it and worked for someone calling the shots. As a rule, well-to-do men in expensive suits who drive brand new Mercedes don't just get themselves stabbed to death in middle-class neighborhoods in broad daylight, house of horrors or not. Bodinger couldn't get his head around why he would leave.

Or more to the point, where?

53

As Frank fought to his feet, the pain was unbearable. As the effects of the Taser began to subside, the more serious pain became more evident. Leaning on the kitchen table, he forced his right hand underneath and around his back, finding the cause. The knife handle was sticking straight out with the blade lodged deep between his left shoulder blade and his spine. Severed nerves were firing, causing electric pain to shoot all through his upper body. His first instinct was to somehow manage to pull it free, but it was then he remembered his police training. Officers are instructed that if you have a victim of a stabbing and the knife is still imbedded, leave it where it is. Pulling it out will open the veins and arteries allowing the blood to gush. Leave it for the medical personnel. There were no EMTs around, so he decided to leave it stuck where it was. The pain was the worst he'd ever felt, but he cleared his mind enough to realize Parker had gotten out of the house with Susan.

Frank stumbled through the house to the front door, spying Susan's cell phone on the table by the door. He grabbed it, knowing Bodinger's number was in there and he'd need to call him fast. Outside, he managed to crawl into the small car, the knife hitting the top of the door, sending excruciating pain through his chest and shoulder. He screamed as he forced the door shut, leaning all of his six foot-two inch, 215-pound frame sideways in the tiny car. It was the first time since he got the thing he regretted letting that prick Tully talk him into it.

"It's too small," Frank had told him.

"You'll adapt," the weasel assured.

Adapt.

"Fuck you . . . Tully," he groaned. "Adapt to Bullet . . . cutting your . . . nuts off!"

Frank fired the engine as the Z4 roared to life. Leaning on the rest between the seats, he had to rest his right elbow in the passenger's seat to shift the five-speed. Steering was the other problem; he'd have to do it with his left arm, the one on fire with the kitchen knife buried to the handle in his left back.

"*Agghhh!*" he screamed, turning the wheel counterclockwise backing out of the driveway. He punched the gas and jumped to the side street just in time to see the azure blue Hummer turning right a block away. He cranked the wheel to the right and popped the clutch. The sports car leaped, leaving tire marks a good twenty feet before catching hold and zooming the block ahead. Without slowing, Frank turned right; the BMW slid sideways, went up on the curb, forcing another scream of pain, but he saw that Parker was headed to the highway. It was several blocks away. Frank knew he'd catch him if he just kept going in a straight line.

"*Don't turn, fucker, don't turn!*"

As Frank closed in, the Hummer made a sharp left turn, causing Frank to hit the brakes, forcing him forward, the knife seemingly digging farther into his body. He was past the intersection. Cutting the wheel left, agony shooting through him, he managed a u-turn and was back in pursuit. Parker was speeding up, and he'd have to catch him and ram the BMW into the Hummer to get him off the road. The problem was that the H2 would squash the two seater like a beer can and never slow down, but it was his only option. He knew Parker was trying to get her out of town, to the woods. On a fall day with this lousy weather, he could have any place he wanted to himself. Given their starting point, Frank thought of Barton Springs or McKinney Falls. Affluent in their own right, but with a lot of secluded spots, perfect for what he wanted to do. One was west and the other east. As long as he could keep the azure H2 in site, he'd know which one he was heading for.

As far as he knew, Parker had no idea he was following, but he was still under the clock. He had to believe that even if Frank didn't die, he'd call the cavalry and tell them to look for an azure blue Hummer, not many of those around. The quicker he got off the streets, the better.

In minutes, Frank knew where he was heading. Too many right turns—he was headed west to the Barton Creek Wilderness Park. Frank cursed himself. If he was physically able to function in the vehicle without constraints, he would have caught him in no time. But shaking off the Taser and having a six-inch knife lodged in his back was making it almost impossible to drive the tiny car. He barely fit in it as it was, now lying sideways with his right arm in the seat and his steering arm partially immobilized, Parker and the Hummer were getting away.

Bodinger!

In the chase, he'd forgotten he'd picked up Susan's phone. After shifting the five–speed, he fumbled with her phone, trying to pull up her contacts. With one eye on the H2, and the other on the phone, he scrolled down until he found **STAN**. As he hit the call button, he said aloud, "I hope you two aren't fighting." The pain in his left arm was beginning to burn as he gripped the wheel, using his right to call. One ring. Two rings. Three rings. *"Answer the damn phone, you bag of shit!"*

Parker turned right onto an access road toward the park; rain was falling softly as the sun was beginning to set. Frank managed to ease the car into the right gear with the phone wedged between his ear and right shoulder.

"I'm a little busy, honey," Bodinger answered.

"It's Frank," he said back.

"What? Frank? What the hell—"

"Shut up! I got Susan's phone, she's in trouble. I'm following . . . Or trying to."

There was a second of silence on the other end. Frank thought Bodinger hadn't heard, but instead it was the realization that something bigger was brewing, and he should have seen it. He'd been feeling it for hours.

"What? Where, Frank? What's going on?"

"Parker grabbed her at your . . . your pl-place." Frank felt himself getting light-headed. His mouth was dry, and he was sweating profusely.

Bodinger was standing in the kitchen of Parker's house surrounded by noisy cops and technicians. "Everybody *shut up!*" he screamed. "Parker has my wife, and Frank Castro is chasing him!" The room fell dead silent, Cordova and Saunders pushing their way through among whispers of "He got Stan's wife" and "Frank Castro?"

"Talk to me!"

"I'm having trouble, Stan. I got a knife in my back."

Bodinger thought of their history, relying, "Enough about old news!"

"No . . . You asshole," Frank managed. "The fucker stabbed me . . . The knife's in my back, you prick!"

He felt stupid. He told the others, "Parker stabbed him, he's hurt." The million-and-one questions Bodinger wanted answers to, like why are you even in this and how do you know who he is, were squelched by the fear for his wife's safety. As long as he had a breath, Frank Castro would catch whoever he was chasing—that was a given—but he was hurt. Bodinger wanted to both punch him and hug him. Right now, he was the only thing between Parker and his wife's horrible death.

Kerndon be damned!

Bodinger calmed himself. "Talk to me, Frank. Where are you?"

"He's headed for Barton Springs . . . Maybe the . . . wilderness park."

"What road?"

"Three sixty . . . North."

Bodinger kept the phone to his ear, telling Saunders, "Capital of Texas Highway, north. He's headed to Barton Springs."

Saunders whirled to the room. "Prince, Reyes, grab three units and go! *Now!* Stan, I'm with you and Cordova. We'll get more on the way. Everybody else, stay and keep at it."

"I'm losing him, Stan . . . ," Frank said, fighting the pain, getting dizzy.

Bodinger, Cordova, and Saunders were already outside and heading to their car to lead the run. "Keep him in sight, buddy. Stay with me." He called to Saunders, "We need to get the sheriffs out there with trucks."

Saunders was on his cell phone. "I'm a step ahead of you."

"How the hell did he know?" Cordova asked as Bodinger peeled out with Saunders in the backseat.

"Your guess is as good as mine." He knew Frank would never be able to keep his nose out of it, and right now, he was glad the stubborn son of a bitch hadn't.

"Frank Castro is the biggest renegade the Austin police ever had," Saunders explained to Cordova, still holding the phone to his ear. "He was a cowboy and a loose cannon, but at nut-cutting time, there's no one else you'd rather have."

"So I've heard."

"Believe it. I once saw Frank take a slug in the chest, Kevlar saved him. But before they could get off more rounds, he took down three without pulling his weapon. They guy's a nut job, but when he's on . . . He's *on*." He returned to his cell. "I want every Travis County cop with a badge heading to Barton Springs, and I want it happening twenty minutes ago. Scramble two EMT units to the same locale, and tell Captain Short his old friend may have just saved a few lives."

"Frank, Frank, you there?" Bodinger asked.

"Yeah . . . Barely. By the way, the Hummer you're looking for . . . ain't black."

"What do you mean? We have a witness."

"Witness . . . was right. He . . . painted it."

"To what?"

"Blue . . . azure."

"Azure?"

"Sky blue . . . you . . . idiot."

"How do you know this? What's going on, Frank?"

"We'll split one . . . Later, you can . . . catch up," Frank slurred, his lungs filling with blood. When Frank refocused on the road, the Hummer was gone. He lost them at the wilderness park. The winding road they'd been on came to a stop at a T intersection.

"*Fuck . . . me.*"

"What? What, Frank, what? What is it?"

He couldn't tell Bodinger. He couldn't tell him he lost them, not yet.

"Gotta go, buddy," he said, "need to concentrate," closing the phone. He sat there at the T in the road, idling.

"Frank? Frank, you there? *Frank*!" Bodinger turned to his partner, "I lost him." He hit his callback button, but instead of Frank's baritone, he heard his wife's sweet voice answer, "Hi, this is Susan. I'm sorry I missed your call, but if you'll leave a number, I'll call you back just as soon as I can. Promise! Bye-bye." A lump grew in his throat. He knew that may be the last time he heard his wife's voice. He and Kerndon both told her there was nothing to worry about. She'd been terrified and they each agreed, telling her to live life normally. He punched the steering wheel and hit the gas.

"No fucking way! Not like this!"

"Calm down, buddy," Cordova said. "We'll get there. If Castro's as tough a son of a bitch as you guys keep telling me, he'll stop him. We'll catch the prick before anything happens."

"Frank's in no shape, Eric," Bodinger told him. "Even if he gets there, he'll be easy pickings. We gotta find them."

Saunders knew he was right. Tackling a psycho with a knife in your back was no way to go to war. But if there was one man who could match crazy for crazy with the likes of D, it was Frank Castro. "Get us there, Stan," he said. "Get us there, and we'll end this damn nightmare once and for all."

The road where Frank was sitting dead-ended at a crossroads, a T intersection. It was either left or right, everything hinged on it. His head said left, but his gut said right. The reason? There was no reason, but following his gut got him this far; it wasn't time to stop now. He turned the BMW right down the small one-lane road, slick with rain and falling leaves, thinking of both Susan Bodinger and Tiffany.

And the steel hanging in his back.

54

Adam had the ultrasonic heavy metal music blaring in the hold ever since he drove away from the Bodingers' house. Once he dropped Susan inside, incapacitated, he took the time to remove her clothes and zip tie her feet together then did the same with her hands behind her back. She tried to fight him off, but he tased her again and out she went. Satisfied that his quarry was subdued, he dropped her clothes outside the Hummer and casually drove away. There was no need to hurry yet. Castro was dying on the kitchen floor, and Bodinger was looking for a black Hummer, not a blue one.

Adam wanted this to be special. After all, it was most likely his last, and it was both the wife of the cop chasing him and a near–dead ringer for Deloris. Ever since her death, he'd tried to meet other women, but being socially awkward left him with little success. He'd been having sex with an older woman since he was eight and found it difficult to achieve an erection with girls or women his age. As repulsed as he was by having sex with his own mother, he discovered he'd been programmed to perform for someone his elder.

The only sexual stimulation he ever felt that wasn't tied to older women was his killing jars. Watching the bugs and mice fight for breath gave him erections. When he applied it to young women, the result was mind-blowing. Inside Adam's world, young women were like specimens to collect. He could admire their beauty, enjoy their bodies and soft veneer, but the only sexual gratification he could ever experience from them was to treat them like the vermin in his killing jars. To watch them fight for breath, their lean, soft bodies writhing in agony as the bag robbed them of their vital oxygen. Watching them die bound, naked, and suffocating was the biggest sexual thrill of his life.

He'd done it three times. Three times he felt he'd touched the floor of heaven.

Adam could enjoy pornography like any normal man. Watching two young people have sex was as much turn on for him as it would be for most people. But in person, one-on-one, he was a failure with women his age. Deloris had made sure of that. She destroyed normality for him. He was robbed of the pleasure of knowing the soft and supple flesh of a young woman his age, of looking into the eyes of a person who had no more years of life than he and enjoy their insecurities and bumbles along with his own. Deloris, his *mother*, took away his youth. She stole his childhood, his innocence, and his ability to interact with women his age. Women of his ilk, women of his own cut.

I'm your mother, your lover, your woman. I gave you life, and I give you sex. What more could you want?

Now he had Susan Bodinger naked and tied up in the back of his killing jar. A handsome woman in her mid-forties, blonde, and perfect. This was the best of both worlds. He had always separated his true sexual desires into two halves. There was the mature older woman he could jump through hoops for; then there were the rodents in his collection.

Susan fit neatly into his cast of deviance.

After he drove to the end of the highway, he exited off and started the snake trail of service roads that would take him to his point of destiny. The true meaning of who he was as a person, as a sadist. Deep inside, Adam knew he was a disease that needed to be banished from existence, but the drive to find his definitive satisfaction was so strong that innocence had to take a backseat to the stronger cause. He was a monster, and all monsters need victims. Just as shadow swallows light, the beast swallows the innocent in order to feed the devastation in its soul. The world grieves for the victim. But no one sheds a tear for the tortured fiend.

362

How does it feel to be the banished? The outcast full of self-loathing and hate. The boogeyman in the dreams of children. The one sent off the playground of life just because you didn't match up with some preconceived notion of morality. Scorned by people who would trade their souls for one solitary, blissful moment as the one he felt when Amy Crowder faded away inside his bag.

To feel the total bliss of ultimate release.

To be both creator and destructor.

To be what Deloris wanted him to be.

To be a God.

After a few miles of the small winding roads, Adam went off road in the H2, clicking on the four-wheel drive, cutting a path through the wet grass and mud. There was a hill in front of him, and his feeling was that the trees on the far side of it would serve nicely as a setting for his ultimate masterpiece. The Hummer climbed the slippery hill with ease, and to his gratification, there was a small grove of trees nestled together on the far side, just yards away from the tree line of the main woods. Once he found the place of his liking, he parked and killed the engine, cutting the music. As soon as the roaring thunder of the heavy metal stopped, Susan began screaming. She had no way of knowing that there wasn't another person within miles to hear her, nor that her captor was only inches away from her behind the customized wall at her head.

Adam took a deep breath and looked at himself in the mirror. His almost-feminine face scared no one. That was why he always wore the ski mask even when he was alone with his doomed victim. He never wanted to lessen their fear with his feminine appearance. He wanted them to be terrified of him. With the mask and gun, he could get them to do anything with promises of their release, but they had to fear him. The mask served the purpose well.

However, this was different. He wanted Susan Bodinger to see his face. He wanted her to be shocked at how boyish and delicate-looking the *Capital Hangman* really was. He wanted her to see, absolutely, who he was. And see him she would, because he wanted to talk first. He hadn't talked to anyone in nearly four years, much less a woman.

Now, he could.

He climbed from the cab and shut the door softly as Susan screamed for someone to help her. He was wearing tan jeans and hiking boots. The tails and cuffs of his shirt protruded from beneath the long-sleeve pullover sweater he'd donned that morning. His hair was a mess, and he felt like a schoolboy as he walked to the back of the Hummer. He felt the same way he always did when he came home from school. Apprehensive.

With Susan having already been prepped, he left his pistol and knife in the cab; this was the one time they weren't necessary. Taking a deep breath, he opened the back of the dark H2. The dwindling daylight shone into the hold, and there she was. Naked, tied, and terrified for her life. Adam climbed in as Susan screamed even louder. He squatted inside like a baseball catcher, his forearms resting on his knees, tilting his head sideways like a dog trying to hear a certain sound.

"Let me out of here!"

He shushed her. "Shhh."

"Let me go! You don't have to do this!"

"Calm down."

"Somebody help me!"

"There is no one."

"Somebody, please help me!"

Adam stepped out of the hold, cupping his hands to his mouth, shouting, *"Somebody help her! Somebody please save this poor woman!"*

His action startled Susan, and she stopped screaming. Adam leaned back in the door, saying, "The only ears out here belong to the squirrels. It's just you and me. Okay?"

Susan was freezing cold. Naked and petrified, she was shaking so bad the zip ties were digging even deeper into her skin. Again, he climbed up into the hold and squatted by the door. The light was bad, so he went back to the cab and turned on the dome light in the hold. Susan was shocked by the light, but what was more shocking was when Adam climbed back in, and she could get a good look at him. She guessed he was in his mid- to late twenties. Piercing blue eyes and high cheekbones. His raven black hair was covering his forehead, looking like it hadn't been washed in weeks. It also looked like he hadn't eaten in days nor slept. His face was gaunt and weary looking. But the eyes were burning with something she didn't like. She saw pain in his eyes. The kind of pain a twisted mind would want to share.

"You look like her," he said.

Susan had to muster the strength to respond. Finally, she croaked, "Who?"

"Deloris. My mother. You are similar. How old are you?"

Again, she cleared her throat and managed, "Forty-six."

"Ah. When she died, she was forty-five. That was four years ago," he paused. "You're contemporaries."

"I guess so," she said. She wanted to cover herself, but it was impossible. Her hands were bound behind her back, and her legs were crossed at the ankles and bound as well. All she could do was lie there naked, vulnerable to whatever this sadistic man was planning to do. She thought about Frank in the kitchen. Before she could stop herself, she asked, "Frank?"

"I'm sure Castro's dead by now."

Her eyes welled. He'd come to save her. He knew who this man was and what he was planning, and he came to save her. Now, he was dead, and there was no way for Stan to remotely know what was going on. She was going to die like those other poor girls. The image of herself hanging like this from a tree . . . Tears rolled down her cheek.

"Calm down, Susan. I just want to talk," he said, studying her.

She didn't respond.

"Are you a good mother?" he asked.

Again, silence. It was fine with him. After all, he didn't care what she had to say. He was the one holding court in the back of the Hummer, his forum to get things off his chest.

"Deloris thought she was a good mother. I always had food and shelter, schooling. I got birthday presents and Christmas gifts like everyone else. She always made sure we had a big tree every December. December first, just like clockwork. I'd come home from school, and there it would be. A big green Christmas tree with all the bells and whistles. Wrapped presents and stockings. You know, all that Norman Rockwell bullshit. She made sure I did my homework and ate my vegetables. Yeah, she was a good mother, I guess." His eyes narrowed as he asked, "But does a good mother teach a seven-year-old how to use his tongue on her clitoris the way she likes?"

The question jolted her. She felt her eyes pop open even wider. He kept staring at her, waiting on an answer to his horrible question. She had none.

"See," he continued. "When I was too young to perform sexually, before puberty, she taught me the finer points of oral sex. So even if I was too young to have intercourse, I could still make her life more . . . pleasurable. A loving son doing his chores like any other kid." His eyes drifted off to a place beyond her, a place steeped in molestation. "It got so routine that I thought no more of it than walking to school. It was just what a loving son does for his most giving mother. After all, who loves you like your mother? Hmm?"

Susan could see where this was going. He was going to punish his mother by killing her. In that instant, all hope drained away. Her heart quit racing as the trembling stopped. Suddenly she was warm in the back of the hold. Fear was replaced with resignation. She was going to hear this poor bastard's sad tale, as tragic as it was; then he was going to kill her. Calm washed over her like a warm bath, and she listened as Adam told her of his mother.

"Once, when I was about eleven or twelve, she woke me for school. I ate my cereal and gathered up my books and all, and she told me"—he grimaced—"she told me that there was enough food in the house for two weeks. That I was supposed to go to school every day just as always and come straight home. Do my homework, eat, shower, and go to bed. Get up the next morning and do it again. Do it every day until she got back."

Susan listened.

"She left that morning when I did. Except, when I came home, she was still gone. And she stayed gone for two weeks. Can you imagine? A twelve-year-old alone for two weeks with no supervision? Now, I was a good boy. I did as she said. Every day up and school, homework, and shower, to bed—the whole thing. I did it just like she said. But she never came home. Two full weeks. Remember, there's no father, no grandma or aunts and uncles. It's just me and her. And without her . . . There's only me."

"You were only twelve?" she asked, empathy in her eyes.

"Hey, old enough to make your mother orgasm, old enough to stay alone, right?" He rubbed his hands over his face then went on. "Anyway, it was Sunday night. I'd been alone for two weeks, and the food was about gone. I didn't know what to do. I couldn't tell anyone. They'd take her away, and without her—"

"There's only you," she said calmly.

"Right again," he said. "You're catching on." The pain in his eyes was heartbreaking. Susan had to keep reminding herself that he was out of his mind and was going to kill her. But resigned to the inevitable, she listened.

"I was in bed. The next day was a school day. Can't stay up. And that big house was so creepy when I was little. By that night, I was sleeping with the lights on. Well, I wasn't sleeping. I was just wrapped in the covers, staring at the ceiling, when I heard a car pull into the driveway. I peeked out the curtain, and I saw Deloris get out of the car and walk to the door. I jumped out of bed and ran, tears everywhere, crying like a baby. I thought I'd never see her again. When she walked in, I ran to her, and she stopped me. She said she needed some sleep, that we'd catch up after school," he told her. "She sent me to bed. Can you image? Not seeing her for two weeks, and when I do, she sends me to fucking bed like nothing had changed." He adjusted himself then proceeded. "The next morning, she was still asleep when I left. I thought she might die before I got home." His eyes drifted away to a place far from where they were. "In a way, I hoped she would. Just die and leave me to whatever there was in the world. Leave me to deal with it in my own way."

Susan pulled back, knowing what was coming.

"But," he said, "she didn't. Nothing's that easy. When I got back, she was still out. She slept for two days. On the second day, when I got home, she was up and had dinner cooked and was waiting for me at the kitchen table. Know what she asked me when she finally took the time to talk to me?"

"I have no idea," Susan admitted, tears staining her face.

"She lit a cigarette then leaned over to me and asked me, '*So what have you been up to?*'"

Susan sat in silence, not knowing what he wanted to hear—if anything at all. He seemed to want to talk, and she was prepared to listen as long as he wanted. Since this was the last of her life, she wanted to live it as long as she could; and if that meant listening to a madman's sob story, as tragic as it was, she was willing to savor every second of breath she was allowed to have.

"About a week later," he went on, "she had some guy over. She really wasn't promiscuous, but there were men around from time to time when I was too young." He lowered his stare at her. "She was waiting on my puberty to show me what my life was really going to be like. Anyway, there was this guy. I think his name was Jeff. Anyway, she told him the story, and he called me into the room and asked me about it. Asked me if I was scared while she was gone, and I said I was. He asked me if I thought she would never come back, and I told him yes. He told her she needed to put a dog tag on me. Dogs have tags so someone can find the owner, so a child should have a tag like a dog. They laughed and laughed all night about that." His face grew even darker. Susan could feel the pain seeping from him. "Well, after hours of coke and whiskey, Deloris passed out, I mean *out!*" He snapped his fingers. "Then ol' Jeff gets an idea. Instead of a dog tag, I should be marked. So as she's passed out, he took it upon himself to mark me for her. Everyone called her D. That's what he called her, and that's what all the men back then called her. D."

A new chill went up Susan's spine.

"So Jeff lays me on my stomach and sits on me to hold me down. Then he took his fat cigar, and on the back of my right shoulder, he burnt the letter *D* into my skin. One . . . dot . . . at a time."

Susan closed her eyes, horrified.

"I screamed bloody murder, of course, but she was out like a light. Never heard a thing. At least that's what I've told myself all these years.

I still have the scar." He stopped and pulled the back of both the sweater and shirt up to his neck and turned to show her. There it was. The letter *D* seared into his flesh from over a dozen burn scars. "I feel it from time to time to remind me how the world doesn't care. That I have that pain to fall back on when I think I'm too smart or lucky for my own good. But then again, I don't believe in luck. All I know is misery. And to a point, destiny. See, I was destined to be this."

Susan had to ask. Before she died, she had to know who was killing her. "So what are you?"

"Well, isn't it obvious?" he asked. "I'm insane."

55

Frank was trying ever harder not to pass out. He could feel that the back of his shirt was wet with blood, but he knew if he pulled the knife out, the bleeding would be worse; and worse yet, whatever arteries or organs that were severed or punctured would either flow or fill with blood. The seat kept bumping the knife, pushing it deeper with every jolt the road made. However, he was determined not to stop.

He'd driven several miles on the small road slowly, looking for any sign at all that the H2 had been that way. The small road was littered with yellow and orange leaves from the fall season, and the day's rain made them stick to the pavement like postage stamps. He fought the urge to call Bodinger and give him his location. If he was wrong, Stan would have a better chance by doing the search himself. Besides, he was doing well enough just to drive the tiny car without managing a distraught husband over the phone. Also, he knew that by now, every park service employee, county sheriff, and free city cop was headed his way. Parker was done for and didn't even know it. If it wasn't for Susan, he would stop and let the authorities handle it from here. He'd done enough and needed a hospital. But time was ticking, and Susan was as dead as a sermon on Bourbon Street if he couldn't find her.

He felt that his bottom lip was wet, and when he wiped it off, there was blood coming from his mouth. Since it was getting more and more difficult to breathe, he figured the knife had now punctured his lung. He was stuck in a catch-22. The longer the blade stayed in, the more damage it would do; however, pulling it out now would mean death if he couldn't get immediate medical help.

"*Fuck me running.*"

The BMW eased around a small hairpin turn then up a slight rise that leveled off into a long straight stretch. About a hundred yards into the straight, he noticed a set of fresh tire tracks that left the road and headed up a gradual hill to his left. The tire tracks were deep in the wet grass and mud, and whoever made them had done it very recently. He stopped. With the big engine idling, he pondered the situation.

Going off road on such wet ground meant the car would get stuck. If he was wrong about it, even if he got out and walked, Susan was dead. If he was right, and he could get the car as far up as possible before it lost traction, the walk would be shorter and he could possibly prevent her murder. The question was is this it? He had to decide quickly, both he and Susan depended on it.

"Well, Tiff," he said to the woman he was avenging, "it's all or nothing, baby. What's the call?"

Nothing. No help.

"Gonna die anyway," he told himself, blood trickling from the corner of his mouth. "What do ya say? Let's punch it." With that, he cut the wheel to the left, popped the clutch, and leaped off the road. The back of the seat did him no favor as the tip of the handle lodged against the cushion, forcing the blade deeper. Frank screamed in pain as the small car fishtailed on the wet grass but caught enough traction to scoot a good thirty feet before the street tires hit mud and spun out. He knew he had to keep the car moving to fight out of the ruts, but the pain shooting through him was more than even he could stand. He blacked out long enough for the car to stop, thus dooming it. When he came around, mere seconds after losing consciousness, the car was stuck.

"*Damn it . . . ,*" he said, his head dropping to the side of the steering wheel. He knew he'd have to make the rest of the trek on foot. He killed the engine and climbed out, falling to his knees. His head was spinning, blood erupting from his mouth. Sitting on his knees, he fished the phone from his pocket and dialed Bodinger.

"Frank?" Bodinger answered.

"*Who's left . . . ?*"

"Where are you?"

Frank gave him the best directions he could. The biggest thing was turning right at the T intersection. "Not even sure . . . I'm close though," he confessed. "I lost them . . . a ways back."

"Jesus, Frank! You lost them?"

"Well, at least I'm closer . . . than you."

"Where are you heading?" Bodinger probed.

"Up this hill," he stopped, coughing. Blood going everywhere. "Oops."

"What happened?"

"Just blood . . . I'll live." With that, he closed the phone. He tried to put it back in his pocket but missed, dropping it on the wet grass. Using his right knee as a base, he pushed himself up and started to walk. After he made five steps up the slope, his eyes danced in their sockets, and he went facedown on the ground. As he lay there, semiconscious, he liked how the cool, wet grass felt on his face.

Then, like the sky was hooked to a dimmer switch, the world faded away.

Bodinger was leading a team of seven cars with lights flashing and sirens blaring off the 360 loop and into the wilderness park. He was finding it hard to separate the cop doing his job and the husband trying to save the life of his wife. Suddenly the past ten years evaporated, and he was back working hand in hand with his old partner, Frank Castro. The last time they worked together, the very last night Frank saved his life. Now, ten years later, all the bad blood was washed away; and it was Frank, once again, going beyond his expectations to save Susan's life.

He wished he had it all back. To go back and make things right. He'd suffered many sleepless nights from then to now, and it always centered around Frank. He knew he'd done the right thing even if 90 percent of the cops on the force viewed him as a rat. Frank was out of control; he did them all a favor, including Frank. He knew he was never forgiven by his old partner, but everyone's life was better for what he did even if no one could see it at the time.

Now, here he was, racing to help Frank find the madman who broke his routine and kidnapped his wife surely to kill her. The memories of the other three women, hanging naked and dead from tree limbs, were firing through his mind like a machine gun. One awful vision after another, each more horrible than the last, all ending with his innocent wife. She'd been frightened by the threats, but it was he and Kerndon that assured her the killer had no desire to follow through with his intimidation. It was a typical terrorist tactic, they told her.

Live your life normally.

When Bodinger snapped himself out of his own mind, he saw the T intersection coming up.

"Right!" Saunders said from the back.

"I'm on it," Bodinger said, slowing to turn just as Cordova yelled for him to stop. Bodinger hit the brakes as three ATVs belonging to the Travis County sheriff's department blew through the intersection, left to right, heading in the same direction they were going.

"And there's more coming," Saunders told them as Bodinger turned right and floored the gas, shooting up behind them in no time. Saunders got busy trying to get patched through to whoever was in the lead ATV. They'd need to be able to communicate, especially if Castro called with more details.

Cordova leaned sideways to Bodinger and said, in as confirming a voice as he could muster, "It's going to be okay, bro. We'll find her in time."

Bodinger said nothing. He gripped the wheel tighter, focusing his attention on the back of the ATV in front of him. But in his head, he was praying for his phone to ring and for Frank to tell him she was safe.

That was all he could think about.

56

"Are you afraid of me?" Adam asked.

Susan thought the question was ridiculous; of course she was afraid of him. She was terrified. She knew what he'd done and, with all certainty, knew the same fate awaited her. She only nodded.

"I guess I should take it that my reputation has preceded me," he said, half mocking. "I mean, if you saw me on the street or in some putrid mall, would I intimidate you? Me? Really?"

She had to be honest. Even though she knew that he'd basically laid out his confession and motivation to her, he was beginning his own inward descent into the place he needed to be to kill her. As he was before, he wouldn't be able to see it through. He had programmed himself into being able to dissolve his morals with a state of mind that would not only allow him to carry out his heinous acts, but also justify them inside his own twisted mind. This was the beginning of the end, but in her gut, she knew she had to be honest with him.

"No."

"Of course not," he grunted, pushing his black hair out of his face. "I look like a woman. I know I'm a man. I have all the urges of a man, all the male impulses—I like women. But I have this face. This face that Deloris used to tell me would be so pretty on a girl. You know I caught hell in school. The weird kid that had the pretty face. Bullies would give me shit all day. I knew I had a face that could get me all the pussy I

374

wanted, but there was that little *mental* issue that drove them away. That and the fact that my loving mother would have destroyed any *split-tail*, as she called them, if any of them showed the slightest interest in her . . . *man*."

Susan sighed. The circulation in her arms was cutting off, and her hands were beginning to tingle. Her feet had been numb ever since she came to; and her skin, once again, was beginning to chill. But as uncomfortable as she was physically, her mind was devastated to think that this was the way she was going to end. Dying at the hands of a psychopath. She'd always thought she'd die in a hospital bed with her children and grandchildren gathered around her. To end up on the end of a rope in the woods, naked and bound for the world to see, to die simply because one man had a terrible childhood and decided on *you* of all people was enough to make her believe that Adam was right.

No one cared.

"From the time I was eight until I was twenty-one, all the sex I ever had was with my own mother. Do you know I can't even get it up for a young woman? Deloris actually programmed me. Like a robot. She took me away from *me*. My life's been a nightmare. I survived instead of lived." He drifted away again, whispering more to himself than to her, "This isn't what I wanted to be." Adam was lost in his own life as always, never seeing that all are connected. Humanity is like spokes on a wheel, each individual is separate and unique, but all are connected to the same common laws of life. He never saw that.

All Adam saw was Adam, and Adam's world.

As deviant as it was.

"In school, and even after, no one ever took me seriously. I was too fragile for the boys and too creepy for the girls. All I had was Deloris."

Susan felt that she should gamble and ask a question. Why not? "How did she die?"

Adam snapped back from his revelry and looked at her pointedly. "I killed her."

Susan wilted.

"I'd had enough. I wanted to be free from her. One night, she demanded I come to her bed, and I said no. I said no and I left." He spoke as though he was trying to convince her. "I guess it made her distraught. She drank a quart of vodka and passed out. You do know an unconscious drunk shouldn't lie on her back, yes?"

Susan nodded.

"Sometime, while she was out, she uh . . . regurgitated. My mother died choking on her own vomit while I was out. I was just walking, you know. Just walking. Wanting to clear my head. I mean I would have come back. I would have done anything she asked. I was gonna fuck her anyway like she wanted. I just wanted her to know I wasn't a kid anymore! I wasn't a toy!" he yelled at her, making her shrink away. "I told her once that if she was divided up into a hundred different parts, all of the worst parts of her were used to make me. Her and that sperm donor that made me. She *made* me! She forged me like a piece of clay! I am what I am because this is the way my *mother* made me!"

Susan closed her eyes, dreading the inevitable.

"She was all I had. If she was gone, there was only *me*. So I looked out on my future and saw nothing. I was staring at the abyss that was the rest of my life. It looked like a gaping black hole . . . Endless. Pointless." Adam was agitated. Frustrated once again by the failure and waste that passed for his life. He slid up the hold, close to Susan. He smelled awful. Everything about him made her want to retch, but she stayed with him, stayed focused. The longer he talked, the longer she lived.

Without thinking, she croaked, "Hope."

As if he'd been slapped, he recoiled, looking at her sharply. "What?"

Susan cleared the fear from her throat, saying again, "Hope. You have to have hope."

Adam huffed to himself and sat back on his knees, inches from her. Their eyes locked. Susan saw nothing but death in the evil blue eyes that bore through her like laser beams.

"Hope?" he asked, shocked. "Let me tell you a thing or two about hope," he said, bringing his face closer that they were nose to nose. "Hope is a violation of life. *All* hope is nothing more than a violation of life. I've become who I am because this is who I'm supposed to be. All of that, all of that shit I went through was required to make me who I am today. It all led me here today . . . with you."

The look in his eye was unmistakable; he was gone. The man he had been ceased to be, and the man he wanted to be was the one staring into her   soul.

"You don't have to do this," she pleaded.

"Yes, I do."

"Why?" she asked, her voice trembling. "Why do you do these things?"

He tilted his head, studying her. "When you have no soul," he told her, "all you can feel is pain. It's all you know how to share." He rubbed his face, asking, "Have you truly lived, Susan? Hmm? I mean do you understand what *real* living requires?"

She gave no response.

"I'll tell you." He moved back to her, close enough she could feel the heat from his body. "If you haven't chosen a person to die, if you haven't looked into their eyes as the last gasp of breath escapes them, if you haven't watched their eyes turn black as death takes them from this earth, if you haven't *done* that, if you haven't *caused* that . . . Then you haven't lived." His eyes narrowed. "And I really don't think you've done that. So since there are only two kinds of people in the world, you are obviously one kind. And I am the other."

Before she could stop herself, she asked, "What am I?"

"The victim," he said, pulling his hands from beneath him, "and I'm the boogeyman."

"*Nooo!*"

In a blink, he slapped a clear plastic bag over her head followed with a zip tie around her neck.

Zip!

"As you're dying, think of your mother!"

Instantly Susan went into shock. Her oxygen was cut off, and all she had now was the poisonous carbon dioxide from her own body filling the bag then refilling her lungs and starving her brain. As she struggled, Adam shifted back toward the door and sat on his knees like a child in front of a Christmas tree. He knew it takes approximately seven minutes for the brain to die from lack of oxygen. With the factor of shock and a rapid heartbeat accelerating the oxygen-deprived blood to the brain, he knew she'd be dead in about five minutes. He cupped his hands in his lap, watching Susan fight for life. Her long, lean, and naked body was thrashing in the back of the H2. Adam was ecstatic. This was more precious than the others. This was his masterpiece. As Susan rolled around, bucking against the zip ties and fighting with all she had to break free, Adam was overjoyed. This was beyond sexual. The other three had been avenues of sexual release. This was far grander. Susan was almost spiritual. The feeling he was having, watching Susan Bodinger die inside his bag, was religious. He felt a part of something bigger. Tears formed in his eyes the way scholars weep at a da Vinci or the music of Mozart. This, Susan Bodinger, was his opus.

This was his right!

This was his moment!

This was his time!

This was his perfect creation!

This was his masterpiece!

He was God!

He was—

It was then that a hand grabbed the inside of his collar and jerked him out of the back of the Hummer and onto the ground. Landing flat on his back, he looked up to see Frank Castro, bleeding from his mouth and nose, standing over him.

"*Remember me?!*" Frank slurred, turning his right arm, making an L shape with his elbow, then dropping all of his 215 pounds behind his forearm down on Adam Parker's face. Adam's nose disintegrated into a pulverized mass of blood, bone, and cartilage. His face exploded in a mist of crimson as he screamed such a wounded, guttural cry it reminded Frank of the squealing pigs in a slaughterhouse. Frank rolled off him and onto his side. Adam scrambled to his knees, his eyes swelling. He gagged and choked on the huge flow of blood, bone fragments, and mucus that cascaded down his throat. In too much shock and pain to retaliate, he instantly listened to his primal instinct of self-preservation. Adam stumbled to his feet then staggered into the woods; he just wanted to get away.

How could this happen? Why wasn't he dead? How did Castro not only find him, but do it twice?! Once after being tased and stabbed?! Adam was in the worst pain of his life. His nose was a lumpy pulp, blood covering his face and sweater. Not able to see with his eyes watered and swelling, he groped through the woods on all fours, climbing to his feet occasionally to lean his head back and slow the bleeding while taking strides toward escape. As the disgusting flow from his shattered face gushed down his throat, he threw up blood and bone fragments mixed with bitter bile.

Frank's first instinct was to jump to his feet and stomp the psychopath to death with his size 13 boot. However, his body wasn't cooperating with him at a high level. All he could do was watch him stagger into the woods as he yelled, "*I'm not . . . done with you!*"

Now, the light came on again; Susan was in trouble. He rolled on his stomach then, with one hand, climbed up into the back of the hold. He saw her. She was naked and bound. Her body was beginning to convulse, but most alarming was the plastic bag secured over her head. "*No! No no no! Hell no!*" Frank barked, crawling to her. Cradling her head, he saw her mouth frozen open in a horrible mask of panic. Her body twitched as Frank used his index finger to poke a hole through the bag directly into her mouth. The rush of sweet oxygen filled her lungs.

"Breathe, baby . . . Breathe. I got you . . . I got you. Breathe." He tore the rest of the bag away, leaving only the zip tie around her neck. Susan coughed and gagged, threw up beside him, coughing more. The rush of air into her burning lungs overwhelmed her shocked system, but she was coming around.

"You're okay . . . You're fine," Frank assured her. Tears started flowing, and the more she began to realize that indeed Frank had saved her, the more she wept.

"*Frank . . . Frank . . . He said he killed you! I thought you were dead!*"

"He tried . . . all right."

"*Oh god, Frank. He's so crazy, he's gone completely mad!*" Realizing she had no idea where he went, she asked, "My god, where is he? *Where is he?*"

"He went into the woods."

Finally noticing the blood covering his face, she panicked. "Frank! My god, you're bleeding! What happened to you?"

It was becoming more difficult to talk with the blood in his lungs. "I fell down coming . . . up the . . . hill."

"Frank, get me loose! Please get me loose."

"Okay . . . Hang on," he said, noticing her hands were bound with plastic zip ties, no way to undo them by hand. They had to be cut off. He scanned the back of the Hummer for a pair of wire cutters or a box cutter with a razor blade. He saw nothing. Susan was crying and needed to get free, but he had nothing to do it with. He needed . . . a knife.

"Stay here," he told her, his voice a raspy whisper.

"No! Where are you going?" she pleaded.

"I have to get . . . the knife."

"What knife?" she asked. Frank managed to back out of the Hummer and stand outside.

"You might not . . . want to . . . watch this," he told her, turning away, revealing to her the steak knife still hanging from him.

"*Oh god, Frank!*" she cried. Now she knew why his speech was so labored and why he was bleeding from his nose and mouth. First she thought it had been his scuffle with Parker. He must have stabbed him in her kitchen because he said he killed him, and that knife belonged to her and Stan.

Frank hesitated for a moment. This was going to hurt. He cleared his mind then thought of Tiffany. The way he found Susan had to be the same way Tiffany died. Suffocated in a plastic bag while that slime sat and watched. Refocused on the task at hand, he moved his right arm behind his back and over to the left side. He could feel about a half inch of steel between his back and the knife handle. Using his index and middle fingers, he slid them on either side of the blade as though he were holding a cigarette. With all the strength he could muster, he used the fingers to inch the blade back.

"*God no,*" Susan sobbed.

The pain was enormous. Not wanting to stop, he pushed harder, sliding to his knees. The blade moved more as the pain grew. His cheeks trembled; his mouth drooled a mix of saliva and blood down his white shirt as he forced the blade back. He used his weakening left arm to

380

reach back and grip his wrist, pulling it closer to the knife. Now he could get a good finger grip on the blade with his index and thumb. As he pulled the knife out, he and Susan bellowed together in a chorus of agony. His in pain and hers at the horror of watching the bloody knife emerge from his back.

"*Aaaagghhh!*" he screamed as the knife finally fell away, forcing him to collapse on the ground.

Earlier, he'd passed out on the hill. He was out for less than a minute, but the clock in his head told him he'd just blown his one chance to save her. Willing himself onto his feet, he logged his way up the wet hill, intermittently going down to one knee or the other every few steps. Once he made the hill, he saw the azure H2 a good fifty yards away. The back door was open, and Parker was kneeling there like a praying altar boy. He scuffled his way to the vehicle, thinking of only two things: save Susan and kill Adam Parker. At the moment, one and a half out of two wasn't bad for a man in his condition.

"*Oh, Frank!*" Susan sobbed, her own face wet with perspiration and tears. She had no idea that the man who'd saved her life was in such a state. She managed to get to her knees at the back of the hold, just at the door, feeling the cool, damp breeze against her skin. It was a welcomed feeling of near freedom. She just needed the binds off. It was horrible that Frank had only one choice to make in cutting her free. The choice he ultimately had to make. For if Parker did come back, Susan needed her freedom.

He pushed himself up, picking the knife from the ground. He fell against the side of the Hummer, nearly face-to-face with her. She saw it. The life force in him was draining away. This entire ordeal was taking its toll on him. He needed to stay with her and let the police take it from here; he'd done more than enough. She turned around and let Frank cut the tie off her wrists. The circulation hit her hands like a million needles. It was wonderful. Next she turned and extended her legs out, and he cut her feet loose. As soon as she was free, she threw her arms around his neck and cried into his thick shoulder, burying her face in his neck. She was crying and ranting at the same time, unrecognizable words flowing from her in a release of joyous exhilaration. She was alive! Not realizing that squeezing Frank's neck so tight was killing him.

"*Oh shit,*" he grunted. "*Susan . . . Please . . . Let go . . .*"

Understanding, she released him, and he sank to his knees. She fell from the back of hold to the ground beside him. "I'm sorry," she cried. "I'm so sorry! Frank, you're so hurt. We have to get out of here. We have to go before he comes back!"

"He ain't . . . coming back."

"No, we have to go. We have to get out of here. I'll help you."

"No . . . no. You gotta wait here. The cavalry's . . . coming."

"What?"

"Stan's on his way . . . with half of Texas . . . coming with him."

The words felt like a rope being tossed to a drowning victim. Stan's coming and bringing a ton of help. She couldn't believe her ears. How? How did Frank do this?

"Let's get you . . . warmed up," he said, pulling at his sports coat. She helped him pull it off; then he helped her put it on over her bare skin. It was warm. A special warm. A safe warm. He helped her climb back up into the door of the H2 where she sat. "Let's call him," he said, fishing in his coat pocket for the phone. It wasn't there. "I used your phone. It's gone . . . Must have . . . dropped it . . . somewhere."

Removing the knife did exactly what he feared it would. During the drive, the tip of the blade worked forward, puncturing his lung. With the blade out, his left lung began to fill with more blood. He coughed up a huge amount of blood and spat it on the ground. The back of his white shirt looked like a sheet from a battlefield hospital.

"My god, Frank, you're bleeding to death. I have to do something," she pleaded.

"No," he said. "You wait here. Stan's coming. He should . . . be here in . . . ten minutes." He snagged the knife from the ground and told her again, "Wait here for Stan . . . He's coming full speed."

"No, we'll wait. Understand?" she cried. "*We'll* wait for Stan. He's in the woods, he can't get away. Let them do this."

"I have to . . . go."

"No, Frank, no! You have to stay here. Stay here with me. You've done enough. Let the police take it from here."

"I have to."

"You're hurt. You can't. You won't make it, you'll die. Please just lie down in here with me, and we'll wait together," she pleaded. "Please, Frank. *Please!*"

He shook his head. She was right, of course. Parker wasn't getting away, and he *had* done enough already. There was just a certain bit of business that still needed to be taken care of. As Susan begged him to stay with her, he climbed to his feet; and knife in hand, he turned for the woods.

"I have to," he said. "I have . . . a promise to keep."

57

When Adam felt he was an adequate distance from Castro, he stopped long enough to try and halt the bleeding from his obliterated nose. The blow not only shattered his face, but also jarred his brain with a slight concussion. Nauseous, he threw up again, falling to his knees. His stomach had been empty, with the only thing in it coming from his broken face. Once all was expunged, he was locked in a bout of dry heaves. Spasm after spasm gripped his body in an agonizing fit of emptiness. When they stopped, he folded forward, resting his forehead on the wet ground.

Satisfied he could stand, he dragged himself to a knee then stood erect, staggering into a tree. Once his eyes cleared enough for him to inspect himself, he was shocked at how much blood there actually was. His sweater looked as though his throat had been cut. The metallic taste of blood still lingered in his mouth as he held his head back, trying to think of something to do.

He needed to pack his nose to stop the bleeding. The only thing he could use in the woods was mud. He cleared away a small patch of wet earth, cleaned away the leaves and pebbles, then began scooping the soft soil into his hand. When he had what he felt was a sufficient amount, he rolled it into a ball then painfully stuffed the mud into his swollen and misshapen nostrils.

"Oh fucking *Jesus*!" he screamed, sinking to his knees. He reprimanded himself for shouting. The last thing he wanted was to give away his location. He had to get out of the woods. He wasn't familiar with the park and really had no idea which way was the fastest route out. Then a thought hit him.

Where are you going?

Home was gone; he was sure of that. Castro had his vehicle. The only other person on the planet he could have called if he was in trouble was dead in his bathtub or maybe even the morgue by now. He had no money on him, no resources, and no time. Indeed, where was he going? It was the instinct of a wounded animal that made him run in the first place. If he hadn't gotten so damaged, he could have possibly gotten to the cab of the Hummer where his pistol was and killed Castro right then, and his masterpiece would still be intact. As it was now, Castro had ruined everything. He was sure he climbed in and saved Susan Bodinger. On top of that, he most likely called the cops. The woods would be swarmed with hundreds of armed officers just itching at the chance to put a bullet in his brain.

He thought about giving up. Spend the rest of his life behind bars as a case study for criminologists. However, he knew he wouldn't last five minutes in a high-security prison. The inmates would rape and kill him the first day.

What was driving Castro so hard? Was it Tiffany Malvern? Was it the voice message he now regretted leaving? Why was he so determined to catch him?

Frank Castro's gonna cut your fucking heart out!

Was that it? If indeed it was, then as long as Castro was standing, he'd be coming after him. The more Adam thought, the more convinced he became. His rage started to build. Castro had taken away his last chance of creating a masterwork so complete it would have made headlines around the country. He would have killed the wife of the very detective assigned to catch him. He would have been unique, different, special. But now, it was all a waste. Suddenly the pain in his face was replaced with a burning rage for revenge. Castro was trying to avenge the murder of the girl; he knew that's what drove him. To kill the mighty Frank Castro, even if the bastard did save Susan, would be worth it. He knew Castro's only goal at this point was to kill him. He simply couldn't allow him to win. He knew he'd never be free again, but he'd rather die at the hands of the authorities than have that bitch's threat ring true.

Frank Castro's gonna cut your fucking heart out!

He wanted to crush the life out of him. He wanted to obliterate the private detective from the face of the earth. Closing his eyes, he tried to remember the encounter behind the H2 before the big Cuban smashed his face. He remembered seeing blood on him. He was bleeding from the mouth. The knife wound had not killed him, but it had done its damage. If he could achieve the element of surprise, he might be able to take him down. He resigned himself to the fact that he would be entering the woods after him; to think otherwise would be to underestimate him. Something he'd never do again.

He searched the ground, studying all the broken and fallen limbs. When he found one to his liking, he took a couple of practice swings and felt it was both solid enough yet light he could get a good swing. The first swing would count for everything. Even in bad shape, he knew he was no physical match for Castro. He'd have to ambush him. Once he had him on the ground, he'd do his best to turn Castro's head into a pulpy mess.

Afterward, he'd charge the police and force them to shoot him.

Without Deloris, all he had was himself. Soon, that would be going away as well. But first, Frank Castro had to die.

It was the longest and most frightening ten minutes of her life. Susan sat in the back of the Hummer just the way Frank instructed. Wrapped in his coat, she listened for any sound coming from the woods. Any sign at all that *he* was coming back. As much as she loved Frank for saving her, she hated the stubborn son of a bitch for leaving her alone. She cried and waited, alone and terrified.

She heard Parker's words again. The horrible stories he told her. She had no way of knowing how much of what he said was true. But even if only one of the stories had any validity, it was cause enough to say he had a terrible childhood. If all were true, then his upbringing was worse than an orphan from a Dickens novel. She felt terrible for the child he once was. She empathized for the boy he'd been. But all she wanted for the monster he became was to be eradicated from existence. The horrible few minutes she felt inside the bag was something she knew would haunt her for the rest of her life. Powerless to move and unable to breathe, she felt her life fading away. She would have died if not for the persistence of a man she hadn't laid eyes on in ten years.

She began to rock back and forth as she cried, unable to shake the feeling of isolation. She could feel the walls closing in even though she had open wilderness in front of her. The longer she waited, the more aware of her surroundings she became. She had no idea where she was. She'd been locked inside Parker's killing jar during the trip while bombarded with thundering music. The woods didn't look familiar, but she knew she was somewhere around Austin and her husband was coming.

When she first heard the faint echo of the siren, her heart leaped. It was then that the real fear started. They were close enough to hear, but they weren't there yet. The Hangman could emerge from the woods at any minute and end her life with help merely yards away. Her crying turned into wailing, and as the top of the Travis County sheriff's ATV crowned the top of the hill, Susan fell completely apart.

Saunders had the deputy in the lead ATV on the phone as they hit the straightaway after the hairpin curve. When Bodinger told him it was Frank's car stuck in the mud halfway up the hill on the left, Saunders relayed the information. "That's Frank Castro's car stuck on the hill. Hit it!"

The two ATVs attacked the hill, shooting to the top, as Bodinger slid left and went off road. The only thought in his mind was saving Susan. He didn't give a goddamn about Adam Parker or Frank at that moment; he just wished he was in the lead ATV so he could get there sooner.

However, at about the same place Frank's car lost hold, so did Stan's. He fought the wheel left and right, bouncing Jim Saunders around the backseat like a ping-pong ball. About ten yards past the BMW, the Ford spun out. Before anyone could say anything at all, three men were out of the car and sprinting up the wet hill.

Bodinger was fighting back tears. Frank was here somewhere, but he was nowhere around. What was he going to find on the other side of that hill? Would Frank be there with Susan safe and Parker at bay? Or would he find Parker gone, Frank dead or dying, and his poor, sweet wife hanging in the trees like the other victims?

Victim.

Suddenly the word had an entirely new meaning. Ten years ago, Frank had saved him from becoming what he himself should have been, a victim. After years of working with victims, the word loses its power. You get desensitized to it. It becomes another throwaway word that litters daily conversation. Popular culture bombards us with victims. Media victims, victims of heartbreak, victims of chance, victims of fate, and victims of love.

A true victim is a person who is struck down without cause, for the sole purpose of fulfilling the twisted desires of a madman left to run loose among society. A true victim is a girl abducted on her way home from school. A true victim is a young woman snatched out of her own yard. A true victim is a young lady kidnapped at her own front door. True victims are three school kids who were in the wrong place at the wrong time. The thought of Susan being a absolute victim . . . He swallowed the tears.

When Bodinger topped the hill, with Saunders and Cordova a pace each behind him as more sirens screamed in the distance, his chest nearly exploded. There she was, wrapped in a man's sports coat. Bare legs, no shoes, her hair looking like a cat had played in it, sitting on the back of the open azure blue H2, crying her eyes out. Bodinger's resolve finally caved as tears flowed freely down his cheeks as he ran to her. Past the four deputy sheriffs with weapons drawn, he ran to her. When he got to her, he lifted her off the Hummer as she threw her legs around him. They both cried into each other's necks.

"I thought I lost you," Stan cried.

"I thought you did too."

Saunders immediately went into command, setting up a perimeter around the crime scene. As more and more officers arrived, he began to coordinate them into groups. Obviously Castro and Parker were in the woods somewhere. It was the APD and the Travis sheriffs who would find them.

Stan set her back inside the door of the Hummer. "You okay?" he asked, cupping her face in his trembling hands.

She nodded. "I'm fine, really. I'm okay."

"You sure?"

"I'm fine."

"Where's Parker?"

She began to cry again and told him that as far as she knew, he'd run into the woods to get away from Frank.

"Is he armed?"

"I don't think so," she told him, calming. "I can't be sure. I mean, I don't know, but I don't think so."

"Where's Frank?"

"He went *after* him!" she said, losing control again. "Stan, he's so hurt, he's bleeding so bad. You have to find him, baby. Frank's dying. You have to find him and save him. *Please*," she sobbed.

Stan told her, "I got it, I got it. I'll find him."

They were speaking over the top of one another.

"Find him, baby."

"I will."

"Help him. He's bleeding so bad."

"I'm here, sweetheart. You're safe, and I'll find Frank, I promise." He turned to Cordova. "EMTs?"

"Right behind us, boss."

"Okay, they're going to take you to the hospital to—"

"No, I want to stay and help with—"

"I'm not losing this argument, not this one. Look at me," he told her, holding her face. "We got you. I've got you. I've got to go help my partner now. Me. Understand?" There was a meeting of the eyes that Susan understood all too well. Frank had now saved both of them. Now, Stan was going to save him, save his *partner*.

She closed her eyes and nodded. He hugged her firmly while asking in her ear, "Is this Frank's coat?"

"Yes," she answered, wiping her face.

He knew it was. For when he looked at his arms that were wrapped so tightly around his wife, they were covered in blood.

After the ambulance left with Susan, Saunders spoke to the squad of men. "Okay, here's the news. We have two men in these woods. One we believe to be the Capital Hangman. His name's Adam Parker. Five nine and 150 pounds. We have no idea if he's armed, so we'll assume he is. The other man is Frank Castro. He's an ex-cop turned private dick. Some of you know him. About six two and over two bills. A tough son of a bitch, but he's bleeding to death. Now, Castro thinks he's doing us all a favor by going after this whack job, but we've got a job to do. First we find Parker. Then we find Castro. But know this . . . Priority is split. We have a man who's dangerous and man who's dying. We don't leave till we have them both. Understood?"

The group all agreed as a helicopter flew over.

"Bird's here," Bodinger told Cordova. "Let's go find 'em."

58

The light was bad in the woods as Frank fell again. His left arm was almost useless. The loss of blood was making him light-headed, and the blood in his lungs was making it hard to breathe. His extremities were going numb. He knew, when he removed the knife, he'd have an hour tops. The longer it took, the less he was going to be able to do anything if he ever found him. The only thing that kept him going was the thought of Tiffany strapped down like Susan, with the bag over her head, as Parker watched and laughed, probably playing with his dick as she fought for life.

What makes men like that? he thought. *What happens to you that is so horrible that you get pleasure from such deviance?*

He already knew the truth. Most men like that are born that way. They're born that way, and all it takes is a few traumas along the way to push them right over the edge. He knew Adam Parker. He was a guy who got a bad break as a kid and was looking to make the world feel all the pain he felt. A man so torn up inside the only relief he feels is to inflict as much misery on the world as he can in one lifetime. There are millions of children who have tortured lives who grow up to be model citizens, but those are the ones without that special X factor in their genes. For the few unfortunate souls who get dealt the bad hand who happen to have the X factor, there's not enough chaos for them to cause that will ever satisfy their need for retribution.

"I'm . . . going to kill . . . your punk ass," Frank hissed to the gray sky.

He heard sirens echoing far away. That was good. Susan would be safe. Bodinger and the cavalry had arrived to seal off the park, and soon the circle would close. Helicopters and four-wheelers would scour the woods until they found Parker and put him away so that he would never harm another soul. Frank knew it was right. It was justice. It was justice for the people of Austin. It was justice for Bodinger and Susan. It was justice for Bryant, Amy, Julie, and the three boys.

However, having Adam Parker sit in a cell waiting for a needle to put him to sleep was not justice for Tiffany Malvern.

Will you, Frank? Will you cut my heart out?

The words danced in his head like a macabre ballet. Taunting, sneering, ugly. All he had was Parker's own words that Tiffany actually said them. *Frank Castro's gonna cut your fucking heart out!* If he closed his eyes and concentrated, he could hear her saying them. It gave him strength to stand. Strength to walk. Strength to hunt. He had a promise to keep. He swore to her as she lay in her casket that he would find him and kill him. He swore it then, and he swore at the cemetery. Bodinger and boys were coming to arrest him.

Frank Castro had an entirely different idea.

When Adam heard the sirens, his first instinct was to run. But then he heard Deloris's voice asking him where he would run to. He never knew his father. Now that he did, and it was the Tidy Man, he was no longer an option since he'd butchered him in his red room. The Tidy Man was the only other person alive who could help him or would even care that he was in trouble, and he was dead now. He was dead because they kept his identity away from him.

Why?

What was so wrong with letting him know the Tidy Man was his father? Was it because he might get involved and not allow Deloris to mangle the mind of his son? Or was the Tidy Man just that? Too tidy, too neat, and too proper to have a son with a woman like Deloris Parker? Whatever the reason, it no longer mattered. He'd been an inexcusable fiend that deserved everything he got. He started to cry at the thought of being locked up with hard cons who would relish his fine features.

He heard Bodain's insipid voice. "You just so damn pretty."

No! He could not be caught, and there was no escape. He had to confront Castro and let the police kill him. Dying at the hands of the cops after ending that bastard Castro would be a fitting end to his life. But Castro was first.

He'd walked through the woods, looking for a trail that might lead to the far side, all along spitting blood and repacking his nose with mud. He'd always been a city boy, so the woods gave him difficulty. The only time he went to them was to scout places to frame his art. Then, once he had the girl, he'd go back and create his aesthetic work. But those were controlled circumstances. To be in the woods, in a wilderness park he'd never been in, on foot—with a freak like Frank Castro on his ass—was foreign territory. He felt he could make it out of the park, but there was no place to go. By now, the face on his driver's license would be all over Austin. Since there was nowhere to run, he'd hide as long as it took for Castro to find him. He'd done it twice; why not believe he'd do it again? But this time, it would be different. This time, he'd be ready.

Bodinger was thankful that Captain Saunders was running the search because he was far too distracted. His wife had almost ended up as another victim of Adam Parker, and she would have if not for the meddling of his ex-partner. To see her that way, so scared and so vulnerable, had Bodinger rethinking if he should even be a part of the hunt.

What would he do if he found Parker first?

His instinct as a husband would be to blow his kneecaps off then stomp the life out of him as he screamed for mercy. But he was a cop. The law says there are certain rules of conduct your must observe at all times, that's what separates our society from so many others. He wanted to act with extreme prejudice but was bound by his badge not to. Even though there wasn't a man in the woods who would argue the shooting death of such a miscreant as Parker. Especially if the shooter's wife was to be his latest victim.

Bodinger and Cordova were flanked by two Travis County deputy sheriffs on either side. They walked ten feet apart through the woods with weapons out, scanning left to right for any movement. Bodinger thought back to his youth and squirrel hunting with his father. "If something catches your eye, turn but don't shoot till you see it clearly." His father was a wise man; his hunting advice worked for both man and beast.

Bodinger forced Susan out of his mind. There was no good to come from worrying about what might have been. Frank saved her; she was safe. There were no *what ifs*. The facts were that Parker tried and failed, and now he was as good as caught. The nightmare of the last six months was about to end.

Justice would be served.

"I've got to find Frank."

The tree looked good. Fat, stout, with huge roots extending from it like crippled fingers. Frank had to rest; his body was giving out. He could no longer feel his feet; his fingers and hands would be next. He sat on one of the large root bases and tried to breathe. Blood pushed its way up his throat, forcing him to cough, spewing red all over himself. He was dying; it was as certain as the coming darkness. His only hope for living would be to get airlifted out of the woods and flown to Breckenridge Hospital right then and there. Since there wasn't a chopper next to him at the moment, the outlook was bleak.

He tried to think like Parker. Where would he go? Surely he knew he was trapped by now. All that was left was closing the net, and he'd be caught in the middle. If he ran west, he'd come out in an open area between the Southwest Parkway and the golf course. He'd have the best chance that way; there was still plenty of growth. If he went any of the other directions, he'd come out in either residential districts or the Barton Creek Mall. He had to run west, but with the cloud cover and the mist, there was no way to know what direction west even was.

Then a thought occurred to him. Would he run at all? Would he try to escape, knowing he was doomed, or would he stay and try to claim what was stolen? Frank had ruined his creation, twice. Twice he corrupted his chance for the ultimate finale to his crimes. Maybe he wasn't running after all. Maybe he was waiting. He had to wait for all his victims. Suddenly it was becoming clearer. Parker was like a spider waiting on the fly to hit the web. It was how all his crimes were perpetrated. There was never blind luck or chance involved. It was planned, thought out, calculated. He'd scouted them. He knew their routines. He knew the path Amy walked home from the bus. He knew when Julie left for work. He knew where Tiffany lived and when she got home late. He knew Susan was home and should have been alone. Felix Bryant was his father. Calm, analytical, logical. He was a machine. A cold, calculating machine that—

Crack!

Frank heard the snapping of the branch and turned in time to see Parker behind him, swinging the limb at his head. With his reflexes slowed, he was barely able to get his right arm up high enough to block the blow, sending him crashing to the ground. As he lay on his back, Parker jumped the huge root, screaming, *"You fucking pig!"* while swinging the limb again. Frank rolled to his left, and he missed. The first blow had knocked the knife free from his hand, and he rolled to his knees empty-handed. The sudden movement threw off his equilibrium, and he swayed backward as Parker again came after him with the broken limb. He held it over his head like a samurai sword, screaming as he ran toward him as if he was going to try to split him in two. Frank was having trouble focusing his eyes, but instinct told him to roll with the blow. As Parker swung down with the limb, Frank rolled over backward while lifting his good arm, catching Parker's wrists. The block turned the limb away from him and exposed Parker's ribs.

If only I had a left arm, I could break his ribs with a body punch!

As it was, Parker stumbled to his left, and Frank delivered a well-placed heel kick to his right knee. Parker howled, crumbling to the ground, as Frank scanned the area for the knife that Parker was unaware of. Once he saw it, he tried to leap, but his body was too weak, and he stumbled on all fours. Parker rose and, thinking Castro was simply trying to get away, took his time retrieving his limb.

"Look at you," he taunted. "The badass cop with no badge. You fucked up my *dream*!"

Frank continued to crawl. His legs were shaking, his left arm buckled, and he fell over. The world was spinning in his eyes. He was dying as it was on his own; he didn't need Parker helping the matter. But he was this far, so he had to try and finish what he'd come to do. However, his blood-drained body and punctured lung were not cooperating with him. If only he'd remembered his .45 when he left the car. He'd sacrifice following Tiffany's threat to the letter just to blow the top off this miserable fucker's head.

"My mother warned me about boys like you. She said bullies may take your lunch money, they might laugh at you." He swung the stick, letting it smack the ground beside Frank as he crawled. "They may even make you bleed a little." He swung again, this time like a baseball bat, intentionally missing Frank's head, letting him feel the wind of the swing behind his ears as he again managed to get on all fours, crawling like a wobbly newborn. "But there's one thing you got that they don't, she always told me," he said, raising the limb high over his head, ready to smash it down. "You have *me*!" he screamed, ready to smash Frank's skull. Just then, Frank felt Parker's feet on either side of his right leg. Parker was straddling it at Frank's knee. With what reserve he had left, he rolled, whipping Parker off his feet. He landed hard on his back with the limb dislodged from his hands, the back of his head thumping the ground.

"*Son of a bitch!*" Frank growled, scrambling for the kitchen knife a few feet away. Parker shook the cobwebs out of his head, rising to his knees. He retrieved the limb, telling Frank, "Your cunt secretary was right. You are a handful." He stood.

Frank fell again, but this time, he lay on the knife. Parker still had no idea. He came back, more determined this time. "Did you like my house, Frank?" he asked, the mud gone from his broken nose, blood again streaming down his face. "I know you found it, you had to," he said, tapping the limb on the ground. "It was that shit Bodain, wasn't it? I

396

hope you at least broke something on him. Personally, I hated the son of a bitch." He grew closer as Frank still lay on his stomach, the ground tipping sideways, making him feel he would roll off the edge of the world.

"I guess you found my jars? My artwork? All my writings? I was going to leave it for the world to see after my masterpiece was complete. But my *father*!" he screamed, "fucked all that up. Then you come along like a pebble in my shoe and ruined my alternative. That's just something . . . I can never forgive." Again, he was standing over Frank.

This was it. He had nothing left, his body was used up. He gripped the knife firmly in his right hand beneath him then rolled onto his left side, looking up at the man he'd sworn to kill. He seemed to sway beneath the gray sky. It was just the loss of blood draining what was left of his senses. Parker took one last step, the limb high over his head, straddling him, and he said, "Before you die, think of your mother!"

"Think . . . of *yours*!" Frank snarled, slashing with his right hand, ripping Parker's thigh open. Parker screamed, falling to the ground, as Frank managed to crawl to him then lay his two hundred pounds on top of him, pinning him in the mud.

"*No!*" Adam screamed, seeing Castro with the knife. "*Not this way!*" He slapped and clawed at Frank's face, trying to get him off; but he was too big, too strong, too determined. Frank sat up on his knees, the knife in both hands. The light in his eyes was fading in and out; humming began in his ears as what life he still possessed teetered like a slowing top.

Will you, Frank? Will you cut my fucking heart out?

"*You . . . goddamn . . . right, I am!*"

With that, Frank slammed the knife as hard and as strong as he'd ever done anything in his life. Down, down into the chest of Adam Parker. Blood erupted from his mouth like a volcano as Frank twisted the blade, spitting, "*Die! Die . . . You worthless piece of shit!*"

Frank never let go. Instead, he ground the blade deeper, trying to find the right spot. The point of his evil soul where Tiffany rested, trying to free her from his grip, setting her free at last. "*Just . . . fucking . . . die!*"

With blood streaming from his mouth, Adam's eyes focused on a place over Frank's shoulder. A place far beyond the woods. He focused on a place so far away from the place he was dying, all he felt was emptiness. With his last act, he mouthed a single word to the gray Austin sky. Adam Parker cried, "*Mother*."

Then he was gone.

The evil of Deloris and Adam Parker was no more.

59

When Bodinger got there, Frank was lying on his back next to the Capital Hangman. The knife was still embedded in Parker's chest as the officers holstered their weapons.

"*Frank!*" Bodinger screamed, running to his old partner. He fell on the ground beside him, lifting his head. "Frank! Frank, can you hear me?"

Frank's eyes rolled then blinked open. Blood nearly covered his entire face, his breathing labored. He had no feeling in his legs; his arms were fading as well. He couldn't hold his head up, slipping in and out of consciousness.

"I got you, buddy, I got you," Bodinger told him before screaming, "*I gotta a man down! I need the EMTs!*"

Frank coughed blood, whispering, "How's . . . Susan?"

"She's fine, buddy, she's fine. How ya feeling?"

"I . . . could . . . use a drink."

"I bet. Sorry, bro, the bar's closed." Again, he screamed over his shoulder, "*I need a fucking medic!*"

"They're coming, Stan," a voice shouted from the back as more and more officers gathered. Saunders arrived; then he and Cordova began sectioning off the scene, telling the others to make room for Frank to breathe. "Give'em some air," Cordova ordered, watching Bodinger with his old partner.

Bodinger tore his eyes away long enough to see the dead man beside them. He was finally looking at the menace D, the Capital Hangman, and more importantly, Adam Parker. His face was shattered, and Bodinger's own kitchen knife was buried in his chest to the handle.

"Looks like you showed him who's boss."

"Yeah . . . He had a . . . bad day."

"I reckon."

Parker was smaller than Bodinger expected, almost fragile. He was trying to imagine how such a non-threatening person could cause so much destruction. This was not only the man responsible for six murders, but had also come within a breath of taking the life of his very own wife, the mother of his children. He didn't know how Frank accomplished it and, at that point, didn't care.

"That was good police work, buddy. I don't know how in the hell you managed it, but that's some goddamn good police work."

"No . . . drink, huh?"

"Sorry buddy," he chuckled, a nervous laugh.

"How about . . . a cigarette?"

Bodinger turned again. "I need a cigarette. Who smokes?"

An officer from the group walked forward and lit a cigarette, handing it to Bodinger. Stan took it and placed it in Frank's mouth. "Here you go, buddy."

Frank took a puff then said, "Ugh . . . menthol . . . *Yuck*," spitting it to the ground. Bodinger laughed, saying, "You're going to be okay. You hear me, Frank? You're going to be okay."

"You . . . believe this? The . . . son of a bitch . . . killed me."

"No, he didn't. You're right here. I got ya."

"Scrawny little bastard . . . He . . . killed me. Of all . . . the shit."

He had no more regrets. He'd closed the book on all his unfinished business. He resolved the issues with his old partner, he avenged Tiffany, he saved Susan, and Austin's finest were there to see it all. For the first time in his life, he finally felt like a cop. A good cop. One deserving of a partner as good as the man holding him.

Even the wolf took a backseat during the day's chase, allowing the man, Castro, to do his best alone—with no help.

Bodinger was fighting back his emotions while talking to the man he

400

owed everything to. Now, he was the one filled with regret. "Listen to me," he said quietly. "You never laid down for anything or anyone, ever. Not you, not Frank Castro. You're the reason this is all over now. You're the reason Susan's still with us. You're the reason we're here, all of us. Now, you relax, and we're gonna get you the hell outta here, get you patched up. You're gonna live to tell this story to all the world. You hear me, Frank? You're gonna live to tell this story."

Frank knew the truth. He shook his head, closing his eyes for a second, then said, "Heaven's . . . hung in black . . . partner."

"No."

"Yeah. Someone told me that . . . once."

"I was wrong."

"I had . . . to . . . look it up. Lincoln . . . I'm impressed."

"Don't be. I was wrong. I should have stood by you."

"Nah . . . I was . . . out of . . . control. You . . . were right, Stan. I . . . forgive you for that," Frank said, his eyes rolling.

"Listen to me, you stubborn son of a bitch, you ain't going out like this, not now. I still have to book you for interference in a police matter. You hear me? You ain't dying on me, Frank, not now." He turned again. "I need a *goddamn medic!*"

"They're coming up, Stan!" another voice called.

"You saved my life. You saved Susan's life. I owe you, Frank. I can't pay it back like this. You have to hang on."

Frank's eyes rolled side to side. The echo in his ears was roaring, and he couldn't feel a thing below his chin. "We're even. I . . . put you through hell . . . I say . . . we're even." More blood gushed from his mouth. "Wanna know . . . the funny . . . part?"

"What buddy?"

"I wish . . . I had something . . . smart . . . to say. Guess I . . . have to . . . leave that to you."

Bodinger was fighting back tears as he told him, "You're my partner. You hear me, you stupid spic? You're my *partner*."

Frank focused all the energy he had left on Stan's eyes. They were watery and tired, full of regret. But there was also the look of admiration he'd never seen before. In all the years, he never saw admiration in

Stanley Bodinger's eyes. But it was there now. Frank mustered all he had and whispered, "Partner? . . . I . . . like the . . . sound of that." He coughed a last time then told Stan, "Ten years . . . go by . . . pretty fast." With that, his eyes rolled back, and the last of his breath escaped, leaving him an empty vessel. Frank Castro was gone from the earth.

"Frank?" Bodinger called. He shook him, screaming, "*Frank!*"

Saunders, his face wet with tears, cleared the emotion from his throat then touched Bodinger's shoulder, saying, "Let the man sleep, Stan."

Bodinger looked up lost, confused.

"Let the man rest, he's earned it."

60

Susan was sitting on the side of the hospital bed when Stan walked into her room. She was given a sedative so she could relax; however, no drug could ease the whirling torrent in her mind. When Stan walked in, she burst into tears. Not the uncontrolled sobbing that rattled her hours before, but tears of relief that her husband was safe at her side. Before she could rise, he was there for her, arm in arm, a loving embrace. She could feel the grief in his bones. She didn't want to ask, but the words escaped before she could find a better order for them. "What happened?" she asked, wiping her face as he pulled her back, looking at her.

"Frank got him. He's gone, baby. He won't ever hurt anyone again."

"Oh god," she said, falling into his arms. "How's Frank?"

When there was no answer, only the tightening of his back, she knew what had happened. "Oh no," she sighed. Tears welled, and soon she was crying fully as was Stan. They held each other in the hospital room, crying into each other's necks, shedding tears for a man that had saved both their lives.

Frank paid for his frailties with his career. He paid for his persistence with his life. He was a loose cannon, a renegade, and a wild card. Now, he would live with both of them for the rest of their lives.

*

Chief Short ordered a full investigation into how Castro found the Capital Hangman before the authorities. Saunders didn't want Bodinger anywhere near it, but both Short and Bodinger himself insisted on it.

Bodinger also had another insistence. "Frank gets a police burial. If not, I resign. Today." The chief was so pleased to have Parker gone he sold the idea up the ladder with little resistance. Frank was buried in full uniform with a color guard and a twenty-one gun salute as bagpipes played "Amazing Grace." Just the type of thing he would have hated.

Stanley Bodinger got the last laugh after all.

Susan slipped the photo of Tiffany Malvern and her sister inside his casket during the viewing. Her husband told her Frank loved that picture. She slid it beside him, to rest with him in his long sleep. "She's safe now, Frank," she assured him through tears. "We're all safe now. And we thank you—all of us."

A thousand citizens turned out for the hero's funeral. The unknown ex-cop was a bigger celebrity in death than he ever was as a member of the APD. Something Bodinger made certain of. As the guns fired their salute, Bodinger, in full dress uniform, shed a tear for his old partner, his lasting words coming home to roost in his heart. "Heaven's hung in black, old friend," he whispered to the echoes. "Heaven's hung in black. Save me a seat at the bar, will you? I think I'd like to catch up some day."

When the ceremony was over and the gathering began to disperse, Bodinger heard a familiar voice behind him. "Detective Bodinger?" When Stan turned, he was surprised to see Russell Malvern, Tiffany's father, standing before him. The man wore a grim expression, still aching from the loss of his daughter.

"Mr. Malvern," Bodinger said, extending his hand. "Seems the circumstances of our meetings are always bitter," he finished, shaking hands.

"When I heard, I had to come," Malvern confessed. "My wife couldn't make the trip. She couldn't bear it. You understand."

"Of course, sir." There was lasting grief etched on the man. New lines of sorrow that would never fade. Stan was moved that he found it necessary to pay his respects at the cost of irritating his still-fresh wound.

He knew before that Malvern was a strong man; now it was even more apparent.

"It's a good thing what you did here today, Detective. A damn fine thing. Frank deserved this, we all know that. Must have been a hard sell."

"Actually no. The city owes him as a fallen son. It was easy enough."

"I didn't know him that well, just what Tiffany told us," Malvern said. "When she'd come home, he's all she'd talk about. She respected him, admired him. That was enough for us," he said, blinking the emotion out of his eyes.

"He had his ways, Mr. Malvern," Bodinger told him. "Frank was a hard man to pin down. I know that better than anyone. But I know no matter how he lived, his heart was always in the right place. His methods, well . . . ," he trailed off.

"None of us know, Detective, to what extent a man will go."

"Agreed," Stan said as he studied Malvern's face. There was something there, something beneath the surface, like a jagged stone hidden below calm water. The man's daughter meant the world to Frank. Suddenly he had a question. "Mr. Malvern, if I may, there is something I'd like to ask. Call it the bloodhound in me."

"Okay."

"Did Frank ever give you any indication as to what his actions would be? In any discussion, no matter how offhand they may have seemed?" It was then that Bodinger understood. He was glad he'd never have to interrogate Russell Malvern. They held eyes, and the man showed nothing. A stone-cold poker face hid what Bodinger now recognized so clearly. It had been right under his nose the entire time.

"Good seeing you again, Detective," Malvern said, shaking hands again. "Perhaps someday we could meet under more pleasant circumstances."

Stan shook his hand. "We can only hope, sir." As Malvern left and Susan made her way to him, Stan turned to the hero's casket, grinning to himself. "You son of a bitch," he said in a laugh.

"What, baby?" Susan asked.

"Nothing, sweetheart. Just one last memory I get to keep." He started to laugh. He knew it was wrong, but he couldn't contain it. It was small, but it was still a laugh. Thinking of Frank making a deal with Tiffany's father to avenge her death was so obvious a rookie should have seen it.

"What's so funny?" she asked, confused.

"Nothing, really. It's just Frank being Frank," he said, taking her in his arms. His eyes watered with emotion as he told her with a smile, "Let's go home, baby. Let's just go home. This is Frank's day."

The investigation that followed did little to prove anything. Tully Prichard had left the country, and all they had were Frank's credit card receipts from Louisiana. The Metairie police called Cordova and told him they had a crazy Cajun with two prosthetic legs raving to them that the cop he saw on television was the man who killed his friends and took his legs. He was out of his mind, but they wanted to at least check it out for their own conscience.

"What's his name?" Cordova asked them.

"Bodain. Trevor Bodain. Career criminal. Runs a local chop shop and other…*businesses,*" the Metairie cop informed him. "He's as mad as a hatter, but we thought it was worth a call."

Cordova laughed then lied, "He's crazy all right. We know for a fact Castro never left Austin. We have a witness, a young woman named Carmen Spinoza, says Castro was with her that whole week. Tell Mr. Bodain to find another dead man to blame his problems on. Our guy's clean."

After two months of investigators and criminal psychologists crawling through every inch of Adam Parker's house of horrors, Florence Cabbershaw had it demolished. In its place is the Frank Castro Memorial Park. She erected it to honor a man she respected and to erase the horrible memory of the house where innocence was sacrificed.

A child's playground now stands where once only horror resided.

Epilogue

Bodinger was standing at his desk, filing away the last of the Capital Hangman case, when Glen Young walked into his office. He cleared his throat, forcing Bodinger to look up.

"Well," Bodinger said, "look what the cat puked up."

"Nice to see you too, Detective," Young said, walking to his desk, carrying a folder. "Congratulations."

"I guess," Bodinger said, stuffing files in a storage box. "So to what do I owe the honor?"

Young could see Stan was in no mood for small talk, so he began, "I have a confession."

"What? You cross-dress on weekends?"

Young laughed, "Yeah, the heels kill my back."

"They'll do that."

Young fidgeted for a second then started over. "No. Look, uh . . . Since this thing is over, and we all said our goodbyes to the late, great Frank Castro, I thought about full disclosure."

"Meaning?"

"Meaning, about a month before the end came, I got another letter in the mail. Freaked me out because this one came to my home. I sat on it," he said, waving a hand of truce as Bodinger scowled. "I know, I know, I'm a bad guy and all that. But I'm probably going to write the book about this and get rich. So I figured, what the hell? I got a copy, right?"

Bodinger had learned that the reporter and Frank had shared a drink at Lucky's as all this began, so Young was already on his short list. His patience was wearing thin. "Where?" he asked, closing the box.

"Here," Young said, fishing a sheet of paper from the folder. "You might want to add this to your collection," he said, turning to leave. "Enjoy."

"You know, Young, you may be the luckiest son of a bitch out of this whole thing," Bodinger said, watching him go.

"We'll see if Oprah adds me to her book club. Good night, Detective."

"So long," Bodinger told him, adding after he left, "asshole."

Bodinger sat on his desk, looking at the letter from Adam Parker. The guy was obsessed with words; that was obvious. The letters, the house, the voice message to Frank they found, taunting the bully. Everything about Parker always started with words. He hoped this would be the last time he had to read what went on inside his horrible mind. He turned to get better light then read,

Dear Mr. Young,

Thank you for being a man of your word. My work would be much harder if you hadn't addressed my letters. The detectives would not know of my art unless they had your assistance. So again, thank you.

Now to the matter of this correspondence. I wanted you to be the first to know of the change taking place. The man I was is gone. The boy who was forced to have sex with his deviant mother is no more. With each death, I have grown. I am becoming more than a man. I have reached a status reserved for the gods. I choose who lives and who dies. And when. The power I possess is greater than anyone can fathom. I will be worshipped, idolized, and praised. My art is perfection, one of a kind. My work is truly beautiful. And you, Mr. Young, will tell the world of my changing. I am not a monster, just a higher form of being. I am not evil. Evil is subjective. I am simply who I am. The world will learn of me.

With your help, they will learn who I was and who I've become. Even if they must learn it one body at a time. Maybe they'll understand, or maybe they won't. In the end, it doesn't matter. I'm fulfilling my destiny. I would pity you "people," but I have no pity

to give. I will watch your world burn as I revel in its flames. And when my demise comes, I'll embrace it. For at last, I will be free from this world's blithering hypocrisy.
Until we chat again,

D

Bodinger read the letter word for word.

Then he balled it up, and tossed it in the trash.

THE END